CW00556806

Praise for The Metiks Fade Series

"Thomas Welsh has woven an engrossing and fascinating world where artists literally change the landscape of reality. This exciting debut will stick with you like a fever dream."

—Jaye Wells, USA Today bestselling author

"Welsh is not just a great writer, but a smart one. He's constructed a story that's full of bravado and color and lights, in Anna's otherwise bleak world. This is a magnetic tale full of dark adventures, mystery, and our worst demons. With a combination like that, it undoubtedly unfolds brilliantly."

—Sarah Noffke, Amazon bestselling author of The Reverians series

"...absolutely unputdownable."

—Martina McAtee, *USA Today* bestselling author

". . . a compelling and unique voice. Managing to be both lyrical and poignant, *Anna* is more than a story of dreamers and undreamers...it's a story of hope and healing, a reminder that even ashes can still carry a spark. This is a dark fantasy for fans of *Labyrinth* and Holly Black, a story that will seep into your consciousness and keep you dreaming long after you've closed the pages."

—Sherry Ficklin, bestselling author of the Stolen Empire series

"A brilliant piece of writing...a fantasy novel filled with energetic writing that pulls the reader in and doesn't let them go."

—Amanda J Evans, Summer Indie award-winning author of *Finding Forever*

"Highly addictive. What's not to love about *Anna Undreaming*? It's an inspired, atmospheric fantasy, accessible for the genre and is sure to leave fans shouting for more."

—Louise White, New Apple Award winning author of the Gateway series

"...absolutely stunning..."

—Odd and Bookish

"This book is like reading a dream. It has hints of *Alice in Wonderland*, and I felt like both Anna and I went through the looking glass into a fantastical Inception-like world. The book is fast-paced and captivating, and I really enjoyed it."

—Kal, Reader Voracious

"The *Matiks Fade* trilogy has already won its spot in my heart with *Anna Undreaming* and all I can do now is trying to survive until the sequel comes out."

—Life of a Simple Reader

"Welsh creates his descriptions beautifully. The way he describes the scenes is brilliant and makes it easy for the reader to picture his world easily, from the beautiful scenery to the somewhat haunting creations seen in the Hazes."

—Parchment and Quill

Thomas Welsh

OWL HOLLOW PRESS

Owl Hollow Press, LLC, Springville, UT 84663

Library of Congress Cataloging-in-Publication Data
Anna and the Winterheart / T. Welsh. — First edition.

Summary: One year later, Anna and Teej's partnership has ended, and the companions face a new legion of enemies alone.

Cover design: Les Solot

ISBN 978-1-958109-77-9 (paperback)
ISBN 978-1-958109-78-6 (e-book)

It's not hard to write a heroic woman when you're married to one. Nana, your smile is my sunrise. Forever.

one

One Year Later

"One please."

The ticket vendor grunted as he wiped the back of his knuckles on his greasy vest. He smeared the yolk from his egg sandwich in an inverted arc, like a crooked smile.

"Ya lookin' to take a twirl on the Dipping Dragon roller coaster tonight, Mister? If you've got a friend along, I can do ya a deal: two-for-one on ride coupons! Just don't tell ma boss."

"I'm here alone," said Teej. "And I'm not here for the rides."

"What are ya here for then?"

Teej pointed to the end of the pier. "I'm going to sink this whole thing to the bottom of the sea."

"How's that?" replied the vendor with a tremble in his voice. "For real?"

"Go home," said Teej. "Tomorrow, all of this will feel like a bad dream."

He left the man staring open-mouthed as he walked through the broad gateway from the boardwalk onto the pier. The faded sign overhead frowned down at him. Above its arch, a manic clown face leered.

Sleep all day, Party all night at Centrale Pier!

Stepping across the planks, he felt a low rumble beneath his feet. Someone else might mistake that rumble for the crashing of waves, but Teej knew what it truly was. Breathing in deeply, he stretched out his senses and attuned himself to Rolo's Haze.

The wood beneath his feet creaked ominously, the stormy sea visible through the cracks. Vertigo rocked him on his heels, but Teej took another deep breath and steadied himself. He pushed onwards.

The night air was fresh and though the winds blew fiercely, it wasn't cold. Crowds of teenagers talked and laughed as they bustled past. Teej watched a pack of skateboarders race past a cotton candy stall, grabbing handfuls of bright pink sugar as the red-faced owner shouted after them, "I told you kids to stay off the boardwalk!"

Every inch of the pier was lit with flashing neon signs. The Ferris wheel, green and red, turned creakily, while the roller coaster glowed yellow as it curled like a dragon overhead. Electronic tunes blared from little stalls where arcade machines and claw games offered cuddly toy prizes. But although it was flashy, the funfair was run down. Graffiti scarred every wall. One tag in particular, large purple letters scrawled on the side of a burger stall, caught Teej's attention: "Who is Kas?"

Who indeed?

That was one of the many questions he hoped to answer tonight. Who is Kas? Why has Rolo kidnaped Amara? Whose side is Rolo on? Teej had no shortage of questions, but in truth, only one really mattered to him. *Where is Anna?*

He moved on down the pier. A gang of leather-clad bikers rolling dice against a wall scowled at Teej as he walked past them toward an antique Love Tester. The brass machine was covered in faded heart and angel decals.

Fishing in his pocket for coins, Teej slipped all the loose change he had into the machine. It lit up a garish red and cooed *"Put your finger on my spot and I'll tell say if you're hot!"* The recorded voice was an Italian woman's, so tinny and loud that it made him wince. Chuckling to himself, Teej put his finger on the metal plate, which was already warm. The red lights shot up the machine from "cold fish" to "Casanova."

"You're one hot tamale! Make a wish, you tasty dish, and a card will reveal your fate."

Teej licked his lips as he considered his next move. This wasn't a fun distraction; it was part of a game Rolo was playing. He was listening. Teej spoke from the heart.

"I wish I knew where Anna was," he said under his breath.

"What you say, Mister?"

Teej flinched. A girl had sneaked up behind him and tried to rest her chin on his shoulder, but Teej shrugged her off. She was young, maybe nineteen, and punky, with purple hair, a leather choker, and tight denim shorts. A baggy loose-knit sweater hung off one shoulder, exposing a black bra strap. She chewed gum loudly, blowing pink bubbles over her black lipstick.

"It says you're hot," she said, putting a hand on his chest. Black fingernails.

She pouted. "It's never wrong, you know."

"Shush!" chastised Teej. "I'm thinking."

Focusing his Will, he sucked his teeth then said, "Why did you kidnap Amara?"

The machine fell dead silent; its lights winked out. It rattled twice, then spat out a small card from a slot near the bottom. The card almost slipped between the cracks in the floor before Teej caught it.

"What does it say?" The girl tugged at his shoulder. "Who are Rolo and Amara?"

Teej grinned at her. "Who are *you*?"

"I'm Bianca. And you're old enough to be my dad."

"Many times over, Bianca!" said Teej with a chuckle. "But if you'll walk with me, I'll tell you a story."

"Wait, what was the answer to your question?" Bianca pointed at the card.

Teej held it up for her.

"*To unmask her?* What does that mean?"

"I have only a faint idea."

Bianca blew another bubble, then took his arm and pulled her body close to his.

"Will you win me a prize? And buy me a drink? I need a drink."

"Me too, Bianca," said Teej as he started to walk. "How about that story first?"

"Nah," said Bianca. "Just the drink is fine."

Arm-in-arm, they walked past the arcade, the hotdog stalls, and the bumper cars. There was no sign of the Dreamer, Rolo. Perhaps Teej had successfully sneaked in without being noticed. It was difficult to get the drop on a Dreamer within his own Haze, but not impossible, especially if he was distracted. And Rolo had more than just Teej to worry about. He certainly seemed in no rush to greet him.

"Who are we looking for?" asked Bianca.

"Amara."

"That's a funny name," she said, wrinkling her nose. "Does she work here? Is she a fortune teller?"

"In a way," said Teej. "But no, she doesn't work here. She has been kidnapped by Rolo. He controls everything in this Haze."

"You mean Rolo owns the boardwalk?"

Teej ignored her question. "There's someone else here too, Bianca."

"Yeah," she said, squeezing his arm. "Me!"

He gave her a concerned look. "No, someone more dangerous. Another Metik maybe?"

"Who?"

Teej shook his head. "I don't know."

Bianca was bored with the conversation. "You like games, Mister? Should I call you Mister?"

"It really doesn't matter."

"We could play that game" she said, pointing. "The one with the water guns. Not all games are for kids you know."

"You're only interested in me because of Rolo."

Bianca pulled away. "What do you mean? Who is Rolo?"

Teej looked closely at Bianca, squinting as he tried to discern her nature. She was innocent. Just another sleeper swept up in Rolo's Haze. Most of the people on the pier were innocents, perhaps all of them. Teej had to be careful. There was potential for tragedy with so many in thrall to Rolo. They deserved their freedom.

"There's something special about this place," said Teej as he disentangled himself from her. "And you're not quite yourself here. Rolo loves to play games, but the stakes are always a little too high."

"I know what you mean," Bianca said as she stretched her arms to the sky. "It feels amazing at the moment! Win me a prize, Teej. I want you to play games for me."

"How did you know my name, Bianca?"

Wrinkling her nose, she seemed unable to answer. Teej started walking again. Bianca scampered after him.

"Where are we going?" she asked.

"Well, I thought I'd walk to the end of the pier and see if Rolo is there."

"Who is this Rolo guy again? And why is he avoiding you?"

"He's the Dreamer who made this place. And he's toying with me. With us. That's why he won't face me."

"Uhhhh, and who was the other one? Alana?"

Teej sighed. "*Amara.* Rolo kidnapped her."

"And Kas?"

"Quiet!" snapped Teej. He felt a gust of Vig in the air sweep through the Haze like a cold winter wind. Stepping in front of Bianca, he looked around the boardwalk for signs of danger.

"Someone else is here."

"Who?" asked Bianca.

"The other Metik I sensed. It's Kas!"

Bianca looked confused. "But who *is* Kas?"

Teej let her go and started walking again. "Every single Dreamer and Metik alive is asking that same question right now, Bianca. W*ho is Kas? Where did he come from? Why does he keep attacking Dreamers? Is he out for revenge? Is he hunting the Doxa?* No one knows. So, let's find out."

They were closing in on the roller coaster. Halfway along the pier, Teej felt the winds of Vig blow stronger. The Haze was changing now, blooming into something more sinister. The changes to the environment were obvious, even without his Haze Sense. The world reformed around them. One by one the stars winked out of the sky. Floating green lanterns climbed into the air. Emerald flames lit up the torches along the rails. The ride attendants and stall vendors' faces became animalistic: dogs and foxes and a few wolves. Looking over the edge of the pier, Teej noticed the sea was now an unnatural green.

"We're getting closer, Bianca. Rolo will be here soon. This Haze is unstable. Maybe it's time you went home."

"You want to take me home?" she asked, taking hold of his hand and biting her lip. Teej didn't pull away but didn't squeeze her hand back. He could see her expression twitch as her will strained against Rolo's control. The Dreamer was too strong. Bianca was his puppet, and though she could strain against her strings, she moved at his will.

"My parents are out of town for the weekend." Though she seemed to be flirting with him again, Teej could see the fear in her eyes. The conflict. Deep down, she knew this was all wrong. She was wrong. Rolo was controlling everything here. Especially her.

"That's not the direction tonight is headed, Bianca."

Her frown was so severe he felt momentarily guilty. But she wasn't disappointed he was turning her down. She was afraid he was abandoning her to her fate. It was too late for her to run. Though the swelling of Vig had slowed, Rolo was still coming.

They had a little time. Teej tried to reassure her it would be alright.

"We have a little time. I'll buy us some food, then let's see what happens. I'd rather not eat alone anyway."

She smiled instantly. "Buy me a drink too?"

"Maybe."

Teej led Bianca to a nearby fried food and ice cream stall, and they sat at the counter on high stools. The server wore a smart ice cream parlor uniform, starched white, with a little paper hat, but his face was blurry, his features smeared out like an out-of-focus photograph. He had tall rabbit ears, but it wasn't clear if he wore a mask, or if he was monstrous. Bianca didn't seem to notice.

"Two deep-fried chocolate bars with powdered sugar and ice cream," said Teej.

"It'll be a few minutes," said the blurry rabbit. Teej nodded. They watched as the chocolate bars were dipped in batter then dropped in the fryer. Bianca was uncharacteristically quiet.

"There's someone else isn't there?" she asked after a few minutes of silence. She didn't sound jealous. She was concerned. "Another girl?"

"I lost her," replied Teej.

"Oh," said Bianca, shuffling in her seat nervously.

"Not completely. I fully intend to find her again."

"How long you been lookin'?"

"A year."

Bianca frowned. "All that time searching for some girl?"

"She's not *some girl*," said Teej gently. "She's Anna."

"I got your food, folks!" shouted the server. He sprinkled each treat with powdered sugar, topped it with a dollop of half-melted ice cream, then handed them the cardboard containers. Teej was relieved to see the food looked normal. He dropped a ten on the counter, then stood up.

Taking a big bite of dripping, battered chocolate, Bianca seemed happy.

"Could go for some beer with this," she suggested, but Teej ignored her. Lifting the stick, he bit into the sugary batter, then immediately spat it out.

"That good, huh?" asked Bianca.

"I hate coconut. Tastes like shredded newspaper."

Bianca cheered as Teej threw his food into the sea.

"Good throw! You should win me some prizes. Let's look at the games."

Teej shook his head grumpily. "I'm here to find Amara, not play games."

"But I think Rolo, whoever he is, wants us to play *all* the games. Then maybe we should look at that dragon roller coaster. Do you think it will come to life one day?"

"I'm done with Rolo's games," said Teej as he grabbed her firmly and pushed her ahead of him. "Take me to him, now."

"Getting rough," Bianca bit her bottom lip, her eyes sparkling. "Are you just like Rolo? Deep down?"

Teej shook his head. "I'm nothing like him. It's time for us to meet. Rolo knows I have a secret to share, and I know he loves secrets almost as much as he loves games."

Bianca's expression was conflicted. The Dreamer affected her mind, but she still had a modicum of free will. The path she walked was fixed, but within that narrow lane she could shift a little, and right now she was shifting towards Teej.

"Please don't hurt him," she muttered under her breath to her master. "I like this one."

"Everyone likes me," said Teej as he shook his head. "But it never stops them from trying to kill me."

two

Leaning on the railing, Teej looked out to sea and caught his breath. The pier seemed to stretch on forever, and they'd be walking for what seemed like hours. Below them, the waves glowed radioactive green, but the gray skies were pleasantly dramatic, the layers of dark clouds offering a distant promise that all this ugliness would soon be washed away by the rain. But not before this Haze resolved and Teej faced Rolo.

Who is Kas?

Teej wasn't surprised so many Metiks and Dreamers were asking the question, but he was surprised any of them thought *he* had the answer. He remembered the graffiti he saw on the wall back at the start of the pier. Why was it there? Perhaps a sign that Rolo thought Teej knew who Kas was? Perhaps he could bluff his way to some positive outcome here. When he confronted Rolo he'd need something to trade. If the only thing he could offer was information, this might be his best chance, even if he'd have to lie.

"What now?" said Bianca breathlessly.

Teej ignored her, stretching out his Haze Sense. He felt nothing. Rolo was powerful, and even if Teej had a partner, finding Rolo or Amara would be a challenging task. On his own, Teej was out of his depth. He remembered his fight with

Mustaine, and how it almost cost him his life. Rolo was a dangerous dreamer, and Teej wasn't sure he had the stomach for another solo fight.

"Who are we looking for again?"

"Rolo," replied Teej wearily.

"There was someone else too…"

"Amara. A wise old Dreamer, long since fallen into madness. She's harmless enough, but I need to know why Rolo has kidnapped her."

"He doesn't seem to want to meet you," said Bianca, her hands on her hips. Her voice was lower when Rolo was controlling her. "Tell me about Kas instead."

Teej pushed her away. "That's Rolo talking, not you Bianca."

"What do you mean?"

Teej shook his head. "It's not your fault. You're affected here. Nothing you do or say is in your control."

Bianca's eyes were wide, and she shivered a little. A single raindrop fell on her cheek, and a cold wind whistled as it blew through the night.

"I wish he'd just face me," Teej whispered under his breath.

"Very well," said Rolo. His gravelly voice seemed to come from all around them.

The Dreamer warped and distorted the air around his body as he appeared in front of Teej. Behind him, the funfair melted away, leaving an empty, silent boardwalk that led out to the sea. Rolo walked with his arms out in a gesture that was both a welcome and a vulgar display of power: his hands glowed with green fire.

Rolo was scruffily handsome. He wore a baggy wool coat over a leather jacket with fingerless gloves, and his fingers twitched unconsciously as the flames danced around them. His spiked, bleached blond hair was artfully tousled, and his rough stubble highlighted his strong jawline and deep-set blue eyes. His smile was playful on his baby face, but his eyes were infinitely old and wise,

"Who *is* Kas?" he rumbled, staring hard at Teej.

Teej reached into his hoodie, his fingers curled around the space where his Periapt would materialize if he needed it.

"I can't make it that easy," said Teej, affecting nonchalance. He needed to know what Rolo knew before the Dreamer discovered he was bluffing.

"Sure you can," said Rolo with a razorblade smile. "But we can start with something easier if you like."

"Like?"

"What are you doing in my Haze?"

"You know that already."

"You're looking for your Undreamer friend."

Rolo was trying to look indifferent, but Teej felt the tension in the air. It was hard to appear relaxed while your hands were wreathed in green flame, even for Rolo. The Dreamer fidgeted with the flames, making little patterns in the air. His movements looked casual but remained a threat. Teej hoped there was some room for diplomacy.

"I lost a lot of friends, not just Anna. Alby too. Taken by Rayleigh."

Rolo nodded like this was all old news.

"At Kanna Island. I heard about that. I hope you're not bringing that kind of trouble into my town, Teej. Bad luck follows you around. You don't have many friends these days."

"We're all friends here," said Teej as he slowly put his hands up. They stood ten feet apart now, and every time Rolo moved, Teej tried not to flinch. The music and laughter all around had stopped, and though the pier was still busy, most of the people stood still, their eyes empty. Above them, the curve of the roller coaster cast a long shadow, and every twenty seconds another car would twist over and above them, though the passengers on board remained motionless. Bianca was shoulder to shoulder with Teej, but she didn't feel like an ally.

"Friends?" whispered Rolo, his demeanor calm but his eyes fierce. "These days it seems there's scarce a pair of Dreamers or

Metiks that would call each other friends. We're all at war now. The Dreamers are tearing each other apart."

A shadow flickered across Rolo's face. A flash of white teeth. Teej shuddered.

"It doesn't have to be that way. Why did you kidnap Amara? You should let her go."

"I'm protecting her," said Rolo with a smirk. "You got me all wrong. I took her in to save her from the ugliness that's all around. I like the old girl. She's mad, you know, but she's safe with me."

"I doubt your intentions."

"And I doubt you have any information," said Rolo, his voice rising. The sound from the arcade games stopped. "You don't know anything more about Kas than I do. You've got nothing to bargain with."

"Don't you want to dance around a little longer?" goaded Teej. "I thought you liked secrets Rolo."

Rolo licked his lips, watching Teej closely.

"You know I do, but carnival games are my thing these days. You witness every aspect of life at the carnival. Danger, laughter, romance. Circuses, clowns and games of fun and peril. Competition: the glory of winning and the humiliation of defeat But secrets? Secrets will always be my *first* love. Tell me a secret Teej. Let the game of truth begin."

The roller coaster roared overhead, the sounds restored now, and for a moment neither of them could talk. It gave Teej some time to think. He watched Bianca as she fiddled absent-mindedly with a life preserver by the railing, pretending not to listen to them.

"I came here for your help," confided Teej. "Rayleigh either has Anna, or he's trying to get her; I've been dodging his goons for a year. Either way, I have to find him, and I think Amara can help."

"You think your Anna's still alive?"

"I know it."

Rolo rolled his eyes but didn't argue. "You said you needed my help, not Amara's."

Teej hesitated for a moment and then decided to answer truthfully.

"Maybe you can help me, too. You're an expert on secrets? The entrance to the August Club is a kind of secret."

Rolo clapped his hands together in glee, sparks flying from his fingertips. "The August Club! Whatever could you want from there?"

"It's the only lead I have left. I… don't know where else to look. If I can get to the August Club, I can get help from… an old friend. I can't find Rayleigh without help. Whether it's from someone at the August Club or from Amara, I need to find Rayleigh. Face him. That's the only way to help Anna. *That's* my truth. Now, will you be honest with me in return?"

"I will," said Rolo.

"Can you help me find the August Club? Will you let me talk with Amara?"

"No."

Rolo took a step back, adjusted his stance. He was preparing an attack.

"Dammit Rolo, we don't need to fight. Just let Amara go."

"She's right there," said Rolo as he nodded to their left. Bianca and Teej followed the gesture and turned to see a small, old woman sitting on a low stool next to a hot dog stand. She was wearing a mask that looked like a fox's face, and her shoulders rocked gently up and down as if she was sleeping, though she sat bolt upright.

"Why did you take her? What are you *protecting* her from?"

"No, my turn," said Rolo firmly. "Who is Kas? Where did he come from and what does he want?"

The winds of Vig abated, and the tension eased. Rolo's curiosity caused him to let his guard down. The Dreamer had always been dangerous, and this wouldn't be the first time they'd fought. Still, Teej hoped for a little more time to find a peaceful solution.

Turning away, he walked to the railing and leaned on it, looking out to sea. A moment later Rolo joined him, and together they stared out at the waves in silence for a long time. Nearby, Bianca lingered, held in Rolo's thrall.

"Honestly, I don't know who Kas is," confessed Teej. "But I do have one more secret to share."

"Save it," said Rolo. "I like you Teej. I like that you came here to talk. I liked Garret. Hell, I even like Amara, and she's nuttier than a fruitcake. But if you don't know who Kas is, you're no good to me. Save your secret. It's time for you to leave."

"I'm not going anywhere," said Teej calmly. "I know why you have Amara. You're going to use her blood."

Rolo grabbed his arm and turned Teej around. He was defensive. "It ain't like that! I know half the Dreamers are taking blood from Muses these days, but it makes them sick. I don't want to play a game when there's no way to win."

"What about taking another Dreamer's blood then?" challenged Teej.

"She's on her way out, man! I won't harm her, but when the inevitable happens, what's the big deal? She doesn't need her blood when she's dead."

"So, you just keep her here, and then when she dies, you're what? A vampire?"

"It's a game, man," said Rolo with exasperation. "It's *all* a game. An arms race. We're eating each other, and I need to get as far up the food chain as I can. If you're not a predator, you're prey. I won't hunt—I'm not a monster—but I'm not above scavenging. Whatever it takes to stay in the game."

Teej shook himself free of Rolo's grasp.

"I'm not leaving without her. This is wrong. Amara deserves better."

Rolo reached into his top pocket, pulled out his sunglasses and put them on, then gave Teej a wide smile. "Sorry about this, friend."

Bianca pounced from behind, slipping a coiled noose around Teej's neck, then pulling it tight. The other end was tied in a slipknot around her neck.

"No!" protested Teej, but it was too late.

"I'm sorry," she said, tears in her eyes as she ran to the railing, swung her legs over the side and jumped into the sea.

"No hard feelings," Rolo said over his shoulder as he walked away. Teej grasped for his Praxis, summoning his Will. *Too late.*

The rope snapped taut and Teej was dragged across the wooden slats of the pier before his back slammed hard against the railings. The slipknot cinched tight, and his hands went to his throat. *Six to ten seconds.* That's how long he had before he lost consciousness, but he didn't want to drop Bianca in the sea. That's if her neck wasn't already broken.

The rope bit into his skin, making his vision swim. Teej grasped the knot with both hands, ready to snap it if he could, but he had to hold onto Bianca too. Summoning Vig, he failed to break it at the first attempt. His arms went numb. He'd delayed too long. His world went dark. *Not like this.*

Snap! The pressure suddenly eased as the rope broke and he could breathe again.

Teej glanced up to see Kas leap out of the sea and over the railing. Kas flew above all of them. He dropped Bianca's limp body on the ground, his red cloak and hood fluttering in the wind as he flew overhead.

Pulling the broken rope from around his neck and casting it aside, Teej managed to croak, "You … should have let me share my last secret, Rolo. I don't know who Kas is. But I knew he was already here."

three

Cloaked in red and emanating a pale orange aura, Kas radiated demonic power. Neither Teej nor Rolo was ready for him. The fading sunlight seemed to bend and shimmer around him, making it hard to perceive his form. As he hung in the air his clothes rippled in slow motion like he was underwater, and his hood obscured his face completely, a black void where light dared not go.

Rolo backed off. “Teej, you bastard! This was a trap all along! They call you the Diplomat, but you’re just as sneaky as the rest. Well, I ain't standing for it. I’ll send every single person in this Haze to their death at the bottom of the ocean! You can try to save them, or you can chase me, but not both. Make a choice!”

As Kas touched down, Rolo turned to run for the end of the pier. Kas shot out an arm, summoned his Praxis and manifested a long golden chain from his right hand. With a flick of his wrist, the chain shot out fast as a bullet, wrapping around the top of Rolo’s arm. Pulling back for a moment, Kas rocketed forward and hit Rolo in the back, delivering a brutal blow with both knees. Rolo collapsed to the ground in a heap as Kas rolled into a crouch. He retracted his long chain Periapt, which curled in a loop in the air above his head, coiling and writhing like a snake.

"I'm sorry," wept Bianca as she lay across the deck, wet and shivering.

"It wasn't your fault," said Teej as he conjured his Periapt and eyed Kas cautiously. The wood of the tonfa creaked in his hand as he grasped it tightly. He fell into a crouch and summoned Vig, ready to move at a second's notice. "What now?" he whispered under his breath.

Kas spun, swinging his chain at Teej, who ducked just in time. It missed his head by inches. Scrambling to safety, he prepared to sweep his Periapt forward to counterattack, but hesitated. Kas had just saved his life. Why would he be trying to hurt him now? Teej turned to see Kas' true target: a creature with a blurred face, clutching a long blade in one hand, splayed unconscious on the ground from Kas' blow.

"Uh, thanks," muttered Teej, but it was already too late. Kas flicked his wrist upward. His chain wrapped around a roller coaster support beam directly overhead, and in a flash, he was in the air. As Kas flew into the riggings, Teej reached down to help Bianca to her feet. Mascara stained her cheeks, but she wasn't crying anymore.

"What did he do to me?" she asked as they both looked down at Rolo's unconscious form. "I told him I didn't want to hurt anyone."

"You're in his thrall," sniffed Teej. "I can't break you out of that; you have to do it yourself. Try to get clear before he wakes up. *If* he wakes up."

Teej took a second to consider his next move. Should he help Amara? She was in the same spot, sitting on the same chair, still seemingly asleep.

"Is that guy in the mask going to stop that roller coaster?" asked Bianca.

"What?" asked Teej, snapping to attention.

She pointed at the track above them. Teej followed her gaze to the spiraling rails and saw a massive dip at the end dropping straight into the sea. This was Rolo's doing. He'd altered the rails and made the ride into a death trap. Strapped into the roller-coaster carriage, the passengers were already screaming.

"Was it like that before?" asked Bianca. "Will they be alright?"

"Think Bianca! You're going to have to be smart to escape this place. I know you can do this."

Bianca looked numb. Teej touched her face gently.

"We're playing his game, but we don't have to follow his rules."

Turning on his heels, Teej broke into a run. Pooling Vig into the ground below his feet, he took two steps, three, then exerted his Praxis and leapt into the air. Teej soared, the wind whipping at his clothes and hair as he arced through the sky towards the roller coaster above. He was aiming for the end of the track, but almost overshot. Reaching out a hand at the last moment, he caught hold of a support rail and spun himself around to balance precariously on a thin beam. The wind stung his face. Tiptoeing onto the tracks, he looked up to see the roller coaster carriage was perhaps half a minute away. The terrified passengers wept as they struggled against their straps. They sped around a bowline twist and the screams grew louder. As the roller coaster straightened out on the final stretch, it accelerated towards Teej.

"What exactly is my plan here?" he muttered through gritted teeth.

Teej had to do something, and quickly, but was out of ideas. The carriage was fast; its momentum would be hard to redirect. He could try to form a new track, but materializing matter out of Vig had never been his strong suit. The coaster was going too fast anyway. They'd be in the sea before he could create anything. Perhaps he could twist the rails just enough to form a ramp, sending the carriages crashing onto the deck below instead of into the sea? Would more of the people survive? Probably not.

Levering his tonfa under one of the rails, he pooled Vig and prepared to bend the track. His arms strained against the groaning metal as he heaved with all his might. *This isn't going to work.*

Teej glanced up as the roller coaster rattled closer. The hazy silhouette of Kas was balanced precariously on the front carriage. *What is he doing!*

Kas' Periapt wrapped around the nose of the lead car like he had a wild beast on a leash. What was his plan? The chain creaked around the metal of the front carriage, and though the rollercoaster slowed, it didn't stop. Kas was using his Will to try to wrest control of the carriage, but the momentum was too great. The whole thing started to topple. His chain was pulling it apart.

As Kas took the strain, the carriage slipped away from the rails and it tipped sideways, causing passengers to slide out of their seats. They were falling.

Just like at the frozen lake. Teej remembered Anna's fall from the riverbank. He'd formed a whirlwind to guide her safely to the ground. Could he do the same thing here? With this many people? He had to try.

As the first woman slipped out of her seat with a scream, Teej swung his Periapt hard, and concentrating his Will, produced a whirlwind a few feet from the tip of his tonfa. It arced into the darkness silently, catching the woman just as she approached the ground. It was a rough landing, but the wind spun her, slowing her fall. She landed with a dull thud, then slowly rose to her feet, dazed but uninjured.

"Let go!" Teej commanded the remaining passengers, augmenting his directive with the power of the Word. Most of them were already losing their grip. As the carriage hit a corner, one by one they all let go and hurtled towards the wooden pier. Teej closed his eyes, focused his Will, and reached for his Praxis once more. His arm caught the tail of a whirlwind, and he threw it forward, enveloping the falling bodies in a mighty cushion of swirling air. A heavy blanket of fatigue fell over him immediately, and he almost lost consciousness. Cracking his eyes open, he breathed a sigh of relief when he saw the passengers splayed across the deck, disheveled and hurt, but alive.

He had saved the passengers, but now was in trouble himself. The carriage was still coming towards him. Teej reached for his Praxis, but it came too slowly. His arms and legs were still heavy, his reactions lethargic. The rails shook under his body. It was too late. Before the carriage hit him, he closed his eyes and braced for the impact.

Nothing.

Teej opened them again in time to see Kas wrench the carriage completely off the track, then back-flip away as the roller coaster flew off the pier into the sea. Teej watched him drift to the ground like a leaf in the wind as the carriages splashed and sank into the waves without a trace.

"Thanks again, I guess," mumbled Teej.

Teej unzipped his jacket and tossed it aside, then pulled Vig into the air around his feet and pushed off from the coaster track, this time aiming straight down. He channeled his downward momentum into a cushioned blast as he hit the ground, landing close to Rolo's unconscious form. Turning the Dreamer to check on him, Teej recoiled as Rolo's eyes sprang open. His hands shot out and grabbed Teej's collar.

"You led him here. You led him all around the world!"

"What do you mean?" asked Teej.

"Help!" Bianca's cry cut their conversation short.

Rolo's Haze was devolving into a nightmare. Bianca was being chased by a demon clown that looked like it had crawled out of the sea. It was the same clown that had been on the sign at the funfair entrance. With a chalk-white face and a blood-red nose, its portly body was draped with baggy, colorful overalls covered in stars and moons, but its eyes were inky black. It held giant balloon animals floating on the end of string: a dog, a bird and a snake, that moved and snarled as if alive.

"What now?" complained Teej as the clown unleashed his inflated legion. They closed in on Bianca.

"Your Art is a mess," said Teej as he wrestled himself free of Rolo.

"You need Anna," croaked Rolo. "You're no good on your own. We're all soldiers now, even you, *Diplomat*. But when the war begins, you'll need a proper fighter by your side."

"What do you mean?" asked Teej, but Rolo was already gone. The wooden planks beneath him broke away as his body fell into the sea. The green waves swallowed him without a sound. Rolo was losing control of the Haze and losing his ability to manipulate the Vig here. Maybe Rolo could swim to shore and escape. Maybe not.

"Teej!" Bianca shouted in desperation. A dog balloon animal floated overhead, then came down and started to chase her.

Behind her, Kas battled more of Rolo's monsters. A biker gang, now red-eyed and with long claws, swarmed him, but Kas danced and weaved between their attacks. Kas didn't seem even slightly concerned for his safety, as he dodged between his enemies, smashing them to pieces with his flaming golden chain Periapt.

Teej walked slowly toward the clown at first, then broke into a run, lifting his tonfa over his head as he charged the creature. The snake balloon-animal flattened itself into a sheet as it moved to envelop him, but with a flick of his wrist, Teej shot out a blast of hot air, drying it to a brittle, hard panel. Teej ripped through like paper, coming out the other side to ram into the clown shoulder first. He barreled his adversary over the side of the pier into the sea, grabbing hold of the clown's red nose and tearing it off as he fell. Turning, he imbued the red globe with charged Vig and threw it at a pack of bikers closing in on Kas. It exploded like a handful of fireworks, setting several of them on fire. The flames died within a few moments, and the creatures crumbled to dust.

"Slower than you used to be," said Amara.

The old woman was awake now. She sat alone on the pier, the arcade machines and fairground rides all gone. Meanwhile, Bianca girl was struggling to break free from the balloon dog, which was trying to absorb her, wrapping its body around hers. She reached out for Teej, and as he grabbed her with one hand, he pushed Vig toward the balloon dog with his other. A blast of hot air made the rubber dog roar in pain, then disintegrate into dust.

Bianca gasped for air as Teej held her by the shoulders.

"You're fine. Just breathe."

After she calmed down, she nodded mutely. Satisfied she was safe, Teej turned to see Kas. Standing stock-still, his burning gold chain Periapt laying passive across the wooden deck, his enemies defeated, Kas waited for Teej.

Teej walked slowly towards him, but as he passed Amara, she grabbed him by the wrist. From behind her fox mask, she whispered something, but he couldn't hear her properly. Leaning closer, she repeated her words.

"You won't like what you're about to see."

four

As the Haze faded like a quickly forgotten dream, the heavy banality of the real world reasserted itself on Centrale Pier. Teej reluctantly tossed his Periapt aside. Hopefully he didn't need it anymore. He ran his fingers through his hair and waited for Kas to speak. As the sun cracked the clouds, Kas turned away before Teej could make out his face in the shadows of the red hood. He seemed to shrink, becoming smaller and thinner as he walked away.

Teej hesitated, unsure whether to follow Kas or stay with Amara. He looked closely at the old woman. She now wore a wolf mask.

"Do you know what's happening Amara," asked Teej. "Do you remember me?"

"Through the bitter winter, the sun clung to the horizon, but wood holds both the memory of water as well as the dream of fire. Though the flames burn out, the fire waits. And it watches you. The winterheart bleeds."

Teej scratched his chin. "So, I'm the fire? Or the wood? Is it the bitter winter now? Or is the bitter winter what we've just been through? You know, the *actual* winter? Who is the winterheart? I can see why people get annoyed with you."

"You are also annoying," chuckled Amara.

Teej laughed in return. He leaned in close to the old woman and whispered in her ear. "What do you think? Chase him?"

Ignoring Amara, Bianca came close to Teej and pulled him by the arm. "I hope Rolo is dead." She spat, bitterly. "He told me I could be like him. He lied. I don't want to be like him. I don't want to be like any of you. You're all monsters."

Teej ignored her and started walking after Kas who was striding towards the exit of the pier.

"But... thank you for saving my life, I guess," Bianca shouted after Teej.

He struggled to keep up with Kas, who was already at the pier gateway.

"Wait!" he shouted. Kas didn't stop or slow down. They were both running along the beachfront now. Teej worried Amara might not stay where he left her while he chased Kas. What was he going to do with the mad old Dreamer? What was he going to do when he caught up with Kas? Teej hoped one of the two would be able to help him find Anna, but he was grasping at straws. Was she even still alive?

A whole year.

The rain eased off, and as Teej left the pier farther behind, the localized weather system created by the Haze broke down, giving way to patchy sunlight as the gray clouds parted. On the doorsteps of the beachfront cafes and bars, waiters set up tables and chairs, expecting the sun to make an appearance before lunchtime.

Ahead of him, Kas darted up an alleyway. Teej hesitated. That alley was a dead end. Flashes of the battle at Avalon came back to him: Garret and Raguel broken on the rocks, Alby with a smoking hole in his chest, Drowden falling through the portal into the Sump. Since that day almost exactly one year ago, Teej's whole life had been on hold. The reverberations of the battle echoed across the weeks and months, and still shook him now, wracking his soul with guilt and regret. How could he abandon

Anna to Rayleigh? How could he let his best friend die? All he did now was run. He was chasing Anna, scouring the globe with little real hope, each lead seemed more tenuous than the last. Maybe he wasn't even running after her anymore. Maybe he was just running away.

Teej turned the corner into the alleyway to find Kas waiting for him. Head down, face concealed by the cloak, he gestured for Teej to come close.

"Why the red hood?" asked Teej. "Why hide your face?"

"I don't run from the wolves anymore. They run from me."

Teej's mouth fell open. He knew that voice. "It can't be..."

She pulled the hood back. "Sometimes you change so much your old name doesn't fit you anymore."

"It's you!"

Her hair was shorter, her eyes clearer and brighter, and she stood with confidence now. But it was her.

"I'm Kas now," she said with a warm smile that almost burst his heart. "But my friends still call me Anna."

five

"Well? Are you happy to see me?" The words felt all wrong in Anna's mouth, but she didn't know what else to say.

His face was just like she remembered, except for the dark circles under his eyes. Tousled brown hair, thin cheeks, deep turquoise eyes, and a narrow frame—athletic but with an almost undetectable limp. He was handsome too. And charming. Standing amidst trash in the shadowy alleyway, confused and tired from the fight, he would be the most wonderful sight she had ever seen, if only he would smile at her.

"How?" he asked flatly. This was going badly. They weren't holding each other. They weren't kissing or cheering or even smiling. This was all wrong. It was like a meeting of two strangers.

Anna had prepared herself for this moment, but not enough. Teej had been through Hell, but he could never understand what *she* had been through. Worst of all, Anna didn't know how to explain it to him. Rehearsing this moment in her head over and over, she had never been sure what to say. *When the time comes, I'll find the words.*

Anna opened her mouth to speak, but no words came.

Teej took a step closer, but his expression was dour.

"Was this all some sort of trick?" he asked quietly.

Anna pushed her shoulders back, stood tall and forced herself to remember she wasn't the same woman he once knew. Teej would come to understand in time, but right now he had to know one thing: her safety wasn't his responsibility anymore.

"It's not a trick. I had to be away from you for a while. I had to be away from *everyone*. There are reasons for this all, and I'll explain later, but I'm... happy to see you Teej."

Teej shook his head dismissively. "I thought Rayleigh had you."

"No, I was free. Properly free."

Teej stepped closer, his eyes dark.

"You broke my heart."

Anna's guts twisted in a knot, but she swallowed hard and remained firm. "It had to be like this. It wasn't easy for me to stay away either."

"Not one word from you. Not a single message. Not a phone call. Like you were dead."

Anna didn't know what to say. "I..."

Teej leapt forward and threw his arms around her, and they held each other. For the first time in over a year, Anna let herself feel vulnerable. Let someone near her. Pulling away, she grabbed his shirt with both fists then put her forehead on his chest and breathed a sigh of relief.

"I didn't picture our reunion like this," she whispered.

"Me neither. Why are we in this dirty alley?"

Anna gestured toward the pier. "To get away from the Haze. It's going to draw attention."

"Oh yeah," said Teej distractedly, like he had forgotten how things worked Behind the Veil.

"Look, I am going to explain everything when we have time," Anna said as she tried to steer them back on course.

"You sound like me. *I'll explain later.*"

Anna laughed. "I have stories to tell." She took his hand and looked deep into his eyes. "Still trust me?"

"Always."

"Then go and get Amara. I know you tried to save her. I think we need to protect her now."

"We do," he said firmly.

"Get her and meet me at Central Station at 2 o'clock. Three hours."

"We're going somewhere?"

"Yes, somewhere dangerous, for you at least. Be ready to defend yourself."

"I'm ready," he said with a nod. "But where are we going?"

"Don't be so eager," said Anna with a chuckle. "I'm taking you to meet my mom."

Standing in the middle of her tiny apartment, Anna put her hands on her hips and scanned the mess. What should she take and what should she leave behind? It didn't take long for her to decide. She'd leave almost everything.

The one-bedroom squat in Chinatown had been her base for a month now. Above a restaurant, it was constantly filled with the smell of food, and the only window provided a view of a comically ornate dragon gate. It was centrally located, clean enough and cheap, though Anna didn't have to worry about money anymore.

Rooting around under her mattress, she pulled out a large plastic bag filled with high denomination currencies and twenty different credit cards in different names. She thumbed through them, picking out five with the highest credit limits along with a wad of bills, then jammed them into her pocket. She plugged her phone to charge, threw off her red cape, then flopped down onto the messy bed to bury her face in the pillows.

What a day. What a year!

Running from Haze to Haze, meeting Dreamers, fighting some and helping others, Anna had learned more in the last year than she had in her whole life. Everything was different now. No friends, constantly on the move, it had been a wild ride. She was lonely, but she was also rich and healthy, and for the most part, happy. Throwing herself into her training, finding teachers where she could, she had travelled to every corner of the globe. Physically, she was strong and fit. Her mind was sharp. Taking a moment to reflect, she thought back to the three teachers who had changed her the most.

The lessons she'd received with the reclusive Dreamer Chegu had made her both strong and fast, a competent martial artist, if still somewhat reluctant to hit people in the face unless she had to. Meanwhile, time spent gambling and networking with celebrities and politicians in Monaco with Gahan had sharpened her social skills and made her comfortable mingling with the wealthy and the powerful. Most importantly of all, she'd located the hermit Metik Nylah, and together they'd worked on her Praxis, improving her skills while developing her unique style of Undreaming. Now that she was back home and with Teej, she had to find a way to explain all of that and more. A whole year of adventures. Where to start?

Anna fidgeted with her ring for a moment, worried it felt loose on her finger. She held it up to her face. No, it was the same as always. Her new Periapt had seen off another enemy.

Kicking off her sneakers, she started picking splinters of broken wood out of her jeans and socks. The fight at the pier had been exhilarating, and though it hadn't been her best performance, she hoped Teej saw the difference in her. He didn't need to worry about her anymore. Anna could keep them *both* safe.

Balling up her dirty socks and throwing them across the room into the trash, she pulled another pair from the drawer, put them on, then considered what else she should wear. The one constant had to be the red cape, so she searched for clothes that didn't clash. Pulling on a yellow cardigan, she checked out her outfit. She'd been avoiding mirrors for months, so a piercing glance was all she allowed herself these days.

I look like a children's TV host.

She swapped the cardigan for a plain white cotton t-shirt and then rustled through a pile of clothes at the base of her wardrobe looking for suitable shoes. *How did I make this much mess in a month?*

Reaching deep into the shadows, she pulled out the most unsuitable shoes possible and laughed out loud. Black with six-inch heels, sleek and shiny. A Dreamer had asked her to wear them, and it had sounded like fun till she tried to walk in them. *I've learned to fight, run, shoot, climb, swim and even dance, but I still can't walk in heels for shit.*

Placing the fancy shoes back in the wardrobe with a chuckle, Anna grabbed an old pair of sneakers instead and slipped them on. Halfway through tying the laces, she was interrupted by her phone vibrating. Anna picked it up.

"Elise, he knows," said Anna.

"What? Oh wow! Do you still want to go ahead with your plan? Did you kiss?"

Anna slumped down on the bed. "What? No… we just talked."

"How did he look? He's not been good, you know? Are you sure this was a good idea?"

Anna sighed, "Well, it's a bit late for that now Elise!"

"Ok, yeah, sure. God, I can't believe you saw him again! It's been so long. How did he react? Did you look hot?"

Anna stifled a laugh. "I was flying through the air fighting blurry-faced monsters on a roller coaster."

"So, you *did* look hot!"

Anna laughed. "What am I going to do, Elise? As soon as I saw him, I felt so guilty. Did I do the right thing? I feel like an idiot."

"You're not an idiot," said Elise patiently. "You're so much better now, Annie. All the things you've done, all the places you've been! Teej will be impressed. He *already* thought you were amazing."

"I was useless last time we were together! I had no idea what I was doing."

"You always tried your best."

Anna put the phone on speaker and pulled her socks up. "You always know the right thing to say."

"What? Me? Believe it or not, no one's ever said that about me before."

"I've gotta go. I'm going to see him in an hour. We're going to visit mom."

Elise paused. "*Your* mom? Uh-oh. I'll see you when I get back?"

"Yeah. See ya."

"Hey Anna!" shouted Elise just before she hung up. "What are you wearing?"

"Nothing you would like Elise."

"Wear something sexy! He's barely spoken to a woman for a year."

"Something sexy? Do you know me *at all*?"

"I saw the stilettos at the back of your closet," teased Elise.

"Bye, Elise!"

six

"Tickets please."

Teej flashed three ticket stubs at the train conductor with a half-smile. He sat opposite Anna, who was texting on her phone, and Amara, who was whispering incoherently under her breath. The Dreamer wore a goat mask, but the subtle influence of her Art made her seem mundane to the other passengers. For those without Haze Sense, it was like she was invisible. The conductor didn't even look at her before moving on.

Teej shifted uncomfortably in his seat. He was ill-at-ease, both because of unanswered questions, and because he was unaccustomed to letting someone else take the lead. It had been a long time since Teej had been the sidekick.

The train chugged out of the station, and in a few minutes, Teej was looking out the window at empty apartment blocks and industrial graveyards. He let out a long sigh as the sun slipped behind a thick bank of clouds. The summer had slinked away, like a pretty girl slipping out the back door at a party without telling anyone.

Anna's phone underlit her face as she texted, and Teej found himself staring at her. She wore sensible clothes under her red cloak. Her short hair was buzzed at one side and longer at the other, parted to the left. It made her look older, but also trendier. She even wore a little eyeliner, but as she put her feet up on the chair opposite, he noticed her beat-up sneakers.

He couldn't tear his eyes away from her. How many nights had he pictured that face? Finding Anna had been an obsession, and now that he was with her again, he worried that if he looked away, she'd vanish like a shadow in sunlight. Dark brown eyes, a fine jawline, high cheekbones, pouting lips, a brow furrowed in concentration. He'd always found her features attractive; her fine jawline, high cheekbones, and pouting lips... but now there was more. Teej almost chuckled to himself when he realized he was nervous around her. Had he developed a crush? How had that happened? It could be her newfound confidence that attracted him, or maybe he had become obsessed with finding her over the last year. Maybe it was just the make-up, and the fact he hadn't spent any time with a woman in a long time. Maybe it would pass. Maybe it wouldn't. He hoped it stayed.

Seated next to Anna, Amara seemed content. It was hard to tell, with the mask, but her babbling had settled down and now she rocked back and forth very slowly. Teej wasn't sure how much the Dreamer understood of her situation, but she seemed happy to come along with them. Occasionally she would say something that seemed profound, prophetic, or at least lyrical, mixed in with the nonsense.

"The deceiver clouds his mind as we speak. He no longer knows friend from foe."

Anna frowned at Amara, then looked at Teej. "Every time she speaks, no matter what she says, it feels like pure truth. She uses the Word constantly."

"Amara was once very wise," replied Teej. "Even back when I first met her, her mind was already slipping. I know we must protect her, but she's a bit like a big human-shaped tracking device."

"With a funny mask."

"Exactly. And our enemies won't struggle to find us while we're with her."

"That's not quite right," contradicted Anna. "As long as you're with me, you're hidden."

Teej narrowed his eyes. "How? The cloak?"

"Yup," she smiled, swishing it around. "Not bad, right?"

Teej shook his head and frowned. "So that's why you were able to move around freely. I guess you didn't want *anyone* to find you."

Breathing out slowly, Anna put the palms of her hands on the small table and leaned back.

"I owe you an explanation. And like a million apologies. And-"

"Just some answers would be good," said Teej as he folded his arms. "But you don't *owe* me anything."

"Jeez, if you're gonna be like this the whole time, maybe we should get coffee. It might cheer you up."

"Behold, it approaches!" shouted Amara as the concession cart came down the aisle. Anna ordered two coffees and a carrot cake. Teej noticed the name on the credit card.

"Thanks for the coffee, Anastazja Brzozowska."

"Oh, so that's how you pronounce my name!"

Teej had to fight hard to hold back his grin. "You're the worst credit card scammer I've ever met."

They sat in silence a moment longer.

"Well, are you going to drink your coffee, or are you just going to sit there and frown?" asked Anna.

"Why can't I stay mad at you?" he replied, not expecting an answer.

"Cause you think I'm cool?"

He frowned. "No, that's not it."

"You can shout at me if you like. Do you want to shout at me?"

"No!"

"Go ahead. You can. It will make you feel better."

"I don't want to shout at you!" shouted Teej.

"See," said Anna with an annoying grin.

They sat in silence again until her playful grin finally broke him. Anna laughed first, and Teej couldn't help but join in.

"I'm having the cake," he said as he grabbed it.

"Well, if you have the cake, then we're equal."

"We are not equal!" he snapped, still laughing. Unwrapping the cake, he devoured it in two bites.

Anna bit her bottom lip. "Teej… I thought of you every day. Every single day."

Teej let out a long breath. "Me too." He took a sip of his coffee, then smiled at her. "Too cold, but not bad."

Anna sipped her coffee, wrinkling her nose. "Where do I start then? With the 'Kas?'"

"You changed your name," said Teej. "Why?"

"You changed yours too. Many times, right? We probably did it for the same reason."

Teej nodded. "To start again."

Anna frowned. "No. Not just that. To leave stuff behind. To leave… people behind. Anna did terrible things. Ran away from her friends. Failed her husband. Failed… herself. But Kas was different. Kas was strong, and Kas didn't need any friends. Kas had no one to leave behind."

Teej was beginning to understand. "You wanted to forget your husband. I did the same. I wanted to forget what happened to Linda."

Anna shrugged. "Yes. And there was more. The name change wasn't just for me. It was for the Dreamers, too. I had to create a persona. Someone new who would distract them and take the heat off you and Elise. You know the Dreamers need stories to use their Art. Well, I created a new story. A new character to shake up their mythology. I became Kas, and then I was free."

"And the cloak?" asked Teej. "You got it from Charron?" It was the only explanation he could think of, although it still left a lot of questions unanswered.

"Yes."

"I don't get it! You went back to the Sump?"

"*I don't get it*!" repeated Amara, mocking Teej's voice.

"Quiet you," chastised Teej before turning back to Anna. "Why did you go there?"

"I went to a *lot* of places, but yes, I started from the Sump. The Moonlight Road took me there."

"Drowden was there, too."

"Our old friend," said Anna with a smile that faded quickly. "Either the Moonlight Road got screwy because of Drowden's portal, or I was *supposed* to end up in the Sump. Either way, that's where it took me. I arrived just *after* Drowden. We both went into the Black Water together. Only I came out."

"Oh God, Anna, I didn't-" Teej reached out his hand, but she pulled away.

"No, don't worry about me. I'm fine. I made it here and I'm telling you this story, so everything turned out fine. I'm serious that it's not like before. Don't give me that look."

"What look?"

"Sympathy. I don't need it. I don't want it."

"I understand," lied Teej.

"What happened in the Sump… that seems like a long time ago now. But I guess after that, I was different. I realized something about myself when I was there."

She held his gaze when she spoke. Anna was trying to show him she wasn't afraid. She started to talk, then held back.

"Go on," he prompted.

"It sounds dumb when I say it," said Anna with a frown.

"Just say it."

"I changed. I changed how I use my Praxis by changing how I think about Hazes, and about myself. When I go in a Haze, everything that happens requires my permission. But now, I don't need to let anything happen that I don't want to. Do you understand now?"

Teej nodded. "We all have our own way of comprehending a Haze. I don't see it like that, but then I'm not the Undreamer."

She narrowed her eyes like she didn't quite agree, but she didn't contradict him.

"Seeing things this way has made me stronger. The old Anna was weak. I'm not. The old Anna couldn't fight her way out of the Sump. The old Anna couldn't beat Charron in combat and claim a piece of his cloak as a reward. The old Anna was always afraid. I'm not afraid of anyone."

Teej believed her. "So, you killed Charron?"

"Killed?" She shook her head with a playful smile. "No, we're friends."

Teej started to laugh, then realized she was being serious.

"He wanted a good fight, so I gave him one. Then afterwards, he said, "*Take this gift*" and he ripped a piece of his cape, and it became, like, a *mini-cape*. He said it would keep me safe, and if I ever needed him to sail me anywhere, I just had to dip it in water. All Ancestrals like Charron have a unique method of travel between realms, and if you defeat them, they can share that power with their conqueror."

"And it also hides you from Dreamers?"

"It... blurs me. Makes me hard to pinpoint. That's how I've slipped away from everyone who has chased me for the last year."

"That's why I couldn't find you with the Fetish."

Anna pointed at his pocket. "Your spoon?"

"Yes. It told me you were alive. It even told me when you were close, but it couldn't find you. I travelled thousands of miles, but it was like chasing a rainbow. You kept disappearing over the horizon. I guess your cape is a Fetish too. My Fetish finds things, yours hides things."

"The spoon is how you knew I was still alive?"

Teej nodded. "I didn't need the spoon to know you were alive. But... Dammit, Anna! I thought Rayleigh might have you! For the past year, I thought you were held captive."

He sighed heavily. "I thought I'd lost you."

Amara tutted loudly, but Anna reached across and took his hand.

"I could feel that you were following me. I knew where you were there the whole time. I was safe, and I kept you safe. When they came close to you, I lured them away."

"Who are *they?*"

"Everyone trying to kill you. Dreamers, Etune assassins, creatures sent by Rayleigh."

"You lured them away by yourself?"

Anna shrugged. "Yeah. It was hard at first, but, you know, I got better."

Teej fumed. "Why? Why didn't you come back to me?"

"I was running, fighting, learning. Two months in the US, a week in Paris, three days in Rome, a month in Nepal. I had to learn how to move quickly, how to stay safe and how to keep *you* safe. And it worked. Now we have Amara, we have our first real lead on Rayleigh. It was all part of my… plan."

Teej understood her words, but they still hurt. "Your plan. It didn't involve me."

Anna sighed and looked out the window. "It did, but not until now. After I got out of the Sump, no one could find me. Including you. I had a chance to be alone. I had to take it. I ran as far as I could. It wasn't an easy choice, but it was the best one. For all of us."

Exasperated, Teej grasped for some way to make her understand the pain he felt. "What about your friends? We needed you. Why did you need to be alone? Why didn't you tell us you were safe?"

"I knew everyone would be alright without me for a little while. And the less you knew the better. I was… running interference. And the only one I worried about was you! Everything I did was to keep you safe. And it worked. You're alright. The plan worked."

"What about everyone we lost at Avalon?"

Anna closed her eyes. "I know, Teej. But what could I do to help them? Garret's gone. Vinicaire too. Pappi just wants to be left alone. No one knows where Alby is. But now we have a lead on him with Amara."

Every time Teej thought of Alby, his stomach sank. "The Apoth shot him, and when Pappi went back to save him, the body was gone. Rayleigh *must* have him. I thought Rayleigh had you *both*. Wait… Who were you texting earlier?"

Anna looked nervous. "Don't be mad."

"Elise?!" said Teej as he slammed a fist on the table. "She knew! But I see her almost every day."

Anna reached for his hand. "She was just looking out for you. Keeping in touch with her helped me keep you safe. It stopped me from worrying about you too much."

Teej threw his hands up in anger. "That little…"

"Don't have a heart attack. Elise means well. She cares about you. And she couldn't tell you anything. We needed our enemies to think I was missing. We needed you to keep looking for me."

"Girls and their secrets! She watched me scour the globe for you and she knew you were safe all along. I cannot believe it."

"*Girls?* Believe it Teej. Look at me. Look at this haircut. Who do you think recommended this?"

"I like it," said Teej reluctantly. It was the truth.

"So do lesbians!"

"Really?" asked Teej, surprised.

"No… but that's what Mom will say. She's gonna give me a hard time about losing the curls."

"Why did you let Elise choose your hairstyle?"

"She's cooler than me."

"She has a crush on you," observed Teej. Anna gave him a quizzical look, as if he'd just solved a mystery for her.

"You might be onto something," confessed Anna. "She tried to kiss me. Thrice."

"Thrice," said Teej with mock solemnity. When she smiled back at him, it felt like sunshine on his face. They shared a moment of silence. Teej looked out the window, then back to Anna.

"Anna, I just…"

"Two miles!" shouted Amara.

Teej had no idea what she was screaming about.

"Two miles to what?" asked Anna.

"I guess we'll find out pretty soon," said Teej.

seven

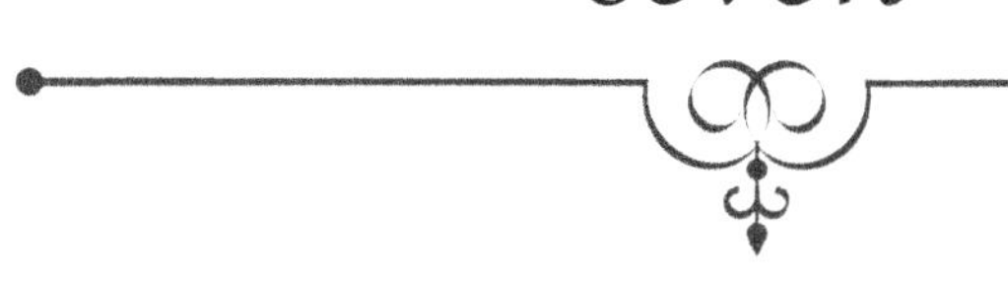

Despite all the answers she had given Teej so far, Anna knew he hadn't forgiven her. She had to share more so he would understand. Not sure where to start, she started talking without thinking.

"Hey, this kinda reminds me of the last time we were on a train together. Do you remember?"

Seeing his frown, Anna felt a pang of guilt. She was avoiding the important subjects, and he knew it.

"Not really. I was in a coma."

"Only a *kind* of coma," said Anna with a grin. "Not a *coma*-coma."

"A mile and a half!" shouted Amara.

"The tension is killing me," said Teej, rolling his eyes. Anna was glad he wasn't worried about Amara's countdown.

"Ok, I'm just gonna say it," said Anna finally. "I have to tell you something. After I got the cloak from Charron and I escaped the Sump—"

"On his boat?" interrupted Teej.

"On his boat, yes. When he gave me a fragment of his cloak, it let me command him to take me wherever I wanted. Now, as I said, if I dip the cloak in water, I can call on him to sail me anywhere I need to go. Anyway, I knew your fight was already over in Avalon. When I called Elise, you were in the hospital, and she was lying to the cops about what had happened."

Anna noticed Teej wince when she mentioned Avalon. She wasn't sure if he was reacting to the memories of his injuries, or the memories of everyone he had lost there.

"I could have come back then," said Anna with a sigh. "But I had a feeling… a very strong feeling, that I shouldn't.

Teej didn't respond, so she kept talking.

"And the feeling only got stronger the longer I was away. At first, I thought it was guilt. After The Midnight Man's thugs attacked you and put you in a coma, I looked after you. I won't lie, it was hard. I… don't like being around sick people. At first, I thought I was shirking my responsibilities. But I talked with Elise on the phone every day, and she told me you recovered quickly. I knew you were going to be fine. How is your hip now, by the way?"

Teej snorted. "My hip? Makes me sound like an old man. It's better. Drowden broke my nose. Now I can do this."

Putting his index finger on the tip of his nose, Teej moved it around. "See? No cartilage now."

Anna narrowed her eyes. "Everyone can do that. That's not a thing." Putting her finger on her own nose, she moved it around too.

"It's not the same," replied Teej, glumly.

"Your nose is fine," Anna reassured him. "It's no weirder than it was before." A tiny smile showed him she was teasing.

"One mile!" shouted Amara as she fidgeted with her mask, which now looked like a grumpy bull.

"I told Elise to keep my call a secret. At first, I thought maybe it was for your benefit. When you got better, I knew you didn't need me to nurse you, but I figured maybe Rayleigh was more interested in me than you. That's when I decided that if I stayed away, maybe I could keep you safe. As long as I was near-ish, I could come help you if you needed me.

"Every day I was away from you, I felt different. Being on my own again was hard, but it felt right. Something snapped into focus down there when I was back in the Sump. I thought back to what you told me about training. Do you remember? You told me I had to learn to run and jump and fight, and use my Praxis better, and learn to see through people's lies. I remembered all that, and I knew you were right. And" she took a deep breath. "The only way I could learn all those things was without you."

"I still don't get why," confessed Teej. "Why did you need to be alone? I still don't understand why you couldn't help us when we needed you. Or at least send word that you were alive. You knew I was looking for you. You knew Alby was in trouble. He still is! But you didn't come back to help me. Help *us*."

Anna swallowed hard. Taking a moment to compose herself, she fiddled with her ring as she struggled to get the words out.

"Teej, I've started to think about my past."

"Oh?" He was watching her closely, but she had no idea what he was thinking.

"I've started to think about what happened to me," she went on cautiously. "I swore I would never talk about him. My husband drowned, you know? Two years ago. There was a suicide letter and I burned it without reading it. I haven't talked to anyone about it since. Not my family. Not friends. Not *anyone*."

"I don't know what to say." His voice was full of concern. Anna thought she didn't want Teej's sympathy, but it felt comforting, nonetheless. She was skirting close to the truth now. A truth that would destroy her if she faced it. A truth that she couldn't share with Teej, because she couldn't even face it herself. She had to redirect the conversation. If she lingered on this subject, she would begin to unravel. Questions that would destroy her would come from his lips. *Are you being honest? Why was your husband trying to kill himself? Did he really write the letter?*

"There's nothing *to* say," said Anna dismissively. "I haven't even cried for him, but I will one day. When I find the right moment, and a friend is nearby, I'll tell them everything that happened. I'll say my husband's name and I'll explain how it all happened, then I'll be at peace."

Then I can die. *Desolation.*

"That sounds like a good plan," Teej said softly. He laid his hand out on the table, and she held it.

"We're going to be doing this together for a long time, right?" asked Anna hopefully. The longer she could keep fighting alongside Tej, the longer she could distract herself from the truths she had suppressed. "Me and you?"

Teej nodded. "If we manage to make it out of our present situation alive, yeah."

"That's why I stayed away. We're going to be together after all of this is over, and we're going to go places and see things."

"Amazing things!" he said with a laugh.

"Exactly. But before that, we have enemies who want us dead, and we have friends that need our help. That's why I had to leave. Before I could be your partner, I had to figure out who I was *without* you. I had to discover what I was capable of on my own."

Teej nodded like he understood. "Your new Periapt is quite something. A flaming golden chain. Not subtle at all. I like it! How did you learn that?"

Anna felt herself blush a little. "Thanks. The ring on its own wasn't enough anymore, but I didn't know how to make it into something new. I trained with a Metik called Nylah in Iran who showed me how."

"I've heard of her," said Teej. He sounded impressed. "She's reclusive, but powerful."

"I came across her right away, but I think maybe she was looking for me. When I asked her to train me, she took some convincing. I don't think I made a great first impression. Maybe she was expecting someone who already knew what they were doing. I guess she thought I'd already had some training. When she eventually took me on, she was harsh, but fair.

"Nylah taught me a lot about my Praxis. When she saw I used the ring, she told me its limitations were based on my beliefs, not the properties of the ring. *If you can command a ring, ask yourself what in this world is not made of rings?* She was right. Rings are everywhere. Wheels, shields, cities, friendships, life, the cells that make up our bodies. In a Haze I found my ring could become lots of rings, then a chain. I dunno, I just kinda liked it and stopped there. I always felt a bit foolish: all the men have staffs and weapons, and I had a wedding ring. Your funny stick seemed so much more practical."

"Now you have your own weapon," said Teej with pride. "And you can fly, too."

"Not quite," said Anna with a grin. "But I can swing around a lot. It feels natural now."

"Half a mile!" shouted Amara. Anna gave her a look of concern, but Teej shook his head dismissively.

"Don't worry, I'm sure it's nothing. Tell me about who else trained you. When I was tracking you, I lost you in Iran, but felt your presence in Dresden. Then I thought I followed you through Austria-"

"Yeah, all the way to Ljubljana. I met an Aesthete who could trap people in photos."

"I know him. Gahan."

"He's like a modern-day Warhol."

Teej tutted. "More like a modern-day asshole."

Anna gave Teej a teasing smile. "I dunno. He's very handsome..."

"He's a very handsome asshole. Did you kill him?"

"What? God, no! I learned a lot from him. He took me to parties, and we travelled around Europe. I met a lot of interesting people."

A darkness came over Teej's features. Anna touched his arm. "It wasn't like that. We became friends. He was a manipulative, sneaky scoundrel, but I kinda liked that. I could handle him. I learned how to mingle with politicians, models, and pop stars. And get this: I actually learned how to walk in heels!"

"Really?" asked Teej.

"It's the truth," said Anna.

"It approacheth!" shouted Amara. She was getting increasingly agitated.

"What approacheth?" asked Anna.

"Never mind her," said Teej irritably. "After Gahan, where?"

"Oh God, let me think… Singapore. It was while you were still in the desert. I knew the trail had gone cold, so no one was after you. But I went via China, and when I was there—"

"There was a Haze that Spiraled in Shanghai."

"Yeah, that was me. I killed a Dreamer. It was horrible. He was drinking people's blood."

"The blood curse spreads!" shouted Amara. "We will arrive in moments."

"She's right," said Teej. "The blood curse *is* spreading. Dreamers all over the world are killing each other for blood. That was Rolo's plan."

Anna nodded. "I saw a lot of it on my travels. But even the Dreamers who aren't drinking blood are still being influenced by Rayleigh. A lot of people tried to kill or capture me."

"And me," admitted Teej. "Although not as many as I expected. Because of you?"

"Yes," said Anna reluctantly. "I know half the time you were following me with the spoon, and half the time you were trying to track down Rayleigh, but *the whole time* I was thinking of ways to protect you. When I could, I drew them off your trail. When they came close, I fought them off as best I could. Even the Green Knight."

"That can't be," breathed Teej. "He died at Avalon."

Anna shook her head. "A fall can't stop him and even I can't stop him. He first appeared six months ago when you were in

Canada. Remember the logging mill by the lake? He came out of the reflection in the calm surface of the water."

"Reflections," said Teej as he stroked his chin thoughtfully. "The mirror blades must be some sort of Fetish that lets him transport himself through reflective surfaces."

Anna nodded. "Like I said, every Ancestral has a unique method of travel. Charron has his cloak. I guess I have that power now. Raguel uses his mirror blades to appear through reflective surfaces. I've been avoiding mirrors for six months; I must look like a complete mess."

"You look better than me," said Teej reassuringly. "He didn't appear in *my* mirror."

"Raguel's attention is entirely on me now. The day after you left from the Shanghai airport last February, I fought him in the snow by the river. All I could do was slow him down. I almost didn't make it."

Teej looked into the distance. Anna could see the Green Knight still haunted him. She tried to offer comfort. "Teej, there might be a way to—"

"We are here!" thundered Amara. She began laughing violently.

Anna leaned forward to look out the window. "You have *got* to be kidding me."

The train shuddered to a stop. The conductor's voice sounded through the speakers, "This stop, Stanpoo Station. Please be careful when stepping off the train onto the platform."

"Be careful so you don't... *stan* in *poo*!" wailed Amara. Laughter rocked her whole body.

"That's it? *That* was the countdown?" said Anna, incredulously.

Teej smirked.

"Oh, come on, that's not funny," snapped Anna. "How old are you?"

"*Stanpoo*," he repeated with a smirk.

"Woman," said Anna grumpily, "If you could keep your ominous countdowns to yourself from here on out, that would be great."

"Oh Anna," said Amara, suddenly serious. "I assure you; the fun is over for all of us. I'll take my masks off now, and answers to your questions will follow, none of which you will like."

eight

As they waited for Amara to speak, the steady *chuff, chuff* of the rails was the only noise in the train cabin. After what seemed like an eternity, Amara pulled off the first mask, but she wore another underneath. The angry bull gave way to a feral bunny. Anna let out a weary sigh.

"Another mask," Anna said sarcastically. "I did *not* expect that."

"How many of these does she have?" asked Teej.

"My time is up," said Amara. "Up and down. Downtown. Down and out. Get down!"

"This isn't making sense," complained Teej.

"No, it is," said Anna. "Just a little. Do you feel the change?" Anna's Haze Sense tingled. Amara's Vig was unfocused, like television static, but slowly something was coalescing.

"I do," he agreed.

Amara shed another mask, exposing a grumpy frog face. "Back, back, back we go. Hoppity hop, fast not slow."

"She might take a while to get lucid, but I think her head is clearing," said Teej. "While we wait, why don't you finish telling me about the last year. Tell me where else you went."

Anna hesitated, eyeing Amara cautiously. Teej was right, though; the old woman was a long way from lucidity. Maybe they had a little more time.

"I'm not sure you want to hear every little detail," said Anna. "But I guess I can tell you more about the places I've been and the people I've met."

"Sounds good. Then maybe I'll understand *why* you went away. Alone."

"Maybe," said Anna hesitantly. She doubted he would understand, but she owed him an explanation. And a story.

"After I travelled, I fought, I trained. I even got in shape."

"You joined a gym?" teased Teej.

"Gym, gym, sing a hymn, I'll tell you a story of her and him," rhymed Amara.

"Nope. I told you about Chegu, right?"

"The monk martial artist?" said Teej. "He was a friend of Garret's. And he was dangerous."

"He still is. I almost fell off a mountain learning how to spin kick on a collapsing rope bridge."

"A spin kick? Show me!"

"Maybe later."

"And after Chegu?"

"There was more training, but after that, our old friend Raguel started to pop up more regularly. I got used to sleeping in three-hour chunks and avoiding anything reflective."

"The Green Knight!" proclaimed Amara.

"That's the guy," said Anna. "You knew him personally?"

"I was a child when he was a fossil. But friends we were not."

"I think she's making more sense now," said Anna. Touching Amara's arm gently, she examined the old woman, who shed another mask. New ones seemed to appear from thin air, but the discarded one just piled up on the floor. Anna was left looking at an owl.

"I am coming back to myself. Each form I shed returns a little spark, but this is my sunset. When I remove the final face, I'll vanish."

"Then stop taking off the masks," protested Anna.

Ignoring her, Amara took off another and was, temporarily, a gorilla.

"It is almost my time. I want to help you, as you tried to help me, useless though the effort was. As I go backwards, I remember things long lost. In these moments ahead, a great deal of knowledge will be lost to the world. All that can be saved is what you hold onto as I slip away."

"Wait, this is important," said Teej, suddenly interested in Amara. "What do we need to know? She has a lot of information. Quick, what should we ask her?"

Anna's mind raced. "Where is Rayleigh?" she blurted out.

"I don't know this," said Amara, now a turtle. "Nor have I ever known."

"Dammit!" exclaimed Teej. "Uh, where is Wildey!?"

"Cuba," said Amara.

"That's not right," snapped Teej.

"How do you know?" asked Anna.

"Because he's at the August Club, right?"

"Is he?" said Anna. "Maybe he moved."

"No," said Teej with a frown. "We've talked on the phone a few times. He's still at the August Club. He hasn't been in Cuba since... wait. Amara, what year is it?"

"It is 1997," replied Amara.

"Yes, that would be right!" exclaimed Teej. "I was with Wildey in Cuba in the late nineties."

"She's already gone too far back," said Anna. "Each mask she takes off sends her further into the past. What can we ask her that won't have changed by now?"

Teej rubbed his chin. "What we really need to know is how we stop this civil war. And how we can find Alby and save him from Rayleigh. We could ask something like: where is the entrance to the August Club?"

"It moves," said Amara.

"How do we find it?"

"Follow the instructions in The Gentleman's Guide to Night Life. It will illuminate the path."

"Dammit," said Teej, slamming his hand down on the table. "Wherever that book was back in the '90s, it's gone now."

"Nineteen eighty-eight," corrected Amara with a cheetah's face.

"Well, where is… uh, where *was* it back then?" asked Anna.

"There's a copy in the Groven Museum."

"A copy?" said Anna. "Then it could still be there."

"It's a lead," conceded Teej. "If we could get to the August Club, we could meet Wildey."

"Are you ready for that?" asked Anna.

"I am."

"So, after we see Mom, we head to the Groven and try to find this book."

Teej nodded, but Anna could tell he had reservations. He wrinkled his nose.

"About that, why *are* we heading to see your mom?"

"I don't expect I'll see her for a while after this. I've been on the road for over a year. I need to visit home while I still can. And besides, I want her to meet you."

"Why?"

"So I can take *you* into a dangerous situation for a change."

Teej looked worried. "I can't tell if you're kidding. Is she that bad?"

"You'll see," said Anna with a chuckle. "Quick, what else can we ask Amara?"

Teej shrugged. "How are you feeling, Amara? Can we do anything for you?"

“Save our future.”

“That’s it? Just that one small job?”

Anna nudged him. “Teej, if she’s asking us to do that, she thinks we can.”

“There will be no future if the Dreamers keep killing each other for blood.” said Teej “And beyond asking them nicely, I don’t know how to stop them.”

“Oh, Donnel,” said Amara, her mask now a doll’s face, porcelain and sinister, “You can do much more. The blood plague has been once before. And there was a cure.”

nine

Teej and Anna were the only passengers on the Number 18 Trans-City Express train who seemed to notice the pile of animal masks threatening to fill the whole cabin. There was less than an hour left on their journey, and Amara had travelled back to the year 1353 A.D.

"Why doesn't she talk like someone from the olden times?" asked Anna. "Why isn't she saying things like *betwixt* and *thine* and *wherefore art thou*?"

"Because she's not in a Shakespeare play," explained Teej. "And she's not really back in that time, she's just reliving memories from her past. As she removes the masks, she unlocks parts of herself that she had closed off."

"So, taking off the masks is revealing her true self?" asked Anna.

"I think so."

"Where did you live back in the 12th century, Amara?" asked Anna.

"I was in Edinburgh."

"At the castle?" asked Teej.

"On a farm. I lived with a Frenchman named Jacques."

"A Frenchman? Was he your husband?" asked Anna.

Amara giggled. "He was tall."

"Speaking of fine Frenchmen," said Teej turning to Anna and changing the subject, "Did you think of Pappi during your adventures?"

Anna's stomach sank. She had seen Pappi only once in the last year, and it had broken her heart. Spying on him from the hospital window, she'd watched the nurses serve him a cocktail of pills: antidepressants and sedatives. Being separated from his brother had crushed his spirit. Anna didn't know if saving Alby could bring Pappi back to his senses, but they had to try.

"That's not fair, Teej. I wasn't on adventures, I was… working. And I know what happened to Pappi. He lost his Praxis and fell into depression. But we're going to help him now. After we see Mom."

"I don't mean to keep giving you a hard time," said Teej. "I wanted to—"

"The blood plague you speak of has visited us once before," interrupted Amara, her voice suddenly deep and grave. "The Dreamers took the feast of blood when the temptation grew too strong to resist. At first, they drank from the Muses, though that brought illness. In time they started to consume one another. Though the epidemic ravaged our communities, in time a cure was found, and we healed."

"What was the cure?" asked Anna.

"I have memories of it, but they are incomplete. The final face will know."

"What year are we on again?" asked Teej.

"Thirteen something," said Anna. "When were you born Amara?"

Amara smiled. "Eleven-eleven. Ones by the four."

Anna checked her watch. "We have some time. At this pace, she should get to her final mask just before we arrive. I'm going to use the restroom."

"I'll tell you if you miss anything," said Teej as Anna stood up.

"When she gets to it, ask if the dark ages were really that dark!" shouted Anna over her shoulder as she clambered across piles of masks to the rear of the train. Glancing out the windows as she went, Anna watched the trees whisk past. There was no one else in their carriage, so she took her time, stretching her arms over her head and letting out a moan as she yawned. This was a longer journey than she remembered, but she wished it could go on forever. Wouldn't it be amazing if they could just stay on this train till it reached the end of the line, then get on another and just keep going?

Anna let out another, longer sigh, then pushed through the heavy door to the next carriage, bumping into a stranger on the other side.

"Sorry," she said as she bounced off his broad chest.

"My fault," he said with an easy laugh. "I shouldn't have stood so close to the door."

The man was a little taller than Anna, maybe twenty-two, with big glasses and dark hair swept to one side. He wore a t-shirt with a logo that said, "*I donut want to work out,*" with a picture of a cartoon donut on it.

"I'm looking for the restroom," explained Anna.

"It's right here," he said pointing to a door nearby. The *occupied* light was on. "I'm waiting too. Someone's been in there since the last century."

"Since the Renaissance," said Anna, chuckling at her own joke. To her surprise, the man laughed too.

"I think the guy inside is trying to dodge the ticket inspector. I'm Richie, by the way."

"Emma," said Anna. "I shouldn't have had all that beer and coffee."

"Really," laughed Richie, confused.

"Nah, not really. I'm joking."

"Where are you going?" asked Richie, his arms crossed, his eyes twinkling. He was quietly confident. Anna faced him square on, her arms folded too.

"Why? Are you with the feds? I can't believe you finally tracked me down!"

"You're not going to believe this: I'm actually a cop."

"You are not!" protested Anna. She looked him up and down. "You are the least "cop" person I've ever seen."

"Well, I'm a *kinda* cop person. I'm a data analyst on contract with the traffic enforcement agency."

"Traffic enforcement? Wow."

Anna walked past Richie to look out the window. She considered sitting further away but decided to linger nearby. Richie was fumbling with his phone. Anna decided to keep the conversation going.

"At least I know you're not lying. No one would make that up."

"I know, right?" Richie grinned. "Too glamorous. No one would believe me."

Anna smiled politely and then bit her fingernails, not sure what to say next. Richie had really nice eyes.

"What's *your* glamorous career then?" he asked.

"Professional lay-about," she responded glibly. "My parents are wealthy so I'm a faux intellectual. Academia is easier than real work."

"True," said Richie. "I mostly play games at work. I'm really good at alt-tabbing to a spreadsheet when the boss comes around to look at my screen."

"What do you play?" asked Anna.

"Mainly retro stuff, to be honest. I'm into old eight-bit euro games. Commodore 64 stuff."

"Wow, that is a deeply uncool flavor of nerd."

"You mean you don't like 90s videogames on obscure consoles?"

Anna nodded. "Oh sure. But I prefer obscure 90s dance tunes. Euro-trash."

Richie perked up. "Wait, for real?"

Anna wasn't sure why she was talking with Richie so much, but it felt natural.

"Oh yeah. I was born in the wrong era. Does my musical taste disgust you?"

"Absolutely. I only like Eastern European industrial music. The kind that sounds like a broken washing machine falling down stairs."

Anna laughed. "Oh my God, you're a hipster nerd. I bet you have a mini-fridge full of craft beers."

"Ouch" he replied, holding his chest like she had wounded him. "My wicker sandals can't take this much abuse."

"I can't believe you don't have facial hair," said Anna. "I'd buy you some beard wax to cheer you up."

"My girlfriend made me shave it."

"Oh," said Anna, not sure what to say next.

"Before she dumped me."

"Oh!" she said, noticing her own smile and turning away so he didn't spot it.

"Are you going all the way?" he asked.

"No, my parents live in the middle of nowhere. Two more stops."

"Dammit," said Richie. He looked genuinely disappointed. "You wanna keep me company for two more stops? I got no one to talk to about pixel art and chiptunes."

Anna bit her lip. "Tempting though that may be…" The restroom door opened, and an old man stumbled out. Anna ducked inside quickly.

"Too slow," she shouted playfully as she closed the door behind her.

When she came out a few minutes later, Richie handed her a scribbled note. "Call me when you get back to the city? I've got few friends and even less money, but I can get you out of parking tickets."

"Is that true?" asked Anna as she took his number.

"No," he confessed. "But give me a chance, Emma."

"We'll see," replied Anna as she went through the heavy door back to Teej, her cheeks bright red.

ten

Anna avoided Teej's gaze as she returned to her seat. She looked out the window.

"Were you talking to someone?" asked Teej. Anna, cheeks flushed, shuffled in her chair and ignored him. After a moment of fidgeting with her phone, she looked up to see he was still waiting for an answer.

"It was no one?" she said evasively.

"The guy with the glasses?" said Teej. "I saw you through the window."

"Just some guy. There were no mirrors in the restroom, so I was safe. What year are we on?"

"My time is coming to an end," said Amara.

"She's been saying that for an hour now," said Teej.

"Well, the train is running late anyway. She has some time left."

"Yeah, I guess." Teej shifted in his chair uncomfortably. "Look, it's just that I don't think you should be talking to random people. You have to be smart about this."

Anna faced him head-on. "What are you going on about?"

"I need you to focus. We have so many enemies. You shouldn't be so naïve."

"Hey!" snapped Anna, "Who I talk to is none of your business."

"It's my business when you're putting us in danger."

Beneath a lion mask, Amara began to laugh. Teej and Anna shared a frustrated glance.

"He's no one," said Anna under her breath.

"You took his phone number."

Why was he being possessive? Anna didn't want to have this argument right now. She didn't need any man to tell her how to behave or who she could befriend. Why was Teej being so nosy anyway? Didn't they have more important things to worry about?

"Are you spying on me now? Teej, you're my friend, and that's it. If you're lonely, call up the girl you saved in that last Haze."

"What has Bianca got to do with this?"

Anan turned on him. "Oh, you know her name? You have her phone number too, right?"

"Yes!" he protested. "I wanted to make sure she got home safe."

"Whatever," Anna muttered under her breath, turning away from him to look out the window again.

Teej sighed heavily. "I'm sorry, okay. You just need to be careful."

"*You* need to be careful," she said pointing a finger at his chest. "A year of watching your back, keeping you safe, leading Dreamers away from you, fighting off Raguel, and you get pissed the first time I talk to a random guy."

Anna knew she should stop, but her mouth kept going. "You need to recognize things have changed. I've done a better job keeping *you* safe than you ever did keeping *me* safe."

Shit. Anna regretted the words as soon as they left her lips.

"Why are we fighting?" he asked, leaning back, and putting his hands on his head.

"Because you're being an asshole. And I'm grumpy because I'm not appreciated… for things you didn't even ask me to do.

And I left you alone for a year without telling you where I was, so I guess *I'm* an asshole too."

Teej shook his head sadly. "What a pair of assholes."

"When we meet Mom, don't swear," warned Anna. "She's really weird about swearing. And you'll need to take your shoes off at the door. And don't slouch at the table."

"My shoes?"

"I'm serious, even if she seems relaxed, don't slouch!"

"Hey Amara," asked Teej offhandedly, "Do I slouch?"

"Try this mask!" shouted Amara. She was looking straight at Anna.

"What?"

Jumping forward suddenly, Amara thrust the mask onto Anna's face.

"No," shouted Teej.

Everything went dark. Anna reached up to take the mask off, but it was already gone. She was in Amara's spot now, facing Teej and herself. They had switched bodies.

"What happened?"

They both stared at her, Teej and the woman who wore her face.

"Here, I'll help you take the mask off," said Teej.

"Something's wrong. I'm not wearing a mask," protested Anna.

"Sure, you are."

Both Teej and the Anna clone reached for her face. They grimaced with malice. Pinching her skin, they began to pull. But Anna wasn't wearing a mask. They were clawing at her skin.

"Stop!"

Anna screamed as they clawed at her face, their nails scratching her flesh.

eleven

The scratching stopped and Anna was alone. She gently pulled her hands away from her face and opened her eyes. It was dark. Everyone had disappeared. She was no longer on the train. *What did Amara do to me?*

Anna was kneeling on the cold, wet ground. Clambering to her feet, she looked around, her eyes taking time to adjust to the darkness. The air was chilly, and she could hear water flowing nearby. Ahead of her, a line of torches flickered in the constant, howling wind.

Anna stood on a bridge. Edging closer to the low wall, she could barely make out the river below, but she heard its fury and felt its spray in the air. The tide was high, the riverbanks flooded. The night sky was a heavy black canvas, completely devoid of stars. Her old friend, the moon, was a pale, slim crescent. Where the hell was she?

Trying her best to remain calm, Anna reminded herself of all the prisons she'd escaped already. The Sump, the Moonlight Road, Rayleigh's Church—if this were another then it couldn't hold her. But before she tried to escape, she had to figure out where she was. Scanning the horizon, she could make out an indistinct line of trees at either end of the bridge. The dark forest was chillingly familiar. Anna squinted hard, sure there was some clue she was missing. It was too gloomy to see anything beyond the bridge, so she stretched out her Haze Sense. Immediately, she felt a familiar twinge. She hadn't been here before, yet this place felt familiar, as though she'd seen it in a photograph or movie.

The Train. Amara. A mask. Anna pieced together the events that brought her here. The old woman had thrust the mask on her face, and moments later Anna had appeared in this Haze. Had that actually happened, or was it part of the Haze? This must all be part of Amara's Art, but why was Anna here?

If sending Anna here wasn't an act of aggression, this must be an attempt at communication. Amara had something to say, and it was only meant for Anna.

In the distance, a man came out of the shadows. He cut a lonely silhouette, stooped against the flickering light of the torch on the far side of the bridge. He was short, and with his head down and shoulders drooped, he looked defeated. In one hand he carried an oil lamp that struggled to penetrate the gloom. In his other hand, he held a heavy book. Heedless of Anna, he trudged ever onwards, towards her.

"You know him."

The voice startled her. Anna turned to see Amara standing behind her. The old woman had abandoned her masks; her face was creased with lines from laughter, tears, and time. Her eyes shone, and she smiled serenely. She wore a shawl over her shoulders and a plain baggy brown dress, but she didn't seem to notice the cold. In this Haze, she seemed even shorter than back on the train. She was barely four feet tall. Holding her arms behind her back, she rocked on her heels distractedly as she watched the man on the bridge.

"How do I know him?" asked Anna. "And why did you try to rip my face off?"

"You and the boy were irritating. I couldn't abide the googly eyes."

"So you tried to rip them out? And switched bodies with me? Why?"

Amara tutted in dismay. "I was playing with you, girl. A bit of body swapping. A bit of masquerade. To keep you on your toes. You incurred no real harm."

"Where are we?" Anna asked firmly. "And who is he?"

"The last question is fair," replied Amara with mirth in her tone, "Take a guess. You already know the answer. Say a name out loud. You will be right."

"Mott," breathed Anna. It was obvious. Though the young, frightened man looked and acted nothing like the Midnight Man, her Haze Sense was incontrovertible. Anna was looking at her old enemy.

"He is Mott," replied Amara. "And you are seeing him a long time ago. We are at the Blackened Bridge. It's famous amongst our people. Or it was. Few remember it now."

"We're in the Realm?" asked Anna.

"Not really," huffed Amara as she waddled over to the side of the bridge, swung her short legs over the edge, and sat on the wall. "The borders were blurred back then. The Realm, Basine—it all ran together. The worlds clung together at the edges like fabric from carpets woven into one."

"What is special about the Blackened Bridge?" Anna was still adjusting to the transition from the train to this Haze, but she tried to keep her emotions in check.

"It is a ripped seam. If you fall off the bridge, you slip between the margins of the Firmament."

"To where?" asked Anna. Up ahead, Mott was only twenty feet away, but he didn't notice them. He was looking at a small book and gently weeping, his soft features pale and boyish.

"No one has come back to tell us."

"You spoke of a cure," said Anna. "Is this where we find it?"

"Cure?" asked Amara. She regarded Anna with suspicion, her smile completely gone.

"For the blood plague," explained Anna. "That's what we were talking about back on the train, remember? The Dreamers are at war, killing each other for blood. You told us the blood plague had come before. That in the past, the Dreamers had taken each other's blood, but some cure had been found and peace was made. You were going to tell us what it was when you got to the final mask."

"I said what I needed to say in front of *him*. Now I speak to only you."

"No, wait," complained Anna. "Teej is my partner. We're in this together. Don't try to separate us."

Amara didn't respond. Anna clenched her fist.

"You know what? Take me back. I've had enough of this already. If you want to speak to me, speak on the train. I'm not interested in your Haze or your history lessons. I've faced worse than you. I'm not scared of *any* of you anymore."

"Child, I don't bring you here to patronize or intimidate you. I bring you here to conspire with you."

"Against Teej? No way."

"Against them *all*," said Amara smiling again. "Against *every* man. We must manufacture a way to save them from themselves."

Amara was changing before Anna's eyes. The wrinkles were fading, and her features were becoming sharper, her eyes bigger. Her hunched back was straightening, and she moved more smoothly. The years were peeling away from her. Her voice changed too, becoming husky and commanding.

"I have waited a long time for a competent woman to appear and I grow impatient. My time is up, and you will have to do."

Anna put her hands on her hips. "Lay off the charm, huh? You're not exactly flattering me into submission here."

"There is no time for flippancy," said Amara as she pointed at Anna's chest. "You need to take this burden on your shoulders. It is time you accept that these men will ruin this world, and only you can stop them. And if you choose to turn away, you are responsible for the disaster they bring about."

"How the fuck does that work!" snapped Anna. "How am I responsible for the actions of a bunch of power-mad Dreamers? If they're murdering each other, they can make things better by, I dunno, *not murdering*."

"It is in their nature to seek power."

"This is all bullshit," complained Anna. "I'm not taking *anything* on my shoulders. I'm looking after Teej and my friends, and that's it. *That's* my responsibility."

"Look to Mott," commanded Amara.

Anna turned to see him standing on the edge of the bridge, about to jump off. She was caught flat-footed.

"Should I stop him? Did this already happen?"

"You catch our friend at a moment of profound revelation," explained Amara. They both watched Mott carefully. He took a half-step like he was about to jump, then hesitated.

"Mott has the genesis of an idea. Desperation brings insight."

"Why was he thinking of killing himself?" asked Anna.

"The Night Collectors."

Anna's shuddered. "The monsters that chased me to the Purple Desert? But he commanded them."

"*Those* were his monsters, but they were inspired by real men. The Night Collectors were thugs sent to recover a debt. Mott's family defaulted on loans on their farm. He was a gentle soul back then. Mott wrote poems of great beauty, until the Night Collectors took his sister. They carried her away in a sack and threw her in the river."

"God…" said Anna.

"You wrote poems, too, did you not?" asked Amara.

"No," said Anna with a shiver.

"Really?" challenged Amara. "Pull down the sky./Turn the sun to rain./Tip over the mountains./Never love again./Turn off the stars./One by one they blink out/ They cut a neat smile, a wrist abrasion. That old foe always finds me—"

"Shut up!" snapped Anna. "One more word and I swear."

Amara put her hands up in surrender. "Very well. It is not a bad poem for one so young. But I need not continue, for you already know the ending. Let us return to Mott."

Anna let out a long breath. "How long ago did this happen?"

Amara sucked her teeth, thinking. "A thousand years? I struggle to keep track."

"This isn't where he discovered a cure for the blood plague?"

Amara shook her head. "Think harder girl. Catch the thread of truth."

Anna took a step back. "There *is* no cure."

Amara clapped. "Of course not. How could there be? This is how the ignorant men think the world works. They go on a quest, fight a dragon, climb a mountain, all to find a magic object that will save the world. And every step of the way, they kill and maim and harm everyone who cares about them. In the end, they think the treasure will justify the sacrifice. They think the treasure will solve all their problems. But no! There are no easy cures for our problems. There is no treasure, no solution that is sufficiently heroic or worthy for these men, including *your* man."

"He's not *mine*."

Amara snorted dismissively. "I don't care whether the boy likes you or not."

Anna put her hands on her hips. "You want me to take you seriously? Talk to me like a grown woman."

"Very well, though I'm not sure you're ready for truths this harsh."

Amara walked towards Mott. Cautiously, Anna followed her. Amara moved like a younger woman now, confident and upright. Up ahead, Mott was poised, ready to leap, but he repeatedly turned back to look at the book that was lying open in a nearby puddle.

Amara took Anna by the arm. "He has already decided not to jump. Mott stands on the edge, not because he seeks to end his life or explore what lies outside the Firmament. Mott stands on the edge because it stimulates his mind and clarifies his purpose."

"What purpose?" asked Anna.

"He has decided he will save the Dreamers. Once more a desperate, broken man thinks the only way to fix himself is to break everyone else in the same way he is broken. He will write a new story for us all, and the story he writes will spread and change the world. In a thousand years, his plans will come to fruition and your *friend* Teej will almost be killed. His previous partner Linda *will* be killed. And in using blood to create a new deity, Mott and his companions will scar the Firmament. That will heal, but we will all be marked by it. That mark will be—"

"The blood plague," finished Anna.

"Yes. It will take him a long time to learn the skills, develop the confidence and accrue the allies to aid him, but at this moment, Mott has conceived a new story. We now live in the margins of a tale he couldn't finish."

Anna shook her head. "No, I don't see it like that at all. Everything that went wrong didn't come from this one moment. Lots of things happened along the way. Lots of things *will* happen. There's got to be a way to stop this war. The Dreamers and the Metiks and everyone else—they don't *have* to fight over blood. There must be a way to make peace."

Amara grasped Anna's arm tightly. Her grip was surprisingly strong. "Yes girl! Now you have it. There must be peace, and we must *manufacture* it. Just like Mott made a choice here at the Blackened Bridge, you must make a choice now. You must take a higher path, even if that means making sacrifices."

"What sacrifices?" asked Anna as she wrenched her arm away.

"Oh, but you already know," drawled Amara. The old woman licked her lips. "I see a darkness in you that only another woman can see."

"You don't see anything," said Anna.

"Your soul is desolate."

A cold chill ran down Anna's spine.

"I know everything about you. Will you tell Teej all your truths?"

Anna stepped back. "I will. I said so on the train. You were there. I will tell him when I'm ready."

Amara raised a finger to scold Anna. "You'll tell him the same lies you tell yourself."

Anna shook her head. "No. I don't want to hear this." She started retreating as if Amara would attack her.

"Your mind is split, but half of you remembers the truth. Your husband did not jump into the river of his own accord."

"Shut up!" snapped Anna. "Take me back to the train."

"In a moment. First, you will hear my plan."

Anna clenched her fist, her Praxis manifesting as a red flame that engulfed her hand. With a flick of her wrist, she could summon her Periapt and smash this old woman's body to pieces. Still, Amara didn't react. Behind her, Mott had stepped away from the brink of the Blackened Bridge and was gathering his book from the ground.

"Don't antagonize me. I've killed so many mad Dreamers like you already."

"That's not true. You've fought plenty and killed a handful, and what has it gotten you? You're the best hope I have for passing on what I know, and you're a mess. Self-loathing and delusional, ten times more powerful than those men, and yet you feign weakness. You're smarter and more resilient than the lot of them, and yet you torture yourself. Pretending to confront your denial, you paint over your past with a fresh coat of lies. If I had your youth and your power, I would not hesitate to take on this burden."

"Which burden?"

Amara groaned. "I am at my end, Anna. I have almost unraveled. Do you hear me truly? I promise you these are my last words to anyone. I will say this, then I will be gone."

Anna uncurled her fist, the flames dying away. No matter how much the old woman antagonized her, Anna knew she had to listen closely.

"Say what you have to say."

"When you go back to Teej, tell him there is a solution to the blood plague in the sacred lost city of Selmetridon. Tell everyone you will find the Winterheart. It's credible, but it's not true."

Anna held back her anger as best she could. "Why lie?"

"Listen to me girl. I know things about the past and the future. I have no time to convince you with sweet words. Let me be blunt. Your husband drowned. You burned the suicide letter. With Teej's help and a renewed sense of purpose brought on by your time Behind the Veil, you pulled yourself out of a deep malaise, but you are *far* from well. You are a woman in pain. I have seen pain before, but no woman alive has burned like you burn."

"That's what he said." Anna shook her head. "Rayleigh."

"He?" asked Amara quizzically. "Never mind that. I know a little of your past. Would you admit that to be true?"

Anna shrugged.

"Well, I will tell you of your future. And the future of our people, what little I can see of it, at least.

"No one wants this war. Even the ambitious and the bloodthirsty know it diminishes us all. Attempts are being made at peace. Rayleigh has invited the Dreamers to a Grand Council on Christmas. Rayleigh is the only Dreamer with the authority to do so. There will be talk of peace, but unless you act—crash his party and have your say—peace talks will fail. The embers of age-old petty rivalrics and squabbles will ignite, and we will burn each other up. This is not a metaphor, Anna."

"So how can I stop them from killing each other?"

"Lies and deceit. Not your strong points, but those are the cards you've been dealt. These men would ruin the world. We must play their game. You understand what this means?"

"No," admitted Anna. She walked over to the edge of the bridge and leaned on the side. Mott was already walking into the distance and would disappear into the heart of the dark woods soon, leaving them alone.

Amara came to stand by her side. "You must wear a mask. That mask is hope. False hope. You must tell Rayleigh and all the rest of those power-hungry men that a cure exists in the Winterheart. They cannot hold on to peace without that lie. If they believe a cure is coming, they will delay. They will hold off on war in the hope that someone will return with a miracle cure. In the delay, there is an opportunity to heal. Not a great chance, but I have observed the workings of men for a long time, and I can see this path. I know it could lead us to a future we could endure. All other paths will see us devour each other."

"I'm a terrible liar." Anna exhaled loudly. "What is the Winterheart?"

"It is nothing. It does not exist. But you must convince them there is hope found in its discovery."

"Sure."

"When we lie best, we lie with actions, not words. Don't just *tell* them a cure exists in Selmetridon in the Winterheart, send Teej to *find* the cure. They will wait for his return. It might buy us enough time."

"But there is no cure," complained Anna.

"And no hope. No one can reach Selmetridon. The Winterheart is a fairytale. The mists of The Fade will take Teej. He will not survive the journey."

"No!" shouted Anna.

"It's the only way."

"You old crone! I don't believe you. How do you know peace talks will fail? How do you know sending Teej to die will stall them?"

"I know. All other ways lead to failure. You must not tell Teej the truth. You must convince the Dreamers that there is a cure. You must not deviate from the plan I have set out."

"I can't believe I'm listening to this," muttered Anna.

"It is truth. And there is more. A traitor is in your midst. If you fail to follow the path I set for you, if you do not sacrifice Teej, one of your allies will stab you through the heart. I have foreseen it."

"You can see the future now, can you?" asked Anna with derision.

"I can make predictions, but there are some facts that simply can't be ignored. Like the Green Knight. You cannot defeat him, and if you keep trying, he will end you."

"I've come close to beating him twice now."

"Close is nothing. Raguel will break you. I have said all that I will say on the matter."

Her demeanor changed in an instant; a smile split her face. Anna didn't know why.

"Such a bother, isn't it? If only we could go back to the old days, the old ways. It was so much better."

"You're telling me one of my friends is a traitor, that I must send Teej to die, and if I don't, the Green Knight will kill me. Well, I don't believe any of it. You have not convinced me, Amara. I'll tell Teej the truth."

The old woman touched Anna's hand. She looked tired again, tired and wrinkled and ready to sleep for a very long time. She stifled a yawn.

"Do you want some life advice before I leave this world?" Amara stepped towards the wall of the bridge, swung her legs over and balanced on the edge. "Kiss more boys. Or girls if you prefer. Anyone who makes your heart flutter. I should have kissed Malcolm. And Cynthia. And even Ronald, because it would have meant so much to him. Those are my regrets. Insufficient heart flutters in my long life."

"Wait, Amara, I…"

It was too late. Amara stepped off the Blackened Bridge and fell into nothingness.

twelve

Anna and Teej followed the twisting garden path, weaving between the petunias and the rose bushes. The evening breeze rustled the trees. The low sun shone between the leaves as it lingered wearily on the horizon.

As they climbed the hill, every step Anna took felt unsteady. She was excited to get home, but nervous, too.

They had followed a dirt road that cut through acres of well-kept orchards and parkland, overlooked by weather-beaten statues that watched them every step of the way. Anna's childhood home, number twelve Abby Park Street, stood at the crest of a small hill. A wrought iron gate marked the end of their journey. *The old country mansion.* Anna thought that the windows and door seemed to frown at her in disapproval.

"Remind me of our cover story one last time," prompted Teej.

Ignoring him, Anna leaned on the fence and looked out across the perfectly flat green lawn. She needed a moment to herself. Walking partway down a narrow path, she spotted the little summer house next to the old pond. It all must look very grand to Teej, but Anna remembered how much work went into building it and renovating the draughty old house.

"You're my old college friend from out-of-town," Anna called out finally. "You're married, and you're in the city for a conference."

"What kind of conference?" asked Teej. "And which town am I out *of*?"

"Well, if you go with your accent...wait, where *is* your accent from? Where are *you* from?"

"I'm from lots of places."

"That's very unhelpful," said Anna with a shake of the head. "Pick somewhere."

Walking up to the gate, Teej looked at the huge house again. "How old were you when they bought you that first pony?"

Anna chuckled. "I didn't grow up with all this privilege. We lived near here, but in a smaller house, where we struggled to make payments. Dad was a draughtsman back then and Mom didn't get tenure until I moved out."

"You don't talk about your dad much."

Anna sighed. "He had a stroke three years back. He's happy enough, you know? He's not who he used to be, but Mom and I made peace with that. There are hugs and smiles, just not many words anymore. Even before it happened, he was always a quiet kind of guy. When Mom got the big research grants and was made professor, she wanted to use the money to build a new house, but he wanted to buy this old one at the top of the hill and renovate it instead. They bought it for a pittance, and as Mom got more and more consultancy money from big pharmaceuticals, she gave every penny she earned to Dad, and he just kept repairing and decorating. Now they live in this comically oversized house, and when mom is too busy working to speak to anyone, she has a million different rooms to hide in."

Teej looked like he was going to hug her, so Anna edged away.

"I had no idea your father was ill."

She wrinkled her nose and shrugged. "It is what it is. He's not suffering. We treat him the same now as we did before."

Suddenly reluctant to go on, Teej lingered at the gate. "I don't know about this, Anna. I feel like I'm intruding."

Anna grabbed his arm and pulled him close. "It's all getting a bit too real, right? Sick father, over-achieving mother, wealthy family, big house? I'll tell you a secret though: none of it made me happy. I ran away from this place to live in the city, and I'm glad I did."

"Because you got to start over?" asked Teej.

"No, dummy. Because I got to figure out who I was."

"Oh."

With Teej momentarily disarmed, Anna grabbed him before he could protest, and in a flash, they were knocking on the front door. She swallowed nervously but gave him a reassuring nod.

"You'll do fine," said Anna as she brushed some dirt off his shoulder. "Tuck in your shirt."

She reached out to turn the handle, but the door was already open. Stepping into the hall, Anna breathed in the familiar smells of home: freshly brewed coffee, peach-scented carpet freshener, the smoky embers from the fireplace and… wet paint?

"Mom!" shouted Anna at the top of her lungs. "We're here! You'd better not be painting my old room."

"We're in the kitchen," came a distant voice. "We haven't touched your room."

Anna strode down the hallway, noticing every little detail that had changed. The old carriage clock by the phone had been replaced with a laptop, the phone itself replaced by a wireless router. The coat rack had been taken down, and next to the cupboard under the stairs, a little bench with shelves held a tidy collection of shoes and slippers. Anna waved impatiently for Teej to follow as she stomped down the corridor. She paused at a photo frame hanging on the wall.

"Is this you?" asked Teej with amusement, looking closely at a photo of a little girl.

"Yeah."

"What's wrong?"

"It's just… there used to be a different photo there. A photo of me and him."

"Oh," said Teej. He coughed nervously. "Should I take my shoes off?"

"Probably best," she agreed.

"This is a nice house," said Teej while hopping on one foot, struggling to remove his sneakers.

"I guess," said Anna. She felt a gnawing dissatisfaction but wasn't sure why. "Mom! Why didn't you tell me you were decorating again?"

"Tell your friend to take off his shoes!" came the response from the next room. "I've made cookies."

"Something's wrong!" said Anna in abject terror as she grabbed hold of Teej's arm. "She never bakes!"

She left Teej behind as she ran into the kitchen. Mom was at the sink cleaning the coffee filter, and Dad was at the kitchen table with a screwdriver, assembling something that might have been a transistor radio in a past life. All around them were pots of paint, dirty brushes, and rolls of wallpaper. The kitchen wall was half-painted. Dad groaned as he got to his feet, then strode across the room and grasped her in a tight hug.

"Hey, how are you doing?" Anna squeezed him back. "Mom, what's wrong?"

"What do you mean?" said Mom with that familiar smile.

"Cookies?"

"What? I can make cookies!"

"What flavor?" asked Anna cautiously.

"Oatmeal and raisin."

"Gross! Raisins are like—"

"Dead flies," said Teej as he cut into the conversation.

Everyone turned to look at him. "Oh, sorry, I love raisins! I mean *Anna* thinks they're like dead flies. Not me… My name is…" Teej suddenly turned to Anna in desperation.

Why hadn't they thought of a proper name for him!?

"Peej," said Anna. "PJ."

Shit.

"And *PJ* is short for?" asked mom in confusion.

"Paul… Johnson," said Teej weakly.

Mom's eyes narrowed. "Nice to meet you, Paul. Anna tells me you studied together?"

"I'm married and from out of town," blurted out Teej. Anna shot him a look, but Mom just laughed.

"Me too Paul. It's nice to meet you." Mom dried her hands with a towel then came over to shake his hand. "Pamela. And my husband over there making a mess of my kitchen table is Mike. He prefers Mikey."

Teej seemed to be slowly recovering his equilibrium. "Nice to meet you," he said finally.

"Take a seat kids," said mom as she went back to the fridge. She brought over a jug of lemonade, and they sat around the table together.

Anna shuffled uneasily. "I can't believe you baked cookies. And you didn't tell me you were changing everything."

"It's hardly *everything*," said mom with exasperation. "It's a coat of paint. Anyway, never mind that. How are you? And what is this?"

Mom ran her fingers through Anna's short hair. Anna flinched. "You hate it right?"

"I love it," said mom with so much conviction, Anna almost believed her. "Change is good, especially when you get older. Change your house, change your job, change your lover."

Dad made an angry noise and pretended to thump his fist on the table. Everyone smiled.

"Well, Paul," said mom with a sigh, "You're the first friend Anna's brought home since little Peggy Armstrong came over to play Nintendo. It's nice to have company, and it's nice to meet someone from Anna's secret life in the city. She doesn't tell us anything you know?"

"There's nothing to tell, Mom," said Anna.

"Oh, come now, there must be some adventures. For one thing, you look great! Have you been going to the gym? Is this your influence, Paul?"

"Not me," said Teej with a chuckle. "I never make it as far as the gym. There's a pizza place on the way." Anna leaned back in her chair, relieved. Teej was starting to loosen up.

"What do you do for fun, Paul?" asked mom. "I heard somewhere you shouldn't ask people what they do for a living."

"Fun? I like juggling."

"You what?!" interjected Anna. "You never told me that."

"I'm pretty sure I did, actually."

"I did not expect that answer," said Mom with a laugh. They sat in silence for a moment, sipping lemonade. Anna looked at them each in turn. In her loose-knit cardigan and yoga pants, mom looked relaxed, her green eyes clear and bright. She was watching Teej carefully as she tried to get a read on him. She fussed with her long gray hair, tying it back with an old hairband. Dad, meanwhile, looked sleepy. He rubbed his eyes and yawned, his smart shirt and tidy, trimmed beard at odds with his general scruffy demeanor. No matter how much mom nagged him to dress nicely, he always looked like he should be wearing an old sweater and jeans. They both looked very slightly older and more tired, but genuinely happy to see her.

Teej meanwhile, still looked nervous.

"Your father will set up the guest room," said Mom finally. "For Paul, although we don't mind if you want to *'shack up'*."

"Mom!"

"What? I don't know what your set up is."

"Friends, mom."

"I'm married," repeated Teej.

Dad got to his feet suddenly, stomped over to the fridge and brought back two bottles of beer, placing one in front of Teej.

"Just for the men?" complained Anna. Dad shrugged then slapped Teej on the back. Even without words, dad had always been a master at defusing tension. Living with Anna and her mom, he had learned through necessity.

"Well, Paul," said mom carefully, "Would you prefer to see embarrassing photos of Anna when she was five or hear the story of the time she got her head stuck in a toilet seat?"

"Tough choice," said Teej.

"I'll get the photos." Mom got to her feet and shuffled out of the room.

They sat in silence again for a moment. Anna held Dad's hand and gave him a big grin. His fingers were warm, and he squeezed her back.

"It feels strange to be back here," said Anna. "Any little change feels so huge. I guess I need to remember they have their own lives too. I'm really selfish sometimes."

Dad shook his head, leaned forward to kiss her forehead, then went back to working on the radio.

"I guess all families are kinda weird, in their own way."

Teej leaned his elbows on the table and gave her a serious look. "Remember our… friend on the train? Are you ready to tell me what she said?"

Anna looked at Dad, but he was carefully twisting a pair of wires together, oblivious to their conversation. She cleared her throat. "I need some time to think about it."

"Alright then," said Teej. Sipping his beer, he waited.

"I have the photos!" shouted Mom from the corridor. "I can't find the one where you have all the melted chocolate on your face though."

"That's a shame," said Anna.

thirteen

Teej looked around with a sigh. The guest bedroom was the embodiment of tacky. Floral embroidery and tapestries hung from every wall, rugs were scattered across the floor and the bed was littered with dozens of cushions, each a different shape, size, and color. The décor throughout the rest of the house was modern, but this room felt like it was a hundred years old.

Teej peeled off his socks, slipped his shirt over his head and lay back on the pillowy soft bed, fearing for a moment the mattress might swallow him completely. He closed his eyes and tried to rest, but his thoughts swirled like a storm.

When Amara disappeared in front of their eyes, was she really gone? What had she told Anna? Why wouldn't Anna confide in him? Most pressingly, why were they here? The questions disturbed his mind, preventing sleep or rest. Teej decided he might as well speculate wildly. Closing his eyes, he let his mind run free.

Amara must surely have shared some secret with Anna. Was it a secret only an Undreamer should know? He tossed and turned, then rubbed his stubbly beard as his mind raced. Why didn't Anna trust him?

Maybe Amara simply didn't think he was up to the task. Worse, maybe Anna didn't either. She was stronger than him now, and by necessity, she had become harder too. Her nature was less open to compromise, her willingness to fight more pronounced. Anna was out for revenge. He hoped he could temper her anger.

Teej kicked off his pants with a moan as he tried to settle his mind. What was he doing here? Anna said she wanted to see her parents one more time while she still could, but that felt like an incomplete explanation. There was something *personal* about her choice to come back home and about her choice to bring him along. Her memories, long-buried, were bubbling up now. Did she trust him enough to finally talk about her past?

Teej groaned and rolled over on the bed. On the bedside table, he noticed a curious clean patch in the dust. On a hunch, Teej pulled open the drawer and found a framed photo inside. Reluctantly, he closed the drawer without looking more closely. He didn't want to see photos of Anna with her husband. He told himself his reluctance came from his respect for her wishes, but there was something else, too. Teej didn't like seeing Anna with *anyone* else.

"Dammit, get a grip on yourself!" He jumped to his feet and paced, his mind racing faster now. Anna told him she had fought off Raguel. Could that be true? He had no reason to believe she lied, but it seemed so unfeasible. He couldn't shake the memory of Garret's broken body splayed across the rocks, but in that image, the Green Knight had been broken too.

Forget the Anna you once knew.

No, Anna was telling the truth, and she had saved him. The Green Knight couldn't be stopped by a simple fall, and he wouldn't give up the chase either. She had fought Raguel off without his help, and in doing so had given him the gift of a year's life that would otherwise have been cut short by those mirrored blades. His feelings had been hurt when she left, but so what? He was still alive because of her will, strength, and devotion to him.

Anna had saved his life over and over, and if she wanted to hold back information from him, he had to trust her.

I should apologize.

Pulling his pants back on, Teej slipped out of the bedroom, closing the door silently behind him.

He tiptoed down the pitch-black corridor, making it halfway to Anna's bedroom before he stubbed his toe on a side table, knocking over a vase of flowers. Dropping down on one knee, he snatched the vase out of the darkness just before it hit the floor.

"Dammit," he whispered under his breath before placing the flowers carefully back on the table. He was rubbing his bruised toes with one hand when Anna's bedroom door creaked open and she peaked out.

"The hell you doing?" she whispered.

"Sorry," he said as he skulked along the wall.

"Were you trying to be stealthy? You'd be a terrible ninja."

"I was going for Don Juan, sneaking into your bedroom at night."

"What, really?" asked Anna in confusion, leaning her head against the doorframe.

"No, not really," confessed Teej. "I just wanted to say I'm sorry."

Anna smiled gently. She was wearing pajamas with ducks printed on them, and seeing her so relaxed in her old home, Teej felt very fond of her.

"You've got nothing to apologize for," said Anna.

"I do," said Teej a little too loudly.

Anna punched his shoulder. "Shush!"

"Sorry," he said more quietly. "I *do* have something to apologize for. Something *else*. I was ungrateful. Looking out for me for a year, chasing off our enemies, fighting the Green Knight—that's a big deal. A *huge* deal. You saved my life, and not just once. I guess my pride got in the way. If you needed time by yourself to figure things out, that's fine. You can take a year. You can take ten years. If you never wanted to see me again, well, as long as you are happy and safe, that's all I care about. But you went away, *and* you were looking out for me the whole time—and that's something I need to thank you for."

Teej leaned a little closer, but Anna pulled away.

"That's what friends are for," she said firmly.

"Right," said Teej.

Anna gave him a sympathetic look.

"Teej, about what Amara said—"

Teej put his hand up. "Save it. Whatever she told you was for *you*. If there's something you can't tell me right now, that's fine. I trust you."

Her dark eyes looked huge in the low light. She licked her lips softly before she spoke.

"I trust you, too. I'll explain when the time is right."

"Of course," he said slightly too loud before wincing. They stood in silence for a moment.

"Teej… is something else wrong?"

"I was just thinking about how Amara disappeared. She was the oldest Dreamer alive, and she's just… gone."

Anna sighed. "It's sad that she's gone, I told you, we have to keep moving. We have to be strong. You can be a big softie sometimes."

"I know," he said with a shrug.

"Something else bothering you?"

"Hmm? Oh, just, uh, hungry I guess."

"I have to sleep. It's late."

"Sure."

"Listen, at the back of the fridge there are some scraps of ham and there are pickles and cheese. Go make a sandwich. Mom will love it. Tell her in the morning. It's what I used to do when I was a kid. It will make her happy."

"You don't wanna come?" he asked.

"G'night, Teej." Anna gently closed the door.

Teej put his forehead on the wall and let out a long breath.

"G'night, Anna."

Tiptoeing through the dark house, Teej found his way to the kitchen. He rummaged in the back of the fridge in search of the elusive mustard. His sandwich was almost complete, but without mustard, it would never be his magnum opus. In frustration, he shifted aside mayonnaise, ketchup and a whole jar of peaches in syrup. *Who has guacamole, hummus and sriracha, but no mustard?*

"It's in the cupboard."

Startled, Teej banged his head on the shelf. He turned to see Anna's mom sitting at the kitchen table. On the plate in front of her, his sandwich had a huge bite taken out of it.

"Did you steal my sandwich?" he asked incredulously.

"It's my fridge, Paul, so it's *my* sandwich."

"Oh, of course, I—"

"Relax!" said Pamela with a broad grin. "I only wanted a bite. It looked so good."

"We are close to sandwich perfection," said Teej with aplomb. "Which cupboard for the mustard?"

Pamela pointed behind him. "Couldn't sleep, huh?" she asked. "Me neither. Anna's father is out like a light. He has an on/off switch. When my head hits the pillow, my mind starts to race immediately."

"What do you think about?" asked Teej as he came back with the mustard. Pamela was awake, but she looked tired, bags under her eyes, her shoulders hunched. Her green eyes were bright though, and they followed him closely.

"Everything," said Pamela. "Work, my research proposal, Mickey's medication dosages, whether pale blue is the right color for the kitchen, how disgusting the cookies tasted, why Anna is back here now when she has avoided home for so long, who the hell you are."

"Hmm," said Teej as he placed the mustard jar down on the table carefully.

"Don't get me wrong, I don't think you're a bad guy. But I'm worried about my daughter, and I know she's far from ready to fall in love with someone new. And thankfully, she knows that too. I just hope *you* know that. If I knew you better, I might worry that you're going to get your heart broken. I don't know you well though, so all I'm worried about is how you'll react when Anna tells you she just wants to be friends."

Teej straightened in his chair and faced Pamela head-on. Mother and daughter didn't look much alike, but they shared many mannerisms, not least their blunt, confrontational manner. Pamela was just as steely as Anna when she needed to be, perhaps more so.

Teej decided to be completely honest.

"We've been friends for a while. We drifted apart, but now we're close again. I know she's been through a lot, but we don't talk about it. I'll be there if she ever wants to talk. Being her friend is important to me. And I care more about her wellbeing than anything else."

"More than your wife's?" asked Pamela. Teej opened his mouth to speak, but she touched his hand and silenced him. "No need to say anything else. Eat your sandwich."

Teej took a bite. It was a good sandwich.

"You know, I think everyone in the world asks themselves *'Am I a good person?'* I think less than half ask *how* to be one. But I think you do."

Teej licked his lips and thought about what she said. "Anna is a lot like you."

Pamela shook her head. "That's nice of you to say, but you don't know me. We're both stubborn, but beyond that, we're very different people. Anna's sorrow is so great, it squeezes everyone else's feelings out. She can't be there for you like you want her to be. She can't be a good friend or a good daughter right now."

Teej shook his head. "Anna *is* a good friend. A good person."

"She's trying," admitted Pamela. "But I'm her mom, and no matter what she shares with you, I know her better than anyone. She's in trouble. If Anna pushes you away, you know why. She's not ready to get close to anyone. She's not ready to admit to herself, or anyone else, what really happened with her husband."

Patting him on the back once, Pamela got to her feet and walked out of the kitchen. At the doorway, she turned.

"Paul," she said.

He looked up from his food.

"Don't *let* her push you away, even if that means upsetting her. Understand?"

Teej nodded. "I do."

fourteen

Closing the front door of her childhood home behind her, Anna stepped into the misty morning, breath steaming. She thrust her hands deep into the pockets of her hoodie, and though she wore her red cape, the cold still penetrated her clothes and gripped her bones.

Dew soaked her sneakers as she cut across the lawn. Hustling past the rosebushes and the garage, she headed straight for the lake house. That's what her mom called it, though it was little more than a wooden shack overlooking a shallow pond. Still, it was what she needed right now: a retreat where she could watch the sun from the top of the hill and think about her next step. And maybe face her next enemy.

Blowing on her hands to keep warm, she hustled along the pebbled path till she came to the flimsy wooden door of the lake house. It was locked. Anna thumbed the padlock, trying to decide whether she should go back to get the key or smash it with a nearby rock. She fumbled with the metal till her fingers got too cold, then swearing under her breath, gave up and sat on the rusted metal bench on the front porch.

Fidgeting with her ring, she looked out across the pond. Just beyond the water, two rabbits were sitting completely still, watching her closely. One was ghost-white, the other tawny brown. Their noses twitched, their little bodies pulsing with each breath. Self-consciously, Anna waved at them. They broke and ran, disappearing over the hill.

"What the Hell am I doing?"

She let out a long groan. Bringing Teej here had seemed like a good idea at the time, but she couldn't remember why. Her mom and dad didn't know what to make of him. She came here to show her parents they didn't need to worry about her, but all she did was make them worry more.

Paul? What a terrible choice for a fake name.

Anna let out a little laugh. Teej had once lectured her on subterfuge. He'd told her she had to lie better, but five minutes with Mom and he'd become a stuttering mess. He was acting strangely, and Anna couldn't determine if she was the cause.

Their relationship was different now. Teej said they were partners, but he was uncomfortable when she took the lead. If he was any other man, she would think he just couldn't handle a powerful woman, but no, Teej wasn't like that. He was intimidated by her because she was powerful, but also dangerous and unpredictable. And he wasn't just afraid of that power in her, he was attracted to it too. She saw it in the nervous glances, the unnatural coyness. Why had he come to her room last night? Did he have genuine feelings for her, or was he just aroused by this new competent, powerful Anna? It was a role she had learned to play, but it was all an act. Had he fallen for her, or had he fallen for Kas? Kas was the persona she created to fight the Dreamers, but to protect herself too. To segment herself and hide the part that was vulnerable. Now Teej was back, she found it hard to set Kas aside.

There would be time to figure out Teej's true feelings later. Now, she had a task to complete. She had been preparing for this moment for a long time, rehearsing how events might play out over and over in her mind. Her discussion with Amara had made her second guess herself, but only for a moment. It was almost time.

Anna eyed the pond with suspicion. Still and silent, it reflected the morning light like a mirror. Anna cast her mind back to the Endless Purple Desert, and the stagnant pool that had concealed Mott. That place had been a vivid nightmare. This was more serene, like a dream that hadn't quite faded in the morning light.

Getting to her feet slowly, Anna peeled off her red cape and hoodie, and dropped them on the ground behind her. Holding her left hand up high and squeezing her fist tight, she walked to the water's edge. She glanced down at her reflection. Her image shimmered. There was a low rumble. Her reflection blurred, and her image was slowly replaced with a much larger shape. Indistinct at first, but it didn't take long to come into focus.

The Green Knight.

"You must be stopped," said Anna under her breath. "No matter the cost."

fifteen

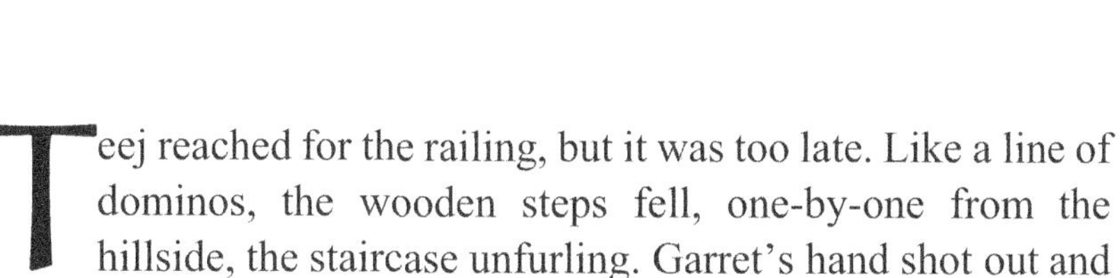

Teej reached for the railing, but it was too late. Like a line of dominos, the wooden steps fell, one-by-one from the hillside, the staircase unfurling. Garret's hand shot out and Teej tried to grab hold, but their fingers missed by a few inches. Teej fell. He closed his eyes as the world spiraled around him and the ground rushed up to meet him. This was the end. Bracing his body for impact, he seemed to fall forever.

Dreaming!

Teej sat bolt upright and stifled a moan. Rubbing his eyes, he struggled to figure out where he was. He dreamed of Avalon every night, but most mornings he knew where he was when he woke up. In the pitch-black, he stumbled around looking for a light switch. His phone screen was the only light in the room. Someone was calling him. The ringing had woken him up. Picking up the phone, he used it as a makeshift flashlight and located the lamp. As he hit the switch, the phone stopped ringing and he remembered where he was. *Anna's parents' house. The guest bedroom.*

“Uhhhh.” He felt hungover. It was early. seven a.m. Who was calling at this hour? He checked his phone to see three missed calls from Elise.

Crawling back into bed and pulling the duvet up to his chest again, he coughed a few times, then drank from the glass of water by the bed. His sleep had been deep and full of nightmares, and the heavy blackout curtains made it feel like it was still the middle of the night. He rolled over and pulled the curtains open wide, grimacing as the early morning light flooded the room.

No one else seemed to be awake. The morning was quiet, barring the chirping of some very loud birds by the window.

Teej took one more gulp of water, rubbed the crust out of his eyes, then picked up his phone again. He called Elise back.

“Hi! So, I tried to find a way to Malamun again. I know you told me not to bother, but I figured it was worth a try because maybe we could get a lead on Rayleigh, you know? But it seems like all the ways to Malamun are closed off now. And I took Pappi grapes, because that’s what you take to someone in hospital, right? But he’s not *sick* sick. He’s just, well not *sad* exactly, but like, depressed, I guess? But you can’t blame him, right? Poor Alby. Then I thought maybe we could look for that old Lady Almeria? Remember her? I went to some old folks’ homes, or I was gonna, but you need to make an appointment, and I didn’t even know her proper name.”

“Elise!” snapped Teej. “Never mind all that. Why are you calling me at seven a.m.? Is there some kind of emergency?”

“No,” said Elise nervously. Even though they were talking on the phone, Teej knew she was chewing her nails nervously. “Are you mad at me?”

“Yes!” snapped Teej. “Extremely. We talked every day for a year, and not once did you tell me you knew where Anna was all along. That’s 365 opportunities to tell me the truth, and 365 times you lied to me.”

“Three hundred and sixty-six,” corrected Elise. “Leap year.”

“Elise!”

"Teejay, I called you every day 'cause I was worried about you. Anna was too. We wanted to protect you."

"Why is everyone suddenly trying to protect *me*?" complained Teej.

"I dunno. Maybe because Anna *can* protect you now. And I can too, although not as well as her. I can't do all the jumping and destroying and flames. But remember Drowden and my knife?"

Teej let out a groan. "I remember. You saved my life."

"And Annie saved you too, over and over again."

"Oh, don't worry, Anna and I have talked about that. My problem is *not* with Anna."

"It's with me?" asked Elise nervously.

"I know that face you're making. That face doesn't work over the phone."

Elise giggled. "Yes, it does."

Teej started to stand, then realized he was naked under the bedcovers. He pulled the duvet to his chest and sat down again, feeling suddenly exposed.

"Look, Elise, we're at Anna's parents'. We can't do anything here. I want you to do something."

"You're at Anna's parents' house? Really? What are they like?"

"They seem like good people. Her mom is just like Anna."

"Curly hair?"

"No, I mean personality. She's tough. I like her. I'm not sure if she likes me back though."

"Pfft, everybody likes you."

"Thanks. Listen, I need you to—"

"What's the house like? It's a huge manor, right? I can't believe anyone would ever live in the suburbs, or worse, out in *nature.* I need good internet. And shops, and places that sell bubble tea. I'm actually kinda glad you didn't invite me to come along. I bet they have, like, *no* vegan cafes *at all!"*

"Elise, do you want to help us or not?"

"I dunno—" trailed off Elise. "Is this a real job, or some dumb busy-work?"

"We need to find the August Club."

"What? Oh, really!? The weird fantasy fetish mystery club? I swear to God Teejay, if you and Anna go there without me, I will *actually* sword you."

Teej chuckled.

"We need to find it first. We met an old Aesthete who told us there's a copy of *The Gentleman's Guide to Nightlife* in the Groven. If we can get that book, we can find the August Club."

"And then what?"

"And do you think you can sneak into the museum and confirm that they have it? Maybe even take a photo?"

"A heist?"

"It's not a heist, Elise. Don't take any risks. Just check to see if they have it."

Elise went silent for a moment.

"Look, it's a big ask," said Teej. "You can say no."

"No, I'll do it! I'm just thinking what my disguise should be. A beret, dark glasses, maybe a wig."

"Whatever. Just be careful, and call me if you find the book. Oh, and check on Pappi again if you have time. We'll be back soon, maybe tonight."

"Ok. I'll report in later today."

"Not a heist!" shouted Teej one more time, but Elise had already hung up.

sixteen

Teej felt like a ghost haunting Anna's empty house. Where was everyone? The loud tick-tock of the carriage clock was the only sound in the empty living room. Worried he might wake someone, he tiptoed towards the kitchen in search of coffee. He was halfway there when he felt the low rumble. The air trembled beneath his fingertips, at the base of his spine, and on the hairs at the back of his neck. Frozen in place, he attuned his Haze Sense, pushed out his feelings and searched for the source. A Haze was nearby. Anna was there, and a fight had already begun.

Along the hall, through the front door, out the house, stumbling down the steps, his fall became a run as Teej raced to get to Anna in time. Sprinting across wet grass, he cut through the garden and headed for the pond. The early morning was misty. Too misty to be natural. The periphery of the Haze was closer than he expected. The fog was chokingly thick, but Teej pushed on. His hand was already in his jacket, ready to grasp his Periapt as soon as he could summon the Vig he needed. The mist swirled gray and thick, then a deep green as he left Basine and entered the Haze.

Hold on Anna, I'm coming.

Barreling down the hill at full speed, he heard a battle ahead, but he couldn't see anything yet. Shapes in the fog seemed to morph all around him. There were dragons with long fangs, and demons with spiked claws, but they were half-formed, little more than ghosts. Forging ahead, Teej pulled his Periapt from his inside pocket and clutched it tightly. Before he cleared the mist, he already knew what he was going to find.

As the air cleared, Teej saw Anna first. Her loose clothes fluttered in the wind as she backflipped through the air, landing on the rooftop of a wooden shack. Her Periapt whipped around with a life of its own, spiraling over her head in an animated coil of golden metal. Her breathing was even, her stance poised, her balance perfect.

A moment later, that old familiar nightmare followed. The Green Knight cut through the mist like broken glass through flesh. He stalked Anna, moving slowly, turquoise flames flickering between the joints in his armor. Teej reeled, the memories of his last battle with Raguel flaring up in his mind. How many times had he dreamt of that monster and his best friend, both broken on the rocks? How many times had he replayed their battle in Avalon? Breathing heavily, he remembered how weak his arms had felt while fighting Raguel and how easily he had been lifted into the air. Like a toy. This monster would surely smash Anna to pieces. How had their doom found them so quickly? Had Anna been careless?

No. Teej realized now what had happened. Anna had planned this all along. She summoned him here.

Pull yourself together.

There was no time to second guess her decision. They were both in danger now. Pulling Vig into his body, Teej fell into a crouch and leapt into action. As his Praxis thrummed through his fingertips, he watched Anna smash her Periapt at ghostly enemies as they formed from the fog. Long snake-like dragons took shape, their eyes glowing green, red flames spewing from their mouths. Before they coalesced, Anna's chain shot out, whipping left then right, scattering them like chaff in the wind. Raguel called upon dire thaumaturgies, pulling monsters out of thin air, but Anna's Praxis flowed through her quickly and she exerted that power with ease, smashing aside stillborn monsters faster than he could conjure them.

Massive in his impenetrable green armor, Raguel closed the distance to Anna, and at the last second fell into a crouch. The ground rumbled underfoot. Teej lost his balance and landed on one knee, his Praxis momentarily failing as his concentration was broken. More enemies rose from the ground, made not of air or smoke, but formed from earth and stone. They resembled oni or yokai: Japanese trolls with long mandibles, bulging eyes, and hideous clawed arms. One by one, Raguel forced them up out of the stone and mud. Their mouths stretched into rictus grins as they stumbled towards Anna.

She jumped off the roof of the lake house, swinging her Periapt up to loop around the chimney. Defying all laws of physics, she fell then swung back up, catapulting herself into the air over the demons. Whipping the chain around her body, she smashed her Periapt down left and right, each blow punctuated with a percussive thud as she smashed the creatures back to rock and dirt. Landing behind Raguel, he turned slowly to meet her, his henchmen defeated within seconds of their creation.

"Kas," said Raguel. Teej had never heard the Green Knight speak before. He didn't even know it was possible. The voice was whistling and broken, like wind blowing over rusty metal.

"One of us burns on," said Anna, her voice thick with potency. "The other is ash."

"Why seek me out when it hastens your demise?" asked Raguel.

"Ask that question to your mirror," spat Anna. Holding her Periapt with both hands, she squared her shoulders and faced him head-on.

"I need no help to overcome you!" roared the Knight as he charged at her. "I'll tear your flesh apart!"

He carried a mirror blade, but only one now. Garret and Teej combined hadn't managed to stop him, but at least they'd destroyed one of his weapons. Still, it made little difference. No human could stand against Raguel.

Or that's what Teej thought. As he struggled to join the battle in time, his footsteps heavy across the uneven ground, Anna seemed unafraid. The Green Knight swung for her, but her Periapt was imbued with a life of its own and moved even faster than Raguel's blade. He swung high then low, countered, crouched and spun—a savage riposte aimed at Anna's neck. She twisted and moved quickly, her Periapt filling the gaps in her defense. The chain coiled around his blade, pushing it aside in one direction then the other, uncoiling suddenly and whipping at Raguel's face, forcing him to duck and weave.

When Garret and Teej had fought Raguel, they had fought within the limitations of what a human could do. They augmented their weapons and their blows with Will, but Anna's approach was different. She had trained and developed her martial prowess, but it was her Periapt that was infused with immense supernatural power and a life of its own. Again and again, Raguel's swings were beaten away as the chain snapped back, denting and chipping his metal plate armor. Anna could make more than one attack at a time. The chain was so long that one loop could snap at her opponent's knee while the tip lashed his torso.

Teej's legs felt like lead as he ran to join them, but he was closing the distance. Anna had looped her Periapt round Raguel's foot, and as she ducked below his blade, she landed on her back as both feet slipped away from under her. Teej shouted in dismay, but then realized this was Anna's maneuverer, not Raguel's. Tugging on her Periapt, she slid across the ground between his legs. Raguel swung his blade down, but Anna was already clear. As she sprang to her feet again, she twisted the chain, catching the Green Knight's other foot. It took him a second too long to realize his predicament. Throwing the slack of the chain around the branch of a nearby tree, Anna tugged with immense strength and all her reserves of Will.

Raguel tried to right himself, but inertia and surprise overcame his resistance, and he was catapulted round the tree. With a flick of her wrist, Anna recalled her Periapt, and sent Raguel flying through the air. His heavy body seemed weightless for a second, but then crashed down like a bomb. Raguel smashed into the lake house with a boom that echoed across the whole Haze. The building collapsed around him.

The winds of Vig swept past Teej and flowed into Anna. She took a deep breath and renewed her reserves. She gathered her red cape from the ground and wrapped it around her shoulders. It danced like it was alive. Anna didn't look like Anna anymore. Her pupils were massive, her eyes dark and full of righteous fury. Teej wanted to call out to her, but the words caught in his throat.

She strode towards the ruined lake house, her hands out at her sides, fingers crackling as they raked the air for Vig. Could she actually defeat a creature like Raguel? Under that armor, did he possess human skin and flesh, and below that, a human heart she could plunge a blade through? Or was the beaten, battered metal all that remained of his physical form? Teej had no answers.

The wreckage of the lake house began to twitch, wooden timbers and dust shaking loose. Everything went still, then Raguel burst free with a mighty crash. He roared with fury, rising above Anna before twisting in the air to plummet down, his sword aimed at her head.

Teej called out without thinking. "Stop!" Augmented with his Will, the Word wasn't strong enough to compel Raguel, but it threw him off for a moment, and he aborted his attack. He landed short of Anna, his mirror blade imbedding itself in the dirt.

"No more!" called out Teej.

"Teej!" warned Anna. "Stay back."

Her warning came too late. Teej froze as Raguel changed targets and raised his blade high. *The mirror blade, Raguel's hand around his throat, Garret falling*: flashes of the battle at Avalon clouded Teej's mind and locked up his muscles. The Green Knight lunged and swung for him. Though he clutched his Periapt tightly, Teej didn't raise it quickly enough. The sword curved towards his neck.

The chain swung between them, and the tip of Anna's Periapt deflected the blade at the last minute. Another coil knocked Teej aside roughly, separating him from Raguel. As Teej fell backwards, Anna jumped into the space to challenge the Green Knight once more. Teej tried to keep his footing, but he slipped in the mud, and before he could right himself, he was rolling down the hill. He reached out desperately for something to arrest his fall, but his reactions were too slow. Eventually, his Periapt embedded in the dirt, and he swung his body round, regaining his footing. He was at the bottom of the grassy knoll. As he dusted himself off, the fight continued above.

"I am going to kill you," said Anna. It sounded like a promise.

"You can't kill me in a way that matters," replied Raguel.

With one massive, armored leg, he kicked a tree stump at Anna. The trunk exploded, pulling dirt and roots out of the ground, the pieces flying at her like shrapnel. Anna dodged under the debris before falling to a crouch once more. Her body was untouched, but dust was in her eyes, and she rubbed her face with her cloak, her Periapt momentarily falling limp.

Raguel's green armor seemed to darken, his body swelling. He was eight feet tall now, and dwarfed Anna. His distended legs powered him towards her, each step shaking the earth. As he bore down on her, she still couldn't see him properly. Raguel's blade curved through the air.

"I'll bury you," roared Raguel as he swung downwards.

Anna saw the blow late and though she dove backwards, the tip of his mirror blade caught her, just above the hip. The sword tore her flesh like tissue paper. She screamed. Raguel moved in for the kill, but Anna's Periapt came to life again. She intercepted another blow, the chain suddenly white-hot as Anna's Praxis took on a new level of intensity. She sent Raguel reeling with a blow to his head, the chain denting and scorching his helmet. He stumbled, then fell onto his back, and for a moment, it seemed he might not rise again.

Ignoring her injury, Anna swirled the white-hot metal over her head, ready to finish him for good. Raguel rolled out of the way, and where the Periapt hit the ground, it scorched the earth. The grass began to burn. Anna's Periapt snaked out to strike at him once more, but this time Raguel grabbed hold of it with a massive metal hand. Tugging with immense strength, he hauled Anna towards him.

Teej lost track of the fight as he scrambled up the hill, feeling too slow again. The rattling and humming of the battle reverberated through the Haze, but Teej was barely a consideration for the two combatants. His mind burned with the image of Garret, broken and defeated by the Green Knight. He had to help Anna. He had to be faster.

When Teej reached the summit, Raguel held Anna's head in his hands as he threatened to crush her skull. Reeling, Teej forced all the Vig he could into the ground underfoot, leaping towards them. He landed nearby, but Anna had already freed herself, scorching Raguel's hands with her flames. She was an avatar of fire now, an inferno extending from her Periapt to her hands, up her arms. Even her eyes were wreathed in flame. As Anna pushed her flaming palms onto his chest, Raguel began to smolder and singe.

But his broken sword lay within reach. He groped for the blade with one hand, even as the other struggled to hold Anna back. In the mud, his fingertips almost grasped the weapon. Teej had to stop him.

"No, you don't!" shouted Teej as he kicked the blade away.

"Out of the way, Teej!" shouted Anna. Before she could finish him, the Green Knight brought his feet into Anna's chest and, while she was distracted, kicked hard, throwing her backwards. Her Periapt was still in her hand, and she swung at him, but it was just out of range. She landed too far away to help Teej. As he realized with dismay that he was vulnerable, the Green Knight's hand shot out and caught hold of Teej's ankle. *Crunch.* Raguel's vice-like grip snapped Teej's leg like a toothpick.

He would have fallen, but once again the Green Knight had a hold of him. Teej struggled, but it was no use. One metal hand went round his neck, the other clutched his shirt. Raguel lifted him with ease, holding his body up as a human shield. For a moment, Teej considered summoning Vig into his body to fight back, but he had dropped his Periapt, and when he focused his Will, Raguel squeezed him by the neck till his vision began to swim and fade.

Dammit.

He had failed to stop Raguel once more.

I'm sorry Anna.

Teej fell to blackness.

seventeen

Anna's heart beat loudly in her chest, but she closed her eyes and tried to compose herself. Her flames burned too hot. For precise use of her Praxis, she had to focus. Exhaling slowly, she let some of the Vig in her body diffuse away with each breath.

Holding Teej's prostrate form in the air like a sacrificial offering, Raguel stood battered but not yet beaten. His armor was bashed and scorched, and the blue flames beneath the metal burned lower and cooler. Anna felt the Vig within him sputter. He had been close to defeat, but now he held Teej's life in his steely fist.

All the lessons she'd learned, all the fights she'd fought—none of them had been enough to prepare her for Raguel. She had faced him twice before, and both times she'd gotten this far: battered his armor, slowed him down, and drained his Vig. Every time she came close to victory, he found a way to undo her advantage. In their first fight in the mountains, her footing had given way and she'd fallen off a cliff face, almost to her death. Anna had been too focused on her enemy and hadn't paid attention to their surroundings. When they fought for the second time on the frozen riverbed, she'd misjudged his stamina, and when he'd feigned weakness, she had taken a second too long to finish him. His blade almost took her arm off at the shoulder, and she'd been lucky to escape the Haze with her body in one piece. This time Raguel had found a new weakness: her feelings for Teej.

But Anna had not chosen this location at random, nor had she failed to plan for this eventuality. Lessons learned in the past year had made her cunning. Yes, other Dreamers called him an '*Ancestral*', but to Anna the term was meaningless. He was just another Dreamer, older and more powerful perhaps, but he still used his Art, and he still created Hazes. Anna could manipulate, co-opt, and destroy those Hazes at will. She was the Undreamer, and this place was her home.

Never play their game.

"I will break this boy's body," said the Green Knight, his voice a wheezy rasp.

"You will listen to me," said Anna. She jammed her hand into her hip, stemming the blood and using a little Vig to seal the wound.

"My kin pre-dates yours by millennia," roared Raguel. "I am the last of my kind and I have defeated a thousand—"

"You will listen to me!" interrupted Anna, her voice imbued with the Word. Raguel rocked back on his heels. His grip on Teej's body loosened.

"This is my home. I know every inch of this place, and I chose it for a reason. You're holding my friend. Release him."

Raguel flinched but he didn't drop Teej.

"You are vulnerable to my powers," said Anna. "You can't fight like this for much longer."

The Green Knight was immensely strong, but he was not a man. He created this Haze, but he was part of it too. Pushing through into Basine, he used his Art to sustain himself. Raguel was not like Drowden or the Apoth or even the Midnight Man. They were men and could live in the human world; Raguel could not. His physical form was a part of this Haze, and as such, Anna could compel him with the Word, as long as her Will was strong enough. At full strength, he could resist, but she had hurt him, and his strength was wavering. To succeed, Anna had to fuel her Word with memories from her past. She had to find the deepest, strongest emotions in her soul.

"My mom and dad moved here when I was a kid," said Anna. "We didn't live in the fancy house. We weren't rich. I had no friends. I hated it here. In a way I *still* hate it. All around this place I smell death. All around the spot where you stand *right now*."

Raguel let Teej slip from his grasp. He fell to one knee, weakened. Anna's words were weaving a trance, and she could hold Raguel here if she kept talking.

"Every part of my childhood *died* here. My bike is rusting at the bottom of that pond. I threw it into the water after my dad stopped talking. At the time I thought he was dying. In the end, he wasn't gone, but his voice was. And part of me died too. My pets are all here as well. Two cats, buried beneath your feet. And Charlie, the best dog a girl could ever have. They've rotted away, nothing but bones left now, I guess."

Still restrained by her voice, Raguel watched Anna closely as she crouched down and touched the ground. She exhaled and let her ring Periapt contact the dirt, then let her Praxis flow through her body and into the Earth below them.

"One day, Dad caught me trying to dig Charlie up from this patch right here. He told me it wasn't safe. Rabbit warrens all through the hill make the ground unstable. I could fall down a ditch and never get out again. I ignored him. That night I sneaked out and dug a hole. I fell in. Little fingers scrambling against the dirt walls, screaming till I almost passed out. I remember his strong hands pulling me out. Dad found me. When I was safe, I reached my arms up to him, hoping he would hold me. He did not. Instead, he shouted at me."

Raguel strained against Anna's use of the Word, but she was strong enough to hold him. He couldn't fill the silence, couldn't talk, couldn't move.

"He told me that if I dug a hole here again, I'd fall through the ground to the middle of the Earth and burn up in lava. I didn't believe him and told him he was a liar. Do you know what he said?"

Anna licked her lips nervously. For a moment her gaze rested on Teej's still form, but she wrenched her eyes away. To have any chance against Raguel, she had to close her heart to his suffering for a moment longer.

"Dad said to me, *I'd lie to God himself to keep you safe, Anna.*"

Suddenly free, Raguel charged, stepping over Teej's body as he came forward. Anna had already set the trap, and Raguel's first step took him into the center of it. The ground broke up like it was made of twigs, crimson lava bubbling beneath his feet. Raguel sank to his knees instantly. Behind him, Teej was just far enough away to be safe. Anna's precision and patience had paid off.

"This won't stop me," roared Raguel, but even as he spoke, he sank deeper. Boiling steam hissed all around him as the lava crackled and bubbled. Anna held him in place.

"This is my home, and I have made your Haze my own. I know every inch of this place. It's all burned into my mind, a hundred happy memories, a thousand sad ones. This is my domain. I control everything here, especially when it comes to unmaking this place. I am an Undreamer! *I* choose who lives and dies here."

Anna glanced at Teej. His eyes had cracked open, his chest rising and falling as he took shallow breaths.

"He lives," said Anna.

Raguel sank to his waist, the lava fizzing and popping as his armor went from green to black. She cast a dire look in his direction.

"And you die."

Raguel's body began to implode, the metal creaking inward as the pressure built around him. He was becoming a crumpled scrap of metal.

"I would speak before I am gone." His voice almost sounded human now, and desperately sad.

"If you have something to say, say it quickly," replied Anna. "The Vig in this Haze fades, and I would rather heal my friend than watch you die."

Raguel groaned in pain.

"Hurry! Say what you must," snapped Anna.

"The mirror blade. The remaining one is yours."

"I don't want a broken sword."

"It is a Fetish. It will allow you to travel."

"Where would I go?"

Raguel coughed and wheezed. "Anywhere… and no one could catch you. You could simply disappear from your enemies. Your troubles. The world you know."

"Why are you giving this to me?"

"*Giving?* Not giving. You… earned it. By defeating an Ancestral. We have rules I will follow even in death. You beat me. You earned a piece of me."

Anna considered his offer. "I could use it to go to the Realm? To Selmetridon? To find the Winterheart?"

For a moment there was no answer. Anna feared Raguel was already gone, but the broken piece of metal spoke one last time.

"There is a mighty mirror on the outskirts of the sacred city. You could go there, but you would never reach the spires. The Fade has spread. You can never reach Selmetridon now. No one can."

"What is the Fade?" asked Anna. "How do I get through it?"

All that was left of him now was a crumpled mask, and the ground began to close around him.

Steam came from Raguel's open mouth, but no more words. The Green Knight was gone.

Hesitating for just a moment, Anna summoned the remaining Vig in the Haze and ran to help Teej.

eighteen

Anna's mom went from the kitchen sink to the fridge, to the cupboard then back again, muttering under her breath the whole time. "No good. Told your father a hundred times. A thousand times! That place was a deathtrap. No good! Where is that medical kit? I swear I left it right… Not here, dammit! What were you both doing there at this time of the morning anyway?"

"Mom!" snapped Anna from the kitchen table. "We're fine. Calm down."

Ignoring her, Mom continued to scuttle back and forth fruitlessly.

"You know, I think that's the first time I've heard her swear," Anna said to Teej. He sat next to her at the kitchen table, holding an ice pack to his head where a large bump was swelling larger by the second. Together, they'd used the last of the Vig in the Haze to cure the worst of their wounds, but they were both dirty, bruised, and tired. Worst of all, they had to manufacture an excuse for Anna's mom. Anna worried they'd only escaped blame by implicating her poor father.

"That's not the first time you've heard me swear. It won't be the last today, either. Dammit, where is your father?"

"He's back at the collapsed lake house pretending to fix it, but really he's hiding from your wrath."

Anna's attempt to calm her mom failed. "He could have killed you both. Oh Paul, is the lump going down? You come all the way here and we almost kill you. What must you think of us?"

"It's not Dad's fault," pleaded Anna. "That lake house has stayed up for years. The building was fine, it's the whole hill that's subsiding. You have to cut Dad a break. He feels terrible."

"It was his choice to build it," countered Mom. Anna gave her a withering look.

"You know you encouraged him. It's good for him to keep busy, and we're fine. Really! We were on the porch when it collapsed. Paul took some shrapnel in the head, and that's it. He's barely scratched."

Anna nudged Teej with her elbow.

"Yeah, just a bump. I think I lost a tooth though." Teej pulled his top lip back and showed Anna.

"It's only chipped," she said.

"I can whistle through it," replied Teej. "Thee?"

"Oh, good God!" said Anna's mom. She looked faint.

"Don't do that," admonished Anna. "I'm sure your dentist can, I dunno, fill it in or something?"

"Thure thing," he replied with a smirk. Anna punched his arm. "Don't make Mom feel bad," she whispered under her breath.

"Thorry."

"That place *was* a deathtrap," said mom with a heavy sigh. "But you're right. I'll let your father off the hook when he comes back. He's probably beaten himself up enough already."

Mom slung a towel over her shoulder and came over to check on Teej. He pulled the ice pack away, and she gently touched the bump, then shook her head. "I've seen worse. There's a medical kit out in the garage *somewhere*. I'll go find it. Anna, make him some fresh coffee. He likes it extra hot."

"I know," shouted Anna as her mom left the room. Anna touched Teej's hand and smiled, hoping he would smile back. Eventually, he did.

"That was one brave, stupid, dangerous, amazing thing you did."

"I have to tell you something," she whispered.

"So do I. You avenged Garret. *You* did that, not me. I was useless."

"No Teej, I just caught you off guard. I had to—"

"No, *you* defeated Raguel. I don't know how, but you avenged Garret *and* Vinicaire. When I tried to help, I was just in the way. From here on, where you go, I follow."

"Teej," pleaded Anna. "We're partners. Equals. We *could* have fought Raguel together, but this time I had to face him alone. Now just listen, would you? I have to talk with you about something else. It's about what Amara showed me."

Crash. From the next room, a loud noise made them both jump.

"Just me!" shouted Anna's mom. She had slammed the door behind her. "I couldn't find the medical kit, so I'm going to buy some groceries, including medicine."

"Stop fussing, Mom!" shouted Anna.

"No, I insist. And I'm taking Dad. He feels terrible, so he's going to make pancakes when we get back. No arguing."

"I would never argue with pancakes," Teej said to Anna hopefully.

"Sounds yummy!" shouted Anna. As her mom left, the front door rattled loudly, and together they listened to feet hammering down the garden path.

"Alright, what did Amara show you?" asked Teej.

Anna took a sip of her coffee while she got the story clear in her mind.

"Mott, but he was younger. Back when he first got the idea for forming the Doxa. He was going to kill himself, then he changed his mind."

Teej rubbed his chin, lost in thought.

"That's the moment it all began," explained Anna. "He had the idea for the Doxa, then he became the Midnight Man. I guess after that he met Drowden and the Apoth and Ozman."

Teej nodded. "Sounds about right. Eventually, they created the Fluxa Haze that Spiraled and left us with the Blood Plague. And a big bump on my head."

"There was more," said Anna. "Amara told me there is no cure for the Blood Plague."

Putting down the ice pack, Teej rubbed his head and frowned.

"And she told me not to tell you," Anna went on. "Amara told me to lie to you. She said I should tell you there *is* a cure, and it's in Selmetridon. It's called the Winterheart."

"Why?" asked Teej. "I've heard of the Winterheart. But I thought it was a fairytale."

"It is. She wants to martyr you. Amara says the Dreamers will tear each other apart unless we give them hope that a cure exists. There will be a meeting at Christmas. They will make some attempt at peace, but it will fail unless they all believe a cure is *real* and it is *coming*. Amara's plan was to send you to die on a hopeless quest for something that doesn't exist to postpone the war."

Teej took a deep breath. "And Amara foresaw no other route to peace?"

"Well, that's the thing," said Anna as she leaned forward. "Amara foresaw a lot of things, one of which was my defeat at the hands of Raguel."

"So that's why you faced him."

Anna nodded. "It was always my plan to fight him here, on my home turf. I *knew* I could beat him. But when Amara told me I shouldn't face him…"

Teej nodded. "So, you had an opportunity to prove someone wrong. Well, Amara didn't know you very well at all."

"Teej," said Anna as she clasped his hand. "You're not useless. We *are* partners, but sometimes one partner needs to park their ego to let the other partner get shit done."

"I dunno. Garret..."

"Is avenged and can rest at peace. The Green Knight will kill no more."

Teej shook his head sadly. "Good. Thank you."

Anna rubbed his arm gently, then stood, and went to refill her coffee.

"What did it feel like?" he asked over his shoulder.

"To kill Raguel?"

"No," he said darkly. "To burn like that. To fight like that. I've never seen anything like it."

"The fighting I can take or leave, but the flying..."

"How do you do it?" asked Teej with a half-smile.

"You know, I'm not even sure. I think the heat helps me rise or something. And it's not *really* flying, it's just jumping with style."

"But it *feels* like flying."

"It does. I've always dreamed of flying, every single night. It feels like my dreams."

Teej shook his head, but he was smiling. "So, what now?"

"More coffee and pancakes?" she offered with a shrug.

"No, after that. Whatever you want to do, I'm with you."

Anna turned and leaned on the counter. She watched Teej closely. He was a little battered and a little bruised, but his green eyes were serious, and he held her gaze. He would stand by her side no matter what, and that was exactly what she needed.

"For now, we get that book. Then we find the August Club, and Wildey. We hope either Wildey knows where Alby is being held captive, or he knows where this Christmas meeting will take place. We can't wait any longer. We need to face them all."

Teej nodded resolutely. "Sounds good to me."

Anna brought the coffee pot to the table. "So, what do you think of life out in the country?"

"No offence, but I think I'm ready to get back to the city."

Anna nodded in agreement as she poured the coffee. "I agree. Nothing ever happens out here."

When Mom and Dad returned from the store, they talked, but the whole time Anna was checking the clock. It was hard to say good-bye to them, but not as hard as Anna expected. The fracas around the collapse of the lake house made for a good cover story. Teej (or Paul rather) had to head back to the city to get his chipped tooth replaced by a dentist before they closed for Christmas. Anna apologized to him for failing to fix it in the Haze, but she also found the new gap in his smile hilarious.

Mom packed them off with minimum sentiment and maximum fuss. *Do you have a packed lunch? Does Paul have painkillers? Did you remember to pick up your phone? Don't forget your present. Will you call me when you get home?*

Anna tried to reassure her that they *had* enjoyed their visit. It was half true. The pancakes had been good, and defeating Raguel had been better, but Anna worried she hadn't told her mom everything she needed to say. Perhaps that could be done in a phone call.

A few hours later, Anna and Teej stood together at the train platform waiting for the city express. Anna fidgeted with the strap on her bag.

"She wasn't so bad," said Teej. He was peering over the edge of the train platform. Anna grabbed his jacket and pulled him away from the brink.

"Mom? Yeah, she was in a good mood. She didn't try to speak to you in private about me, did she?"

“She did,” said Teej as he wandered over to lean on a vending machine. He seemed restless.

“And?”

“Your mom thinks you’re in trouble. She said she knows you better than anyone else, and she thinks you push people away.”

“Thanks for the amateur psychology, Mom,” muttered Anna.

“I told her I thought you both were very similar, but she says you are very different people.”

“That’s fair.”

“I don’t think she believes I have a wife.”

Anna grinned. “You mean she saw through your cunning charade?”

Teej winced. “Yes, sorry about that. The last thing she told me was that I should stick by you. That we should stick together.”

Anna nodded. “That seems like good advice.”

“I like her.”

“I like her, too,” admitted Anna.

“It was nice to see your home.”

“No,” said Anna with a shake of her head. “That’s not home anymore.”

Teej shrugged, then thrust his hands into his pockets. They both stared at the departure board. Two minutes.

“Should we call Elise?” asked Anna as she fished her phone out of her pocket.

“On the train,” replied Teej. “It will be here in a minute. We’ll tell her to meet us at Maxines, then we’ll try to get that book. When we have *The Gentleman’s Guide to Nightlife*, we should be able to find the August Club.”

“Sounds good. I still have the thing too.”

Teej put his hands on his hips. “What thing?”

Reaching deep into her backpack, Anna pulled out Raguel’s broken mirror blade.

Teej’s eyes widened. “Oh, that thing. What do we do with it?”

"Raguel told me the blade allowed him to travel through mirrors. That it could take us to the Realm, but not all the way Selmetridon. He said if we go, we will get lost in the Fade." She rubbed her chin.

"You're scheming again. What's your plan?"

Holding the broken blade up to the light, she admired how the shards refracted the sun.

"I don't know yet."

nineteen

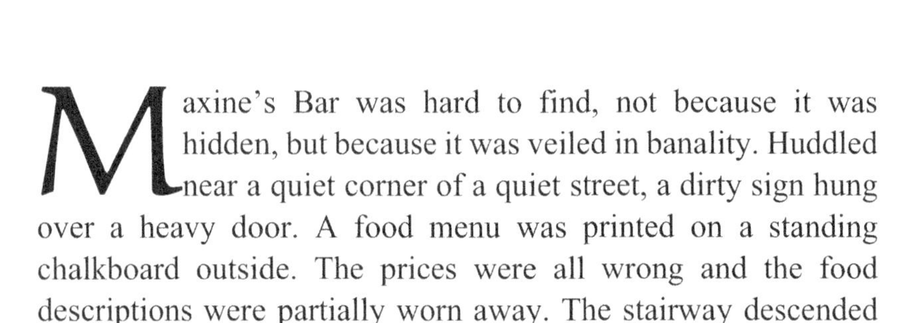

Maxine's Bar was hard to find, not because it was hidden, but because it was veiled in banality. Huddled near a quiet corner of a quiet street, a dirty sign hung over a heavy door. A food menu was printed on a standing chalkboard outside. The prices were all wrong and the food descriptions were partially worn away. The stairway descended to a basement entrance that smelled of stagnant water and mold. It was unpleasant enough that the only people who would go beyond those stairs were those who already knew what lay inside.

Teej followed Anna down the stairs. When they stepped through the door, the old familiar smells assaulted his senses, filling his mind with memories both happy and sad. All the Vig was long gone from this place, but there was still a metaphysical aftertaste—a melancholy that was neither unpleasant nor unwelcome. As he stepped up to the bar and ran a hand across the dusty countertop, Teej licked his lips and examined the bottles.

"The spirits are still good, but only ghosts remain to enjoy them."

The voice came from a shadowy corner. Pappi was hunched over a table. As he leaned forward, a shaft of light cut through the window shutters, and for a moment Papi's bloodshot eyes and gaunt face were illuminated. He wore an ugly shirt, far too baggy for his slim frame. His hair, normally immaculately styled, was combed but untidy. Pappi emanated an aura of sickness.

"Do I look very terrible?" he asked.

"You looked very tired, my friend," said Teej. "Like a man who might still need to be in a hospital."

"No, no. There are no cures there. It was just a place to languish. Tell me, is Anna here too?"

"I'm right here," replied Anna. She stood at Teej's side.

"You seem to be here with us, but for a long time, you were not. Is this Anna, I wonder? Or Kas? Neither of them seemed interested in the plight of my brother."

"Pappi, I…" Anna trailed off.

"Hey!" called out Elise cheerily as she burst out of the men's restroom. They all turned to look at her. "Whoa! Who died? You could cut the atmosphere in here with my sword."

Teej was glad to see her. Elise was bright-eyed as she skipped into the room. Her outfit was remarkably subdued for a change: tight jeans, crystal-white sneakers, a purple baggy t-shirt and purple braids. She wore a baseball cap with Japanese writing on it.

"Pappi is mad at Anna because she didn't help us find Alby," said Teej. He stepped across the room to Pappi. "But he should not be, for she had no choice. Anna spent the last year fighting to protect me. This was not her fault."

"Phew!" breathed Elise. "I'm just glad you're not mad at *me* anymore. Keeping secrets is *not* my thing, in case you hadn't guessed."

"Are you sure you should be here?" Teej asked Pappi with concern.

Pappi frowned. "I feel this is *exactly* where I should be."

Elise came to Teej's side and whispered in his ear, "When I visited him in the hospital, I might have let slip that Anna was back and we were going to try to save Alby. He insisted on joining us."

"If any of you has anything to say to me," said Anna firmly, hands on hips. She took a step forward. "You should say it now and get it out of your system. I know you're all angry. Or disappointed."

Elise raised her hand. "Me first! Did you really kill that Green Knight guy?"

"We stopped him," replied Anna. "For good."

"Thank you," said Elise. Her voice was lower than normal, more serious. "We lost too many friends to him."

Anna gave Elise a nod. "Anyone else got anything to say to me?" challenged Anna.

Teej thought for a moment. "I've said everything I needed to say. Now I just want a drink."

Teej went to the bar, swung his legs over the countertop, then went in search of a bottle of something that would make him feel better. Finding a single malt, he twisted the cap off with his teeth and turned his gaze back to Anna. She walked towards Pappi, as the tall Metik struggled to get to his feet, leaning his weight on the back of a chair. He narrowed his eyes and examined Anna critically.

"You remember at the Groven? We talked properly for the first time."

"I remember," said Anna.

"We talked about what was most important to us in life. We talked about what we fight for."

Anna's voice cracked. "I... I thought about you and Alby every day I was gone."

Pappi was unmoved. "This is interesting. Every day I thought about you too. At first, when I found my brother's body was missing at Avalon, and you were gone too, I thought about whether I had lost my new friend as well as my family. When we found evidence that Alby had been kidnapped by Rayleigh, we assumed our enemy must have you too, and my mind went to the tortures that might be inflicted upon you both. As we searched in vain, every day I thought about how I had failed you. How we had sent you to our enemy knowing the horrors he could inflict.

"As those horrors plagued my mind, I fell into a form of madness. My Praxis failed me. My hands would not stop shaking. Teej and Elise cared for me, but soon my nightmares were too much. To allow our companions a better chance of finding my brother, and my dear friend Anna, I consigned myself to a hospital run by an old Doctor who owed me a favor. A private place, where I did not sleep and struggled to eat, but still, that care kept me sane. Every day, I spent hours looking at these hands—"

Pappi held his hands up, and his voice became angry.

"These hands!"

Everyone winced as Pappi's voice broke. Teej wanted to step in, but he had to let this play out. Anna had to face Pappi here and now.

"I willed the shaking to stop so that my Praxis might return, and I could help my friends save my brother and my dear friend. As recently as this morning, I looked out my window and I imagined you were out there in need of help, and I felt great guilt. Now I find that for the last year, all of that guilt was misplaced. You were *fine*. You were not just fine, you were *well*. And while you travelled and ran from your problems, not a single step was taken to find or save my brother. So, tell me, Anna, when you *thought* of Alby and Pappi every day, why did you *do nothing?"*

Teej couldn't take it anymore. Putting his bottle down, he pointed an accusing finger at Pappi.

"Dammit, that's not how this went down, and you know it. Anna lured the Green Knight away from us all. She wasn't here, but she didn't leave."

"No," interrupted Anna. "Pappi is right. I had a plan to save Alby, but I was too slow. I should have done more."

Elise started to speak. "This seems…" she trailed off.

Pappi stumbled across the room, moving towards Anna like an old man, in obvious pain and deathly tired. Teej wanted to intervene but restrained himself. Pappi laid a heavy hand on Anna's shoulder. She faced him squarely.

"Tell me, Anna. Has anything you've done this past year made you stronger?"

"Everything" replied Anna.

"Then if you are now strong enough to save my brother, I beg you to try."

Anna put her hand on his. "That was always my intention. I promise."

Pappi's expression softened and a shadow of a smile appeared. The tense atmosphere evaporated.

"I'm pouring us all a drink," said Teej.

Pappi slumped down on a stool at the bar, and Teej grabbed four glasses. Elise and Anna sat on either side of the old man. Elise threw her arms around Pappi's waist and hugged him ferociously, and he put a long, lazy arm over her shoulder.

Teej lined up four shot glasses and filled them to the brim.

"This is the bottle I was looking for" explained Teej. "Garret told me to save it for a celebration. McAlan '26."

"That is a serious bottle," said Pappi. "None of the whiskies in the world can make me feel joy today." He held his glass up and examined it in the low light. "But if they could, it would be this one."

"What are we celebrating?" coughed Elise. Teej turned to see her glass was already empty. "Elise!"

She waved the glass at him. "Just fill me up again and do the toast."

Teej poured her another glass then held up his own. "Garret, you old miserable bastard, we got him for you."

"And Viniciare," said Anna as she nudged Elise.

"We miss you," said Elise.

"To absent friends," finished Pappi, and they all drank.

The whisky burned Teej's throat the whole way down, and it was glorious. He watched Anna with amusement as she first wrinkled her nose and then eventually raised her eyebrows in approval. Even Pappi seemed a little happier. Before Elise could grab the bottle again, Teej swiped it away.

"Hey!"

"We need clear heads," he replied. Noticing Anna hadn't finished her drink, he clinked her glass with his. "Drink up, boss, then tell us your plan."

Anna drained her glass, shook her head then coughed. "Smooth. Alright, here's what I've got so far. The only lead we have on Rayleigh is Wildey. We know that Rayleigh is calling a Council of Dreamers at Christmas, but we don't know where."

"And it's safe to say we're not invited," said Teej. "We still have two weeks. We can't just wait around. We need to get to that Christmas Council. Maybe we can convince the Dreamers to pursue peace. Maybe we can expose Rayleigh and turn the Dreamers against him.

"But most important of all, we can save Alby. It will be hard to find Rayleigh in his hideout, but when he meets the Dreamers for their Council, that's when we can make our move."

"A Council?" said Pappi. "For what reason?"

"We've heard mention of peace talks," said Anna. "That's all conjecture for now. All we know is that the Dreamers are tearing each other apart in some bloody civil war."

"Like, really bloody," said Elise. "Because they're drinking each other's blood."

"Exactly," went on Anna. "We can only do something about it if we make it to that Council. We can face Rayleigh and save Alby. To do that, our only lead is Wildey. Either Wildey knows the location of Rayleigh's hideout or at least where the Christmas Council will meet."

"And Wildey is in his super-secret club?" said Elise.

"Yes," said Anna. "And when we *do* find him… Well, that's as far as I've got. You're sure he's still there? The last time I heard from him was back outside the Groven Museum when he called you."

Teej nodded. "Oh yes, I'm sure he's there. We've spoken on the phone since then, and he still wants to meet me, as long as I bring you along. He says he has the information we need. And he hates Rayleigh. An unlikely ally maybe. What do you think Pappi?"

Pappi swirled his glass absentmindedly. "It is as you say. Finding Rayleigh is the first challenge. He is a political manipulator, and you see how successfully he has turned many of the Dreamers against you. His Art is like chess, but played out with people, not pieces. He will be surrounded by supporters and protectors. We have taken his knight, but no doubt he has many other pawns he will throw at us, and not all of them will be soldiers deserving of death."

"We'll worry about that when we face him," said Teej eagerly. "And if we confront him at the Christmas Council in front of the Dreamers, he can't just kill us. We still don't know what he wants from this meeting, though."

Pappi rubbed the back of his neck. "If this Council seeks to bring about peace but fails, we will all be doomed. The Dreamers will feel the pang of their mortality and hide in their Idylls for a time, but that calm will not last."

"I think he's right," said Elise. "Vinicaire was super-brave, obviously, but when unexpected things happened, we would always hide out for a while. He said it was to come up with a plan, but sometimes we wouldn't plan that much."

Teej and Anna exchanged a glance.

"Anyone who's not trying to kill us is an improvement right now," said Anna. "We don't have any other friends left. There's only Wildey."

"We're really going to the August Club?" said Elise in wonder.

"Yeah," said Anna. "That's his base. First, we need to find that guidebook that tells us how to get there."

"This one?" asked Elise. She slammed an old brown hardback on the bar.

"How did you…?" asked Teej.

"One-woman heist," explained Elise. "And seeing as I got the book, don't even *consider* leaving me behind!"

Pappi let out the smallest of chuckles. "Elise, we would face the monsters without fear, but when there is such fire in your eyes, none of us would dare argue with you."

twenty

Grandiose plans had been derailed by the most mundane concerns. Anna and Elise were hungry, and everyone needed new clothes. Meanwhile, the two men seemed unable to read a map properly. Anna finished her maple-glazed cream-filled donut, threw the napkin in the trashcan, then sipped her coffee while watching Teej and Pappi argue about where to go next.

Their guidebook, *The Gentleman's Guide to Nightlife*, explained step-by-step the route to the August Club. Unfortunately, their quest to the most sought-after and exclusive venue in existence had stalled at Millie's Shopping Mall. Pappi, Teej, and Anna stood outside a trendy vintage boutique called 'Miss-Thrifts' as they waited for Elise to buy a suitable outfit. The men had complained that now was not an appropriate time for Elise to go shopping, but Elise had retorted that retail was an essential step in their quest. Anna sided with Elise, and the decision was made. She had asked Anna to join her in the changing rooms, but Anna had demurred, opting instead for distraction of the glazed and cream-filled variety.

"I can't believe we're hanging out in a mall again," said Anna.

"There used to be a dragon on the top floor," said Teej.

"You told me that last time we were here. I still don't believe you. How old is that book again?"

Teej's furrowed his brow as he flicked between the same two pages over and over. "Eight hundred years."

"Read that last line to me one more time."

"*Ye first entranceway that you seek is secluded betwixt the cronut stand and the gentleman who maketh the balloon animals.*"

"You have got to be shitting me!" Anna put her head on his shoulder. "Show me the book."

Teej held the page up, and right enough, though the script was cursive and hard to read, that was exactly what it said.

"Wild," responded Anna as she sipped her coffee.

"I can't believe you're indulging Elise like this," grumbled Teej.

"Our fashionable friend is having a more successful journey than we are," said Pappi. He leaned on a pillar nearby, his expression pained. "I am sorry; I must sit for a moment."

Anna offered him an arm, and together they stumbled to a nearby bench. The mall wasn't busy, and everyone who passed by ignored them. They sat, and a moment later Teej joined them, still absorbed in the book. He was squinting and holding it sideways now.

"You should be home resting," Anna scolded Pappi. "You're skin and bone."

"You did not share your donut," he teased.

"I'll buy you a whole box if you'll eat them!"

Pappi laughed a little then held his chest as he coughed. "I cannot eat, I am sorry."

"Is there anything we can do to help you?" asked Anna.

"No. The connection between me and my brother is deep and strong. When we are apart, we suffer greatly. It is a result of being in so many Hazes together for so long. My sorrow manifests physically. Do not worry about me. In trying to save him, you are doing everything you can for me."

"We're going to get him back," promised Anna. "Isn't that right?" She nudged Teej.

"Hmm? Oh yeah, sure. I just don't understand why the book says there's a door when…"

"The book shifts and changes like the tides," explained Pappi. "It is mercurial, and the requirement for reaching the August Club is different for every group. The journey requires those who walk the path pay a price. If you make it to the end, you will all lose something on the road."

"Isn't that always the way?" replied Anna.

"I am serious, Anna," replied Pappi. "The book is treacherous. Do not mistake its anachronisms for whimsy. It is possessed of a will of its own. I can feel its malevolence."

Teej tried to pass the book to Pappi, but he recoiled. Anna snatched it from Teej's hand instead.

"Let me try." Rubbing her fingertips over the rough cover, the book felt warm in her hand. The leather binding had a fleshy consistency that was deeply unpleasant. It smelled too, a mix of stale coffee and human sweat. Anna flicked to the third page; the first two were all dire warnings and vague threats written in abysmal old-timey prose. Whichever gentlemen had written *The Gentleman's Guide to Nightlife* had no discernible literary talent.

"So?" asked Teej impatiently.

"So, why don't we just go through the door between the cronut stall and the balloon stand?"

Teej gestured broadly in the direction of where the door should be. There was no door.

"Maybe it's some kind of riddle?" suggested Anna.

"I am sure you will crack the code soon," said Pappi wearily. "My Praxis is stunted, but I discern some path is close. Do you not?"

Teej looked suspiciously at the clown manning the balloon stand but didn't say anything.

Anna stretched out her Haze Sense and quickly found Pappi was right. This place felt like the elevator to Malamun or the first steps on the Moonlight Road. She could feel there was an entrance here, but it was obscured.

"I know you did not expect me to come along today," said Pappi. "I will do what I can in your absence."

Anna put her hand on his shoulder. "I don't think there is much you can do to help us."

"There is," he contradicted with a smile. "I can keep track of where the shrapnel lands when you blow this new place apart."

"Hey!" protested Anna. "I don't blow up *every* Haze I enter."

Teej and Pappi exchanged glances.

"Very well," chuckled Pappi. "I will keep my ear to the ground. I still have many connections and even a few friends. When you get back, call me. I will arrange a sanctuary for you all. We can regroup and make ourselves safe until this Christmas Council. We *shall* meet again."

"Remember to bring the rest of that bottle," commanded Teej. "And we'll bring Alby."

Pappi said nothing, but he closed his eyes and held Anna's hand.

"I'm done!" shouted Elise as she skipped between shoppers with a bag in each hand. She had already changed her clothes and was now wearing a purple berry and an off-the-shoulder cardigan with a loose tartan skirt and orange leggings. She'd bought another pair of brand-new white sneakers too.

"Elise," complained Anna, "We have no idea where we're going to end up. Is that the best inconspicuous, all-weather, all-terrain outfit you could find?"

"No. That's why I bought a ton of different outfits for each of us. And I got us a backpack each too. You know, to carry useful supplies and stuff."

"That's actually a good idea," conceded Anna.

"Who knows where this path will take us?" said Teej. "It surely won't start and end in a mall. We could end up travelling all across the firmament. The book says we might travel through nightclubs, bars, restaurants, temples, theatres at the top of mountains or illicit raves under the sea."

Elise held her bags up. "That's why I bought smart clothes, casual clothes, hiking gear, swimwear, sunglasses, scarves, scuba gear…"

"Scuba gear?" questioned Anna.

"Well, more like rubber clothing. We're going to a fetish club, right?"

"No." protested Teej. "That's not right at all!"

"Jeez, what's his problem?" muttered Elise.

"You did great," consoled Anna. "I think Teej just wishes he had a sat nav for the August Club."

"I'd settle for any map that made sense," said Teej.

"Has anyone tried just going through the door?" suggested Elise.

Anna frowned. "There *is* no door."

"Sure, there is," said Elise. "If the book says so. It's not going to appear if we're not serious about going through it, right?" She stormed off to the cronut stand, pushing the clown with the balloon animals aside when he approached her.

"Elise, that's not how doors work. It's not going to just-"

Before Anna could finish, Elise had located a nearly invisible door in the recess in the wall. She pulled it open and smiled back at them.

"This should be a lesson," lectured Pappi. "All three of you must go boldly on this journey. Timidity will lead to torpor."

"You have a better way with words than the idiot who wrote this," said Teej as he closed the book, stuffed it in a backpack and slung it over his shoulder. He turned back to Pappi. "You will be all right?"

"I am not someone you need to worry about."

"Goodbye, Pappi," said Anna as she hugged him and pulled her red cloak tight around her shoulders. "Look after yourself."

"Come close, Elise!" shouted Pappi as he waved her over. She lingered at the open door, then reluctantly joined them.

"Read the book's instructions carefully," said Pappi as they huddled around him. "I have heard talk of this book. It is dangerous. I do not believe it will contradict itself, nor will it lie to you, but it may mislead you. The book's purpose is to show you the way, but also to *guard* the way. My Praxis, long-dormant, stirs in proximity to this tome. I sense malign purpose, but also quixotic mischief. The book whispers lies in your ears. Do not allow it to succeed. Cleave to one another. You are my dear friends, and together, we can achieve a great deal. As you follow this path together, remember the way to succeed is to grasp the reins of friendship close. That is how you will prevail."

"I won't let you down, Pappi," promised Anna.

"I know," he replied. "I can always see what is in your heart."

Pappi put his hand out and Anna held it. Then Teej put his hand on theirs, and finally, Elise slapped her hand on top.

"And if this book tries anything," growled Anna. "I will burn it to ash."

twenty-one

Elise skipped eagerly into the darkness, but Anna followed more carefully. Behind her, Teej rested a hand on her shoulder.

"I can't see a thing," complained Elise. "Maybe we should… Whoa!"

The darkness gave way to blinding light as Elise opened a door. and Anna collided with her. Holding her friend, Anna took a moment to let her eyes adjust. They had emerged from complete darkness, through a side door into a narrow alleyway glowing with lamps and neon signs. The air was warm and humid. Signs written in Japanese were all around them, and the smell of fried chicken and grilled fish filled Anna's nostrils. Elise gasped in excitement then started to stray, so Anna grabbed hold of her arm and pulled her back.

"What the Hell…?" Teej joined them a moment later, his hands protecting his eyes as if he'd just woken up with a hangover. Trying to get her bearings, Anna turned to see she was standing next to a bubbling fish tank full of sea urchins and gently bobbing lobsters.

"Tokyo," explained Teej. "I've been here before. To this street food market. It's a nest of bars and restaurants squeezed into tiny alleys below overhead rails."

"I knew that," countered Anna. "I've been places like this before."

"It's not a competition you two," snapped Elise. "What do we do now?"

"Let's get out of this street and find a quieter alley," suggested Teej as he motioned for them to follow. Hesitating for just a moment, Anna followed with Elise in tow. It was busy; people hustled past, laughing, ordering food, shouting and eating. Anna examined a nearby stall featuring mochi and melon-bread, and despite herself, started licking her lips. Wrenching her gaze away, she looked to her friends.

"We're in a little warren of alleyways beneath the train tracks," said Teej. "I think I recognize that shop, but it changes constantly. It's all street food stalls and bars. I guess we're on the right track."

"I've always wanted to come to Japan," said Elise with wonder. She was about to poke her finger into a tank of live fish, but Teej pulled her back at the last moment.

"Don't. Touch. Anything. We need to make sure we do *exactly* what the book tells us, and no more. If we fall off the path, who knows if we'll be able to join it again."

"What happens if we get lost?" asked Anna.

"Then we have to pay for a very expensive flight home."

Elise started to wander away again, and again Anna pulled her back by the scruff of her shirt. "We're doing this for Alby," she reminded her friend.

"I know! I've just never seen deep-fried black sesame ice cream before."

"It's not that good," said Teej absentmindedly as he examined the book again. "We're looking for a place called Ryo's. It's an izakaya."

"A what?" Asked Elise.

"A tiny little pub with only a few seats," explained Anna.

"I could go for some sake," said Elise.

"Me too," said Teej. "It's north of here. How do we find north?"

"I have an app," said Elise. She fished for her phone in her pocket.

"Jesus, it's cold," complained Teej. He zipped his jacket up to his neck.

"I have an extra sweater," offered Elise with a mischievous grin.

"Let's just find the place."

"There it is!" exclaimed Anna. At the opposite end of the alley, she spotted a sign with some English poking out from amongst the tangle of neon and billboards. *Ryo's Quality Spirits.*

"Great," said Teej as he patted her on the back. As they approached the entrance, Anna stretched out her Haze sense but felt nothing. The izakaya didn't seem dangerous, but it didn't seem welcoming either. The doorway was narrow and covered in red signs, but they were all written in kanji. Through a small, misted-up window, she could see three empty stools by the bar, and a sweaty man with a hotplate cooking fish. Over the door was a heavy curtain. She turned to Teej, and he nodded in encouragement. Taking the lead, Anna stepped inside.

The floor was sticky and the place smelled like stale beer and the air stung her eyes. The walls were plastered with newspapers—perhaps they were reviews of the bar, perhaps they were wallpaper. Red lamps made all the bottles on the back wall glow eerily. The steaming hotplate next to the foggy window made a constant, worrying crackle, as though it might spark an electrical fire at any moment.

The room was so narrow that Anna had to slide along the wall to the furthest stool. The seat was slightly too high and far too wobbly, but she balanced as best she could and put her elbows on the counter. Teej and Elise joined her, and together they sat watching the barman closely.

Ryo continued working and didn't acknowledge their presence. Eventually, he grunted, but Anna couldn't tell if he was greeting them or complaining. He had a dark beard and deep-set lines on his forehead that were filled with sweat. His thin, white shirt was so saturated it was transparent. Finally, he turned, and mopping the counter ineffectually with a dirty rag, let out a long sigh.

"What now?" Elise asked Teej. "And why do *you* get to hold the book?"

"Have it," said Teej as he passed the book to Anna.

"Hey!" complained Elise. "What about me?"

"Sake?" Teej asked the barman.

"Shouldn't we be doing what the book tells us?" asked Elise.

Anna scanned the page then found what she was looking for. She put her finger under the line and let Elise read out loud. "*In Ryo's, all travelers must order forth a sake.*"

The barman grunted again, but he brought them three glasses, lined them up, then filled them to the brim.

"Cheers," said Teej as he held his glass up.

"Kampai!" cheered Elise.

The sake was bitter. Anna had to hold her nose and close her eyes to swallow. When the burning abated, she opened her eyes again and examined the book. New writing had appeared on the page.

"What the...?"

"Yeah, it does that," said Teej casually. "I'm beginning to think we don't see the next task till we complete the last one."

"Another please, my fine man!" said Elise loudly, but Teej clamped his hand over the top of her glass.

"Maybe a little later," he told the barman.

"But..."

"We have to do *exactly* what the book says," admonished Teej.

"That book?" said Ryo gruffly. Surprised that he spoke English, Anna almost fell off her wobbly chair.

"What about it?" she asked.

"Seen it before. You be careful. People that follow the book; they come in here bruised, hurt, crying. They're always having a bad time."

"But we just started the journey." said Anna. "You saw people who were hurt when they got here?"

Ryo shrugged.

"Maybe this isn't the first stop for everyone," mused Elise. "Maybe the route gets mixed up for different people."

"Maybe," said Anna. "I can almost read the next instructions. Let's see…"

Oh no.

"Let me see that," said Elise as she snatched the book. "*Order a number 18 bar snack.* What's a number 18?"

"Unagi," muttered Anna. "Eel."

"Oh no, I'm good, thanks," said Elise.

Teej called out to the barman, "Three unagi, please."

Ryo nodded gruffly, reached under the bar and wrestled a glass jar onto the counter. It was filled with what Anna could only describe as rancid slime.

"Oh, is that strictly necessary?" she complained.

"Not happening," said Elise.

"It's going to get much worse than this," warned Teej. "We'll be very lucky if the worst thing we experience on this journey is eating some eel."

The barman struggled to remove the lid, and when it popped off, Anna gagged at the smell of fermented fish. Ryo impaled three slippery eels with a skewer then laid them on dirty, chipped plates.

"Maybe we should reconsider—" Before Teej could finish, Elise grabbed her eel and swallowed it whole. Her face puckered, but closing her eyes to concentrate, she managed to swallow. Anna followed suit. The eel was salty and slimy, but when she managed to suppress her gag reflex, it slid down her gullet with no resistance.

"Shit," complained Teej as he hesitated.

"It's good," said Elise with a hand over her mouth.

Anna nodded in agreement. "*So* good."

"I hate you both." Teej swallowed his unagi with great difficulty. "What now?" he said as he stifled a belch.

Anna glanced at the book again as words scribbled themselves across the page.

"This thing has a sense of humor," said Teej.

"Oh my God, you lost a tooth, Teejay!" interrupted Elise.

"You didn't notice before? I can whistle through the gap, so that's something."

"Shush, it's coming through!" said Anna. "*Find a new locale, have another drink.*"

"That's vague," said Teej. "And the book seems to have abandoned the archaic parlance."

"Yeah, no more old-timey words," said Anna.

"Come on," said Teej as he got to his feet. Halfway out the door, he turned on his heels. "Oh wait, we need to pay our host, right?"

"No, this one is on the house," said Ryo. "Be careful tonight."

Anna gave him a nod and followed Teej and Elise through the curtain and out into the snaking streets again.

They wove through the crowd, Teej forging ahead like he knew where he was going. Anna watched him from behind, noticing how confident he seemed. He was in his element, exploring a new place, meeting new people. Though she was ready to take control if they stumbled into danger, she was happy to follow him for now.

It didn't take them long to find a little bar at the end of an alleyway, with two foldable tables and a few aluminum chairs outside. They sat.

"Good enough?" Teej asked. Anna nodded.

They were slightly off to the side, but the crowds of people nearby created a constant din. They were mostly Japanese, though Anna saw a few westerners too. Closing her eyes for a moment, the crowd became a distant rumble, like the ocean. The sake settled into the creases in her mind, making everything feel smooth and calm.

"I love it here," she said to no one in particular.

"Right here?" asked Elise.

"Yeah," said Anna wistfully. "The people, the buzz of the place. It's so alive. The air is cool, the food looks good. I mean, most of it anyway. And the people have this way of giving you space to just… I dunno, *exist.*"

A waiter came to their table, and Teej asked for three more sake. "It's a wonderful place," he agreed. "When this is all over, the three of us should come back for a holiday. Just go to bars, visit temples—"

"Karaoke and arcades," suggested Elise.

"Ryokan's, and that island with all the bunnies," finished Anna.

The waiter brought their drinks, and Teej raised his sake for a toast, but before he could speak, Elise nudged him. "Wait! We shouldn't have a regular toast. We should have, like, our own *special* toast! For just the three of us."

Teej turned to Anna expectantly.

"I have no ideas to contribute," said Anna. "I'm not the creative one."

"To peace?" suggested Teej. "To friendship?"

"Too dull," said Anna. Elise nodded in agreement.

"How about…" Elise held their attention before raising her glass high. "To Undreaming Anna and the Sunrise Warriors!"

"I'm not sure," complained Teej. "We're not really warriors. And Sunrise? Is that because we're in Japan? Because that's not accurate either. You see—"

"To my Sunrise Warriors!" shouted Anna. "The best friends an Undreamer could ask for."

Anna and Elise gulped their drinks, and after a second's delay, Teej shrugged and joined them. They huddled together and looked at the book again.

“Now what does it say?” asked Anna.

“*Collect your shopping tickets from the food stall with the animatronic octopus,”* said Teej.

“Shopping!” exclaimed Elise. “Fuck yeah!”

twenty-two

It didn't take them long to find the animatronic octopus, though it was less impressive than Anna had expected. At a tiny stall in a quiet corner of the Tokyo food market, a ticket booth and a red velvet curtain sheltered under eight moving arms. Teej pulled a lever on a little rusted ticket machine and passed one ticket to Elise then one to Anna before examining his own. The ticket was golden with red cursive. *Welcome to Mrs. Abbot's Second Chances Thrift Store.*

As they stepped through the heavy red curtains and left the crowded Tokyo streets behind, Anna felt the winds of Vig blow strongly. For a moment she thought she heard someone call her name, but when she turned, it was too late. Behind her, the market had disappeared. There was only a blank silence.

Anna pushed through another set of curtains and stumbled out of a changing room cubicle into a thrift store. Momentarily dazed, she bumped into a clothes rack and then held it for a moment to steady herself.

"Everything all right ma'am?" drawled the store assistant from behind the nearby counter. Her accent was American

Southern, her hair was tightly permed, and she peeked out at Anna over round, silver spectacles balanced on the tip of her long nose.

"Umm, yeah," said Anna as she scanned her surroundings. "Peachy."

She was surrounded by shelves straining under mountains of old, dusty brick-a-brack. Porcelain dogs, sugar bowls, broken teacups, ostrich feather hats, tarnished silver cutlery, dusty Chinese vases, a stuffed and mounted beaver—the thrift store had everything no one would ever want. It was huge too, stretching for hundreds of feet in all directions. It still felt cramped though, with a low ceiling, narrow aisles, and a residual smell of damp.

"Oh no!" said Elise as she burst out of the adjacent changing room. A second later, Teej joined her.

"I know this place," he said. He reached for Anna, but he seemed faint, and his legs almost gave out. Elise caught him.

"Whoa, dude! You don't look so good. Take a knee."

"Catch your breath," said Anna. "I'll try to figure out where we are."

"I'll be fine in a second," said Teej. "Just overwhelmed with how many Fetishes and objects of power there are here. So much Vig."

Anna nodded. She knew what he meant, but she maintained strict control of her Haze Sense. Now wasn't the time to lose focus.

Wandering past a rack of fur coats, a bin filled with umbrellas, a dusty bookshelf and a huge chest stuffed with what appeared to be odd socks, Anna approached the old lady at the counter and tried to smile.

"Excuse me ma'am, could you tell me where the nearest… umm… where are we?"

"The South, ma'am," said the lady with pride.

"Of course. But more specifically?"

"Why, you're in Mrs. Abbot's Second Chances Thrift Store."

"Mrs. Abbot's." said Teej as he stumbled to Anna's side. "*Where every lost thing goes that must one day be found.*"

"That's us!" said Mrs. Abbot. "I remember you, young sir. You were here—"

"A long, long time ago," finished Teej.

"So, this is what?" asked Anna. "Another Staid Haze?"

"Yes," said Teej. "Like the Sump."

"Perfect," said Anna under her breath.

"No, it's not as bad as it seems. It's more like the *opposite* of the Sump. This is a place for things to be found, not for things to be lost."

"So why are we here?" asked Anna.

"Well, best ask the book," he replied with a quick smile.

"This is just like the Moonlight Road all over again," she complained as she wrestled the book open. "We're just popping in and out of these completely random places, and in every third one someone will probably try to kill us."

"No one was trying to kill us back there in Tokyo," said Teej.

"But this isn't exactly a wild night out," complained Elise. "I like thrifting as much as the next person. More! But I thought there would be more clubs. Pubs. Dancing. Wild, drunken adventures! It's *The Gentleman's Guide to Nightlife,* right? She picked up a broken teapot. "Not the Gentleman's Guide to discount kitchenware."

"Hang on, I'm getting a call," said Teej. He fished his phone out of his pocket, looked at the screen, frowned, then put it back in his pocket.

"Who was it?" asked Anna.

"No one."

"What do you mean no one? Why didn't you answer."

"It was Bianca," said Teej with a shrug.

"The girl from the pier?" Anna frowned. "Why is *she* calling?"

"I dunno," said Teej with another shrug.

"What the Hell, Teej! She tried to murder you!"

"It wasn't her fault. Anna, sometimes going into a Haze is about saving people, and then making sure they are alright afterwards."

"News to me," muttered Anna. "I notice you don't check up on everyone. Just her."

Elise put her hands up and backed off. "I can't stand it when Mom and Dad fight. I'm, uh, gonna let you two figure this out. I'll be over by the antique coin collection."

"It's complicated," said Teej.

"That's not an explanation, that's a social media relationship status update. Look, I don't care about the girls you string along, but we have to be more careful."

"Careful!" Teej pointed a finger at Anna's chest. "You were flirting with some guy on the train while you dragged us off to see your mom. Then you fought Raguel by yourself! You're not exactly taking the cautious approach either."

She was about to snap back, but Anna felt her hands get warm. The flames threatened to dance across her fingertips. This was getting out of control. She had to calm down. Closing her eyes, Anna took a breath.

"Anna, I'm sorry," said Teej as he smoothed down his messy hair awkwardly. He seemed suddenly aware of how angry she was. He wasn't frightened, though. His eyes were filled with concern.

"What for?" she said irritably. "You didn't do anything wrong. It's me, I'm grumpy. This book is fucking with us, and I know that. We're being manipulated and I'm already tired of it."

"It's not just the book, though, is it?" Teej asked astutely.

"No. I also keep thinking about Amara. Maybe she was wrong about everything? She was wrong about Raguel. And her plan was—"

"It's not a terrible plan. I just wish she told us where this Council meeting is taking place."

"Not terrible?" complained Anna. "She wanted me to send you to your death!"

"If I was in her place, I'd probably do the same. She possessed cold wisdom and a broader perspective of our problems than anyone else alive."

"A cold wisdom? I don't get it. She told me…"

Anna considered holding back and then changed her mind. If she couldn't trust Teej, then she couldn't trust anyone.

"She told me someone would betray me. Someone close to me."

"I see." Teej stroked his chin, lost in thought.

"So? Should I believe her? She told me that I should let you die, and she told me someone would betray me. Someone close? That can only be Elise or Pappi, right?"

"Or me," he said with a shrug. "Are you sure that's what she said? She specifically said one of *us* would betray you?"

"More or less. But she also said we couldn't beat Raguel."

"Well, you proved her wrong there."

Anna put her hands on her hips. "Her plan can't work though, right? Even if we found the Christmas Council and could convince the Dreamers that some cure existed for the blood plague, would they stop fighting each other? Can they ever find peace?"

Teej shrugged. "What other choice do we have? It's peace or… well, there are no alternatives."

Anna let out a long sigh. "Teej what are we doing? Following some book, chasing Wildey, hanging out in a thrift store? Be honest, are we lost?"

"You ain't lost, honey!" shouted Mrs. Abbot. "Nothing and no one can be lost here in ma store. That's *not* what this place is about."

Anna smiled politely at Mrs. Abbot, then took Teej's arm and led him over to a nearby patchwork chair. He flopped down heavily on it, letting out a long sigh of relief.

"I don't just mean lost right here," said Anna. "I mean lost in general. Is this a real plan? Or are we just killing time until Rayleigh or some other enemy comes after us?"

Teej let out another long sigh. "We don't have a better plan, so this is what we do. And your plans have worked thus far, so I'll follow you, Anna. What did Garret say? *Only two things ever happen: things change, or things stay the same.* Well, we can't let things stay the same. Not for us. Not for Alby."

Teej was right. They had to keep moving.

"Hey guys!" said Elise as she skipped towards them holding a raggedy doll with rough woolen hair and one eye hanging from a thread. "Look at this! It's awful, right? But it looks just like Stinky Susie, my first ever doll. I *need* this."

Teej shook his head firmly. "Unless the book says we should take it, we are not buying and carrying a hideous doll."

Elise narrowed her eyes. "Hideous! You know nothing about fashion."

"Elise could you just not…"

Elise's grinned, and it was too mischievous for Anna to resist. Elise threw the doll over her shoulder as they both giggled.

"I could eat another eel about now," grumbled Teej.

"How are you feeling?" asked Anna. "You look tired. How's the tooth?"

"*Thore*," said Teej. "And I'm always tired. But happy to be with you and Elise. Your Sunrise Warriors."

Anna chuckled. "Enough stalling, folks. Let's have a look at this book again."

"I would very much like to have a copy of that book in my store one day!" shouted Mrs. Abbot.

"If we could give it away, we would," replied Anna.

"Oh Madam, that ain't how this store works. Things gotta be lost before they can be found."

"Yeah, we'd be pretty happy to lose it," said Anna as she brusquely flicked to the next page. She read the instructions out loud.

"The August Club requires a key. The last group to attempt the journey failed. The surviving traveler lost the key and was

stranded outside the entrance. As with all lost items that must one day be found, the key appeared in Mrs. Abbot's."

"And?" prompted Teej.

"That's all it says," replied Anna.

"Great, an old key. That should be easy to find!" Elise scuttled off to the shelves and started rifling through piles of old junk.

"Can you help us find stuff?" Anna asked Mrs. Abbot.

"I'm afraid not, my dear. If something's meant to be found, it finds you as much as you find it."

"Uh-huh," said Anna skeptically. She put her hands on her hips and scanned her surroundings. Where to start? The wall of shoes, each without its twin? The mountain of old clothes? The pile of sweaters stacked over suit jackets, trousers and dresses stretching up till they almost touched the roof? Maybe she could check in every pocket.

No. Best to start with the large bins filled with household items. Anna peered inside the nearest one. Old rotary phones, batteries, dolls heads, empty glue bottles, CD's, beermats, picture frames and TV remotes.

"Do people buy stuff from here?" asked Anna as she raked through the detritus. She didn't expect an answer.

"No, child, this is a place where you're reunited with what you already own, or what wants to be owned by you."

Suddenly curious, Anna asked, "Have you been here a long time, Mrs. Abbot?"

Her smile was inscrutable, and she closed her eyes and chuckled. "Oh yes. Almost feels like I've been here forever."

"Oh hey! I found a key!" shouted Teej as he pulled something shiny out of an old shoebox. "No wait, this is for a padlock."

Anna didn't hear him. She spotted something familiar. The first piece of jewelry a boy had ever bought her: a silver chain with "Ann" spelled out in sparkly letters. Poor Stevie hadn't been able to afford that last '*A*'.

It hung around the neck of a vase as if it had been planted there for her to find. Anna eyed it suspiciously, then turned to look at Mrs. Abbot, but the old lady was distracted, thumbing through a magazine with a disinterested look on her face.

"You know," shouted Elise as she tried on an old beret she'd picked up from the hat mountain, "This is kinda a weird location for the book to take us. It's T*he Gentleman's Guide to Nightlife*, right? Isn't it weird that we're in some store?"

Elise turned quickly to Mrs. Abbot. "No offense, lady."

"It's because we need the key," shouted Teej. "The book wants to send us on a wild adventure, but it also needs to lead us into the August Club, and to do that we need the thing that unlocks the final door."

"I'm ready to get back to the debauchery," responded Elise.

"I'm not," said Anna as she examined tiny gym shorts that might have been the pair she lost in first grade.

"This is creepy," said Anna. "I keep finding things that look familiar. It makes me feel like we've done this before, like I'm drowning in déjà vu. Is it the same for you guys?"

"It is," said Teej. "And the effect is much more disorientating when you are hundreds of years old and have already forgotten more than you'll ever remember."

Anna scraped the bottom of a bin but still found no sign of a key. When she narrowed her eyes and scanned the store, she caught sight of Mrs. Abbot waving her over surreptitiously. She wanted to talk to Anna alone.

Anna tiptoed over while Elise and Teej were distracted with their searches.

"Have you checked the lost correspondence?" whispered Mrs. Abbot. She pointed to a network of mail trays stuffed with documents and papers piled high against the wall.

"I'm… not sure I want to look there," said Anna.

"Hey guys, I hope I don't meet any of my old boyfriends!" Elise was shouting from the far end of the store. "Or girlfriends.

Like, that psychobilly double bassist with the mohawk. She was wild. I think her name was Jade… or Jayhawk?"

Anna ignored her and glanced nervously at the letters, biting her bottom lip.

"Hey," said Teej.

Anna jumped. "Jesus, you scared the shit out of me."

"Oh, sorry. I was just thinking about what you told me on the train… about the letter."

Anna turned away. Teej misunderstood her reaction. He kept talking.

"You know, because you burned it before you read it. But this place is a chance to get anything you lost back. Right? There are letters over there."

"I know," Anna said under her breath. "I burned it for a reason."

When he touched her shoulder, Anna pulled away. Why was that letter still haunting her? How far did she have to run before her old problems couldn't catch her anymore?

"I don't want it."

"But wouldn't it give you some closure?" asked Teej gently. "Won't you regret it if you don't read it?"

"You don't get it," said Anna with a sigh. "What's written in that letter won't help me. It won't even surprise me. There's two of me Teej. Don't you get it?"

Anna shuddered. She was so close to the edge now.

"Two of you?" Teej didn't understand.

"The Anna that can survive can't look back. She can't be honest about what happened. Lies are what keeps me alive. And anything that keeps me alive I have to hold onto."

"What has that got to do with the letter?" asked Teej, confusion written across his features.

"I'm lying to myself Teej. Lying to you too. The letter is just a trick to keep me going. A trick I'm playing on myself, and if I stop denying the truth, I'm done for."

Teej reached for her. "We can't keep moving forward while something is holding us back. We need to face the things that follow us."

"Even if it kills us?" snapped Anna as she turned to face him and thrust a finger in his chest. "What do you know about letting go of the past? And why are you taking responsibility for *my* grief?"

"Look, I just know a thing or two about regret. When you get a chance to resolve things in your past—"

"You don't know what the fuck you're talking about."

Anna saw her words hurt him, but that made her angrier. Her mind was splitting in two, and the Anna who knew the truth was taking over. Anna couldn't face that truth. It would destroy her. She forced down her feelings and redirected them at him with spite. Anna scrambled for the worst thing she could say. She wanted to burn everything in her sight—including his friendship. Wanted to hurt him. Get him away from her. Her blood felt hot.

Desolation.

"I'm sorry. I just care about you and I—"

"You don't care about me, you're just lonely." She spat the words. "I'll never let anyone take his place in my life. Never!"

"I don't… I wouldn't…"

"Hey, guys!" shouted Elise. "I found it! I mean I think it's this big ugly key. It looks good, right?"

Elise skipped over and held up an old wrought iron key as big as her hand. Anna smoothed down her clothes, stood up straight, and tried a smile.

"Looks like a good candidate. Mrs. Abbot, what do you think?"

The old lady looked sad and shook her head. "I can't say for sure, but that key certainly did find you. If I had to wager, I'd say the young miss has found what you're looking for."

"Alright then," said Anna authoritatively. "Let's see what the book says."

Teej edged closer. "Anna, I'm sorry. I—"

"Save it, Teej," said Anna. "We've got to keep moving. We're all on edge. This book brings out the worst in us. Let's finish this journey as quick as we can. For Alby."

Teej nodded.

Anna opened the book. "It just says *go back the way you came.* I guess we found what we were looking for."

"Good luck folks," said Mrs. Abbot as they moved towards the changing rooms again. "Y'all have a safe trip! Don't get lost."

twenty-three

After the thrift store, they went to an underground rave where the patrons drank bubbling green liquid, a submarine was alive, while looking at a rainbow bridge over a frozen pink wasteland. Now they were on a very ordinary train, and when Anna looked at her friends, she noticed even Elise seemed tired of the wild goose chase the book imposed upon them.

As the train doors slowly slid closed, Anna was glad they were on their way again. The train interior was sterile and empty. They had a hundred free seats to choose from, but all three of them stood and held onto the railing as the train slowly chugged out of the station. The engine whirred louder as the locomotive built up speed.

"I hope no one asks for our ticket," said Teej, breaking the silence.

"I hope no one sees us like this," said Anna.

"I can't believe we went on a mystical all-night bender, but I got filthy from the insides of slimy, living submarine," complained Elise.

"We should be on guard," said Anna. "We're getting close. When we get to our destination, are you both ready for a fight?"

"Wildey didn't invite us to the August Club to kill us," said Teej.

Anna tutted. "Every time I meet someone who tells me they don't want to kill me, I find out they do, it's just they want to do it in a really specific way."

Elise grasped her arm. "If we *are* going into a fight, there's no one I'd rather have by my side."

"Who would you take into a fight if your life depended on it?" Teej asked Anna. "Anyone in the world, real or imaginary?"

"I dunno, but if I were you, I'd take me."

Anna knew she sounded cocky, but she was just being honest. She hoped her friends were both ready for whatever lay ahead because she was.

"Do you think we can save Alby before the Christmas Council?" asked Elise. "Will Wildey know where to find him?"

"I don't know," said Teej. "Rayleigh has maintained power for so long because he is untouchable. Unfindable. The Council is our best chance to find an opening, both to confront him in front of the Dreamers, and to save Alby."

"What a weird Christmas we'll have this year!" said Elise. "The holidays are always a party. Mulled wine and split-screen videogames and trying to kiss the hottest person in the room under the mistletoe."

As the train *clack-clacked* hypnotically along the rails, Anna closed her eyes and smiled. "Stealing an extra roast potato when mom isn't looking. That old Christmas tree that smells like vanilla air freshener. Running out into the snow and hitting the old drainpipe with a stick till all the ice falls in one clear tube like it was made of glass.

She allowed herself to revel in the memories. "Our first night in the cabin. Our first night without heat, because we couldn't light the old fireplace. That scratchy old patchwork blanket that gave me a rash. That night when we went out into the forest and got lost, so we had to trace our footprints in the snow to get back to the house."

Anna's voice became dreamy. "We saw a deer in the woods. It was so still, like a stuffed mannequin. Then it just disappeared. We looked at each other because neither of us could believe we'd really seen it."

"You and your mom?" asked Teej.

"No," said Anna.

She opened her eyes and saw her friends looking back at her, and she could tell they both would say anything they could to make her feel better, but they didn't have the words. There were no words.

She gave them a look that said *I will pull myself out of this.*

"Does the book say anything new?" asked Elise, changing the subject.

"Let's see," said Anna, flicking to the last page. "What have you got for us next, you total piece of… Oh! It just says: '*Your final task is to navigate the labyrinth. The entrance to the August Club awaits, but take a step backwards, and the maze will keep you forever.*'"

"It feels like we're entering another Haze," said Teej.

"We're not supposed to use our Haze Sense," said Anna.

"I can't just *turn it off.*"

"Me neither. So I guess we get ready for—"

"Back to the party," said Elise as the train slowed to a stop and the doors slid open once more. They stepped out into the narrow, dark streets of the labyrinth.

twenty-four

The train stopped without rolling into a station. As Teej stepped out onto the street, he turned to see the doorway shimmer and fade behind him, transforming into a bare brick wall. The train was gone completely, replaced by the bricks. Elise and Anna were already there. When Teej reached back and brushed the surface of the wall with his fingertips, it was cold and solid once more.

"I hate trains anyway," he muttered.

The trio stood in a narrow alleyway below a starless sky. The night was dark and still. Shops and bars on either side of them were shuttered and barred, but they could hear laughter and music. The deep thump of bass traveled through Teej's feet into his bones. Up ahead, the street twisted off, winding down a hill before fading away to blackness. There were no cars, no people, and no sign of the August Club.

"The book says that as long as we don't linger or go backwards, we will reach the end of our journey." Anna slammed the book shut and put it in her backpack. Teej was glad to see it go.

"Are we in a Haze now?" asked Elise with a shiver. "It sure feels like we're in a Haze."

"Yes. This is the Labyrinth," replied Teej. "That's what the book said, right? I guess it's a maze with—"

"With a minotaur," finished Anna.

"Come on," said Teej as he gestured for them to follow.

Wandering along the quaint narrow streets of the little town, they passed an old barber's, a music store, a jeweler's and a pharmacy, all closed and deserted. The cobbled streets seemed too uneven for cars. The muffled echoes of laughter and music still sounded in the distance. The tall lampposts gave off a mellow yellow light that failed to dispel the shadows, but nonetheless gave them a path to follow through the night.

Teej felt a pang of nostalgia. *A ghost town by gaslight.* Had he been here before?

"So, is this like *the* labyrinth, or just *a* labyrinth*?"* asked Elise.

"I don't see that it matters," Teej said over his shoulder. He pointed up ahead. "It's a maze. It's meant to get lost in, but it has an entrance and an exit."

Anna was moving slowly, looking down at her feet as she followed. "Remember what the book said. We're not to go backwards. We've made it this far. Just a little farther now."

They crept their way to the end of the street. At the junction, Teej looked left then right, unsure which way to go next. The streets looked the same in all directions, though they seemed to narrow in the distance. Anna tapped him on the shoulder and pointed to a signpost. With a giant glowing arrow, the sign was purple neon, and buzzed and flickered constantly, and though several letters were dark, it nonetheless spelled out three distinct words: *The August Club.*

"This way I guess," said Anna. Her brown eyes shone in the darkness.

"That seems a bit too easy," warned Teej.

"Well, what do we do?" asked Anna. "Go the *opposite* way the sign tells us?"

"No," he said. "Maybe. I don't know."

Teej stood with his hands in his pockets, his mind racing.

"Let's just follow the signs," suggested Anna. She turned to Elise. "And we stick together."

Together they shuffled nervously down the narrowing street. When Teej realized Elise was already lagging behind, he stopped and turned. She was staring into a bar window.

"What did our boss *just* say?"

"Sorry," whispered Elise. "Come look at this."

Teej crouched to look into the window of a small basement bar with a faded sign outside and a bright orange lamp in the doorway. The window was foggy. Through the glass, they could see the outline of people laughing and drinking, but something was wrong.

"They're not real people, right?" said Elise. "They're, like, moving wallpaper. They loop around."

Elise was right. The silhouettes inside looked real from a distance but examined up close, it was clear they were performing the same actions over and over. Animated mannequins, or projected reels from a film that was stuck repeating the same frames. The sounds of their laughter and the music were on a loop as well, the same noises coming back around every ten seconds. There was no life in this place.

"You're right," admitted Teej. "The city is a maze, and the streets are the walls. The noises and the building facades are just set dressing."

He walked to the door and tried to pull it open, but no matter how hard he tugged, the door wouldn't budge. "The door is painted on," he explained. "We should keep going."

"What's that noise?" asked Elise.

"I hear it too," said Anna. "Singing."

"I can't hear anything but the noise from the bar," said Teej.

"Come over here," said Anna. As soon as he stepped away from the doorway, he heard it. A sad, creaky old voice, though the words were indistinct. It was coming from behind them, echoing down the winding streets. Something about the voice made Teej's nails dig into the palms of his hands.

"We should get away from whoever that is." He waved for his companions to move quickly.

"The ground is covered with something gross," complained Elise. Her sneakers had sunk a half-inch into the tarmac, and when she tried to lift her feet, the sticky surface clung like long strands of glue.

"Feels kinda tacky to me," said Anna. "That's not good. The book says we have to keep moving, right? We're not supposed to linger or go backwards."

Teej grabbed Elise's arm and tugged, and with some effort, her feet came free.

Behind them, the singing was getting closer and Teej could pick out some of the words now. "Drawn onward to new era… Here in you lost…"

"This way," said Teej. "Not a single step backwards. We have to keep moving."

They hurried down the empty streets as the laughter and music became a rising and falling wave of background noise that seemed less human and more sinister with every passing second. Every street looked the same. Their footsteps echoed and came back to them, like a counterpoint to every move they made, contradicting their progress.

They were speeding down dark alleys, twisting and turning along streets that got narrower and narrower till there was barely enough space for all three of them to stand side-by-side. The signs for The August Club popped up every three or four junctions, but now different letters were illuminated each time. They stopped under one that read, "*T e Au u t Cl b.*"

Wheezing, Teej put a hand on the nearby wall and caught his breath. "We might be going in circles. I think we've put some distance between ourselves and '*Mr. New Era*' back there."

"You're right," said Anna as she rubbed her forehead. "We need a system."

"To solve the maze?" said Teej. "Maybe Trumeaux's algorithm?"

"Sure, *maybe*," said Anna. "Or we could just follow the left-hand rule?"

"Won't that mean we double back on ourselves?" asked Elise.

"Well, the streets are still wide enough that we're not walking over the *exact* same spot," said Anna. "We're going around the edge, making sure we're always touching the left wall. That should guarantee we will find the exit eventually, right?"

She didn't sound confident, but Teej didn't have a better idea. He shrugged. "If the ground gets sticky again, we know we're in trouble. If we keep moving, we should be fine."

As Anna took the lead, touching the back of her hand to the left wall, she hustled along the street with Teej and Elise in tow. Teej glanced back nervously, but there was no sign of pursuit. The music and laughter from the bars died off, replaced with an eerie stillness, punctuated every few minutes by the buzz of another flickering neon sign that told the same lie: that the August Club was just ahead.

"These signs mean something," said Teej as he tried to keep up with Anna's brisk pace. His thighs ached. Without his Praxis, his body was starting to feel its age.

"We're doing the left-hand thing," she said without slowing down. "You don't think it will work?"

"If this was a normal maze it would."

"What if the walls aren't connected to the outside wall?" asked Elise. "We would just keep going round."

"I don't get it," said Anna, stopping suddenly. She looked as confused, but Teej was beginning to understand.

"She's right. The left-hand method only works if the maze is *simply connected.* If all the walls link up to the perimeter wall. Even then, I think there's *something* about the signs…"

"Maybe it's a puzzle," said Anna.

She walked to the end of the street where it split into a three-way junction. "I can see a sign at the end of two of these three streets. This one on the left has four missing letters, and this one on the right," she pointed down the other street. "Has two. Maybe we follow the path with the most lit up letters?"

"*Here in you lost…*" The sing-song words caught up to them. Their pursuer was closing in again.

"Worth a try," said Teej, and they set off as fast as they dared.

They were running again, careening down one dark street after another. The routes twisted left then right, the signs sometimes missing only a few letters, sometimes most of them. Each time they reached a junction, they stopped and chose a new route, but the further they went, the more lost Teej felt. The whole time, the singing of the old man was getting closer. He was speeding up.

"Wait!" called out Elise as they took another turn. "We're going the wrong way?"

"What do you mean?" complained Teej. He turned to run again, but Elise grabbed him by the arm. "It's this way," she said, pointing to their left.

"No," said Teej. He looked straight ahead, and for the first time, all thirteen letters were lit up. "It's straight ahead. We're almost there."

"What are you talking about?!" shouted Anna. "It's to the right. All the lights are on the street to the *right*."

"Wait!" shouted Teej. "Just… wait a second. I think the maze is manipulating us."

"No time for this!" protested Anna. "Look." She pulled her foot out of the ground, breaking long, gluey strands with a groan.

"The maze wants us to split up," said Teej as he walked straight ahead. "It wants us to each follow the route where we see the sign fully illuminated."

"We all see the sign differently?" said Elise as she slowly realized what was happening.

"Yes! But we can't *let* it split us up," said Anna. "That's what it wants."

"If we don't, we'll be going around this maze forever. We don't have any choice."

"Drawn onward..."

"Yes, we do!" snapped Anna. "I'm tired of running around like this. I think I can use my Praxis and get us into the August Club."

"It's forbidden," said Teej. They'd followed this path so far, and they were so close. Using their powers now was too dangerous.

"I'll do what I always do. I'll get us through and out the other end." She put her hand on the wall nearby. "I'll burn this all down, and beyond it, we'll find the August Club."

"Will that work?" asked Elise.

Teej shook his head. "If it was some normal Haze then maybe, but if Anna tears this place down, we don't know where we'll end up. The book is taking us on a journey, and if we're near the end then sure, she might be able to tear a hole in this Haze to our destination, but that hole could lead us *anywhere."*

"I don't like this, Teej," said Anna. "We're lost. That voice is getting closer."

He noticed how her hand twitched, how she struggled to hold the leash on her fire as it strained to break free.

"I don't like it either," he confessed. "You need to get control. If we don't keep moving—"

"I'm almost stuck!" said Elise as she struggled to lift her feet out of the sticky sludge that was forming all around them.

"Drawn onward..."

Anna relented. "Alright, we split up, but we need to go quickly! Hopefully, the path loops back around and we come back together. Or maybe we all meet at the entrance to the August Club."

Anna turned to Elise "Keep going as fast as you can. Follow the signs."

After a moment of struggling, Elise managed to pull her feet free. She gave them a brief nod, then set off at a run, the ground now solid beneath her.

Anna pulled the straps of her backpack tight around her shoulders and took a deep breath. She looked ready to face anything, but Teej already felt like this might be a mistake. The book wanted them to get to the August Club, but it wanted them to make a sacrifice to get there. Had he made the right choice?

"We're going to make it," said Anna. She must have seen the fear in his eyes. "The book must want us to separate as a kind of final test. We can do this. Just keep moving. If you lose track of Elise, use your spoon to find her."

"What about if I lose you?" asked Teej.

"You don't need to worry about me," she said firmly, and he believed her.

"He's there," said Anna as she pointed over his shoulder.

The old man was here. He was a shambling, emaciated nightmare. Was this really the Minotaur? He was stooped with sunken cheeks and nearly naked. His putrid skin was loose and wrinkled, and he wore a dirty gray loincloth. Straggly gray hair fell over his shoulders, and his huge unkempt beard went down to his waist. Two large bumps on his forehead strained the skin, and he shambled rather than walked, singing his song the whole way. His head was down, and he didn't seem to notice them, but he walked straight towards them.

Teej turned to warn Anna, but she was already moving. After a moment's struggle, she pulled her feet clear of the sticky ground and began running. Teej watched her round a corner and disappear.

"Where's Ariadne when you need her?" Teej muttered before turning and running the opposite way.

twenty-five

As Teej ran along dark, narrow streets, they twisted and turned but never ended. He felt like he was trying to outrun his mistakes, but he'd made too many. He'd left Anna to fight the Midnight Man before she knew how to use her Praxis. He'd been too slow to stop Drowden from sending her to the Sump, then he'd sent her to face Rayleigh alone. Splitting up could be his biggest mistake so far.

With his breathing ragged and legs trembling, Teej let his frustration and fear push him on as his mind raced. Why was he leaving Anna behind when she had saved him so many times before? The last time they split up, she had faced the most dangerous Dreamer alone, and for a year he had tried to make up for that mistake. He had chased her all over the Firmament, trying to fix the mess he had created.

After a year of running, he discovered Anna had *chosen* to be alone. In that time, she'd become stronger than ever before. His mistake had paid off, but only because his failure to protect her meant she had learned how to protect herself. In the process, she'd become stronger and more resilient, but colder and more distant too. Now that they were together again, a horrible question lingered between them: would Anna be better off on her own?

Splitting up had been Teej's idea. Should he have let Anna unleash her Praxis instead? Now that he was alone in the labyrinth running from the old man, it was easy to second-guess himself. Instead of following his plans and schemes, they should be trusting Anna's instincts.

"Here in you lost..."

The Minotaur's wheezy song drew close, but Teej's legs burned. He took a moment to catch his breath, leaning on an old lamppost. When he rubbed the back of his thigh, a throbbing pain shot down his leg. There would be a massive bruise above his knee, and he might have torn a muscle. Once more, a fight with Raguel had caused more damage than he realized. The pain was worse when he stood than when he moved, so he set off again as fast as he could.

Anna wasn't the only one he had abandoned. Twice Elise had saved his life, first from the cyborg sent by the Apoth, then in Avalon she had saved him from Drowden. And for what? To die here in this maze?

Even if they made it out, what awaited them at the August Club? If they faced Wildey, and a bitter enmity that might not have faded with time, they might be better off without Teej. Perhaps the best outcome for their journey would be if Anna and Elise escaped the labyrinth without him.

Teej dared not look backwards, but the wheezing sounded like it was just over his shoulder. At least the Minotaur pursued *him*. He was good for a distraction at least.

What would Garret do in this situation? Probably turn on his heels, introduce himself to the old man and offer to take him out for drinks. Would Garret hold back on his Praxis and follow the instructions in some dusty old book? Probably not, but then Garret had always been willing to risk his body and mind recklessly, and in the end, it had been his undoing.

The August Club – Entrance.

The purple neon sign was clear and bright and didn't flicker or crackle like the others. It hung over a huge oak door, and it straddled a three-way junction at the end of the street. *I made it!*

This was the entrance to the club and the exit of the maze. Now all Teej needed was for Anna and Elise to get here too.

It was time to face his pursuer. Teej stopped underneath the sign and turned to look back along the street where he had come. Though the old man sounded close, he moved slowly and was still a good fifty feet away.

Teej reached into his jacket and felt for his Periapt. Anna was right; they had to be ready to use their Praxis if there were no other options. He had to be ready to fight.

Dammit, where are they?

The old man's singing came clear and echoed loud now. His voice cracked with suppressed spite; the words spat from hateful lips.

"Drawn onward to new era. Here in you lost."

The old man spoke gibberish, but Teej felt the potency of his words. He wasn't sure what effect they would have, but the closer he got, the more dangerous those words would become.

Teej backed off to the door. It cracked open without the need for a key. Perhaps it was enough that they held it. He considered pulling the door open but hesitated. This was a portal, and if he went through without Elise and Anna, he wouldn't be able to come back.

Unless they're already inside?

Could they have gotten here before him? It was possible. There was no guarantee his route to the entrance had been the shortest, and he certainly wasn't the fastest of the three of them right now with his wounded leg.

No, he couldn't go through that door. His friends wouldn't leave him behind. The old man had reached the entrance before Anna and Elise, and they would need to fight their way past. No matter what happened next, Teej would face this enemy here and now. His fingertips crackled with Vig as his Periapt materialized.

"Teej!"

It was Elise. She was sprinting towards him with a look of relief on her face.

"Be careful!" he shouted back. She had already seen the old man and slowed her pace. Teej couldn't tell if she could make it to the doorway before their enemy intercepted her.

"Teej, just go through!" shouted Anna. She was running from the opposite side street and pointing at Teej. "Don't wait for us."

Teej shook his head. "You won't make it. He's too close."

"We'll make it!" shouted Anna.

Teej reluctantly turned to the door, but in that instant, the words of the Minotaur caught hold of him.

Agony. Like a steel trap, he felt the Will of the old man lock him in place. Teej's hands involuntarily clenched into fists, and he gnashed his teeth. His back arched like his spine was going to snap. His skull lit up with pain like his mind was on fire. All the bones in his body were grinding against each other. He tried to speak, but his jaw was locked shut. His Periapt fell from his jacket and clattered to the ground uselessly.

"Drawn onward to new era. Here in you lost."

The words wrapped around Teej's brain, coiled down his spine and took control of his nerves. Muscles spasmed, and he began to move against his will. He took a step backwards away from the door. He strained uselessly against the Will of the old man.

"Teej!" Anna called out, but she was too far away. Elise, meanwhile, was too close. If Teej could speak, he would have shouted a warning. Instead, he was compelled to take another step backwards and away from the entrance to the August Club and towards their enemy.

What would happen to his friends when he was gone? Would they be better off? The book wanted a sacrifice, and it would not let them continue until they had paid in blood. He was trapped in the minotaur's snare, but it hadn't caught them all. Only him.

When he was gone, it would be satiated. Anna and Elise would be free.

"Let him go!" shouted Elise.

She leapt past Teej, knife in hand, eyes filled with fury. As she swung at the old man, Teej was temporarily released, and all his muscles went limp at once. He flopped to the ground just in time to see Elise *almost* strike their enemy. At the last moment, the Minotaur sidestepped with superhuman speed, and Elise went straight past him, falling face-first to the ground.

She splattered down into a deep quagmire of black glue and started to sink immediately. Her arms and legs thrashed as she struggled to free herself, but long, sticky strands clung to her, and as she tried to lift her head, her body sank deep.

"I'm sinking!" she called out in desperation. Teej tried to move, but he was a rag doll. The old man's attack had left him too weak to stand. On his knees, he struggled to even breathe.

The old man straightened and turned to Anna. He was concentrating all his energies on her, singing that same low song, targeting her Will with his own. His eyes finally opened. Gray and pupil-less, they were filled with malice.

Forcing himself to stay calm, Teej pulled in one long, labored breath and his head began to clear. Anna struggled against the old man's invisible onslaught as she approached him. Her head bent as she pushed onwards, muscles spasming, face contorted into a grimace. She was almost close enough to strike at him, but her Will was fading fast.

Teej was crawling. Still weak as a kitten, he managed four steps before falling at the minotaur's feet. As he tried to grab the clammy flesh of an ankle, the old man pulled away, his song interrupted for only a moment.

But it gave Anna the opening she needed. She pulled the broken shards of Raguel's blade out of her backpack and lunged. The old man let out an inhuman scream. The sharp, broken sword plunged into his chest with a bloodless *thunk*, and he reeled back. Anna held the weapon with both hands and kept pushing, and for a moment it seemed he might fall. The old man lifted a finger and touched it to her forehead. As soon as he made contact, Anna dropped unconscious instantly and fell to the ground next to Teej.

With the blade still embedded in his chest, the old man collapsed backwards and slid down the wall. He groped the hilt, trying to pull it free from his chest, but it was embedded too deep. A long, low moan came from the depths of his soul, shaking the whole world. The Minotaur didn't bleed, but he felt pain.

Teej got to his knees and crawled to Anna. He touched her face with the back of his hand. She was breathing, but completely unconscious. Grabbing her by the arm, he tried to lift her, but his body still ached, and his legs failed him. They both lay helpless.

Despite the knife still in his chest, the Minotaur was recovering, standing up again as he growled. Behind him, Elise was almost gone. Stuck and sinking fast, only her head and hands were visible. She didn't look afraid; she knew there was no way out. Even if he was strong and healthy, Teej wouldn't be able to pull her free in time.

"Get up, Teej!" shouted Elise. "You have to go."

Teej closed his eyes, summoned all his strength, and tried again. It felt like a tank was driving over his back. Every inch of movement was a battle.

Keep fighting.

He just had to get Anna to the door. It was so close.

Heaving himself to his feet, Teej grabbed Anna's arm and pulled her along the ground with all his might. He managed to drag her a few feet along the ground before he fell to his knees once more.

The Minotaur stumbled after them, slow but implacable. He wasn't singing anymore. The broken sword in his chest had silenced him, but his footsteps maintained the same steady rhythm. He wasn't going to stop.

With a final lurch, Teej heaved Anna across the floor. He grabbed the door handle of the August Club and realized he was going to make it. *They* were going to make it.

He hesitated.

Elise.

"Go!" shouted Elise. She was almost gone, her mouth about to dip below the surface. Her face was dirty, and her eyes filled with tears, but her voice was unwavering.

"Teej, you *have* to go. You have to save Anna."

"I can't leave you behind," pleaded Teej. "I can't lose anyone else."

"It's too late for me," said Elise as she closed her eyes. "You have to save Anna. We're all here for *Anna!* She's the only one that matters. We're the Sunrise Warriors. We're just the backup."

No!

With a final look of grim defiance in her eyes, Elise sank without a sound. She was gone.

"Dammit!" Teej took a half step towards the old man, but Anna started to slip out of his grasp. Teej turned on his heels. He had to get her to the August Club.

"I'm sorry Elise. I'm so sorry."

With all his remaining strength, Teej pulled the door of the August Club wide open. He cast one last glance at the old man, blade still embedded in his chest, before turning his back and stepping through the doorway with Anna.

twenty-six

No!

Anna shot out a hand, her fingertips grasping the edge of the doorframe. Teej tried to pull her through, but she strained against him and clung on with all her strength.

"We have to get out of here," he groaned, his voice wavering.

"Let me *go!"* Anna's shout echoed with the power of the Word. Teej released her immediately, and she fell to her hands and knees.

Teej pawed at her, but she shook free of his grasp.

"It's too late," he said.

"We don't leave people behind!" roared Anna. She felt the flames build, flowing out from her ring and engulfing her hand before stretching up her arm. With her free hand, she pushed Teej away. Anyone close to her was in danger now.

"Give her back!" Anna screamed at the Minotaur.

The old man stumbled forward with an arm outstretched. "Drawn onward to new era-"

"No more singing," commanded Anna. "Speak."

He stopped in place, and, for the first time, the minotaur raised his head to look at her. His eyes were deep gray, and his gaze was steady. "I do not have her. The maze has her."

"Well, you'd better get out of my fucking way, then."

With a flick of her wrist, Anna released her Periapt. It stretched out into a long chain and animated by her rage, whipped towards him. He sidestepped at the last moment, and Anna's Periapt crashed into the ground. She maintained her Will and focus. Acting on pure instinct, she didn't allow herself even a second of doubt.

This. Will. Work.

The chain embedded itself in the ground with a solid crunch, and Anna focused all her Vig through it. Her Periapt was a conduit to her soul: a release valve for a rage that was already burning out of control. Her Praxis manifested as pure heat and fire, her arm and shoulder engulfed by flame as she pulled with all her might. She was either going to save her friend or burn this whole place to the ground. *Burn out, burn it all away.*

"Give her back to me!" screamed Anna at the top of her lungs. Her conscious thought faded away, and she became a creature of pure instinct and Will.

I will never lose anyone else like I lost him. I'll pull them out. I'm sorry, Sam.

Anna's Periapt melted through the floor, then the chain went rigid as it looped around something solid. Anna began to pull, but the ground resisted her. Cracks and fault lines spread to Anna's feet. She didn't let up, didn't loosen her grip. Instead, she heaved with all her strength, and the end of her Periapt came clear, coiled tightly around Elise's slim wrist. Teej ran to help, swerving to avoid the old man who stood by watching them mutely.

Teej scrambled to his knees and then reached into the ragged hole in the floor. With a heavy groan, he pulled Elise's dirty, unmoving body out of the ground.

"Till the blood runs cold," he muttered under his breath as he laid his hands on her chest. His fingertips glowed, but she didn't respond. Didn't breathe. She looked like a broken doll.

"There will be consequences," said the Minotaur grimly.

"We'll get out of this place. I always make it out," said Anna. She felt like someone else said the words, though she heard them come from her own lips.

"Of that, I have no doubt," said the old man. "Nevertheless, you have broken the rules and there will be consequences."

Fearing he might attack them again, Anna glowered at the old man, but he was already fading away. Like ice in flame, the Minotaur melted into the ground and when he had disappeared completely, Raguel's broken blade fell from his chest and clattered to the floor.

Anna's flame slowly receded, her Periapt coiling back like a retreating snake till eventually, it was just a ring once more. Her flame went out, and she felt completely numb.

She didn't fall, but she leaned against the wall heavily, her breathing labored. Anna couldn't help Teej, so instead, she just watched as he laid his hands on Elise's chest, closed his eyes, and struggled to pull her soul back from the brink.

As she watched Teej exert his Praxis with increasing desperation, Anna remembered climbing out of the riverbank after she lost Sam. With her clothes soaking wet, she could have done more to save him. She could have run for help. There had been a hope, but the desolation had overtaken her, and she'd let that hope slip away. *Never again.*

Elise woke up with a start, her eyes wide with terror. She tried to take a breath but coughed instead. Her fingers clutched at Teej's shirt.

"Calm!" he said, holding her shoulders. "Just breathe."

She retched up dust and mud and shuddered for a full minute until eventually, the spasms eased, and she was able to sit still.

"How do you feel? Do you know where you are?" asked Teej.

"I was gone!" wheezed Elise. "Actually *gone*. I couldn't breathe and then I went away."

"Now you're back," said Teej as he held her hand.

"Back *here* though," complained Elise.

"I know," wheezed Anna. "But not for long." She pushed herself off the wall and stood up straight. "We are *not* trapped here." She said the words with so much conviction, she almost fooled herself.

Stomping to the door of the August Club, she grabbed hold of the handle even though she already knew it wouldn't open. She concentrated her Haze Sense on the wood, but it quickly became clear there was nothing else here. The entrance was gone.

"I don't want to be here anymore," said Elise with a shiver. "Can't you just break down the door?"

Anna let out a long sigh.

"This isn't the door to the August Club anymore," explained Teej. "We broke the rules."

"But we have the key!" shouted Elise.

"There's no keyhole," replied Teej. "I guess the Minotaur doesn't have to chase us anymore. The maze has us."

"But we can still get out, right?" asked Elise, her voice trembling.

"Sure, this is a Haze and eventually we could escape. Tearing a new exit isn't too hard when you've got an Undreamer to help you, but that won't get us *into* the August Club. Who knows where we'll end up?"

"This maze, that old man…" murmured Elise. "It's all too much." She was unravelling. Elise couldn't take much more. They had to get her to safety.

"No," said Anna. "This isn't about the maze or the old man, this is about the *book*."

She pulled it out of her bag. Running her fingers across the embossed letters on the cover, she read the title once more. *The Gentleman's Guide to Nightlife.*

"What *are* you?" whispered Anna. For the first time she pushed out her Haze Sense to properly examine the malevolent tome, and she felt the Vig within. This book was an embodiment of mercurial cruelty. Within those pages was the pulse of a volatile spirit, one that would play games, but preferred to inflict pain. This book had a soul, and with that soul, it must surely hold life. And if it was alive, it must fear death.

"If we're not getting out of here, neither are you," Anna told the book.

"Oh," said Teej, his voice betraying a hint of hope. Anna hoped he understood her plan. Helping Elise to her feet, they hobbled to Anna and stared at the book with suspicion.

"Check where we left off?" suggested Teej.

Anna thumbed her way to the last page, but there was a problem.

"All of the pages are blank now."

"Well let's see," said Teej as he rubbed his chin. "We're treating this book like it's just some awful person—"

"Some fucking asshole," corrected Elise.

"Right. Well, it's a patient… asshole."

Anna nodded. "Yeah, and it's spiteful. It would be happy to stay here and watch us suffer. Right now, this book is exactly where it wants to be."

"So where does it *not* want to be?" asked Teej.

"On fire?" offered Anna.

"Oh, fuck yeah!" shouted Elise. "Do it!"

"Give me some space," warned Anna. As her friends backed away, she held the book up in front of her face with both hands. Squeezing it tight, she made sure her ring was in contact with the paper. Anna summoned her Praxis once more.

"You will listen to me. We played your games, and now we're done. You *will* lead us to the August Club. We paid the toll in blood and tears but murdering one of us was not part of the deal. We've suffered enough. Open the door. If you don't, I'll burn you to ash."

Anna looked over to Teej, but he just shrugged. What did she hope would happen next?

"Check what it says," suggested Teej. Anna opened the book, but all the pages were still blank.

"Fine," she said coldly, and her ring began to burn hot. She hoped to threaten the book first, but her fire was fueled by suppressed rage, and before she could stop herself, her whole arm was aflame.

"I will never get tired of seeing her do that," muttered Elise.

"Me neither," agreed Teej.

It wasn't working though. Anna didn't need to use her Haze Sense to know the book was immune to her fire, she could see it with her eyes. Teej still seemed hopeful though.

"Check what it says before you burn it completely," he suggested. Anna closed her eyes and her flames cooled. When she extinguished the fire, the book was still completely intact. Dismayed, she opened it again to see the same blank pages.

"Don't hold back this time," said Teej. "The book has to know you're willing to destroy it completely if it won't help us."

"I am!" protested Anna. She closed her eyes and summoned all the Will in her body. Focusing her anger and sorrow into her ring, she allowed her flame to manifest. This book had tried to kill Elise. This book would trap them here forever. It was just like Drowden and Rayleigh and all the cruel and controlling men in her life who toyed with her for their amusement. It had to be stopped.

No more.

Anna's flames burned first red, then white-hot as she pushed the temperature higher and higher. She closed her eyes and concentrated her Will, imagining the book in her hands burning to cinders. Her ears filled with the roaring of a furnace, and she smelled ozone. As her flame sputtered out, she cracked her eyes open again and finally took a breath. The book was completely intact. If anything, it looked more pristine than when she began.

"Tough fucking book," muttered Elise.

Teej shook his head in dismay. "I don't think we can hurt the book with a pure exertion of Praxis. It's too rich in Vig. Maybe… maybe we need to get back to Basine. We'll find another way to the August Club."

"We've come too far," said Anna. She refused to let the book win.

Teej put a hand on her shoulder. "You brought Elise back. If we can all survive this, maybe that's enough."

"Enough for who?" countered Anna. "Enough for Alby? What do we tell Pappi when we get back home?"

"What do we tell Elise's family if *she* doesn't make it home?" countered Teej.

"I wasn't the one who was going to leave her behind," snapped Anna. Teej winced, and she regretted the words instantly, but her hands still shook with anger. The book taunted her.

"Guys," said Elise. "Don't talk like I'm not here."

"Sorry," said Anna and Teej at the same time.

"Honestly," said Elise. "I'm ready to head home *any time* now. Teej's leg is busted up, I nearly died, and you smell like a barbequed dog. I hate it here."

"I won't let anyone else hurt you," said Anna.

Teej let out a long sigh. "Look, I know you think you're doing this for Pappi and Alby, but is it possible you're doing it to get revenge on—"

"Doing it to get revenge on the book?" shouted Anna. "Yes, of course I am!"

"Well…" he trailed off.

"This book wants us to fight and argue and unravel, right? It's having fun with us?"

"I think so," said Teej reluctantly.

"What would *stop* the fun for the book?"

Teej rubbed his chin. "Well, we can't destroy it. Not with Praxis anyway. I have a feeling that even if we tore it to pieces, it would make itself whole again."

Before Anna had time to think about what she was doing, she ripped out the first page of the book, crumpled it up and put it in her mouth.

"Oh no," said Teej.

"This is too weird," said Elise as she turned away in disgust. "I can't watch this."

Anna found the dry paper almost impossible to swallow, even after she'd chewed it for almost a minute. Finally, it became soggy mulch in her mouth. Holding her nose, she stifled a retch and managed to force it down. Even after she swallowed, she felt like a lump was lodged in the back of her throat.

"Could you Praxis me up something to drink?" she asked Teej as she waved him over. "This might take a while."

Teej's mouth hung open in astonishment. "You can't be serious."

Anna tried her best to smile back. She must look insane right now.

"Let's see how the book enjoys a journey through my digestive tract. I wonder if that's going to be '*fun*.'"

"How long will it take you to eat all the pages?" asked Elise with her back to Anna. She couldn't watch.

"As long as it takes. I don't have anything else to do. Nowhere else to go."

"I can think of lots of things I'd rather do than eat a book," replied Elise.

"And I bet there are lots of things the book would rather do than be eaten," said Anna as she licked her lips and crinkled up another page, preparing to pop it in her mouth.

"I can't believe this is our plan," said Teej as he wrinkled up his nose.

"If Elise can drown in a glue pit while chased by a backwards old man who's also maybe a Minotaur, then I can sit here and eat a whole book."

"He was *definitely* a minotaur," said Elise.

"Who cares!" shouted Anna as she chewed on another page. This one was a little easier. She tried to imagine flavorless mashed potato, but it didn't help much.

"Couldn't we just rip up the pages?" suggested Elise. "Couldn't we do *anything* else?"

Teej shrugged. "Regrettably, I think Anna has a point. There's something viscerally horrifying about being eaten, even if you're a book. Maybe *especially* if you're a book."

"I seriously can't watch this anymore though," complained Elise. "I feel sick when I see someone eat broccoli, and that's real food. Kinda."

"Check what it says now," suggested Teej. Anna held up one finger.

"One more page," she said. "One more page and then we—"

Anna dropped the book and stifled a scream.

"What happened?" said Teej as he leapt to his feet.

"It felt like it slithered in my hand. It was like the book… I dunno. Like it was alive."

"I think it is," said Teej as he poked at the book with his foot.

"I know, but it felt like it was moving. As if it was repulsed."

"Same vibe here," said Elise.

Cautiously, Teej crouched down and picked up the book, flicking to the last page.

He read aloud, "'*The door is open'*… The door is open!*"*

"No way!" exclaimed Elise. "It worked!"

"Come on," said Anna as she stumbled towards the door for the August Club, holding her stomach as she went. "We should go quickly."

"Before the book changes its mind?" asked Teej.

"Before I throw up," replied Anna.

twenty-seven

The corridor was narrow and the stairs leading down into the August Club were steep. Behind them, the rain battered a glass door that hadn't existed until they stepped through. The luxurious red carpet absorbed the sound of their footsteps as they descended. The passageway was wider at the bottom and rounded at the top, like the silhouette of a giant keyhole, but this entrance was already unlocked, a toll paid with their blood and tears.

It took a moment for Anna's eyes to adjust to the darkness, but her Haze Sense filled in the gaps. There was no need to hold back her abilities now. Her eyes saw the long strips of purple neon lighting along the walls and the frosted glass panels that reflected cloudy silhouettes, but her Haze Sense penetrated deeper. The air hummed with Vig, but this place wasn't like the Sump or even Malamun. The Vig here was heady and intoxicating, like a sweet dessert wine. Anna's fingertips tingled and she licked her lips and closed her eyes for a moment, allowing the feeling to flow through her.

"Something wrong?" asked Teej.

"Not yet," said Anna. "I've learned to enjoy the little moments in Hazes before the Dreamer decides to kill me."

Teej chuckled. "You sound like Garret."

Anna turned to Elise and gave her the best smile she could manage. "You've always wanted to come here, right?"

Elise shrugged. "Yeah, I guess."

Anna looked at herself in the mirrored walls. Though the frosted glass reflected an indistinct blur, she knew how bad she looked. Her clothes were torn and scorched, her arms dirty and bruised. "Will we even get *into* this fancy, exclusive club?"

"We better," said Teej.

"Look at me though," said Anna as she ripped off a strip of scorched fabric from the sleeve of her top. "I look as if—"

"As if you've fought a minotaur then ate an evil book while setting yourself on fire?" finished Teej. "We can use our Praxis to clean ourselves when we get to the entrance."

"I thought this *was* the entrance."

"Well, like you said, this is a fancy club." Teej adjusted his shirt collar. "I'm sure there will be a doorman and a guest list."

"And we're going to be on it?" asked Anna.

"We sure are," said Teej confidently.

Teej took the lead and Anna followed. They walked down three more flights of stairs before the corridor opened into a broad reception area. Studded red leather sofas lined the walls, interspersed with little booths lit by low desk lights, framed by heavy red velvet curtains. The lighting throughout the reception area was low and moody, but the orange standing lamps showed off expensive paintings of sensually posed men and women. Soft music played in the background, cellos and violas weaving a sleepy spell. Anna was on high alert, but the overwhelming ambience here was decadence. Lethargy. This was a place meant to put its visitors at ease or even to entice them.

Teej was *almost* right about the doorman. A woman was waiting for them at a polished oak reception desk. She was writing on a giant, golden-gilded guest book with a feathered quill. Teej marched up to her, and Anna followed behind with Elise in tow.

"We're here," said Teej definitively. It was a bold opening line.

The woman looked up and smiled at him. She was infuriatingly pretty with blonde hair, dark eyebrows, and little pouty lips. Her big blue eyes lit up when she saw him.

"Yes, absolutely!" she said brightly. "I'll just check the guestlist for your names."

What was she wearing? It was some kind of uniform, like an old-fashioned air stewardess with a tiny hat and an apron, but she was in a corset too, with long, black, shiny gloves stretching to the top of her arms. Her hair was immaculately styled, like a pin-up model. Anna was sure she'd seen someone just like her in a movie, perhaps painted on the side of an American World War Two bomber.

Her finger glided across the page as she ran it down a list of names. Anna was confident her name wasn't there. How could it be? But suddenly the woman stopped.

"There we are!" she said brightly.

"We're on the list?" Teej asked.

"Of course, Mr. Donnel. I believe you prefer '*Teej*' these days, am I right?"

"You are."

"It suits you very much, sir. My name is Clarissa and I'll lead you to your Hostess for the night."

"Hostess?" asked Anna brusquely.

"Yes, Ms. Cassidy. Your Hostess will be Miss Elizabeth Needham. You are privileged indeed! Miss Needham is both our most senior member of staff and the current proprietor of the August Club. As your receptionist, I merely hold open the door for when you want to leave. I can take you back home any time by simply—"

"Not Ms. Cassidy," interrupted Anna.

"Excuse me?" replied Clarissa. Her smile didn't waver for even a second.

"I'd rather be called '*Anna.*'"

"Of course, Anna, that is no problem at all. Now I know the journey can be challenging and our guests often arrive tired and in need of refreshment."

"I could go for a whole case of vodka," grumbled Elise. "And a cheeseburger."

"We're serving champagne," said Clarissa as she rang a small bell on the desk, "which our waiter Mani will bring in a moment. In the meantime, I'd encourage you to use the changing booths to my left and right. Right for women, left for men. You'll find clean clothes inside."

"I guess we still have some spare clothes, too," said Anna as she glanced at Elise's tattered old backpack. Had they really been shopping in the mall a few hours ago? It felt like a lifetime.

"Are you coming in with me?" Anna called back to Elise.

"I'll go after."

Anna hid her disappointment and pulled the heavy red curtain closed behind her. She was alone for a moment.

What the Hell am I doing?

In the opulent changing room, Anna looked at herself in the mirror and saw two different reflections. Like one of those optical illusions, she could perceive one version of herself or the other depending on how she shifted her view. One was the old Anna: soft brown eyes, a blank expression, shoulders loose, head down. The other was the new Anna (or maybe even Kas): eyes fierce, fists clenched, shoulders square, chest out. Ready to fight.

But this wasn't the time to fight, not with Teej or '*Clarissa*', or even with Wildey. Now was the time for diplomacy and caution. Anna had to calm herself. Their next challenge wasn't facing old enemies but creating new allies. When they finally sat down with Wildey, Anna had to be clear of mind and emotionally neutral. Teej had a bitter, age-old enmity with the Metik, but Anna had never met him. As a team, they would rely on Anna to remain calm and keep her head clear.

She ran her fingers through her dirty hair and let out a long sigh. There was a glass of water by the table, and, despite her earlier protestations, she drank it then took a seat.

A box of wet wipes sat on the table, and she grabbed a handful and began cleaning the dirty streaks from her cheeks and forehead as best she could. They felt cool and pleasant on her skin and smelled like chamomile. When she finished cleaning, Anna took off her scorched clothes and examined herself in the mirror, pale and almost naked.

There I am.

There was the real Anna: angry and afraid and still alive. If she had to fight Wildey she would, but if she needed to manipulate or lie to him, she could do that too. Whatever was required of her, she would survive. She would get out of here.

Going back to the table, Anna freshened up. She didn't know if regular Metiks found it easy to clean using their Praxis, but as an Undreamer, she certainly did. Running her fingers over her arms and shoulders, the dirt and grime broke down as her powers manifested as rapid entropy. Breaking down physical material, whether it was dirt or oil or bloodstains, was easy for her now, and after a few moments of brushing her skin and burning a tiny amount of Vig, Anna was clean and refreshed. Now to see what clothes choices she had.

The wardrobe door opened automatically as she stepped towards it, but she was not offered an expansive choice. The '*style*' was significantly more glamorous than Anna was expecting.

An emerald green, strappy sequined dress hung on a solitary hanger. As Anna held it up to the light, it glittered with swirling patterns that she had to admit were mesmerizing. It was a sleek dress with a plunging neckline though. Just looking at it made her feel deeply uncomfortable. Sneakers and leggings were probably out of the question, but she would have settled for smart-casual, and instead, she was being offered sensual and chic.

"Fuck it," Anna grumbled as she stepped into the tiny dress and wrestled it up her body. Halfway through, she feared she might be stuck, but finally, somehow, she got the straps up over her shoulders. Red-faced through exertion and embarrassment, she built up the nerve to look at herself in the mirror.

She looked like a beauty blogger at a New Year's Eve party. Though it wasn't her style, Anna couldn't deny the dress fit her perfectly and accentuated all her best features. Still, she wouldn't be ordering food in the August Club, or even sitting down if she could avoid it. This was a dress for sipping water and standing by the bar.

Alright, what's next?

A pair of broad bracelets and a sleek choker sat on the shelf, all covered in sparkling crystals. She snapped the bracelets on.

This is a lot of bling.

The choker was all that was left, but she held it loosely and regarded it with skepticism. It was not her style at all, but she had gone along with all the other wardrobe suggestions so far. Testing the look, she held it against her skin, and though it was wide and heavy, it coiled around her neck easily and the clasp seemed to click shut by itself.

Well, it's done now.

Gathering up Raguel's old broken sword and her red cape and stuffing them into her tattered backpack, Anna guessed what her friends would say about her outfit. Teej would make some cheeky remark no doubt, while Elise would think it was garish and overly revealing. She would love it.

No more time for frivolity. Mentally preparing herself, Anna reached for the curtain but then at the last moment, she glanced down at her dirty sneakers. *They'll have to do.*

Nervously, Anna stepped through the curtain and grimaced in anticipation of her friend's comments.

"Anna, I trust everything is to your liking?" said Clarissa.

"Not exactly," said Anna. "Elise, how bad is it?"

Elise looked glum, but when she finally looked up and saw Anna's clothes, she smiled. "Love it. Eastern European chic with, like, internet influencer swagger."

"I think you mean Russian call girl."

"But a really expensive one," said Teej as his eyes lit up. When Anna saw him, she couldn't help but grin from ear to ear. He wore a sharp suit, cut perfectly for his lean body, with a smart gray waistcoat, black shiny shoes and a little pocket-handkerchief folded into a perfect point. His messy hair was swept back from his face, and he was clean-shaven, refreshed and completely renewed. He also looked a little nervous, like he was picking her up for a prom date. Somehow, the more uncomfortable he looked in smart clothes, the more she liked it.

"The award for best couple goes to…," Elise said in a sing-song voice. She couldn't keep the grin off her face.

"Laugh it up missy," said Anna. "I can't wait to see what they've chosen for you. I'd like to see you in an old brown cardigan, sandals with socks and a… I dunno… a smock."

"Ha, yeah," said Elise.

"I don't think so ma'am," said Clarissa.

"What do you mean?"

"Your friend is not on the list."

"What the actual fuck?" roared Anna. This was not happening; not after everything they had been through. Anna slammed the palms of her hands down on the counter and stared directly into the receptionist's eyes. Clarissa did not flinch.

"Her name is not on the list," she repeated.

Elise reached out and grasped Anna's arm. "It's okay Anna."

Anna shrugged her off. "It is *not* okay." She pointed a finger in Clarissa's face. "Listen, lady, you have no idea what I've done to get here. You have no idea who I've fought and how many people have told me I have to leave my friends behind. They are always wrong, and most of them are dead. I will not…"

"Anna!" snapped Elise. "Look at me."

Anna slowly turned around, and when she saw Elise's eyes, she realized their journey together was already over.

"I'm going home. That's why my name isn't on the list."

"Home?"

"She is correct," said Clarissa. "If someone does not truly desire to enter the club, their name will not appear on the list."

"She said I can go *home*," said Elise with relief.

"Is that really what you want?"

Elise shrugged. "Yeah."

"But you've always wanted to come here. Right?

"I did," said Elise with a frown, "But this is all too much."

"We made it through together. We don't leave friends behind."

"This is the end of the journey for me," said Elise. "You didn't leave me behind. I'll never forget that."

"I'm sorry," said Anna, tears coming to her eyes.

"No, don't be dumb! You saved me. Don't say sorry. I'm not saying sorry either, because I'm not doing anything wrong. I just need to go home. You have to know when something is too much. Back in that maze when I went under… that was too much. This isn't the right time for me to be by your side. It wouldn't be good for me or you. You have to do this without me."

Anna took her friend's hand. "But you would be so much better at this than me. Cool people, clubs, dancing–I'm not good at all that stuff."

"Shut up," scoffed Elise. "You're good at *everything*. You'll be fine."

Anna cast a stern look in Clarissa's direction. "And she'll get home safely?"

"She will. All Ms. Beauchamp need do is walk out the exit, and she'll appear back where your journey started. I believe you set off from…" Clarissa checked her notes. "Millie's Mall? She will arrive back exactly how she left."

"You're sure about this?" Anna asked Elise.

"Yep. I'll go find Pappi and make sure he's safe and tell him you made it and I'll tell him you ate a book to get us here."

"It wasn't a book; it was only a few pages." Anna reached into her bag, grabbed *The Gentleman's Guide to Nightlife* and thrust it into Elise' grasp. "Take this and throw it in the sea."

Elise saluted. "Yes, Captain."

"You *did* follow the instructions in the book to the letter?" asked Clarissa. "If you didn't, we could all be—"

"To the letter," replied Anna firmly.

Teej came up behind Elise and gave her a big hug. "You'll be back here one day."

"I know," Elise turned to Teej. She put a hand on his chest and winked. "Looking pretty fly in that suit by the way, *Mr. Bond*."

"Thanks."

"You crazy kids be careful, okay?" said Elise.

"We will," said Anna as they walked Elise to the door. "You still have your knife?"

"Yeah. Shouldn't you take it?"

"No," said Anna as she looked down at her dress. "I have nowhere to put it in this outfit. You keep it. Tell Pappi not to worry. We'll find out where the Christmas Council is taking place, then we're going to get Alby back."

"I'll tell him." Elise opened the door then turned to face Anna head-on. She looked tired and relieved.

"Hug me please," said Anna.

Elise lunged, planting a kiss directly on Anna's lips. Anna started to pull away with a laugh, then decided to kiss Elise back.

"You're so hot," Elise muttered under her breath as she turned away, cheeks flushed. "Goodbye Undreaming Anna."

Anna gave her best friend a wave. "Goodbye Sunrise Warrior."

Elise stepped through the doorway and was gone.

twenty-eight

Teej realized he was staring at Anna again. Wrenching his gaze away, he focused on Clarissa as she led them down a long, snaking corridor into the depths of the August Club. Hazy purple strip lighting illuminated swirls and patterns along the walls. Every hundred yards they'd pass a locked door, and sometimes they heard muffled noises coming from the other side.

So far, the August Club had been both more and less strange than he expected. They'd only met one person so far, and Teej was struggling to get a read on Clarissa. Did she treat every visitor with the same hospitality? Clarissa said they would be looked after by the legendary Elizabeth Needham, and that certainly was unusual. Needham was the owner of this place and a formidable Dreamer in her own right. It was doubtful she met with every visitor. If their treatment was preferential, Teej guessed it was more likely because of Anna than him. Everyone wanted to meet the new Undreamer.

"Just a little further," Clarissa called back, her high heels clacking across the floor even though she moved quickly.

"How big do you think this place is?" asked Anna, her arms folded across her chest. It was obvious she felt uncomfortable in her new dress. Teej meanwhile fidgeted with his too-tight collar. He hated wearing a tie.

"I can't tell. Every time I try to feel the edges with my Haze Sense it just…"

"Seems to go on forever," finished Anna.

They walked in silence a little longer before Anna spoke again. "I miss her already."

"Me too," confessed Teej. "She came into her own after we lost Vinicaire."

"She was a flower wilting in his shadow."

"That's very poetic."

Anna nodded. "Her words, not mine."

Teej shook his head. "I forget that when we were apart, she was speaking to both of us every day for over a year."

Anna chuckled. "Who would have guessed she could keep a secret that long?"

"Not me," Teej admitted. "You know, she got stronger after she lost someone."

Anna cast him a glance that hinted she didn't want him to keep speaking, but he pushed on.

"And so have you, Anna. The loss of your husband… it doesn't make you weak. Eventually, it makes you stronger than you ever thought you could be. When I lost Linda—"

"It's not the same," cut in Anna. Her gaze was icy. "Not the same at all. You think because we both lost someone, we're the same? It's not just about who we lost Teej. It's about *how* we lost them. And how we failed them."

"Right," said Teej hopefully. "We failed. But we learned."

"I didn't learn a fucking thing," said Anna under her breath.

"You might think that now, but in time…"

"No," said Anna firmly. "I know you're trying to help. But failing to save Linda from some murderous Dreamers is not the same as how I failed my husband."

"So, talk to me!" said Teej as he put his hand on her arm. "Tell me what happened, and you'll feel better. Then you can start to recover."

Anna looked away from him. Teej felt her withdraw into herself. "Not now. Not with you. Even if I told you what happened… I don't trust myself. I've buried it so deep; I can't face what happened. My memories are a mess. So don't push me. This isn't your business. And my loss is nothing to do with you. Leave me alone."

Before Teej could respond, Clarissa stopped suddenly and gestured towards a nondescript door that looked exactly like the fifty other doors they had already passed.

"Is this it?" asked Teej. The discussion with Anna would have to wait. His Haze Sense didn't give him any special insight. This door felt like all the rest. He licked his lips nervously and then reached for the door handle, but Clarissa put her slender hand around his wrist to stop him.

"The August Club is a place of discretion," said Clarissa.

"Of course," said Teej.

"Follow the rules and we are all safe. No Praxis, no Mimesis. If you are cast out of the August Club, we do not know where you will land. And we do not care."

"We understand," said Teej as he broke free of her grasp and opened the door.

Anna and Teej stood in a busy, chic lounge bar. They were surrounded by smart waiters and waitresses, men in expensive suits and women in sparkly dresses, all framed by a stunning circular view of a city skyline that seemed familiar but was somehow generic too. Jazz beats echoed through the bar, and though everyone noticed their arrival, the low rumble of conversation didn't stop. No one seemed particularly interested in their appearance except for the nearest waiter, who wandered over. He carried a tray with two champagne flutes.

"Sir, Madam, welcome to the August Club. I trust your journey here was not too arduous. Please take your drinks and follow me in your own time. Mrs. Needham and Mr. Wildey are expecting you."

Anna and Teej followed the waiter through the lounge, past an ornate water fountain, a beautiful woman in a cocktail dress sipping a margarita, and an old man snapping his fingers as a waiter carried over a platter of hors d'oeuvres. The August Club was decadent and sprawling, and every time Anna thought they had reached their destination, they turned a corner and entered a new, grander area instead.

"I'm not sure I'm as ready as I said I was," Anna whispered to Teej, but when she saw his reaction, she instantly regretted her words. He was pale and his eyes darted nervously around the room. His hand trembled and he swallowed nervously.

"Teej, forget what I just said. I am ready. *We* are ready."

"I've dreaded this moment," muttered Teej. "Had nightmares about it."

"Coming to the August Club?"

"No. Seeing *him* again."

"Stop," Anna put her hand on his arm and held him. He tried to pull away, but she didn't let go.

"We have to keep moving," he complained.

"Why?" she retorted. "He can wait for us."

"Sir, madam," said the waiter. "I do recommend we—"

"Quiet you," snapped Anna. "We're talking here."

The waiter wrinkled his nose, the pencil moustache above his top lip quivering. "Of course."

"What do you need to hear from me?" said Anna. They didn't have time to dance around each other's feelings. They still hadn't worked as a team since they'd reunited, but now was the time.

Teej shrugged. "Tell me to pull myself together."

"Alright then: Teej, pull yourself the fuck together."

He smiled and nodded resolutely. "I will."

"We got this," said Anna. "Just remember why we came here. We need to find out where the Christmas Council is taking place in order to save Alby. Our friends are counting on us, right?"

"Right," he said. "For Pappi. I just hope I can—"

"You can," interrupted Anna. "Now let's go see your old frenemy and figure out why he made us suffer so much to come to this fancy, huge, and frankly, overrated, bar."

"The views not bad," said Teej. "And the champagne was…"

"It was awful. What's that about?"

"Madam, the champagne is over forty years old," complained the waiter.

"Sure tasted like it."

Teej burst out laughing.

"Come on," said Anna. "Let's get going before Jeeves here bursts a gasket."

They followed the waiter, crossing the dance floor and going up a series of glass steps before ascending a ramp to a cordoned-off area. They stood on a high platform overlooking the dance floor, with luxurious red velvet sofas and clear glass tables. Beautiful waitresses and smart waiters lined the walls, ready to bring more drinks to the VIPs at a moment's notice.

When Teej examined the faces of everyone more closely, he saw the exhilaration in their eyes. Everyone here was living a fantasy, though that fantasy was beyond anything sexual or romantic. This place was euphoria. The guests at the August Club were experiencing their hearts' deepest desires.

Near the bar, an old man was clutching the hand of a young woman, looking deeply into her eyes. They looked alike. This wasn't an old man flirting with a beautiful young woman. It was a father looking at his daughter with pride and longing. Longing to have her back. The old man had lost the daughter, and the August Club was showing him what she would be like now. If she had survived.

Teej's Haze sense revealed more secrets. A nervous young man was on his knees while a woman stroked his cheek with slender fingers. She was a pop star. He was her biggest fan, and now, completely in her thrall. Next to them a postman, still in his uniform, was holding a trophy of some sort. He held it with pride. He'd dreamed of winning all his life. The August Club made everyone feel like a winner.

Shaking his head, Teej looked away. The August Club didn't tempt him.

The waiter lifted a red velvet rope, and Anna and Teej arrived at their table. It was time to move on. Waiting for them were two empty seats. Opposite, their host Elizabeth Needham was already seated, waiting for them. And next to her sat Wildey.

Teej let out a long breath. *Hello, old friend.*

twenty-nine

Anna's eyes went to the owner of the August Club first. Elizabeth Needham was a transfixing sight. Dark, luxurious brown curls cascaded down her shoulders, and she had a tidy, straight Betty Paige fringe. Her pale white complexion was flawless, and her eyes sparkled blue under the glare of the chandeliers. She wore a laced corset and white blouse with a pencil skirt and pointed heels. Anna narrowed her eyes. *I bet she can walk in those just fine.*

"Please, sit," said Needham, gesturing towards the empty chairs. Her red lips curled into a smirk, and though she was poised, Anna detected a current of tension in the air that even Elizabeth Needham's polite manners couldn't defuse.

Anna self-consciously lowered herself into the soft leather chair and waited for Teej to join her. Even seated, the woman opposite was taller, and with her perfect posture, seemed to loom over them. Anna straightened her spine and tried to face Needham eye-to-eye but couldn't help nervously tugging her dress down to hide her bare legs. Slinky, sequin dresses were something she liked in theory more than practice. Anna felt like a Christmas bauble in January.

Teej took his seat a moment later, and when he did, Anna finally allowed herself a look at Wildey. At long last, she would come face to face with the man who had tormented Teej.

He wasn't what she expected. While Needham was poise and refinement personified, Wildey was neither. A snide I-told-you-so smirk played across his lips, and his dark eyes were filled with mischief. He had curly red hair, and he rested his hands behind his head, his feet up on the table. He wore a bright red sweater and brown pants with pristine white sneakers. Everyone else was dressed like they were in a casino in Monte Carlo, but Wildey looked like he was headed to the grocery store.

Anna tried to guess his age. He looked like he was in his mid-thirties, but she knew he was much older. Older than Teej? Perhaps, but of the same generation. However long he'd been here, Wildey looked like he'd be happy to stay in the August Club forever.

"Kas and Donnel," said Wildey casually. "Or Teej and Anna, whatever you're calling yourselves."

Wildey's voice was low and lazy. He sat forward and grabbed his drink: a bottle of beer. "Order whatever you want. This place has everything you could ever ask for."

Anna cast a sideways glance at Teej. He wasn't responding. *Come on Teej, pull it together.*

"We are glad to have you with us," said Needham, her voice confident and authoritative with a subtle English accent. "I am Elizabeth Needham, your Host and the proprietor of the August Club. It is nice to finally meet you. I know the journey here can be difficult, but I'm glad to see you made it here in one piece. You both look very well."

Anna looked to Teej, but he remained silent. She would have to take the lead.

"Thank you," said Anna curtly. "But our friend almost died on the journey."

"That would have been tragic," said Needham calmly. "Nonetheless, I trust Clarissa looked after you well enough upon your arrival. We are not responsible for what goes on outside the Club, but once you arrive, rest assured, you are safe."

"Yeah, that sounds fine… except for all the warnings about throwing us out."

"Again, that serves a purpose," said Needham without missing a beat. "Might I remind you that the rules are binding, but they protect you from harm. They protect us all."

"I believe that they protect some of us," said Anna critically. "So why are you friends with him?" Anna pointed her thumb at Wildey.

"Friends?" Needham looked amused. "He is my husband."

There was a sharp intake of breath from Teej.

"It felt like I fell in love with this place as soon as I arrived," explained Wildey. "But it turns out I only really fell in love with the owner."

He put his hand on his wife's. "We've got a lot of catching up to do. I try to keep up with events in the rest of the Firmament and I have my sources, but sometimes it's good to hear first-hand accounts of what's been happening. You two seem to be involved in all the exciting stuff."

Wildey put his bottle down and leaned close. "So, old friend, what you been up to?"

They all turned to face Teej. Finally, he shrugged.

"Not much. You know everything already."

"Not quite *everything*," said Wildey. "And that's why you're here. But let's dance around the subject for a moment longer, shall we? How is everyone?"

"Garret is dead," said Teej without expression. "Maybe that news made you reflect on your choice to hide here."

For the first time, Anna thought she saw a genuine emotion on Wildey's face, but it was hard to read. Grief? Fear? She couldn't tell.

"I'm sorry," he said, and he sounded sincere. "I didn't agree with Garret all of the time, but he was a good Metik."

"He was the best," corrected Teej.

"He would want us to reconcile," said Wildey. "He wouldn't want us to bicker like this. He always respected me."

"He thought you lost your way," said Teej, his eyes narrowing. Wildey frowned for a second, then his smirk returned, and he leaned back again.

"Might I suggest we all take a moment to get better acquainted," suggested Needham. "And as my husband suggested, we should get you drinks. Anything you like, please just ask."

Anna swallowed then licked her lips. "Fine, I guess I do want something. I guess I want…"

She searched her feelings. "I want a ginger ale with lime."

Teej gave her a confused look and all she could do was shrug.

"I'm as surprised as anyone," said Anna.

A waiter lurking nearby scampered off to fetch her drink. Anna turned her attention back to Needham.

"We'll tell you everything that happened to bring us here," said Anna. "But why don't you speak first?" She considered her words carefully. Her questions should be specific, even when she didn't know exactly what information she wanted to hear. "How did you meet Wildey?"

"My husband had been looking for this place for a long time. When he arrived, I was impressed he found us. Most people who come to the August Club have some secret desire, some taboo desire, or nugget of obsessions that they cannot explore back in Basine."

Anna looked around skeptically.

"I see my description does not match your surroundings," said Needham silkily. "I can assure you, what goes on behind the closed doors of each room here is very different from what you experience in the lounge. The August Club is a multi-faceted diamond; some surfaces are rougher than others."

"Uh-huh," said Anna. "So, he came here looking for his 'nugget of obsession', and instead found you?"

"I'm not the same man I was when I first arrived here," said Wildey.

"You're saying you don't want every Dreamer dead anymore?" asked Teej.

"Well, I wouldn't be much of a husband if I did."

"You're a Dreamer?" Anna asked Needham.

"Of course. Though I rarely need to practice my Art here. The August Club has plenty of other distractions, and the day-to-day running of the establishment keeps me busy enough."

Wildey put his hand on Needham's shoulder. They really did look like a couple.

"I can't believe it," said Teej as he rubbed his forehead. "You? After everything you said. After everything that's happened. Married to a Dreamer!?"

"I told you; things change. People change."

"I heard what you said," said Teej dismissively. "It's just… I don't believe you,"

"I admit, when I first came here, I had a scheme or two, but they fell by the wayside. Now, I just want this civil war to be over as much as you do. Sometimes it feels like I've retired, and that makes me happy. I'm just worried that when the Aesthetes tear each other apart, eventually their civil war will spill over into my retirement home."

"You're saying this place is the neutral ground?" asked Teej.

"Certainly!" chimed in Needham. "Think of us as Switzerland, but with more champagne and corsets."

"So, you're happy to languish in escapism and fantasy while the world burns?" asked Teej.

"More than happy, as are the people in corsets," drawled Wildey.

"The only people getting hurt here are people who come to be hurt," said Needham curtly. "Besides, we're mere facilitators. We just make sure everyone is comfortable and safe and let the players play."

Anna tutted. "You won't be able to hide here for much longer. We need your help. Our friend is in trouble."

"That's not what I want to talk about," said Wildey. "I want to know everything about you, Anna. What's your story? Start at the beginning."

He was deflecting. Anna wouldn't let him.

"You didn't finish your story. How you met each other. How you stumbled into your change of heart."

Teej nodded. "Yeah, you know, the story of how you went from a man who was willing to let his best friend die to kill some Dreamers, to a man who married one."

"You remember when I called you?" asked Wildey as he pointed at Teej. "You were outside the Groven, about to hunt down Andre DeLorde. Anna was there. Pappi too I think."

"I remember," said Teej.

"I was being cruel then."

Teej shrugged. "You were being Wildey."

"That's what I mean," said Wildey. "My thoughts no longer swirl in the same patterns. My attitudes have mellowed. I mean look at me! I'm flabby." He pinched his tummy. "And I'm happy about it. I've gone soft, Teej, like you."

"Hey!" said Anna. "What's that supposed to—"

"He does not mean it as an insult," broke in Needham.

"I really don't!" continued Wildey. "It took strength to let so much hate and anger go. Elizabeth taught me peace."

"You're fine with Dreamers now?" challenged Teej.

Wildey grinned. "Not all of them. Not on principle. Don't get me wrong, I won't shed tears for Drowden or the Apoth. By getting rid of them, Anna has done better than either of us. But I have let the old grudges burn cold."

Needham put her hand on his knee. "I liked his righteous anger and his playful schemes, but I like him better now. He'd grown beyond all that."

"Sure," said Teej. "But what particular playful schemes brought you here one year ago?"

"Nothing as awful as you might imagine."

"Really? How did your Praxis manifest back then? Remind me."

Wildey looked away. "It's different now."

"Back then though?" pressed Teej. "Does your wife know?"

"She knows. I made bombs."

"*The Anarchist*," said Anna. "I guess that nickname makes sense now."

"Let's not judge," said Wildey with a smile. "I used to blow Dreamers up, you set them on fire."

"When my husband came here, he was angry and conflicted," said Needham firmly. "I helped put his mind at ease, and over time, his obsessions became fascinating to me. I saw the depth of his passion and realized it had no limits."

As Needham praised Wildey, she stroked his arm. Anna wrinkled her nose. Something about the pair irritated her. Their mutual affection was cloying.

"So, you came here, met, fell in love and gave up being a… what were you exactly?" asked Anna.

"I was, and am, a Metik," said Wildey. "I never gave up, I just settled down."

"It's *staggering* how much I don't believe you," said Teej. "But let's say for a minute you're telling the truth, and you just want everyone to be friends and hold hands. Are you going to tell us what we want to know? You know about the Christmas Council, right? Where is it? We're going to save our friend, and we're going to face Rayleigh in front of all the Dreamers."

"Sure, I heard about Rayleigh's Christmas peace summit," said Wildey. "I don't believe it's genuine, but I could be wrong."

"Maybe you *have* changed," said Teej. "I've never heard you admit you might be wrong."

"I didn't say I *am* wrong, I said I *could* be. I don't think any lasting peace can be achieved while Rayleigh pulls the strings. One way or another, he has to go. I might compromise in other areas, but never in my hatred of Rayleigh."

"Do you blame him for Linda's death?" said Teej as he leaned forward.

"No," said Wildey. He pointed a finger. "I blame you."

A ripple of tension went around the table, settling in Wildey's eyes. Anna shuddered.

"I've had a lot of time to think since I got here," said Wildey. "I've tried to put the events of that night together. Broken memories like shards of a mirror. The more I piece together, the better reflection I see of myself. What I was, what I am now. I don't think you've done that yet, Donnel. I don't think you've even tried."

"I've…"

Teej trailed off. Anna looked at him with suspicion. Was he caught in a lie?

"You need a dose of self-reflection, old friend," said Wildey elusively. "But I'm still waiting on Anna's story."

They all turned to look at her. Anna bristled. She didn't like to be put on the spot, and she didn't like how Wildey was undermining Teej, seeking out his vulnerabilities.

"Well, it all started in the nineties," said Anna flippantly. "Denim was distressed, sneakers were chunky and filled with air, and a young girl called Anna was born on a quiet Sunday afternoon to two middle-class suburbanites."

"There's no need for the attitude," chastised Needham.

"There's plenty of need," snapped Anna. "If you'll waste my time, I'll waste yours. Why all the questions? Our friend needs us."

"This is payment," said Wildey. "I'll tell you what you want to know, but first, tell me your story. Starting with what happened to Sam."

Oh no.

Anna shook her head. "No."

"No *what*?" replied Wildey. "No, don't ask about Sam? Why not? I think it's time you came clean with Teej."

I can't do this.

"Your drink," said the waiter, interrupting them all. He placed the ginger ale in front of Anna. The ice clinked in the glass while they all sat in silence. Holding the silver tray loosely, he lingered until Needham shooed him away in irritation.

Anna lifted her glass and sipped, aware of their eyes on her. Especially Teej's.

"Well?" prompted Wildey. Anna's head went down.

"She doesn't need to tell you, or me, anything," said Teej. "I trust her. I don't need to hear about her past to know the person she is now."

"How achingly noble," said Wildey with an eye roll. "But, Anna, I know what you did, and I don't judge you. That's the thing about this place. You can't lie to yourself here. By word, by deed, or even by thought, there are no deceptions. So, open your soul, let those memories come through, and leave the judgement behind."

He took a swig of his beer and then shrugged. "I'm the only one who knows the truth about you now, and I don't think less of you for it."

"You don't know shit about me," growled Anna.

"You don't want to test that," said Wildey. "It didn't take Praxis to find your secrets, just a bit of time and some old newspaper articles. Sam had no history of depression before he jumped in that river. But you did."

"Stop," said Anna. "Just… stop."

Needham put her hand on Wildey's shoulder and cleared her throat. "Let's not torment our guests. I'm their host, and my professional courtesy extends to our friends. I do not wish to see them harassed so."

Wildey turned his attention to Teej, his gaze predatory. "I didn't mean to tease her. I can see you care about her a lot."

"We're partners," said Teej. "Like the two of us before you stabbed me in the back."

"That's not strictly true, is it? You always partner up with women. You love to find a wide-eyed girl to hitch on your coattails. The difference is, Linda was in love with you, and you didn't love her back, but you were willing to string her along to get your way.

"But it's different with Anna, right? The roles are reversed. I mean look at her! She's much more your type than Linda was. You're swooning over her, old man! Stop me if I'm wrong. I'd love to hear you try to contradict me."

Teej put his palms on the tables and let out a long breath. "You are the most irritating Metik in the entire Firmament."

"Wildey," said Needham with authority. "This stops here."

Wildey licked his lips then put his hands up in surrender. "I tease!"

Wildey finished his beer then pointed at them. "The truth is I only want to ask each of you one question. If you have a good answer, I'll tell you what you want to know. I'll tell you exactly where to find Rayleigh's Christmas Council. Fuck, I'll even tell you how to save your friend."

Wildey stretched his hand out. "Deal?"

Neither Anna nor Teej shook his hand, but Teej nodded. "Ask your questions."

"Anna first. What is in your bag?"

Wildey motioned to the backpack on the ground that Anna unconsciously held between her feet. She turned to Teej, but he gave her a nod, indicating she should answer him.

"Raguel's broken sword," she said without expression.

Wildey whistled through his teeth. "Now that's an answer!" His head went back and as he looked straight up at the ceiling, letting out a little chuckle.

"*Raguel's broken sword.* Just like that. You are something else. How did you get that?"

"Over his dead body," she replied.

"Of course. He would never give up his weapons. Those Mirror Blades retain considerable Vig. Do you know how to use them to open doors?"

"No," said Anna.

"I am no expert, but I understand they let you travel through reflections. That is how he stalked you."

Anna's eyes narrowed. "You know he stalked me?"

"I know almost all of Rayleigh's plans. I just don't see all the details."

Anna examined him closely. There was something she could use here.

"For someone who hates Rayleigh so much, you talk a lot like him."

Wildey winced. Anna's words rocked him. His smile cracked. Finally, she had found his weak spot.

"I'm nothing like Rayleigh."

Anna didn't say anything; she just let his words hang in the air.

"You did well to survive an attack by the Green Knight," said Needham, changing the subject. "I'm impressed. How did you prevail?"

"I'm an Undreamer, remember?" said Anna. "Every Dreamer and Metik has told me how impressive and dangerous I am, but it took me a while to realize something."

Anna took another sip of her drink, making them wait.

"They were right. I travelled, I learned, and now I'm strong enough to protect myself and my friends. I fought the Green Knight over and over again, and eventually, I won."

Wildey shook his head. "*How* though? I mean this is Raguel. This is an Ancestral–not a half-mad Dreamer like Mott or a petty tyrant like Drowden. This is a being from before our time, with powers beyond our conception. How could a neophyte with a flaming ring and anger management issues stop him?"

Wildey seemed restless now. His jibes were getting more obvious, less effective. She'd gotten under his skin, just a little. *Good.*

"I fought him in a place I knew well. And he underestimated me."

"Perhaps the influence of the Ancestrals wanes?" Needham said to Wildey. "Raguel was the right hand of Gwinn, but Gwinn is dormant. Perhaps in Basine, unmoored from the Realm and detached from their Lord, the Ancestrals no longer hold such power."

"There's something in that," ruminated Wildey. "She lured him out of the Realm. He's an Ancestral so he can spin a Haze as well as anyone, but she faced him in an environment she knew well. She was prepared, and perhaps caught him on the back foot."

"I'm *right* here," snapped Anna.

"Tell me, did Raguel… did he give up? Do you think he was ready to die?"

Anna frowned. So many questions. Was Wildey on to something? Everyone seemed so incredulous about the Green Knight's defeat. Had she beaten him in a fair fight? What did a 'fair fight' even mean Behind the Veil?

"He was trying his best to kill me." Anna paused for a moment, considering whether she should say more. "But when he was beaten, he spoke to me."

"What did he speak of?" asked Wildey. He couldn't hide his fascination. His attention was rapt.

"He talked about the Winterheart. I asked him if it was a cure to the Blood Plague, but he didn't answer. He mentioned The Fade too. What is it?"

"Fascinating," said Wildey ignoring her question. He stared off into the distance, lost in thought.

"Well, Anna," said Needham with a sigh, "You're an impressive young woman."

Anna smiled politely. *A bit patronizing.*

"I know little of the Fade," Needham continued. "It's rumored to be a misty curtain that has closed off much of the Realm and prevents anyone from reaching Selmetridon or this *Winterheart.* And no one who has tried to pass through has returned. This is why I believe exploring the Realm beyond the

August Club is pointless. The Realm is full of danger, like the Fade, Raguel, and the Sump. Why not just stay here? We have everything you need, and anything you desire. I'd like to think that when this ugly civil war is over, perhaps we might talk properly. I know you visit the August Club out of necessity, but when your friends are safe, and the situation is less dire—"

"You mean when most of the Dreamers aren't trying to kill me?"

"Yes, quite. When the dust settles, I'd welcome you back. You say you travelled the world meeting Dreamers and Metiks as you honed your skills. There are things I could teach you, too."

Anna's head spun. Between Wildey's barbs and Needham's veiled compliments, she wasn't sure how to feel.

"It's strange that the two of you are so isolated," mused Wildey. "Of course, you have a *few* friends, but there was a time when all Metiks could be called on to band together in times of conflict. Why do you suppose there are so few of us around to stop this bickering between the Dreamers? I remember whole armies of Metiks working together. Or at least I *think* I do."

Teej picked up Anna's drink and looked at her for approval. She gave him a nod, and he took a sip.

"I don't trust my memories anymore," he said with weariness. "Were the Metiks as righteous as we thought ourselves? Policing the Dreamers, meddling in their rivalries? There's so few of us left. It leaves too much time to think. To ruminate."

Wildey nodded. "To stew in our thoughts. I know what you mean. Back in the day, we went from one Haze to the next, barely touching down back in Basine. That must have affected our minds, our souls. Maybe that's why I like it so much here. When you're in a Staid Haze like the August Club, it's easy to forget how bare Basine has come. How much light has gone out. There's less Vig in the world now."

"Entropy," said Teej in agreement. "We are all fading out, winking out like stars, Dreamers and Metiks alike. This civil war is ugly enough, but it's not an epic battle like the old days. It feels so personal, so petty. We're burning out."

"Oh, gimme a break," complained Anna. She didn't like seeing Wildey and Teej agreeing like this. "Can we dial down the doom in the old folk's home? I know you two have been through a lot, but this attitude is getting us nowhere."

"Quite right, Anna," said Needham. "Time for the boys to set aside their affected melancholy. The Dreamers have waxed and waned throughout the ages, and while no one can doubt these are lean years, it remains to be seen what the future holds."

"You have a point," said Teej. "Wildey, you asked Anna your question; now ask me mine."

Wildey brushed his red hair back with his fingers and put his feet up on the table again. "Don't you two wanna talk some more? Wouldn't you rather spend some more time here, asking each other questions, getting to the truths you both hide so deeply?"

"No," said Teej.

"Oh, come now," said Wildey with glee. "There must be something you want to ask each other. What if we play a game? One question each. The other must answer honestly. If you could ask each other just one question, any question, and get an honest answer, what would it be?"

"We're done," said Anna. She clenched her fist and felt warmth form around her fingers, pulsing through the metal of her ring. "No more games."

"No fun at all," said Wildey. "There's so much tension in you two. *Between* you. You need to find a way to defuse. You'll work together better if you resolve it. Have you slept together yet?"

Teej scowled so hard that Wildey backed off, though his grin remained.

"Love, that is enough," said Needham, her perfect lips pursed.

"Wildey, why are we here?" asked Teej wearily. "You don't care about Raguel or his sword. There's something else you want to know. Just ask. I'll tell you whatever I can."

"I hope you two survive this mess," said Wildey. "I really do. You're cute together. No, I mean it! Anna, I've known this guy a long time. He likes you; he really does. One day you might feel half as strongly about him as he does about you. Whether you hook up or not, I reckon you'll make a good team.

"Me and Linda, we were a good team too. We clicked, you know? But none of that mattered when she fell in love with Donnel. Or "*Teej*" if you prefer. She abandoned me, and the worst part is, I can't remember the day she chose him over me. And neither can you, right?"

Wildey waited for Teej to answer, but he said nothing.

"You see!" Wildey went on. "We're enemies now because I stabbed you in the back, and I'm sure I did, but I can't remember what happened! There are little splinters of memory. I remember some monstrosity that the Apoth had built, and I remember you and Linda. I was looking down on you. I think I laughed. Linda screamed. It happened so fast."

"Do you remember the desert?" asked Teej. "Do you remember when I begged for you to save her?"

"I do remember that," said Wildey. For the first time, Anna thought she saw a look of sadness cross Wildey's face. "But she was my partner, and you took her from me."

Teej shook his head slowly. "There's one thing we both need to learn. Linda was neither yours nor mine. She made her own choice. I shouldn't have used her feelings to manipulate her, and you shouldn't have betrayed us, but the choice to go into that Haze–that was all her."

"Fine," said Wildey through gritted teeth. "But what I want to know is if you are going to do the same thing with Anna? And is she worthy of filling the gap Linda's death created?"

"Why are we debating my worth?" asked Anna. "I don't see you fighting Rayleigh's goons. I don't see you with a plan to stop the Blood Plague."

Wildey smirked. "I investigated your history, Anna. Personal history, work history, medical history. There was a mystery I needed to solve: who was Donnel's partner? Was she really trying to confront Rayleigh and stop the Blood Plague, or was she just trying to destroy herself? I think it's time you were honest. Tell the truth, not to me, but to Teej. And to yourself. Is the same thing gonna happen to Teej that happened to Sam?"

Anna shook her head. Wildey leaned in. "Tell Teej how Sam went in the river, and how—"

Wildey broke off. He pushed his chair back, mouth open. What was happening? Anna glanced down at her arm. *Flames.*

"Anna!" Teej shouted in desperation. "No. You have to stop it."

Too late.

Teej was trying to reach out to her, but the flames leapt up and he recoiled. She burned him. Holding his arm in pain, he was speaking, but the words were too far away. Teej reached out again and again but couldn't get close to her. Someone screamed; people ran for the exits.

"Restrain her," shouted Wildey from out of sight.

"How?" said Needham. "We can't get close."

"Don't touch her!" shouted Teej. He was trying to get to Anna, but waves of heat beat him back.

Needham weaved her hands in a pattern, trying to summon her Art, but the terror in her eyes showed she knew it was too late. A black portal opened at Needham's command, exerting a gravity that began to pull them all in. Wildey waved an incantation of his own, his Praxis an attempt to bind Anna, but she resisted. Wildey stopped abruptly and ran for cover. Only Teej stayed close, his face contorted in pain.

Anna felt the heat rising all around her. The tables burst into flame. She felt her agony melt in the flames. All thoughts left her mind. She was pure emotion. Rage. Anna was gone. All that remained was the fire. Her ring slipped from her finger. She didn't need it anymore.

Desolation.

thirty

Blindingly white walls, a white floor, a line of white sinks and the smell of bleach. Teej was reminded of a hospital, but he had woken up somewhere much less familiar. The air was too warm and humid, the distant rumble of conversation and the drumming of feet outside too urgent. He was in the bathroom of some huge building.

Where the Hell did they send me?

Elizabeth Needham had banished them from the August Club. When Anna's fire had threatened to consume them all, their bodies had been thrown like rag dolls through a black doorway. Needham had been left with no other choice. Anna was out of control.

Evicting her must have been a last resort. Wildey had tried to bind her with his Praxis while Teej had tried to talk her down, but they had all failed. Anna's grasp on her powers had slipped, her consciousness fading as she became an avatar of pure flame. He hoped wherever she was now, she had found herself again.

Teej didn't know how long he had been unconscious. A puddle of drool had seeped into the floor cracks where his face rested on the cool white tiles. With a groan, he pushed himself up onto his hands and knees and looked around in despair. He was alone, and he had no idea where Anna might be.

Dammit. Struggling to rise, Teej found he was weak as a kitten. His arms and legs quivered, and his stomach heaved. Clambering to his feet, he caught sight of his reflection and almost passed out again.

I look like a corpse.

His skin was pale as plaster, his shirt was charred and burnt, and his eyes were bloodshot. Leaning on the hand drier for a moment, he stumbled to the sink and ran the faucet till the water began to flow cool, then he drank copiously.

His strength returned quickly as the cool water brought life back into his body. Though being ejected from the August Club was painful, the burns on his skin were not severe. It was not a disaster. If he hadn't been thrown out, he would be dead. The flames would have consumed the whole of the August Club. Needham had saved them all. If only Teej had been able to get through to Anna, to find the words that would calm her soul. *What the hell set her off like that?*

Teej shook his head and tried to focus. There was no time for self-recrimination. He had to figure out where he was, then get back to Anna. There was no sign of Wildey or Needham here, so he had to assume they were with Anna or had sent her away on her own. Even if she had escaped, their time to find the Christmas Council was ticking by fast. Teej had no watch and no phone. How long had he been out?

Glancing around in desperation, he spotted a backpack on the floor. *His* backpack. Hoping for a miracle, he dropped to his hands and knees and rifled through the contents.

It's all here.

Amongst the wrinkled clothes, Teej found the remnants of the Mirror Blade, his spoon Fetish, Anna's red cloak and most amazing of all, wrapped in a small piece of white cloth, Anna's ring.

Perhaps Elizabeth Needham had been kinder than she seemed. She'd thrown him out of the August Club, but she'd also thrown him to safety, and she'd sent all Anna's valuable possessions after him. Things could be better, but they could also be far worse.

But what about Anna? Had she ended up in a Shard Realm, or back at the August Club entrance? Or had she too fallen out of the Haze and back to Basine? And what about Wildey? He had tried to subdue Anna, but was his intention to restrain her or capture her? Either way, Needham had seemed to rage at her husband.

Slinging the backpack over his shoulder, Teej got to his feet and closed his eyes to concentrate. He'd need to think clearly and move quickly. He considered meditating for a moment to regain his equilibrium, but the second he closed his eyes, his stomach growled. *Priorities.* Leaving the August Club seemed to disturb the body's natural processes, and he was suddenly famished. He couldn't skip steps. He had to establish a plan then follow it through.

Figure out where I am, find food, get a phone, call Elise and Pappi, change clothes, find transport, get back to my friends. Teej hoped that once he started to move, a plan for how to locate Anna would come to him.

Standing in front of the mirror, he wiped away the worst of the bloody marks from his chest and neck, then found a wrinkled but clean shirt in the bag and put it on. He wet his hair and slicked it back, then washed his face and hands again before giving himself a little nod of reassurance in the mirror.

Rifling through the bag once more, Teej's fingers found the hilt of the broken mirror blade. Raguel's weapon: the sword that had almost cleaved Garret in two. He held it firmly and made a few practice swings through the air. Even shattered, the weapon held some potency. There was a way to activate its innate power, but he didn't know how. The store of Vig within was locked away, and even though he knew it could help him travel quickly, he felt a sudden revulsion. There would be a cost to using the blade, and he wouldn't know what it was until he used it. With a shudder, he put the sword back into his backpack and returned to his original plan.

As he made for the exit, Teej wondered why he was alone in the pristine white bathroom. And why was it so spotlessly clean? As he tried to open the door, he realized why. *Locked.* Glancing back, he noticed the stalls were closed off with tape. This bathroom was brand new and hadn't been opened yet. And he was trapped inside.

On a whim, he darted back to the stalls and noticed a sealed package of plastic soap dispensers. He checked the label. 'Dubai International DXB'.

"Oh, come on!"

Letting out a long sigh, Teej allowed himself a moment of frustration. He had a long journey home, but he wasn't in a desert or a jungle or trapped in the Realm. He was in an airport. There was surely a route back home, but only if he kept his head.

What would Garret say at a moment like this? Probably, *stop feeling sorry for yourself and have a beer.* Things were easier when he had the old man to fall back on, but now wasn't the time to second guess himself. Teej had learned a lot of tricks and mastered many skills in the last few hundred years, and he was about to use all of them to escape this situation.

Spotting a bag of tools, he rummaged through till his fingers wrapped around a crowbar. Seconds later, he'd snapped the hinge on the locked door and was out of the bathroom and into the terminal.

The crowded concourse was loud and busy, and Teej was momentarily overwhelmed. Travelers rushed past in every direction, wheeling suitcases, and clutching their passports. Teej cut towards a nearby gate and lingered near a small concession store. Inside, well-dressed sales assistants smiled politely as they sold bottles of water and magazines. This wasn't a good spot.

Moving against the crowd once more, he scanned the departure boards for a gate with no upcoming flights. *Seventeen.* Wandering down a long, mostly empty corridor, he found what he was looking for. He grabbed an empty soda can from the trash, then hustled across to a concession stand. It was closed, secured with a canvas cover with metal eyelets locked at the base of the stand. Teej checked for security cameras, and seeing none, he bent down and checked the lock. Exactly as he thought: a cheap laminated steel bolt.

Pulling the soda can out of his bag, he twisted off the ring, creating a jagged edge. He scored the metal can, cutting out a thin rectangle of aluminum using the ring pull and the sharp part of Anna's apartment keys. *Perfect!*

Crouching down, he twisted the piece of scrap metal into a half-cylinder, then slipped it into the narrow gap between the body of the padlock and the shackle. After a moments struggle, Teej began to worry he had lost the knack, but then the locking bar slipped, and the padlock popped open.

Lifting the canvas just enough to reach inside, Teej slid his hand under and grabbed a can of cold-brew coffee, a bag of chips and a chocolate bar. He examined the wrapper before swapping for another. *Coconut. No one likes coconut.*

Teej ate greedily, the food restoring nutrients stolen by his exit from the August Club and bringing his body back to life, while the caffeine sharpened his mind.

Moving more quickly now, he got to his feet and ghosted through the airport, trying to raise as little suspicion as possible. When he saw a young couple arguing about a late flight, he sat down next to them, placed his bag close to theirs and then surreptitiously slipped his hand into the man's inside jacket pocket that was lying on top of the bag. He got lucky. Dropping the man's phone into his own pocket, Teej slinked away quickly and calmly. Later, he'd drop the phone near the lost and found desk and hopefully it would make its way back to its owner.

Two rings, then she answered.

"Elise," said Teej with as neutral a voice as he could manage. "It's me."

"Who is *me*? Wait… Teejay!? Where are you?"

"Dubai."

"Could you say that again? It sounds like you said you're in Dubai."

"I'm in Dubai."

"Why are you in Dubai?!"

"Elise, calm down. Is everything alright there? How is Pappi?"

"He's fine. We're back at Maxines. I'm packing a bag for this Christmas Council thing. It's Christmas, so it will probably be cold, right? Should I pack—"

"Elise, can you just—"

"Right, sorry. *Focus.* I hear you. Is Anna with you?"

"No. We got thrown out of the August Club and I ended up here. I hoped she might be back with you."

"Sorry. Did you find out where Rayleigh has Alby?"

Teej hesitated. "Uh, is Pappi there *right* now?"

"He fell asleep on the sofa in the back room."

"Is he…?"

"He's still not good," said Elise gravelly.

"We don't know where the Council is. We don't know how to help Alby."

"Teej, what are we going to do?"

"Meet me at the central airport, international arrivals."

"Right! And you're sure you want *me* to come? I kinda bailed on you last time."

"It's your choice."

"I'll make sure Pappi is still asleep, and then I'll meet you at the arrivals gate."

"Thank you, Elise. You still have that sword?"

"Already packed," she said, and he heard her rustle it out of a bag. "What are you going to do now?"

Teej rubbed his chin. "Steal a passport, scam my way onto a plane, sleep on the flight."

"What about Anna?"

"We have to trust that she can take care of herself until we find out where they took her when they threw her out of the club."

"What about your spoon?"

Teej flinched. Elise was right. Why hadn't he thought of using his Fetish? He still wasn't thinking clearly.

"I'll give it a try. I doubt she's close to me though. I'll call you later."

"Good luck."

Reaching into the backpack, Teej grasped the spoon. He closed his eyes and pictured Anna's soft brown eyes, her pink lips, her smile, the smell of her hair when he held her close…

thirty-one

Purple and blue and bright green. Little puddles of stagnant water reflected the blinking neon signs high above. Steam escaped a nearby vent and hissed over Anna's bare legs, making her skin damp. The ground was cold and dirty. A breeze blew over her shivering body, swirling old newspapers and trash in a little tornado all around her. The narrow walls of the alleyway seemed to squeeze in from both sides, pinning her in place. Broken, rasping noises echoed all around. Eventually, Anna realized it was the sound of her own breathing.

She rubbed her eyes, but her hands were filthy. Blinking and swearing, she tried to roll over, but numbness clung to her limbs like a straightjacket. With a groan, she rolled onto her back and looked beyond the narrow walls of the alleyway, until she saw little stars twinkling down at her.

Where the Hell am I?

When she closed her eyes, images were burned into her mind like sunspots. She saw Wildey and Needham sitting at the August Club, Teej by her side as they faced their enemies. Everyone was waiting for her to speak. Teej's eyes were pleading with her.

Burning. Blinding pain. What had she done?

Her spine was locked in place, her body rigid, but she could move a little. Scanning the area, she saw no sign of Teej. No sign of anyone. Closing her eyes again, she stretched out her Haze Sense but felt nothing. Nothing but the lingering damage in her own body and the emptiness all around her. She was back in Basine. Back in the city.

Dammit! Teej had tried to calm her. Needham too. Anger had blinded her, but as her rage died down, she felt old emotions creep up. Fear. Uncertainty. Guilt.

Where was Teej now? How could she get back to him?

At the end of the alleyway, she could hear passing cars. A man laughing. Music, indistinct, with thudding bass, loud but distant. Whistling wind.

I've never felt so far from where I'm supposed to be.

Anna struggled to rise, but her body betrayed her. The repercussions for falling out of the August Club and landing back in Basine were severe. Her balance and her equilibrium were all fractured. She could do nothing but wait for her body and mind to recover and reflect on her failures. And come up with a new plan.

Wildey had gotten under her skin. Pushed her till her flames had burst out of her body, her emotions burning hot. She had failed to control herself. Teej had kept his head, but Anna had lost hers. She had failed.

Focus! There was no time for recriminations. She had to pick herself up and choose a course of action. Self-pity, guilt, and desolation would not help her. She had to stop feeling sorry for herself if she was going to save her friends.

Scraping her wet hair out of her face, she found her hands locked in place. She felt heavy steel and the clink of a chain. She was restrained. Though the lights blinded her, she could make out the outline of metal cuffs placed around her wrists. Trying to pull them away, she felt the steel chain go taut. Her metal cuffs were linked to a collar around her neck.

What the hell!

Who had restrained her? Teej?

No, it was Wildey. She remembered them all trying to control her. Teej trying to hold her, Needham shouting dire warnings, Wildey using his Praxis. Yes, though their powers were supposedly forbidden in the August Club, Wildey had been able to use his. Perhaps Needham had let him off the leash. He had transmuted her necklace and bracelets into chains to bind her, but then she had burned him. She had burned them all.

Oh God, what have I done?

Anna had to escape her bonds. Once she could stand, she would stumble out of this alleyway. The steel cuffs around her wrists and neck could not be broken. They had existed in Basine for too long and had become set and immutable. She had to get to a phone. There were a few friends she could call. With no money, she was injured, tired, and barely clothed. She needed a hideout to recuperate, and she needed heavy bolt cutters to free herself. Once she was clean, rested and dressed, she could contact Pappi and Elise again, explain what had happened and form some sort of plan to find Teej. If he was still alive.

"Hey Tag, look at this, man!"

The voice came from the end of the alleyway. Anna put the palms of her hands on the ground and tried to push herself up, but her strength was gone. She couldn't even turn to see them, but she heard the men's footsteps closing in.

"Jay, come on! The limo's only booked till 5 a.m., and we still haven't cleaned the house. I wanna get to Suzie's party. We should go."

Anna closed her eyes and prayed they would get back in their car and get out of here.

"No way, man, you gotta see this girl first."

Anna heard two sets of footsteps. No, three. Two walked confidently, the other lingered further behind, anxious. This was bad. Anna didn't need her Haze Sense to know she was in trouble.

"It's just some junky. Come on, Jay. You know we gotta get going. Cynthia's going to be at the party. *Cynthia!* Do you remember her? She's that model that got dumped last week, and I've got a shoulder for her to cry on."

The third man laughed, his voice low and brutish. "I'll give her something to cry on."

Anna felt their eyes on her. The hair on her arms stood up. She tried to talk, but all that came out was a croak.

"Tag, she's out of it, man. She was all dressed up, but her clothes are ripped. Shit! What kinky stuff was she up to before she got wasted? She's all tied up."

More laughter. "Jay is right. You gotta see this, Tag."

"Right..." Tag sounded nervous. "So, we should get her help? Or just call someone. We can do it from the limo. We don't even need to wait with her, right? Jay? Cameron?"

Anna finally managed to roll over. She met the closest man's gaze as he looked down on her. Blonde hair, clean-shaven, young and athletic with a long nose and freckled cheeks, and a half-smirk playing across his mouth. So, this was "Jay". He wore a loose baseball jacket over a crisp white shirt, unbuttoned to the chest. Anna locked eyes with him. His pupils sparkled in the night.

"No, I think... I think we should take her with us."

Shit.

Jay licked his lips nervously, his eyes scanning back and forth, checking for witnesses. Behind him, he motioned for Cameron to do the same. The brute was as broad as he was tall, with dark curly hair and a bronze tan. He sprinted back to the end of the alleyway, looked back and forth skittishly, then gave Jay a nod. "All clear man. Let's get her in the car."

"Guys!" protested Tag. "Guys, this is a bad idea. What are you doing?"

Jay smirked at Anna again, then turned back to his friend who lingered by the limo at the end of the alleyway, too nervous to come any closer.

"Listen up," barked Jay. "You still wanna pledge this fraternity or what, Tag?"

There was a moment's hesitation. Anna squeezed her eyes closed and tried to crawl away, but the signals from her brain couldn't reach her limbs, and instead, she just trembled.

"I mean…"

"Yes, you fucking do," said Jay, his voice firm, though he didn't shout. "This is your last challenge for Hell Week. Do this, and you're *in*. If you don't, well everything you went through so far was for nothing. You hear?"

"Come on, Jay!" moaned Tag. "I drank the expired milk. I ate a live *frog* man!"

"Just fuckin' do what you're told," said Cameron. "Jay will take care of everything."

"So… what am I supposed to do?" asked Tag.

Jay let out a long breath, then gestured to Anna. "Open the rear door and keep an eye out for me and Cameron while we get this girl in the car, and don't ever tell anyone we took her. Simple enough?"

Tag didn't hesitate this time. "Sure thing, Jay."

Anna tried her best to wrestle herself free of their grasp, but the two young men were strong and though the feeling was slowly returning to her shoulders and arms, her legs were dead weights. Straining against her clinking chains, she tried to call out, but all she could manage was a moan. The two men half-dragged her down the alleyway, her feet scraping along the wet ground.

"She's making too much noise Jay," complained Cameron. "I think she's coming round."

"Maybe she's not some junky," complained Tag.

"She's a hooker," said Jay. "Cover her mouth."

Cameron clamped a large hand over Anna's face, and as she struggled to fight him, he covered her mouth and nose. *Can't breathe.*

Anna balled her hands into fists as tight as she could, her body shaking as she felt a fire burn inside her. But here in Basine, that fire was not a physical thing but an emotion, and though she was furious, she was afraid and desperate too. She had to bide her time, save her strength for when she needed it most. Hoping that the big one would loosen his grasp if she stopped fighting, Anna allowed herself to go limp.

I will wait and I will be patient, and when I am free, I will hurt you all.

Anna made the promise to herself in still silence, and as Cameron moved his hands away and she was able to finally catch a breath, she allowed them to drag her towards the back seat of the car.

"I dunno, man," said Tag. "Covering her mouth. That's a bad look. That's real bad guys."

"What did I just say?!" shouted Jay. "She's a hooker. We'll leave her the biggest tip she's ever had. We found her in an alleyway. She could have died. Things turned out pretty well for her. She's lucky we turned up."

"Leave her a tip for what?" asked Tag nervously.

Jay pushed Anna into the back seat and held the door open, glowering down at her body. Inside the limo, the leather seats and the blacked-out windows felt like a prison, and she was about to be locked in.

"Leave her a tip for what Jay?" repeated Tag.

"What do you think?" said Jay, his eyes hungry. Moving round to the other side of the vehicle, Cameron chuckled.

"Hey!" someone shouted. It was a woman's voice, far away and unsteady. For a moment no one reacted.

"Hey, what are you doing?!" The voice was closer this time, the woman a little surer of herself. Jay glanced back and forth nervously between his friends, then gestured for them to calm down.

"I'll handle this," he whispered. He slowly pushed the door closed on Anna, but she forced a leg out of the car. Jay leaned down low and tried to quietly wrestle her leg back inside, but Anna fought as best she could, kicking at him weakly. She could hear the woman walking closer. With her leg still trapped in the door, Jay crushed Anna's thigh as he struggled to close her in, but she refused to give an inch. Eventually, the woman came into view and Jay had to give up the struggle. He swore silently under his breath, then turned to face the woman with a smile on his face.

"Hey, lady, we are *so* lost right now. Can you help me and my girlfriend find our way back to the Gisborne Hotel? We're not from around here."

"What are you doing?" asked the woman. She was about Anna's age or a little younger. Brown hair, soft features, hazel eyes, and a big coat wrapped around her small body, with a scarf that hid the lower half of her face. She looked afraid, but she didn't retreat.

"What's *your* name?" asked Jay.

"Why?" said the woman. "What are you doing with that woman?"

"I told you, she's my girlfriend. I'm Jay."

The woman glanced around nervously. "I'm Lilly. What is *her* name?"

"Kelly," said Jay easily. "And she needs to get home soon, so we're just going to—"

"Mind your own business, lady!" shouted Cameron.

Jay shot him an angry look. Anna could tell Cameron was stupid, but Jay was manipulative and sneaky. Every word out of his mouth defused the tension, reassuring this woman that Anna was not in danger. Still, Lilly was not fooled. She looked back and forth between the two men, then stepped forward to look more closely at Anna. Jay didn't move, so she half-shoved her way past him.

"My God, what happened to her?"

"I know right!" said Jay jovially. "It's her birthday. She got carried away. We need to get her back to the hotel for a change of clothes and a shower, right guys?"

Tag, who was half-sitting in the driver's seat, made a kind of murmur of agreement, but he seemed too frightened to talk.

Anna calmed her mind, swallowed once, then tried to call out for help. All that came out of her mouth was a moan, but it sounded desperate and animalistic enough to startle everyone. Lilly reached out, but Jay refused to get out of the way.

"If I don't get Kelly home soon, she might throw up," said Jay as he straightened his back and towered over Lilly. "That will be on you, Lilly. Are you going to pay for the dry cleaning on this limo? Are you gonna take responsibility if she chokes on her vomit?"

"Why is she chained up?" said Lilly, refusing to be intimidated.

"Prank gone wrong," said Jay instantly. "It was her idea. We go to college together."

"Where?" said Lilly.

"Central."

"Which course do you study?"

"All different. I'm in Law."

"How do you know each other then?"

"We all went to school together."

Lilly put her hands on her hips. "Why are you in an expensive limo playing pranks?"

"It's a hazing ritual to get into our fraternity. And her sorority."

Lilly took a half step backwards. "So, this is part of an initiation?"

"Yeah, that's what we're doing tonight. Out partying and pledging"

"I thought you said you were out for Katy's birthday?"

"Kelly's. And yeah, it's her birthday, too."

Lilly shook her head, unconvinced. Anna moaned again, and Cameron flinched like he was going to restrain her. Jay shook his head and shot him another warning glance, but Lilly saw it this time.

"This isn't right. Call her an ambulance and let her out of the car."

Jay shook his head slowly. "No, that's not going to happen."

He barged Lilly aside as he tried to close the door, but she shot out a hand and held it open.

Jay let out a little chuckle, but there was no humor in the sound he made.

"Lilly, are you all by yourself right now? Think about what you're doing here."

She took another step back. Anna moaned again, and Lilly looked at her with concern. Anna could see the conflict in her.

Don't be afraid. Don't let them see how frightened you are right now.

Lilly shook her head. "No, this isn't right. If you touch me, I'll call the cops. I'll take your license number if you drive off. I already have a photo of it on my phone. This isn't right. You all know it's not right."

Lilly looked at Cameron, pursed her lips, then turned to Tag. "*You* know."

Tag slinked into the front seat of the car and closed the door.

"You're making yourself look foolish," said Jay as he put his hands behind his head and leaned back casually. "It's kinda insulting what you're trying to say to me about my intentions. I mean this is my girlfriend. What are you trying to accuse me of? Lying? You think I'm going to hurt her."

Lilly pulled her scarf away from her face. "If she's your girlfriend, prove it."

"How?"

"You have a mobile phone. Show me a picture of you two together."

"Sure. But this phone is new. I got it from my parents as a gift for making it into the fraternity. I don't have any photos on it yet."

Jay took a step forward, put his hand on Lilly's chest and easily pushed her away. She stumbled backwards, a look of shock on her face.

"We've been nice here," said Jay. "Time to just turn around and walk away."

Be brave, Lilly.

She took three steps backwards, turned, and began to walk away. Lilly was leaving. Anna was on her own.

"Stop moaning," muttered Jay under his breath to Anna. "Stop making me look bad. I could have left you behind. We're just going for a little ride."

"My friend is on the other end of this line," said Lilly. She was back, and she was holding her phone up, her voice defiant.

"If you don't let this girl go, my friend will call the cops. If you touch me one more time, she'll call the cops. I sent her your number plate and your names. I don't believe a word you've said. I'm going to get this girl help. Now all three of you, let her out of the car and *fuck off!"*

Anna wanted to cheer. She wriggled and moaned, the feeling slowly coming back into her legs. As Jay reached out for her, she let out a roar of rage, writhed away from him and fell with a heavy thud out of the car and into the gutter.

For a moment Anna feared Jay might kick her, but instead, he turned away in disgust, strode to the passenger door and rapped the hood three times with his fist before getting in. "The Hell with this. Let's go boys. These bitches can take care of each other. Fuck 'em."

The engine roared twice before they drove off, leaving Anna alone with her savior. With a cough, she tried her best to croak the words, "Thank you."

Lilly crouched low over Anna and put her scarf over her shoulders. Desperate to get moving, Anna reached out to her and tried to stand, but her legs were still too weak, and they collapsed together. Anna ended up in the woman's lap. They sat together like that for a few minutes, Lilly repeating over and over that it would be okay. She misunderstood Anna's tears. She wasn't upset, she was furious, but she had no other way to express her rage.

Lilly's phone had fallen just out of reach on the sidewalk, and she reached for it.

"No," croaked Anna. "Just… stay."

She didn't want to get stuck in an ambulance. Her equilibrium was returning, her words coming back to her. In ten minutes, maybe less, she would be able to walk again. Being thrown out of the August Club had taken a huge toll on her mind, but her body was undamaged. As she adjusted back to Basine, her strength was returning, but the situation remained desperate.

"You didn't know those guys at all, did you?" said Lilly. "I'm still going to tell the cops about them."

"I hate them," said Anna. "I hate them. I hate them all."

"All men?" asked Lilly.

Anna coughed and chuckled at the same time. "Well, most of… them."

"What happened to you?"

Anna pulled away from Lilly and sat up straight, matching the woman's gaze. Her eyes were cool, clear blue, and she smiled softly. Anna wanted to be as truthful with her as she could, but she also needed to get moving again as soon as possible. No ambulance, no long explanations, and no interference. Anna just had to get back to Teej, wherever he was.

Straining in frustration against her bonds, Anna realized she also needed help. She had no money, no phone, barely any clothes, and she was trapped in chains. Still, she'd been in worse situations than this, and her training came back to her now. The Dreamer Gahan had once told her, *when you accept someone's help, they feel good about themselves, and that feeling makes them more likely to help you again.* Gahan was a scoundrel, but he knew how to get almost anyone to do almost anything for him. In this case, any help Lilly could offer Anna would be repaid in full one day. Anna wouldn't forget how the young woman had saved her.

"Thank you," said Anna. "I mean it. That was... brave."

"Please," said Lilly. "I couldn't just walk away."

Anna sighed. "I was out with... friends. Some guys tried to start some trouble. We got separated and I hit my head."

"Did you take something?"

"No. I had a few drinks, so I wasn't clear-headed I guess."

"How did you end up like..." Lilly gestured broadly at Anna. "This?"

"Uhh... It was a fancy club, so we were all dressed up for the night."

"I mean how did you get tied up?"

"Right. So do you know much about conjuring?"

"Like, what a magician would do?" Lilly looked skeptical.

"Yes, exactly. So, my best friend is an amateur magician. That's why I'm dressed up. I'm more of a jeans and sneakers kind of girl, but he needed a *'glamorous assistant'*, so I made the effort. Anyway, the... fire alarm went off halfway through the escapology bit, and then before we could get back into the building-"

"Aren't your friends looking for you then? Is the place close?"

Anna shook her head. "As I said, some guys started some trouble. My friend and these guys got in a fight, and we got separated."

"I think you need an ambulance. What's your name again?"

"Emma."

"Well, let me just grab my phone and—"

Anna grasped Lilly's arm. "No, I need to get home. That's all."

Anna leaned forward, and with Lilly's support, she managed to clamber to her feet.

"You might have a concussion," said Lilly. "I think it would be best if you get checked out."

"My mom is a doctor. I'll go home and see her. My friends will be calling by now to see if I'm home in one piece."

"I, uh… yeah, I guess that makes sense. Did those guys steal your phone and purse?"

Anna shook her head. "They're in my friends' car."

"I see. Then can I help you get home or something? Or, like, find you a locksmith?"

Anna laughed. "I have a key at home, I think. Hail me a taxi?"

Even as she said the words, Anna was trying to figure out where she could go. She had a few places she could lie low in the city. Not exactly safe houses but places she could regroup. Or should she call Elise and head back to Maxines? She didn't look forward to facing Pappi and seeing the disappointment in his eyes.

Sensing her indecision, Lilly nudged Anna.

"You remember your address?" asked Lilly as she fumbled for her phone with trembling fingers. She was muttering constantly to herself as she wiped the screen. The shock of the confrontation was subsiding, and now the rush of adrenaline was gone, Lilly sounded nervous and shaken again.

"I'll call you a cab. You must be freezing. What a night! I'll have to tell Maddy about this. She's my sister, and she's always telling stories that start with, *'so we were all totally wasted'*. I'm the boring one, you see. That's what she says anyway. Hey, do you think your friends might want to hear from you? You could call them if you like."

"No need," said Wildey.

Anna turned so fast she almost fell over again. Half of Wildey's face was scarred, his left eye milky. The injury looked old, but Anna knew it wasn't. He walked with a limp and smiled casually. Anna backed off.

"Is this your friend?" asked Lilly. She stepped in front of Anna and confronted Wildey.

"Yes," replied Anna with a reassuring hand on Lilly's shoulder. "We're friends."

She confronted Wildey. "You brought me here?"

He smirked. "Funny, it seemed more like you brought me. But I'm glad to see you're fine. I can't believe I'm back in the city. It's quieter than I remember."

"Teej. What happened to him?"

Wildey stroked his chin. "Exiled from the August Club, just like us. My wife was not pleased with our performance."

"We have to help him," said Anna.

"He isn't the one who needs help," said Wildey. "We're not safe here."

"When am I ever safe?" muttered Anna. "Where is Teej?"

"I told you, exiled. When you're thrown out of the August Club, the journey isn't dangerous, nor is it pleasant. It can take a long time to recover, and your destination can be… random. Suffice it to say, the threat stalks us now, not Teej."

Anna took a deep breath and calmed herself. If what Wildey said was true, she could take a moment to plan her next move.

"Come on," said Wildey, "We have a little time. I'll buy you a coffee. I know a twenty-four-hour place nearby. It might still be open."

"Are you going to go with this guy?" asked Lilly. She leaned in close and whispered in Anna's ear, "Is it safe?"

"Yes," said Anna. "And thank you. He'll drive me home."

Lilly nodded and touched Anna's arm. "Take care then. I hope you get out of your…"

Wildey reached out for Anna, grasped hold of the chain around her neck and twisted his wrist before clicking his fingers. Suddenly, she was free. The metal clasp which hadn't existed a moment before snapped open and the chains clattered to the floor.

With immense relief, Anna rubbed her aching wrists. She sighed, then looked back at Wildey in astonishment. He slipped something that might have been a coin into his back pocket, and both Lilly and Anna stood open-mouthed, awaiting an explanation.

"What?" he asked nonchalantly. "Although chains are fairly common in the August Club, I assume you were done with your bonds?"

"How did you…?" Anna stalled.

"So, *you're* the magician," said Lilly. "I… I think I'd like to see your show one day."

Wildey scowled for a moment and then broke into laughter. "I've been called a lot of things in my life…"

thirty-two

Anna and Wildey sat opposite each other, but they both stared out the window of the steamy coffee shop. On the rainy streets, the storm was getting heavier, the wind whipping the coats and umbrellas of club kids and students as they struggled onwards through the night. In the cafe, coffee machines gurgled and frothed, and smooth jazz played on the radio. Behind the counter, a bored barista with big glasses read a well-thumbed paperback.

"I spent all the money I have on these two coffees," said Wildey as he leaned back precariously on his chair and ran a hand through his curly hair. "The least you can do is drink one."

"It's still too hot," complained Anna.

"A simple *'thank you'* would go a long way right now."

Everything about Wildey put Anna on edge. His mouth was twisted into a perpetual smirk, and Anna still wasn't sure if it was genuine or an affectation. A few of his mannerisms reminded her of Teej, but his demeanor was wildly different. Teej had his share of irritating character traits, but he was never cruel, never spiteful. Wildey though…

"Thank you?" said Anna. "You tried to kill me, and you think I *owe* you?"

"Don't be so dramatic. You don't owe me for the coffee. You owe me for risking my neck to save you back at the August Club."

"You didn't save anyone," said Anna. "You antagonized me and risked all our lives."

"Antagonized?" scoffed Wildey. "I was the one who prevented you from killing us all. Including our good friend Teej."

"Is he chill, dog?" said Anna. She was unable to hide her concern.

"I imagine so. He's too annoying to just *die.* And you're alive, aren't you? Not only do you owe me for saving your life, but you also owe me for the storm of trouble I'm going to face from Lizzy when I get back home."

"Sorry for disrupting your domestic bliss," said Anna. "But might I remind you that you invited us?"

"Any half-decent Metik can make it to the August Club without incident," scoffed Wildey. "And none of them, before you, have set it on fire."

"It's your fault," protested Anna. "You provoked me."

"Provoked?" Wildey stroked the scar on his cheek with the back of his hand. "If light goading and some simple questions are all it takes for your flame to kindle into a pyre, how are you going to handle Rayleigh at the Christmas Council?"

Anna pointed a finger at his chest. "You know where it is."

"We'll come back to that. First, I want you to thank me for saving you. And I want you to apologize for burning me."

Anna scoffed. "You tried to kill Teej, and after luring us to your creepy club, you spent half the time sneering at us and the other half antagonizing us. It's not my fault that—"

"I pushed you to test you, and you failed," snapped Wildey. "And you're too proud to even apologize. Do you *ever* admit you've done something wrong?"

His words were serious, but the smirk didn't leave his lips. Anna noted the way Wildey's eyes lit up when she got angry. He liked to provoke her, but she was in no mood to play games. He sipped his coffee, but she pushed hers aside.

"I'm sure you'll be able to talk your way out of trouble with your wife," said Anna. "But I'm not your wife… *or* your partner *or* your friend. I don't trust you, and I don't owe you an apology, but we're here and we're not trying to kill each other. So where do we stand?"

Wildey narrowed his eyes. "I never wanted to kill anyone. Well, except for Aesthetes, and they're not really people."

Anna held up her hand. "Enough bravado. We're both trying to stop Rayleigh, right?"

She didn't wait for his answer. "And we both want to stop this Blood Plague before the Dreamers tear each other apart."

Wildey cocked his head to one side. "Well…"

"Because if the Dreamers fall into some chaotic civil war, they won't be the only ones affected. A lot of Metiks and regular people will suffer too, right?"

Wildey took a swig of coffee and swirled it around his mouth, making her wait for his answer.

"Right."

"And I want to save my friend Alby," said Anna. "So, while we might not like each other, we're wasting time bickering. We need to move forward, so from this point on, I have questions, and the best way for us to work together to achieve our goals is for you to answer them honestly. And if you want a fucking apology, then you can have it. I'm sorry I burned your face. Now we move forward. Agree?"

Anna hoped her forthright approach would sway Wildey to her cause. It seemed to work.

"Ask your questions," he said. "You wanna know why I helped you?"

"Actually," said Anna, "I want to know how you got me out of those chains."

"A trifling thing," said Wildey with a smirk. "I have an old Fetish for just such occasions. A coin given to me by a Dreamer friend."

"You have Dreamer friends?"

"Not anymore," said Wildey.

"What does the coin do?"

Wildey shrugged. "For me? Nothing. It is drained of its power. I spent it to save you. Before that, I could use it to dispel an object created in a Haze as long as it was fresh."

"Show it to me," said Anna.

Wildey fished the coin out of his pocket and slapped it down on the counter.

"Keep it," he said. "When I spent it to free you from your bonds, you became the new owner. Now you can spend it, but remember, you can't keep a penny *and* spend a penny. Whoever you use it on next, you'll have to pass it on to them."

Anna ran her fingertips over the silver coin. It felt smooth, like it had been passed between a thousand hands, but there was a residual glow and the faint, unmistakable crackle of Vig that told her it possessed some latent power. Anna nodded in thanks and grasped the coin tightly in one hand, before glancing around distractedly.

"I don't even have a bag. Or a pocket."

"Your dress has seen better days," said Wildey.

"This is *not* news," said Anna dismissively.

Wildey chuckled. "What else do you need to know?"

"Why did you do it?" asked Anna with a sigh. "Why did you push me like that?"

Wildey puffed his cheeks and shrugged. "Boredom. Some misplaced enmity with Teej. An innate desire to break rules. This last reason resonates with you I would guess."

"Why do you say that?"

Wildey looked surprised. "You were told not to use your powers in the August Club. You were told to follow the rules in the book."

"I've found the people that set the rules rarely have my interests in mind."

Wildey examined her closely. "That is true. Honestly, I hate them, too. I hate the mad ones and I hate the arrogant ones, but most of all, I hate the manipulators behind the scenes. Damn Dreamers. They think we're all pawns, and they make a mockery of our freedom and the choices we make about how we live our own lives. I'm here now to help you because I hate Rayleigh most of all."

Anna nodded. "Then tell me what Rayleigh is trying to do at the Christmas Council?"

Wildey shook his head. "I can't be sure."

"But you have an idea?"

"Rayleigh is Machiavelli with fewer morals. He could convince you a lemon was a honey cake after you'd taken a bite."

"He has my friend, Alby."

A look of sadness flashed over Wildey's face. "Your friend is in peril. Rayleigh has techniques to attack the seat of the mind. If you're willing to meddle with the brain, you can scar the very essence of the soul."

Anna knew what he meant. "Like the Apoth's creations."

"Exactly."

"If he did that to Alby, can he be saved?"

"I doubt it. Even if some part of his mind is unaffected, what will be left of him? I have seen men whose souls have been ravaged by Rayleigh's cruelty. They haunt this world like half-ghosts. Walking scar tissue."

"Scars can heal," said Anna.

"Maybe," conceded Wildey stroking his cheek. "You need to be ready to fight. And you need to control your Praxis better with Rayleigh than you did with me. Can you do that?"

Anna frowned as she looked down at her hands. "I'll try. But I lost my ring."

"Does that prevent you from fighting?"

Anna looked away. "I'm slower without it… but I'll be ready."

"After you save Alby, what next?"

Anna thought for a moment. "Rayleigh."

"Is that all you've got? The name of the next person you'll kill. Your plan needs to be more than a list of your enemies."

"Is yours?" challenged Anna. "Since I've been Behind the Veil, all I've had is a list of enemies. Mott, the Apoth, Drowden, Raguel. And you know what? They're all gone now."

Wildey was amused. "You need to find a way to use your abilities for more than fighting."

"Says the guy who blows people up! I thought all you wanted was to get rid of all the Dreamers. To kill Rayleigh."

"As a means to an end," said Wildey as he pushed his coffee cup aside and leaned forward. "If Rayleigh could be a part of lasting peace, I'd set aside my hatred. I know I said it before, and I know you don't believe me, but I *have* changed. I want an end to this life. I don't want this drama anymore. I want to get home to my wife, and I want the world outside our door to stop burning because I fear, eventually, we won't be able to hide from the fire."

"If you really wanted to escape the drama, you wouldn't look so happy when you talk about fighting."

Wildey threw his hands up in the air. "Oh, come on! Don't pretend you don't love this part."

"I don't," said Anna.

"I know you. You're not like Teej. You're no diplomat, you're a warrior. You live for that moment before the fight. You can taste it in the back of your throat. Feel the static in the atmosphere. I saw you set yourself alight. You don't burn like that because you need to, you burn like that because your *soul* burns. Letting all that rage and fear and frustration explode out of your body feels good. I *know* it does."

"You don't know how I feel."

Wildey sipped his coffee then shrugged. "I suppose I don't. But I can guess. My point is, you don't need to learn much about fighting anymore, but you might find that soon, you must learn when to stop. Take it from me, a man who took a long time to learn how to stop fighting."

Anna picked up her coffee, swirled it, then drank it in one gulp. It was tepid and bitter, but she enjoyed it, nonetheless. Outside, the wind whistled suddenly, and a heavy metal street sign blew over with a loud crash.

"Maybe you're right," conceded Anna. "If we go to this Christmas Council, I have to keep calm. I have to make sure the whole thing doesn't descend into chaos. I need Teej."

Wildey nodded slowly, then licked his lips. "I think I should come with you to the Council."

Anna laughed dismissively. "Absolutely not. That's a terrible idea. You're the *Anarchist*."

"I don't have to be."

Anna pushed herself away from the table. "That's how they all know you. They think you're a terrorist. The gap between who *you* think you are and who *they* think you are is too wide."

"Well, if I don't go, I'll need you to deliver a message."

Anna nodded. "As long as it's not a bomb."

"Well…" Wildey smiled and shrugged.

"It *is* a bomb!"

"Oh, come on, give me some credit!"

"What message then?"

Wildey pushed himself up from the table suddenly.

"It will have to wait." His eyes were wide. Something was wrong.

"What?" said Anna as she got to her feet too.

"Hello," said Alby from the doorway. The boy was shivering and wet, wearing just a light shirt and shorts. His eyes were glazed, his jaw slack. He held something behind his back.

Anna couldn't help herself. She ran to him.

"Oh God, Alby, are you…"

"No!" shouted Wildey. He grabbed her and together they rolled to the floor. Gunshots rang out, one, then two then three.

Wildey groaned as he lay on top of her. The other customers screamed. Some of them ran past Anna, almost trampling her.

Bang. Bang. Bang. Anna winced with each shot. Wildey let out another long moan.

"No!" cried Anna.

Bang. Then it was over. She forced herself to open her eyes. Anna reached out to Wildey, but her hands were slick with blood. Rolling out from under him, she looked around to see they were alone. Everyone had run off, including Alby.

"Wildey, we have to find him. We have to…"

Wildey reached for her hand.

"Your head. Anna, your head." Anna leaned over him suddenly feeling faint. Wildey stroked her hair, his hands coming away bloody. When she touched her forehead, she felt something sticky.

"He hit me too," said Anna as she felt herself begin to panic. "He hit me too."

Anna's vision swam. She felt suddenly very tired. Letting her body sink to the ground, she closed her eyes for just a second to rest. Then she was gone.

thirty-three

Anna awoke with the taste of iron in her mouth. She heaved, spat blood, and then coughed till she saw stars. Finally able to draw breath, she got to her hands and knees then sat up and looked around.

"Morning, sleepyhead."

For a moment Anna thought it was Teej that spoke, but no. Leaning over an upturned chair, Wildey looked like a corpse. Blood ran from multiple bullet wounds in his chest into the cracks in the wooden floor.

Anna glanced around to find them still in the coffee shop, but everything was different. Everyone was gone, and the place was a mess. Anna crawled past broken cups and saucers and headed towards Wildey.

Reaching out to grasp his hand, a blindingly sharp pain in her chest threatened to stop her in her tracks. Anna touched her heart and a moment later the pain subsided, and she could move again. Brushing bloody strands of her hair out of her eyes, she crawled onwards.

As she got closer to Wildey, she slowly became aware of the extent of his wounds. His left thigh had a bullet wound that was spurting blood. She could see a wound on his neck and two more in his gut. There could be more, but it didn't matter. He was done for. His skin was already pallid. How long had she been out?

"Looking good," said Anna as she reached out to him.

"You too," drawled Wildey. "You're bleeding all over your terrible clothes."

"Happens every time," said Anna.

"I don't feel any wounds," he said as Anna reached for his hand. His skin was ice-cold to the touch. "I just hit my head."

"Took a bullet for you, didn't I? Several. Not such a bad team. So, be honest—"

Wildey winced in pain, then gritted his teeth and tried to smile again. "Am I better than Donnel?"

Anna shook her head. "No way."

Wildey tried to laugh, but it came out as a cough instead. "Come on, you could have lied."

Anna shook her head. "Maybe next time keep an eye out for enemies sent by Rayleigh instead of antagonizing your allies."

Wildey tried to laugh again. "*Next time.* Good one, Anna."

"I'm going to get you some help," said Anna as she looked around for help. "An ambulance must be on its way. I hear sirens."

"Come on," said Wildey gruffly. "You know what happens to someone that's lost this much blood."

He glanced down at the wound in his thigh, and Anna saw the growing pool of blood under his body.

"Shit! We need to put pressure on that."

"You're no fool," said Wildey. "Not anymore. You know how this story ends."

Anna grasped his hand firmly in hers. She didn't know what else to do or what to say. Wildey's head fell back, and he gritted his teeth and then slumped down.

"Wildey!" Anna touched his face. "Is there anything you want me to do? Anything you want me to say? To Elizabeth?"

"She… knows."

"Will she get through this?"

Wildey spat. "Better off without me. She's almost as old as the August Club. She'll forget me in a few hundred years. Maybe a thousand."

Anna glanced around for something, anything to help, but she already knew it was useless. Could she try to drag him out of here onto the street? Moving him would make the bleeding worse. She bit her lip. If they were still in a Haze, she could at least attempt to use her Praxis, but it was far too late for that now. Her rudimentary first-aid knowledge was woefully inadequate for this situation, and she didn't have any tools or tricks left.

Except for the coin.

"Wildey!" Anna turned to him with a desperate hope forming. His eyes were closed, his skin gray.

"Wake up!" She slapped him once, then again harder. "Wildey, the coin! Could we use the coin?"

Wildey's eyes cracked open. "It's gone."

Anna searched her pockets frantically. A sharp pain in her chest made her wince in pain, but once again it disappeared as quickly as it came. Refocusing, she started to scrabble around on the ground looking for the coin he had given her. It must be here somewhere!

"Anna!" rasped Wildey. "It's too late. It... wouldn't work anyway. They came for us in Basine. Sent a kid with a gun. They didn't want a real fight."

"I just had it!" Anna said enraged, her fists clenched.

"It doesn't matter." Wildey closed his eyes again. "Don't let them get close."

"Who?"

Wildey coughed and rolled onto his side. Anna tried to prop him up, but he was too heavy. The wound over her eyebrow was still bleeding, but it was just a graze. Enough to knock her out for a few minutes, but that was it. She would recover, but Wildey was running out of time.

"Anyone," he croaked. "They'll stab you in the back."

Anna didn't know what to say, so she held Wildey's hand again and nodded.

"The Christmas Council is at the Amphitheater in Bulgaria. *Come all in that old spirit.* Tell Teej those words. He will understand."

"I will," said Anna as she squeezed his hand. The sirens were close now.

"I'm sorry Anna. If you were in my place, you would have… done the same. I'm sorry."

"Sorry for what? *Wildey!* Sorry for what?"

It was too late. Wildey was dead.

thirty-four

"There he is!"

Teej heard Elise before he saw her. As he stepped through the automatic doors into the main concourse of the airport, the purple hair and yellow dungarees were hard to miss. Elise burst out of the throng of people and ran straight towards him. She could never blend into a crowd.

"You changed your—"

Before he could finish, Elise slammed face-first into his chest and squeezed him as tight as she could, knocking the wind from him. Teej kissed the top of her head and returned the hug.

"I'm glad to see you too."

"I am also happy to see you," said Pappi. His eyes were gaunt, his skin sallow, but he offered a smile. "Though I hoped you would not return alone."

"We should find somewhere quiet," suggested Teej. "But first I have to say goodbye to someone."

"Who?" Asked Elise.

Teej turned and waived to the flight attendant. She was just coming through the gate, the wheels of her small suitcase rattling across the floor as she hustled towards him. Her name was Carrie, and she blushed as she blew a lock of curly hair away from her face and touched his arm.

"Will I see you again?" she asked coyly.

"Of course! I owe you for the ticket after all. You saved me from the desert sun, Carrie."

"Just buy me dinner and we'll call it even."

She slipped her business card into his hand. It was as casual as taking a breath.

"See you around, stranger," she said as she turned and wheeled away.

"Goodbye, Carrie," said Teej with a wave.

Carrie rushed after her colleagues, and together the three flight attendants cleared security and disappeared from view.

"Who the Hell was that?" asked Elise with a little scowl.

Pappi put an arm around her. "Though current circumstances may conspire to convince you otherwise, our friend Teej has always been more of a lover than a fighter."

"Gross," said Elise. "I'm telling Anna."

"I had to get back here somehow," said Teej in exasperation. "Pappi exaggerates, but I can usually talk my way out of trouble. Or into a free plane ticket."

"His charm has saved more lives than his little stick," said Pappi with a mischievous grin.

"His what?" said Elise. "You mean his Periapt? Or are you making a dirty joke? I don't get it. Shouldn't we be going? Why were you in Dubai?"

"You're right," said Teej as he started to walk. "Let's get out of here. I'll tell you what happened on the way home."

"No, this way," said Pappi as he pointed to the exit. "We have a vehicle waiting."

They moved through the terminal like everyone else. The airport was loud and busy, but when they cleared the crowds and Teej could talk, he still didn't know where to start. Eventually, Pappi could wait no longer.

"Please, Teej, we need to know what happened. On the phone you told Elise so little."

"We did not find Alby," said Teej reluctantly. "We were thrown from the August Club. Anna lost control of herself and…"

Pappi shook his head. "Flames. We knew this was a possibility. Her fate is not your fault. She is not herself anymore. A wild animal you cannot control. I should have come."

Teej tried to calm his friend. "No, you are not ready to face our enemies yet, Pappi. This was my responsibility."

"You are wrong," said Pappi firmly. "I will be by your side from here on, and I will prove my worth, with or without Praxis."

Teej stopped and put a hand on his arm. "If we can find the Christmas Council, Alby may be there by Rayleigh's side. We have no leads though. We thought Wildey could tell us where to go."

"Perhaps we need not lose faith in Anna too soon," said Pappi. "She may yet find her goal." Though his eyes were still haunted, Pappi seemed a little stronger now. Teej gave him a pat on the shoulder and Elise took his arm. It was clear some of her resilience had rubbed off on the Metik. She was a good influence.

"So, where is Anna?" asked Elise.

"I tried the Spoon Fetish," said Teej, "But all I could tell was she was *somewhere* in the city. I don't know if it's failing because our Praxis is a mess after being thrown out of the club, or it's an aftereffect of her cloak."

"What about, you know, *phoning* her?"

"You mean call this?" said Teej as he pulled Anna's phone out of his pocket.

"Ah."

"At least she is alive my friend," said Pappi more cheerfully.

"She's not alone," replied Teej. "Wildey followed her."

"Is that a good thing?" asked Elise.

Teej turned to his friends to see them both waiting for his answer. He shrugged. "It's a thing. If Rayleigh wants Anna,

Wildey will do anything he can to prevent that, even if only to spite his enemy."

"So, what do we do now?" asked Elise.

"We can regroup at Maxines," said Pappi. "Once Teej's strength returns, his spoon may return better results."

Teej nodded. "We have to believe that one way or another, Anna will know what to do next."

"And if we do find the location of the Christmas Council?" said Pappi. "What is our strategy?"

"It could be a trap, right?" said Elise. "I mean, do we really think we can stop this civil war with *talking*?"

Teej put his hand on Elise's shoulder. "No peace has ever been achieved with anything *but* talking."

"But talking with *Rayleigh*?" complained Elise. "After everything he's done? After all the times he tried to kill us and abduct Anna."

"The Blood Plague is bigger than all of us," said Teej. "Even Rayleigh. If we can't find a solution, eventually we're *all* done for. If Rayleigh can't lead the Dreamers towards some kind of peace, maybe we can convince them to overthrow him and install a new leader."

"They have always, and will always, fear Rayleigh," said Pappi. "And rightly so."

"Maybe that's why he wants Anna so badly," said Teej. "He doesn't have the Green Knight to enforce his will anymore. Anna is an example of what happens when you stand up to Rayleigh. A *living* example."

"Then the Dreamers might follow Anna?" asked Elise.

Teej shook his head. "They would never follow a Metik, especially not an Undreamer. But the veneer of invincibility around Rayleigh has been cracked. If Anna stands up to Rayleigh at the Christmas Council and openly defies him, the Dreamers may no longer fall in line with his demands."

"I will bring the car around," said Pappi as they walked out of the airport into the dry, cool morning air. Teej and Elise watched him go as they stood next to the empty car park. Little patches of blue sky poked out between the fluffy white clouds, and Teej smelled the promise of snow in the air. He took a deep breath and sighed.

"What was Dubai like?" asked Elise.

"I only saw the airport, but it was warm."

"And the August Club?" asked Elise. Teej tried to read her expression, but she turned away.

"You didn't miss much. We should get moving."

Pappi's car pulled up and he waved for them to get inside.

Teej opened the door, then realized Elise wasn't joining them. She was looking at something.

"What?" he asked.

Elise pointed at the huge Christmas tree in front of the airport. "I just realized what day it is."

"Weirdest Christmas Eve ever, right?" said Teej. "Come on, the sooner we get this over with, the sooner we can all be back home around the fireplace with some eggnog."

thirty-five

It was six-thirty, and though Anna had evaded the police, Wildey's blood was still on her hands. She'd stolen some clothes and escaped to the riverside district, but she still didn't know how to get to the Amphitheater.

She'd followed her Haze Sense along the grassy riverbank, looking for some kind of tunnel entrance in the darkness. She knew there was a way into the Realm nearby, but as with any passage out of Basine, the doorway was hard to find. Even once she was in the Realm, she had no idea how to travel through it or how to find the Amphitheater. She'd been to Malamun and the Sump, but she was far from an expert on travel through the Realm. Now she stood almost directly under the Foalmouth Bridge, ankle-deep in mud, pursued by an angry swan that hissed at her every time she slowed her pace. As she tipped her head back to let out a moan of frustration, a single snowflake drifted down and landed on her nose. The swan hissed again.

"Hey, Swannie, it's snowing."

The swan remained unimpressed.

"Would you stop hissing at me! I don't want to steal that gross piece of hotdog you're defending."

Recognizing her frustration, the swan edged away nervously before turning and waddling back along the riverbank, leaving Anna alone once more.

Leaning on a bollard, she looked first down into the murky water, then up at the huge bridge towering over her. She was standing in a piece of fenced-off wasteland, but the lights from nearby cars and buses burst through the gloom, illuminating the nearby freeway and the tall Foalmouth Bridge. In the distance, she could see a barge carrying river trash coming towards her, but no one seemed to notice she was there. Though she was in the middle of the city, she was in the middle of nowhere, too.

This would be a lot easier if she still had her phone. She could call Teej and find out where he was, and where to go. If he was still alive.

She'd considered returning to Maxines in case he was there, or even going back to her old flat and calling Elise. She was running short of time, though. And perhaps it was better she went alone. Anyone close to her, especially when she was in a Haze, was in danger now. She'd lost control of her Praxis, and when she faced Rayleigh, she'd probably lose control again. Anyone close to her was liable to get hurt. Better if everyone she loved and cared for was far away right now.

Letting out a sigh, Anna looked down at her mismatched clothes, her gaze running along the sleeves of her oversized sweater to her dirty hands. Her fingers were still smeared with Wildey's blood. She washed them clean in the water. She'd just left him there in the cafe. Just like Amara, Anna had left another body in her wake. No burial for either of them.

What would Needham think? Maybe she should have stayed at the crime scene, faced the repercussions and abandoned the Christmas Council. After evading Rayleigh for all this time, she was running straight into his arms with no plan and no friends. Could she count on Teej and Pappi to be there already? Maybe they'd found the location of the Christmas Council on their own. It seemed unlikely.

If she had her phone right now, Anna might call Mom. Tell her she was tired, that she was lost, that she wanted to come home. Anna was falling into despondency, and she knew it. Her lungs still felt the smoke of the bonfire that threatened the August Club. The scent saturated her, reminding her that once again she'd lost control of her flames and burned herself out of consciousness.

A horn blared and a barge sailed under the bridge, rousing Anna from her reverie. A searchlight scanned the water. Anna absentmindedly followed the beam till it swung around to the shore. For the first time, she noticed a round building near the South end of the bridge. It was an Italian restaurant now, but before that, it might have been something else.

Like an entrance to a tunnel!

Anna set off at a jog towards the building. Long before the bridge existed, there had been a tunnel under the river, and the round building had served as the entry point. It was blocked off now, but a blocked off underground tunnel was exactly the kind of gateway that could lead to the Realm. That *had* to be it.

Anna was halfway up the riverbank when she took a deep breath and felt a sharp pain in her chest. Falling to one knee, she closed her eyes tightly and waited for it to pass. Since she'd escaped Alby's assassination attempt, this had happened every time she moved too fast. Or maybe she had incurred injuries at the August Club that she couldn't remember, but until she got to a hospital or into another Haze, there was nothing she could do. With a grunt, she got back to her feet and pushed on more slowly.

She could read the sign over the round building now. *'The Gatehouse.'* Inside, smartly dressed diners sipped wine and ate pasta. Anna's eyes wandered from the brightly lit main entrance to a little set of stairs leading down into a boarded-off basement. It was dark and hidden, and it thrummed with the familiar vibration of a Staid Haze. Anna felt the Vig flow out from that door and wash over her in waves. It felt like Malamun or the

August Club, but older and earthier. There could be no doubt, this was a route to the Realm.

Anna took a deep breath and steeled herself. Whatever waited for her through the door at the bottom of the stairs, she had to be ready.

The steps were slick with wet moss, and she clung to the walls to keep her footing as she descended into darkness. At the bottom, a puddle of stagnant water came up to her ankles, and she moaned in discomfort. It was pitch black. She ran her hands across the heavy metal security door in front of her, fumbling for a handle of some sort, but she felt only a deadbolt and a heavy padlock.

Dammit.

There had to be a way in. Anna could feel the edges of the Haze, close enough that she could almost use her powers, but tantalizingly out of reach. It was frustrating. If she could edge just a few meters closer to the source of Vig she sensed beyond this barrier, she'd be able to bust through this door like it was made of paper. Since she was in the real world and with no Haze nearby, she'd have to find a way through without her Praxis.

Anna tugged on the chain, rattled the padlock, then ran her hands around the edge of the doorframe searching for a secret latch or handle. In a flash of frustration, she kicked the door hard enough to make her big toe throb.

"Fuck!"

That was stupid. Taking a deep breath, Anna brought her mind into focus and calmed herself. She wasn't some naïve girl anymore. She was not a weak, submissive grad student, but she wasn't an all-powerful Undreamer right at this moment either. She'd learned a lot about her abilities in this last year, but she'd learned even more about herself. She knew she was prone to impatience and bouts of self-recrimination. But she also knew when she controlled her temper, she was resourceful and creative.

I can do this.

She had to find an old key she could use to bump the lock, an old hair clip and a nail file to pick it, or, if all else failed, a crowbar. Climbing the stairs carefully, Anna was almost back to the top when she felt the pain in her lung again. Clutching her chest, she lost her grip on the railing as her heel slipped on the slick top step.

Anna tumbled down the stairs, hands scrabbling in vain for the handrail. She splashed into the puddle at the bottom, and her back slammed against the door.

Good work.

Catching her breath, she touched her knees and elbows to feel scrapes and bruises. The heel of her left hand felt like she'd just caught a softball without a mitt. She sat there in silence for a moment, not sure what to do now.

Heaving herself up, she rubbed her chest till the pain began to subside. Anna realized she could see a thin sliver of light in the dark stairwell, coming from the doorway. She pushed the door gingerly. It opened.

She could see the deadbolt was intact, but the metal eyelet was loose. The rusted screws holding it in place had dislodged when her body hit the doorframe.

Well, whatever works.

Anna entered the tunnel.

The path ahead was dimly lit by exposed lightbulbs that hung along a bare corridor. Most of them had burned out. Those that still worked flickered and buzzed.

Forging ahead, she pushed through curtains of cobwebs, past faded signs, and a dusty old kiosk that had once sold tickets for passage under the river. Eventually, the corridor opened out to a cavern. The only path left to take was a rusted, broken escalator that led down into utter darkness.

Taking each step slowly, holding the railing tightly, Anna descended deeper and deeper into the tunnel. She could hear dripping noises above but felt no water. Her footsteps echoed in the distance. It grew darker as she descended; eventually, there was no light at all. She clung even tighter to the handrail. The old metal felt cold and rough.

In the distance, Anna saw a dim halo appear. At first, she thought it was a trick of her eyes, but as she got closer, she realized the light was bleeding in from somewhere.

Scratching, skittering noises were all around her now, and Anna felt something crawl across her knuckles. She forced herself to hold onto the railing. No matter if this place was full of spiders, or rats, or, God forbid, centipedes, she had to hold on. If she fell now, she was done for.

The air felt heavy down here, the smell of damp increasing as Anna neared the bottom of the escalator. Her route was clear, but it was blocked by another heavy door. The gloom receded as light seeped in from the bottom. As the scratching noises in the darkness intensified, Anna quickened her pace. She felt like a whole army of vermin were closing in on her, and with the exit in sight, panic rose in her chest.

I have to get out of here.

Stumbling down the last few steps, Anna broke into a half-run toward the door and freedom. Though she felt sure it would be locked, she put her shoulder down and hammered into it at full speed. Bursting through the rotten wood into a brightly lit street, Anna covered her eyes and groaned. She was in a Haze again.

When her vision returned, she saw colored lights all around, a huge Christmas tree towering over her, and soft flakes of snow drifting down across a city street.

With a shiver, Anna set off to find the Amphitheater. She only managed a few steps before the pain in her chest exploded, shooting from her heart down her left arm, then spreading through her whole body. Collapsing in a heap, she opened her mouth to call for help, but no sound came.

thirty-six

Amara's voice was a clamoring din, and though she called out to Anna and told her to wake up, Anna felt herself drift further from consciousness.

"I said get up girl!"

A slap stung her cheek. Anna opened her eyes and saw the little old woman standing over her.

"I don't have all day," said Amara with the wag of a finger. "I can't carry you. You'll have to do this yourself."

"Aren't you dead?" asked Anna. Her words were slurred, her tongue a cold piece of meat in her mouth. She rolled over and looked into the old woman's eyes.

"I'm here, and if you don't get to your feet and follow me, you'll be deader than I am."

"Fine," said Anna with a groan. Getting to her feet, she pressed the palm of her hand against her chest to dampen the pain.

"Are you real or a dream?"

"Real enough," said Amara. "You're close, but they won't find you here. Come on."

Amara trudged through the whistling snow, leaving no footprints. Anna followed slowly, her legs leaden, the wind stinging her cheeks.

"Who won't find me?" asked Anna. "Close to what? Are we going to the Amphitheater?"

"Yes," Amara shouted over her shoulder. "But you won't make it. Talk less, walk more."

"If I won't make it, why try?" asked Anna. The outline of Amara was lost in the blizzard for a moment, but her voice cut through.

"Sometimes if you do half the work, someone else will meet you halfway."

Anna stumbled and fell to her knees. The snow was freezing, but it felt like a warm blanket beneath her body.

"Why should I listen to you anyway? You said I couldn't beat the Green Knight. You said my friends would stab me in the back. You told me to let Teej die!"

"Get up, you fool!" snapped Amara.

Anna was so tired. Her mind was fuzzy. "Who are you?" she asked. "Did we meet before?"

"On the train," said Amara flatly. "And long, long ago, we stood together on a Blackened Bridge."

Anna didn't understand. Amara was exasperated. "You failed to follow the path I set for you, just like you fail to follow me now."

Her voice was getting farther away. Anna crawled through the snow after the woman. She wanted to scream at her.

"I didn't fail!"

She was talking to this woman as if she was the real Amara, but Amara was dead. Anna's head was a mess. She tried to bring her mind back into focus.

"I *chose* not to walk that path. And you were wrong."

The old woman chuckled. "I was not wrong. Your allies will stab you through the heart for this."

Anna shook her head. "You told me the Green Knight would kill me. I am still here."

"I did not say he would kill you. I said he would break you. Are you not broken?"

She was right. That was *exactly* what Amara had said back on the Blackened Bridge.

Anna's hand curled into a fist. "He did not break me. I beat him!"

"And lost who you are. Defeat can make you stronger, just as victory can make you weak. You failed to learn any lessons. Raguel infected you."

"Infected me? With what?"

Amara appeared out of the blizzard as the winds abated for a moment.

"Infected me with what, old woman!?" raged Anna.

"With an insidious idea. Your defeat of Raguel has made you callous and has closed your mind. You think you can fight any enemy and win. You are wrong."

"I'm an Undreamer. I stopped Raguel. I saved my friends. I'll stop Rayleigh too You... you don't know what I was like before my training. I couldn't fight for myself, never mind anyone else. I'm an Undreamer now, and no one will hurt the people I love ever again."

Amara's voice softened. "Oh, my dear, I believe you. I do. But no matter how hard you fight, you can't protect them all. To save your friends, you need to be smarter than your enemies. An Undreamer doesn't need to win a fight when that fight is someone else's game. *Never play their game.*"

Anna heaved herself to her feet and stumbled after the woman. Was she a ghost? A memory? Part of this Haze? Anna couldn't tell.

"How do you know that phrase? Are you really Amara?"

Amara smiled warmly. "I am."

"How can you be?"

"You should have buried me."

Anna felt a pang of guilt. "You mean after we left you on the train? There was no time. You disappeared."

"You *made* no time. Do you know how old I am? Or how old I *was*? I deserved to be treated with more respect."

Anna clutched her chest to endure the pain and tried to catch Amara, her legs sinking deep in the snow.

"You stuck around to lecture me?"

"There's barely a shred of my soul left. I'm a whisper of a shadow. I won't last long."

Anna tutted. "And you're using the last moments of your existence to tell me how much of a disappointment I am? I don't need that. I already have a mom."

Amara stopped in her tracks and Anna saw her shrug her shoulders. "You can only disappoint someone who once believed in you. There's still some hope."

"What do you suggest I do, then? What can I do *but* fight?"

Amara turned, and Anna became lost in her eyes. Old eyes, gray and wise. "The Fade. You need to go into the Fade, and when you do, everything you have ever run from in your whole life will catch you. When it does, you need to turn and face it. If you're not honest with yourself when you enter the Fade, it will take *everything* from you. Find the Winterheart. Find yourself."

Anna's head hurt, her legs were jelly, and she could barely see. What was Amara trying to do to her? Was any of this real? The soft snow beckoned, but Anna needed answers before she slept.

"What the Hell is *'the Fade?'*"

Amara chuckled.

"The Fade swallowed the ancient holy city of Selmetridon. The Fade is all the secrets that were never told, made real. It is the choking mist that has closed off the Realm, and it grows. The Fade is why no one will ever be able to reach our old Gods again. Inside the Fade, you will find all your answers, but they will find you, too."

Anna was confused. Another gust of wind obscured Amara with snow, and Anna had to break into a half-run to catch her.

"I thought you wanted me to send Teej to get the Winterheart," said Anna with a wheeze. "Now *I'm* supposed to get it!?"

"Your path has diverged from the one I foresaw. Teej will no longer be able to take on this task."

"Wait, what?" said Anna in alarm. "*Why* can't he go?"

Amara went silent. She stopped in her tracks again.

"Tell me why!" screamed Anna.

"Why do you think, girl? He will be dead."

Anna stopped. "No, this is all lies. You're not Amara. This is all in my head."

A slow shake of the head. "You only wish that were true."

Anna focused her Will and used the Word. "Where is Teej!"

"That won't work on me, girl," said Amara. "You should be ready to move quickly. You will face your foe again soon."

As she spoke, Amara began to fade like mist in the morning sun. Her body became ethereal, transparent.

"Get back here," said Anna as she stomped towards the old woman. With every step Anna took, Amara's hunched form faded a little more. By the time Anna was face-to-face with her, she was almost completely gone. Anna grabbed her by the shoulder and turned her around. Her face was indistinct and blurry, like it was made of mist.

"Lie to them all," said Amara. "Tell them the Winterheart is the cure, then let the Fade take you. That's the only way to find peace. That's the only way you can save the ones you love. That's the only way you can atone for what you did to Sam."

Anna tried to keep hold of her, but Amara became snow and blew away with the breeze.

"I won't let him go!" Anna shouted into the darkness. "I can't do this without him."

Amara was gone.

Head fuzzy, limbs leaden, Anna finally let herself fall to the snow. She closed her eyes and melted away.

thirty-seven

The snow fell heavy and soft, obscuring any landmarks Teej might recognize. Holding up the spoon, the heat in his hand told him Anna was close, but the landscape had changed since the last time he was here. The statue of Alyosha looking out from Markovo Hill was lost in the mist, and the old soviet-style radio broadcast tower that loomed large over Plovdiv's main boulevard was obscured. In their place was a blanket of white, decorated with a million Christmas lights strung around lampposts and trees.

Teej, Elise, and Pappi stood by the old central post office; the only building that remained undecorated. It never changed—a block of concrete dropped into the city center, its ugliness at odds with the sprawling, pristine garden it overlooked. The few people who had braved the cold were hustling home through the park, but when they reached the tree line, they faded like ghosts.

"Are we in the Haze now? asked Elise.

"Yes. Can't you tell?" replied Teej.

"But where *are* we? I mean, in the *real* world."

They'd left Basine behind and come through an old portal under the Foalmouth Bridge, but Teej knew where their destination would be as soon as he saw the snow. The Amphitheater in Plovdiv. The old Bulgarian ruins were one of the few places Rayleigh could hold a Council and hope it wouldn't become a battleground.

"We're in the Realm," said Pappi as he pointed at the tree line. "Just at the periphery. There is little natural Vig here. As we get closer to the Amphitheater you should feel the situation change. You are no Dreamer or Metik, Elise, but you are... sensitive. You can learn much."

"What is this Amphitheater?" asked Elise with a suppressed smile. It was clear she appreciated Pappi's encouragement. "We catching some Shakespeare? In the snow?"

"There will be a show, of that I am certain," said Pappi with a grin. "The Amphitheater is precarious. It is a whole structure held aloft by runes interwoven with Mimesis. Any use of the Art would drain the Vig that supports the platform, sending us all to our doom."

"Do we have far to go?" asked Elise. "You were right about bringing a jacket. It's so fucking cold!"

"I told you to bring a hat too," said Teej.

"And I told you there are no shops open to buy a hat on Christmas Eve."

"You don't have to *buy* one."

"I don't have one that matches this," said Elise as she pulled the ends of her pink parka.

"Please," said Pappi, his voice breaking just a little. "I am not an impatient man, but tonight..."

"You're right," said Teej. "We need to get a move on."

"How far?" asked Elise.

"This way," commanded Teej as he set off at a brisk pace. Holding the spoon aloft "We're close to her. Watch your feet. The snow is getting deeper."

"I'm glad his spoon started working again," Elise said to Pappi.

"And I am glad we have Anna," said Pappi. "Now we must hope that the path she has set for us leads to our salvation, and we find her on that path in good health and good spirits."

They trudged past shuttered shops, restaurants closed for the night, and even a few cafes that were still open, their steamed-up windows bleeding orange light into the night. The going was slow, and Teej's legs burned with the effort while his cheeks were pinched with the bitter cold. He was lightheaded, still weakened from his ejection from the August Club, but when he saw Elise and Pappi following close behind, steadfastly marching in his footsteps, he forced himself to keep up the pace.

They passed the donut stall he remembered, and the smell of caramelized sugar and cooking batter assaulted his senses, but he didn't slow down.

"I wish we had time," he said to himself. Elise heard him.

"We'll come back," she said as she put a hand on his arm. "And we'll bring Anna. And Alby!"

"Elise, I'm not sure—"

"We will," said Pappi. He was a little out of breath but managed a half-smile. "And thank you for the optimism, Elise. Were such things possible, the warmth of your heart would melt this snow."

Elise beamed.

"This isn't much of a Haze. It just feels like the regular old world."

"There's little will to change things here," said Pappi. "We skirt the margins of the Realm. This locale has been chosen for a reason. No *one* Dreamer controls this place, but another Haze cannot be created here either. In the Realm, every Dreamer and Metik has some power, but not too much."

"At the Amphitheater, we must be ready," warned Teej. "We're certainly not invited. When we get a chance to speak, we need to be careful what we say."

"Then we must have a goal in mind," said Pappi.

"Peace," said Teej.

"A fine starting point," said Pappi. "But we need a route to get there."

Teej tugged absent-mindedly at his scarf as his mind raced. Pappi was right; they needed to have their arguments ready. Teej didn't know where to start.

"It's about temptation, right?" said Elise.

"Perhaps," said Pappi. "Go on."

"Dreamers need to overcome that temptation. Like, if the blood will make them more powerful *and* safer, then taking the blood is the logical course of action. But if they don't do it, everyone else will, and they'll be vulnerable. So why are they not all taking each other's blood *already*?"

"Because they are not monsters," said Teej.

"And they don't want to *become* monsters either," said Elise. "So, there is hope, right?"

Pappi nodded. "There is hope. Right now, even when they have all the reasons to turn on their brothers and sisters and tear each other apart, they resist. Some of them at least."

Elise was on a roll. "We need to find a way to change things so that taking the blood makes them *less* safe. They will always be tempted by it, right? We can't change that part, but maybe we can find a way to make drinking blood hazardous to them."

"That would be our plan," said Teej patiently. "We want Rayleigh to formally forbid the taking of blood. Or, failing that, we want another Dreamer to take Rayleigh's place and forbid it."

"I get it," said Elise, her tone impatient. "We're making laws for the Dreamers."

"Only one law," said Teej.

"They don't follow laws already?" asked Elise.

"No," said Teej. "Although, I suppose the Metiks often try to stop them hurting innocents."

"The dream police," said Pappi with a chuckle.

"I suppose we are," said Teej. "But Metiks don't normally have to stop Dreamers killing *each other*. And there are too few Metiks to stop a civil war this time."

Elise frowned. "Couldn't this be a time to make, I dunno, like, a Magna Carta thingy for Dreamers? Some sort of set of rules or guidelines for everyone?"

"We'd probably have more luck getting cats to form a democratic republic," said Teej acerbically.

"Maybe we need not be so cynical," said Pappi as he put his hand on Teej's shoulder. "There has never been a meeting like this before."

"There have been plenty," replied Teej. "They were before our time, and, from what I've heard, they were all disasters."

"Things change," said Pappi with a raised finger. "In your own words, there are too few of us now. We live in a changing world. What once felt like control may now feel like protection. Perhaps the Dreamers need oversight. Perhaps they would even welcome it."

"Perhaps," said Teej skeptically. "Come on, we need to keep moving or we're going to be late."

His friend's words rang in his ears as Teej led the way through the main street of Plovdiv town center. They went down through an underpass then up and out a tunnel, their footsteps silent in the deep snow. It took a few minutes to reach the base of the long twisting staircase that would take them past the old town, up to the Amphitheater. He could see the Amphitheater through the snow, poking out proudly from the hillside as it looked over the city.

Could the Dreamers be reasoned with? Could they be convinced to sign some sort of treaty or pact that would enforce peace? It didn't seem likely. Garret certainly would have scoffed at the suggestion. Teej hoped to control the Dreamers through coercion and threats from Rayleigh, a Dreamer who was manipulative, dangerous, and had already tried to kill Teej and everyone he loved.

Teej shook his head in frustration as his mind raced. He needed Anna. Would they find her on these stairs? Would they find her at all?

"Wait!" said Pappi, rousing Teej to attention and halting them in their tracks.

"Do you not feel it?"

"What?" said Teej, confused.

"This way!" said Pappi, leaving the staircase to follow a narrow side street. Teej looked at Elise, but she just shrugged. The followed Pappi as he sprinted down the twisting, turning footpaths between the fancy gardens of the old townhouses. Teej wanted to call after him that this was a mistake, that they had to get to the Amphitheater, but his lungs burned, and he couldn't get the words out. They ran through the night in complete silence, the snow swallowing even the sounds of Teej's ragged breathing. It felt like a dream. A nightmare. Eventually, Pappi stopped under a little bridge. He was looking at something huddled in a doorway.

"Hurry!" said Pappi. "She is barely conscious."

Teej froze in place. It couldn't be.

"Anna!" Elise shouted.

And there she was. Anna looked like a broken doll. Her skin was porcelain white. The corners of her mouth were cracked from a bloody wound that had dried. She wore old baggy clothes that were not nearly warm enough to keep her safe in the snow. Despite her condition, when her tired eyes met Teej's, they twinkled with recognition.

"Teej," she reached out to him. "I found you."

He kneeled next to her and held her hand. It was pale blue and felt like ice. "You found me."

"You're late," she said, letting out a chuckle before wincing in pain.

"Nice of you to wait for me."

"I'm sorry I lost control," she said.

"And I'm sorry I couldn't help you," said Teej. "But let's agree to both give ourselves a break."

Anna didn't respond, but she gave him a weak thumbs-up.

"I sense something is not right with her," said Pappi as he began to undress. "Take my coat."

"No," protested Anna. "I want my cloak."

"I have it," said Teej. His numb hands raked through his bag till he found the familiar red material. He draped the cloak over her shoulders, but she still held her hand out.

"Do you have it?"

"Yes," said Teej, and he passed her the ring. It might have been his imagination, but when Anna slipped it on her finger, she instantly looked better.

"What happened?" asked Elise. Teej wanted to reprimand her for hassling Anna while she was in this state, but he wanted to know the answer too.

"Help me stand, first," said Anna, and together the three of them lifted her to her feet.

She was unsteady but seemed to be getting stronger by the minute.

"Wildey is dead. Alby… something was wrong with him. He attacked us. Wildey took a bullet for me. A lot of bullets"

Anna reached out for Teej. "I'm sorry. I know your relationship was… complicated."

Teej felt like a pit had opened in his stomach. No more Wildey, no more Garret. All his oldest friends were gone. He was unmoored, drifting away from everyone.

"I'm fine," said Teej. "It's better this way."

Hesitantly, Anna went on. "He told me to send you a message. *Come all in that old spirit.*"

Teej nodded. "It's an old Metik saying. Not one Wildey would normally use. It was about making a compromise. *Come all in that old spirit. Peace answers harder questions than conflict asks.*"

Anna looked to Pappi.

"Alby was not himself. Rayleigh did something to him. We must stop this Blood Plague. The world has gone mad."

"We will!" said Elise confidently. "We're together again. We stopped the Doxa and their monster. We can stop this too. And if Rayleigh stands in our way, we can just—"

"No more fighting," interrupted Anna. "We either find a way to make peace, or we fail. I'm not fighting Rayleigh or Alby or anyone else anymore. No more fire."

She glanced at Pappi.

"We save everyone we can."

He didn't say anything but gave her a nod. Elise meanwhile looked like she was going to protest, then changed her mind and stopped herself.

"Is it far?" asked Anna.

"No," replied Teej. "You came in through the bridge tunnel? We found the locked door. It was smashed. How did you get through?"

"With my butt," said Anna with a straight face.

"We followed your trail, and it took us to the main street, then we climbed the stairs and found you."

"Did you see Amara?" asked Anna.

"What?" Teej looked confused.

"It doesn't matter," said Anna. "Where the Hell did you end up after the August Club?"

"Dubai," said Teej.

"Obviously. And you just got on a plane?"

"He got a free ticket by flirting with—" Pappi elbowed Elise to shut her up.

"We have no time for this, do we?" said Anna.

"We do not," said Pappi firmly.

When they started moving again, it was much more slowly. Teej waved for Pappi and Elise to go ahead, and with Anna's arm around his shoulder, he took her weight, and they shuffled through the snow together. As they began the steep ascent of the stairs once more, Teej paused and let Anna catch her breath.

"I'll be fine," she said. Teej looked into her dark brown eyes and believed her. The moon shone brightly over his shoulder, and he noticed the little freckles on her cheeks. Something had changed. Anna seemed calmer, like she had finally made a difficult decision. She was resilient. Teej suddenly and impulsively wished they didn't have to keep climbing this hill. He wanted to pick her up, take her down the stairs and out of this place. He wanted to take her out of the snow and back to a safe world. A world that they could one day call home, where they would never see another Dreamer or Metik ever again. Where all he had to worry about was who would do the laundry and where they would go for dinner that night.

"Teej," prompted Anna gently. "You're just staring at me."

The sound of her little laugh warmed the cold night.

"Sorry, I was just thinking…"

"Me too," she said. "But we have to keep going. And when this is all over, if we make it through this, there is something I need to talk to you about. To tell you."

Teej nudged her. "Tell me now."

"I can't because when I tell you, you might never want to see me again. When I admit it to you, and myself, I don't know if I'll be able to live anymore."

He grasped her hand and shook his head. "Whatever it is, I'm ready to listen."

"Let's get to this meeting, then," said Anna. "Who knows, maybe there will be some friendly faces in among all the people who want us dead."

The climb was difficult, but when they reached the top, Pappi and Elise were waiting for them. They stood at a big stone archway, beyond which Teej could already see the cobbled road curve towards a narrow street. Once they turned that corner, they would be at the Amphitheater.

"I thought we might see other Dreamers on the way here," said Elise. "Flying on magic carpets, riding in on dragons."

Anna let out a groan.

"Are you still in pain?" asked Teej.

"Yes, and I've already had enough of Dreamers for today."

"There are a great many routes that lead here," said Pappi. "The Dreamers converge on this spot from many directions, and it has been well chosen. I know you realize this already, but I remind you all now, we must *not* use our powers here."

"What would happen if we did?" asked Elise, a look of morbid curiosity on her face.

"The Amphitheater is a place of precarious balance," explained Pappi. "There is just enough Vig in the air to suspend the Amphitheater through the runes scrawled on the foundations. If we are to harness some of that Vig ourselves, the runes will fail."

Anna scowled. "And there's no chance at all that this is some elaborate plan to kill everyone by luring us all here then dropping us off a mountain?"

"There is always a chance," said Pappi with a mischievous grin. "It would certainly solve a great many problems in the world, including our own. I doubt we would feel a thing."

Teej took a moment to look at each of his friends. Pappi's head was held high, his eyes clear. Elise shifted her weight from one foot to the other, the sword in her backpack swinging from side to side. Anna had one hand on Teej's shoulder, and she chewed her fingernails nervously, but she was no longer huddled in pain.

"Are we ready then?" asked Teej. No one answered. "All right, let's go."

thirty-eight

Anna's first experience of the Amphitheater was vertigo. The high steps descended into a distant semi-circular auditorium around a raised podium. At the rear of the stage, a pair of tall portico columns overlooked a sprawling city that stretched to the horizon. Below them, an underground vaulted passageway opened out to a dimly lit cave that led into the orchestra, but it was too dark to see if anyone was inside. Wreathed in snow, illuminated by strings of Christmas lights and the distant city, the Amphitheater was a suitably breathtaking place for a summit to save the world.

Anna pushed open a creaky steel gate and her friends followed her down one of the theater aisles. The carved stone steps were uneven and steep, and they had to move slowly down the slope to reach the seats at the bottom. The higher tiers of the auditorium were still covered in snow, but the front nine or ten rows of seats had been brushed clear and had little padded seat covers. Some of the audience had already taken their places.

There were fewer than fifty people in a theater that could hold thousands, but what an audience they were.

Anna recognized many of the faces that turned to look as she descended. On the left of the stage, Anna spotted the Dreamer Gahan among the crowd. He cut a striking silhouette, his black pinstripe suit and long black hair contrasting with the white snow. When Anna met his gaze, he pulled down his sunglasses to get a better look at her and smiled. Anna gave him a nod of recognition.

Next to him stood an old man with the longest gray beard Anna had ever seen. He looked a thousand years old. One row behind were two women in fancy cocktail dresses, and beside them, the distinctive figure of Elizabeth Needham. She did not turn to look at them. Her view was locked straight ahead, her posture perfect, her lips pursed.

As she followed Teej down the stairs, Anna anxiously wondered which side he would choose. *Bride or groom?* She didn't want to be anywhere near Needham, but she didn't want to be near Gahan either. Not with Teej here. *Too complicated.*

"Do you see Rayleigh?" asked Elise as they walked closer to the stage.

"No," said Anna. "But I don't know what he looks like. Teej?"

"Me neither," replied Teej. "Though I have a feeling we'd know if he was here."

"He will keep Alby by his side," said Pappi. "This is how he will make his point."

"What point?" asked Anna.

"That he is in control."

"You think he knows we're here?" asked Anna.

"Of course," said Pappi. "Perhaps our appearance was part of his plan all along."

"Who is the woman with the short hair?" Anna asked Teej, pointing at the podium.

"Watch your feet," he warned as she stumbled down a broken step. "The steps are icy."

"Her name is Marion. They call her *'The Chronicler of Dream'*. She's an old Aesthete and a historian. That book she carries close to her chest contains all our history. She's respected by most of the Dreamers. Liked by some."

"That book could be really useful!" said Elise with a wheeze as she clambered down after them.

"It might seem that way, but all the pages are blank," replied Teej.

"That seems like an extremely heavy-handed metaphor," said Anna.

"I believe they are only blank for us," said Pappi. "Marion sees them clearly enough."

"An ally?" asked Anna.

"Perhaps," said Teej. "She might at least keep the debate on track. Don't interrupt her when she talks."

"Why? No one can use their powers here, right?" asked Elise.

"Trust me, she uses words like weapons even without powers," said Teej. "And we need her on our side. We need *everyone* on our side."

"Shall we?" said Pappi as he gestured to a row of free seats to their right. The row in front of them held only two people: a young man in top and tails with a handlebar moustache, and an elderly African woman who gave Teej a nod of recognition. He smiled back, and together the four of them took their seats.

Anna counted: they were six, seven, eight rows from the front. The soft snow muffled all sound, but she could hear whispered conversations all around her. Anna nudged Elise, but her friend was too curious about the gathering of Dreamers to notice Anna. Turning instead to Teej, Anna put her hand on his shoulder.

"How are you doing there?" he whispered. "Has the pain gone?"

"I don't feel anything at all," said Anna.

She shuffled close to Teej. He felt warm in the cold night. She found herself wishing for things that would never happen. Maybe Rayleigh wouldn't show. Maybe they could just sit like this forever. Anna sighed contentedly as they waited. It was a long time before any of them spoke. She closed her eyes.

"It's not that I want to disturb your nap…" said Teej.

"Too late."

"I just have this bad feeling."

"Rayleigh is already late," said Anna wearily. "Maybe he won't even show. Maybe all the worrying and bad feelings are just ruining the little time we have left."

"Maybe," said Teej grudgingly.

"Go on then," said Anna as she sat up straight again. "What's this bad feeling?"

Teej wrinkled his nose. "Déjà vu. This feels like the Doxa's Haze."

"At Avalon?"

"No, the one before that. The one where Linda died."

"Well, there's no Wildey this time," said Anna.

Teej shuddered. "There could have been though, right? I bet he wanted to come with you."

"He did," admitted Anna. "That seemed like a bad idea."

"Not for someone who loves chaos."

Anna shook her head. "He didn't seem so bad in the end. I think he just wanted to escape all of this."

Anna looked across at Needham, feeling a sudden twinge of guilt.

"Maybe," said Teej, "But I've forgiven him before. I believed him when he told me he had changed. And then…"

"Wel, he's gone now," said Anna firmly. "And without him, I wouldn't even be here. He saved me."

"Should I get my sword out?" asked Elise as she stood on her seat and glanced around nervously. "I see lots of Dreamers I recognize. Or *think* I recognize. That's the guy who makes photographs come to life, right? And that girl with the pink hair is such a *thirst trap*. I swear she has even more followers online than me. And that old dude with the beard used to drink cognac with Vinicaire. I guess most of them want to kill us. That dominatrix in the corset sure looks grumpy. Wait, is that the August Club woman? Wow, she looks *pissed*."

"Elise, keep it together," said Anna.

Reluctantly Elise slumped down into her seat. They sat in silence, the snow easing off as the clouds parted to show a star-dappled sky. Old lamps around the edge of the Amphitheater gave off a warm glow.

As more and more Dreamers filled the arena, Teej leaned in close to Anna and broke the silence. "What's a thirst trap?"

She patted his hand. "You don't want to know."

Teej opened his mouth, but before he could ask another question, a hush went over the crowd.

"Our host arrives," said Pappi grimly. He pointed a steady hand at the entrance to the tunnel. "There. And Rayleigh is not alone."

Anna didn't *hear* the heavy footsteps, she *felt* them reverberate through the ground. Rayleigh's murder church burst into her memories. Walking along the Moonlight Road, she had arrived at a horrifying facsimile of the place where she'd married Sam, reproduced and distorted by Rayleigh's Art. The footsteps of the knights in that place had shaken the ground, and now they were back.

From the dark, recessed passageway in the middle of the auditorium, a dark knight climbed the steps and entered the arena. Taller and broader than Raguel, his armor was obsidian, and he carried a heavy halberd twice as tall as a man. From the seams in his plate armor, black smoke drifted up into the night air. His faceplate was blank with a narrow slit for eyes, but there was no face inside.

"I killed him," muttered Anna. "Or something a lot like him. Is he like Raguel?"

"He can't be," said Teej. "Any use of the Art here would send us all off the edge of this mountain."

"He's a big mystical knight with smoke coming out of his armor, Teej. He's not exactly '*normal*.'"

"He must be a resident of the Realm," said Teej as he shuffled in his seat. "That's why he doesn't destabilize the Runes that support us."

"Great," said Anna as she threw her hands in the air.

Elise leaned in. "I guess he's what? The *Black* Knight. Is there a Blue Knight? And a Purple Knight after this?"

"We know only of the Green Knight," said Pappi in a soothing tone. "Whatever this bodyguard is, we must not jump to conclusions. Rayleigh would seek to disarm his enemies, spawning illusions and allowing our imaginations to undo us. Do not let him succeed. He must—"

Pappi stopped mid-sentence, his body suddenly tense. Behind the Black Knight, a small figure emerged. *Alby*. He stood by the knight's side, his eyes dark, his gaze unwavering as he looked straight ahead at the stage.

"Easy friend," said Teej as he put his hand on Pappi's shoulder. "Let's see where this goes."

Finally, a third figure emerged from the tunnel to join Alby and the Black Knight. Lank gray hair hung to his shoulders. The figure was hunched over, middle-aged, wearing a dusty black suit. He walked with a cane and came to stand between Alby and the knight before casting his gaze around the audience. A dry tongue licked crusty lips. Those pale eyes examined the audience members one by one till they fell upon Anna. Shaking his head in disappointment, the old man surveyed the crowd.

"So that's him," said Elise. "He's so ugly! You'd think someone that powerful would make himself look, I dunno, better than that."

Anna bit her nails and watched as the old man teetered to the podium. She tried to ignore the suspicious looks cast in her direction.

"If his appearance gets a reaction, it's intentional," said Teej. "He takes on this form for a reason."

"No," said Anna. Something was wrong. Though she wasn't sure why, Anna knew they were being misled.

"That isn't Rayleigh."

The hunched old man cleared his throat. His cough wasn't loud, but everyone fell instantly silent and listened closely.

"I am Gendo. The Orator. We stand here today at the moment of our reckoning."

The Black Knight hammered the shaft of his halberd into the ground, a ringing threat. Most of the crowd flinched, but the old man remained still. There was a moment of silence and then Elise punctured it.

"A moment of *what*?" she whispered.

"Shh!" snapped Teej. He pointed to the old man on the stage and put his finger to his lips. Chastised, Elise crossed her arms and pouted.

"We are here today to save ourselves from a future that seems set in stone," said the old man, his raspy voice reverberating throughout the Amphitheater. "If there is a possible path where we prevail, it will be what Derrida called l'avenir. '*The future to come*'. It will require the arrival of an *'Other'* to save us. That Other is my master."

"Gimme a break," said Elise under her breath. Anna shot her a sideways glance, but when she saw the mischief in her friend's eyes, she couldn't help but smile back at her.

The man was still talking.

"Adorno said art should be oppositional, but we must no longer stand in opposition to each other. Art that makes you happy supports the status quo, but the status quo is now division and conflict. We are not a community, but still, we must heal lest this blood plague end us all.

"Kant taught us that the sublime need not be feared. Though it may overwhelm us, the art we weave into Basine can be beautiful. But soon that beauty will be lost unless we restrain our basest instincts. This Blood Plague must be halted. Today, I speak to you as the announcer for my master. I present to you now, my mentor: Rayleigh."

Anna shivered. This was the moment she'd waited for. She would be face-to-face with an enemy more powerful than the Midnight Man, smarter and more manipulative than Drowden, stronger than Charron. An enemy that knew all her secrets. One who would use Sam's death against her. Anna clenched her fists and waited.

A petite woman dressed entirely in black entered the arena. Her face was painted bone-white except for a black stripe painted across her eyes and nose, like a mask. She walked slowly and carefully. She wore a smart black coat over a tight-fitting black cardigan with black jeans, contrasting starkly with the white cityscape behind her.

"Thank you all for waiting," said the woman apologetically. Her voice was even and neutral, pleasant. The audience regarded her carefully.

"I apologize for Gendo's grand introduction. I'm here to listen more than talk. This isn't about me."

"Well, there *she* is," muttered Teej. Anna could barely process his words, far less what she was seeing.

Rayleigh's dark brown eyes scanned the crowd as she talked. Her pale face paint made her seem ghostly, but her voice was flat and emotionless.

"I see many of you that I recognize as friends, and many more with an axe to grind. If you have words for me, you will have a chance to share them soon. But first, as a point of order, I want to dissolve any hierarchy you may feel exists. This Council will be a place for free and open debate. I do not want any perceived power structure to undermine that. This Council is an attempt at a lasting peace. We all must be equals. I suggest we nominate an adjudicator. Someone fair and wise who will allow us all time and space to express our opinions and put forward our arguments. I nominate our oldest and most esteemed sister, the keeper of our histories: Marion."

A ripple of discussion went through the crowd. Anna turned to Teej looking for some reaction, but he just shrugged. They would have to wait and see where this went.

"Please," said Rayleigh. "If you hold back your opinions, they cannot be recognized. If you feel the need to speak against Marion taking on this role, say so now. If you have another to nominate, do so now."

Gahan stood up. "I have words."

A hush fell upon them once more. Gahan smiled casually, but though he tried to hide it, Anna heard the note of tension in his voice.

"Marion is the Chronicler of Dreams, the oldest and wisest woman anyone could ever hope to meet. She's a good deal less sour than old Amara, wherever the old bat is hiding these days. I'm sure most of us are happy for her to adjudicate, but I have a question before we start."

From the front row, Marion got to her feet and walked onto the stage. She stood far from Rayleigh but surveyed the audience in the same manner. She was tall with cropped, bright red hair, and though her eyes looked tired, there was a hint of a smile on her lips.

"Alrighty, I suppose I'm in charge then," she said breezily. She opened her big book and ran her index finger down the page like she was looking for something.

"I suppose my first action is to accept a question from the floor. Mr. Gahan?"

Gahan stroked his beard. "My question is simple. Why are we here at a Council when they have proven useless in the past? And what is this archaic *Council* hoping to achieve? We are Dreamers and we do not play nicely together. How can we accomplish what we have never managed before? Perhaps this can be an open question for you all to chew on?"

Gahan took his seat again, putting his feet up on the seat to his front. Anna tried her best to gauge everyone's reaction. There were irritated glances but smiles too. One by one, the Dreamers looked to Marion for a response. Rayleigh, Alby, and the Black Knight had retreated to stand by the statues at the back of the stage.

"It's a good question," said Marion. Anna recognized the twang in her accent but couldn't quite place it. Irish perhaps.

"But first, as I'm the Adjudicator, I'd like to set out the rules we should observe. When the first Council met in Andaluz long ago, we developed a format for the meeting. As set out in my little book you see me holding here, the first step back *then* is our first step *now*. As my predecessor was heard to say before we discuss what we must discuss, let's discuss how we will discuss it!"

There were a few eye rolls in the crowd, but when Anna turned to Teej, she saw he was smiling. Marion was taking control of the situation, and Teej liked it.

"First and foremost," said Marion, "There must be no threats of violence."

Marion turned to Rayleigh.

"No one is in danger here," said Gendo. Was he speaking on Rayleigh's behalf? It wasn't clear. "At least not from my master."

"Well, that's an easy assurance to make," said Marion. "But as my late husband would say, fine words butter no parsnips."

"I assure you anyone attempting to derail this peace talk with violence will doom themselves as well as all of us," replied Gendo. "You all know a little of the Amphitheater and its precarious nature. Let's continue on the assumption that we are not about to spiral off this mountain to our doom."

Marion gave Rayleigh, not Gendo, a curt nod. "Assuming we're all safe and tickety-boo and we can talk freely, let's consider the format and structure of this debate."

Teej leaned close to Anna. "Marion is not as foolish as she appears. She is defusing the tension. The Dreamers will roll their eyes as she drones on, but their shared impatience with her unites them."

"That's all fine," said Anna irritably. "But Alby is right there! And Rayleigh is a woman! How did that happen? We're surrounded by people who would probably kill us if they could, and we're not even talking about the Blood Plague."

"Just give it time. We'll get to all of that. We just need to keep our heads."

"Easy for you to say," snapped Anna. "You're not getting as many dirty looks as I am."

Teej nudged her. "They know you're an Undreamer. They know you're dangerous. You should take it as a compliment."

Anna shook her head. "That's not what I need to hear right now."

"My friends, we must be quiet," said Pappi. His warning came too late. Anna suddenly became aware that everyone was looking at her. Face red, Anna put her head down and waited for them to go on.

"You had something to say that could not wait?" Marion asked Anna. Anna coughed and shook her head.

"Everyone will have a chance: Aesthete, Metik, Undreamer or…" Marion gestured broadly at the Black Knight, "Miscellaneous. The Metiks of old were once more akin to allies than enemies. Let us treat them as such today."

Marion walked to the center of the stage.

"I have a suggestion. Maybe we should set aside our current situation. As Gahan so astutely pointed out, we must be clear on how this Council might succeed where others have failed. As Adjudicator, I suggest we call on our most knowledgeable member, or a coalition of such members, who might be able to set out the current crisis in terms as clear as the Mediterranean Sea. As you might be able to tell from my tan, I was just on holiday when I was called here, so you'll forgive me if my mind slips back to sandy beaches and cocktails. What was I saying… Ah yes! Perhaps some of our most clued-in colleagues might share what they know of this Blood Plague. Volunteers?"

"I will speak." The voice was loud and clear, and it came from the opposite end of the arena. Anna leaned forward in her seat to get a better look.

"Oh, no," groaned Teej.

"Who is it?" asked Elise.

Anna noticed the long curly red hair, but it was the white woolly coat that was most familiar.

"Leanan Sídhe," said Teej. "My ex-girlfriend. I think. I forget."

"Really!" said Elise with a leer.

Anna nudged Teej. "What do you think your Ex is going to say?"

"God knows," said Teej. "I hoped we'd never see her again."

"I debated whether I should return here or not," said Leanan wearily. "But now I realize there is no corner of the Firmament where the Blood Plague has not spread. I have travelled far, and there is no refuge from the disaster you have all wrought with the savagery of your petty squabbles. I cannot speak to the origins of this disease, but I can report on its scale. The Blood Plague is everywhere."

Leanan sat down abruptly. It seemed the crowd expected her to say more, but she was done.

"Well, that's certainly a grim picture you paint," said Marion. "We're all in a pickle, that's for sure. And if our friend Leanan has highlighted just *one* issue, it's how far the pickle has spread. I wonder though if someone might more clearly outline how we got here?"

There was a moment of silence, then the Dreamer with the long gray beard slowly got to his feet. Leaning on a cane, he took a wheezy breath as if the effort of merely standing was exhausting.

"Most of you know me as Ossian. I gather tales rather than share them, but today I will make an exception. The Blood Plague that afflicts us now has stricken us before. Our current manifestation was woven into existence by a Spiraling Haze, most likely by Mott. He may have had help from others, but we cannot say for sure. The Fluxa Haze in question happened approximately two years ago.

"The crux of our current situation is this: if a Dreamer consumes the blood of another Dreamer, they will swell with their victim's Vig. They will become more potent, their Art rejuvenated and strengthened. But the Blood Plague brings forth both spiritual and mental decay. At first, it seemed that taking the blood of Muses was the only vice that led to madness, but we have now seen what happens to Dreamers who consume one another. They, too, become monsters."

"Is this certain?" asked Andre from the other side of the auditorium. Their old friend from the Groven Museum was skulking in the corner. His confident demeanor seemed to have evaporated, replaced by temerity as he peaked out from behind dark sunglasses.

"If we are getting the facts correct, we should avoid exaggeration, no? We know taking the blood is bad, but are we certain it is *so* bad as you say?"

"I can't believe we let him go free," said Elise.

On the stage, Marion nodded in approval. "Our friend Andre has a good wee point there. We shouldn't assume things are worse than they are. But we seem to have a bit of evidence that says taking the blood isn't exactly recommended by nine out of ten doctors. And it's addictive. Isn't that right Andre?"

Andre shrugged as he sat down. "I wouldn't know."

"Yeah right," grumbled Anna.

Stumbling onto the stage, Ossian irritably waved away their comments. "We stand here today not because we need to diagnose a sickness. We are here because our community is *dying*. Yes, I use the word *community*, though it's been a long time since we've behaved like one. I am old enough to remember when Dreamers, Metiks and even Ancestrals were commonplace in the world. So common that a meeting like this would fill every seat in the auditorium and still more would stand to observe. A Blood Plague back then would endanger even a healthy community, but a sparse, fractious, and divided community stands no chance. Comrades, we stumble towards oblivion."

"You paint a rosy view of the past Ossian," said Rayleigh. She stood with her hand resting loosely on Alby's shoulder. Every time she spoke, Pappi bristled, but he was holding himself back. For now.

"We all know how things have changed," said Ossian. "And who is most responsible for those changes? I am old enough to remember the days when Metiks and Dreamers knew their place in society. The Dreamers inspired and created. The Metiks protected the Sleepers and oversaw the gaps between Basine and everything Behind the Veil. The balance was there. The order was built on tradition, and it safeguarded the common good. The routes into the Realm were open, and creatures and heroes of legend passed into and out of our world with ease, saturating every corner of the Firmament with Vig. Today, we hold Council with no Metiks invited. None, save those who have made their way here unbidden. Yet *I* welcome them."

Ossian looked directly at Anna, his old eyes clear.

"All good points Ossian, good points well made," said Marion patiently. "And for codgers like me and you, it's relevant, but for these younguns, maybe we need to stay on track, or we'll lose them. You know, less talk of the good old days."

"If we want to know where we are, we must look at the path we walked to get here," countered Ossian. "We must consider how our society operates, or fails to operate. If the way we govern ourselves is broken, then it must change for the sake ofour survival. Whether we choose leaders or not, leaders emerge. They must be held responsible for what has occurred, and if they are found wanting, they must be replaced."

Anna turned to Teej, and he shared the same hopeful expression she wore. Perhaps there was a chance to oust Rayleigh.

"We hear you Ossian," said Gendo. Again, he seemed to speak for Rayleigh. The whole auditorium bristled with tension, but Gendo remained calm. Rayleigh's dark eyes scanned the crowd, and most of the Dreamers avoided her gaze.

"And rest assured, a reckoning is coming for many of us," said Gendo. "But before we get to that, Marion, are we not jumping ahead? There is more information we can share about the nature of this plague" Gendo looked directly at Anna. "Before we pass judgement on those who have wronged our community?"

"Yes, quite right, Gendo," said Marion. "And thank you, Ossian. If you are done, we will now continue. Some good historical context there, for sure. Indeed, the only one who might know more about the history of our people and how we have handled similar cataclysms is Amara. I had hoped she would be able to attend. Does anyone know of her whereabouts?"

The Dreamers exchanged glances and there was murmuring, but no one spoke up. Rayleigh continued to glance darkly in Anna's direction. As those dark eyes burrowed into Anna, her chest began to ache once more.

"Should I say something?" Anna whispered to Teej as she pushed the palm of her hand into her chest to ease the pain.

"Not yet. This is going well. The focus is not on us. We don't need to intervene until Rayleigh slips up. When she says something, we can contradict; that's when we make our move. For now, the longer it is before everyone starts talking about the Undreamer and the Metiks, the better."

Anna was about to agree, but the pain in her chest intensified, taking her breath away.

"You alright?" asked Teej as he put his arm around her.

Pain is temporary. I have to get through this.

"Fine," said Anna as she attempted a smile. "Just not fully healed up yet."

"Has anyone else experienced this Blood Plague?" continued Marion. "Are any of you willing to admit to partaking of the blood? We will not cast judgement on anyone brave enough to make such an admission today."

"I will admit it." A pink-haired girl got to her feet and addressed the crowd. She looked young, with big eyes and a nervous demeanor. Her face was half-hidden behind a woolly scarf, and she shivered in the cold.

"Eleanor, this is no easy thing to confess," said Marion. "Please, dear, tell us what happened."

"You know her?" Anna asked Teej. Teej shook his head, but Pappi answered.

"Eleanor's Art is whimsy. She draws manga that comes to life. A peaceful, shy Dreamer, I did not think she would take blood, or admit to it."

"I lost my mentor," said Eleanor, her head down. "He liked to drink, but I didn't realize how bad it got. You may remember him as Sabra, the Draughtsman. He taught me everything about my Art. About the world Behind the Veil."

Tears came to Eleanor's eyes. She put her head in her hands.

"Keep going, dear," encouraged Marion.

"I don't know what made me do it. I don't know what made me think of it, but he was just right there. He must have hit his head on the desk when he fell. There was blood all over his books. I touched it with my fingertips, and it smelled... good."

"You tasted his blood?" asked Marion.

"I did. I took a lot. It made me stronger, but I knew it was wrong straight away. I knew I should be feeling grief and guilt, but instead, I felt nothing. The blood makes you numb. I had to get help."

"You did well to recognize that," said Marion encouragingly. "It must not have been easy."

Eleanor nodded tearfully. "Only one person was there for me. One person took me in, protected me, helped me come to terms with what I'd done, and to her, I swear I'll never betray the trust she showed in me."

"I don't like where this is going," muttered Anna.

"Rayleigh saved me," said Eleanor. "Without her, I'd be just another monster."

Gendo put his hand on his chest in mock solemnity and took a step towards the audience. "And we forgive you, young Eleanor.

This is how we will heal the community. Through patience and understanding, judgement where it is needed, but forgiveness where it is deserved."

"Thank you," breathed Eleanor.

"But if the blame does not lie with you, and I am sure no one here would be heartless enough to judge you for your actions in a moment of bereavement, is there anyone else you feel *was* to blame for this horrible accident?"

"Gendo!" said Marion with a shake of the head "I was nominated as the adjudicator for a reason. To keep this discussion on track. Don't make me send you to the back of the class."

"I apologize," wheezed the old man as he slicked back his greasy hair with long fingers. "I spoke out of turn."

"I'd like to answer, if that is all right," said Eleanor.

"Alright, go ahead dear," said Marion.

Eleanor bit her bottom lip in a way that rankled Anna immensely. "Well, it's just that Sabra's drinking was always bad, but it got so much worse after his brother died."

"Shit," breathed Teej.

"His brother?" asked Marion.

"Yes," said Eleanor with hesitation. "His brother was killed in a bar fight by a Metik. Murdered."

"This seems to be taking us off track," said Marion.

Anna fixed her gaze on Rayleigh, but her expression was too hard to read, so she looked at Gendo instead. His eyes were eager.

"Mustaine," said Eleanor. "Sabra's brother was called Mustaine, and he was murdered by a Metik who is sitting here tonight!"

There was a buzz around the arena, and nervous glances were exchanged. Anna felt their eyes on her. So many accusing glances. She swallowed and kept her head up. *So, this is our day in court.*

"This is bad," whispered Teej. "Keep cool."

"*You* keep cool," she muttered. His hand shook and his pupils were wide. "You did nothing wrong. If they accuse you of anything, it's a chance to tell your side of the story."

"Settle down," said Marion over the muttering. "Settle down! This Council is concerned with the spread of the Blood Plague and how we can fight it. Eleanor, thank you for your contribution and your honesty. You may sit now, dear. We need to keep this ship on course. We can come back to crimes committed later, and you can bet your bottom dollar, we will come back to the Metiks and their actions. Before that, though, we need to know how this whole thing started and whether anyone else here is afflicted. Now, wee Eleanor here is just a girl, and she admitted to taking the blood. Anyone else brave enough to fess up?"

Andre coughed as he got to his feet. "I am admitting it, too," he said. His head was down, hands behind his back. "I was taking the blood. I also managed to stop, thanks to Rayleigh's support."

"How much did you take?" asked Marion. She was much firmer in tone with Andre than with Eleanor.

"A lot," said Andre, his voice trembling. "And from many who were not already dead. I took from Muses instead of Dreamers, though."

Marion frowned. "That is still disappointing to hear. I know some of us care little for the safety of Muses, but most agree that we should avoid unnecessary suffering where we can. I see you're not completely off your rocker yet, Andre. I thought consuming the blood of Muses led to madness.

"It did," said Andre solemnly. "But Rayleigh guided me back to sanity. She was patient and forgiving. She gave me refuge in her home and once I felt safe there, the temptations faded. I owe her more than my life. I owe Rayleigh my soul."

"Bull*shit*," said Elise a little too loudly, eliciting angry glances from the people who sat around them.

"We're certainly getting glowing references for Rayleigh, even if we did not ask for them," said Marion. "You can sit down again and give your feet a rest Andre. Your mouth too."

"You are supposed to be neutral," complained the Dreamer. "I am being insulted."

"I can *try* to be impartial," said Marion with a scowl, "But I am *not* neutral. Sit down."

"If I might make a suggestion?" suggested Gendo nervously.

"No," said Marion. "It seems clear now that our Ms. Rayleigh is a prominent player in the origin of this plague. Judging by those who have spoken so far, she seems to have done much to help those afflicted within our community. When it is her chance to speak, I'd rather hear from her directly rather than from her surrogate mouth. Before that, can anyone speak to the originators of the Plague? We have all heard whispers that Mott was to blame, but we suspect he had allies. Correct?"

A breeze blew through the Amphitheater, and Anna pulled her cape close around her shoulders. Should she speak now? She wanted to tell them everything; about the Doxa, Drowden, the Sump, the fights she'd fought and won to bring her here, but instead she kept quiet. There would be a time to tell her story, but it wasn't now.

"I would speak," said Elizabeth Needham. As she slowly rose to her feet, she drew in a long, weary breath. *Not easy to do in a corset.*

The two employees from the August Club stood on either side of her as Needham surveyed the crowd, waiting for everyone to give her their attention. Her smooth voice dominated the space.

"We know the Doxa was at fault. Mott did not act alone, he conspired with John Murray Speare, Drowden, and Ozman. They formed a cabal, called themselves *'the Doxa'* and sought to create a Fluxa Haze. They were prevented from doing so by my husband, Wildey. My husband, a hero who is now missing, and I assume murdered, by Rayleigh."

There was a sharp intake of breath throughout the Amphitheater. Elise put her hand over her mouth. Teej reeled back in his seat. Someone shouted, "Lies!" and then more people shouted back, and the Amphitheater erupted into chaos. Elizabeth

Needham remained unmoved. She waited for the noise to die down, but the angry crowd wouldn't settle.

"Quiet. Quiet!" called out Marion. "Everyone will be allowed to speak here. These are serious accusations. Do you have evidence, Ms. Needham?"

"If you want to know more, it must come from the Undreamer and her Metik friends."

They waited for Needham to continue, but she simply sat down again, her stoic demeanor undisturbed by the chaos she had created. Some of the Dreamers seemed outraged, others, afraid. Anna kept her gaze on Rayleigh, who returned the stare. Her eyes were so dark Anna felt like she was falling into them.

"The Metiks have failed us," cried Gendo over the rabble. "Are they not supposed to protect the Dreamers as well as their own kind? Where were they when we needed them? Where were they when Wildey disappeared?"

"Gendo, you have had your say," snapped Marion. "If Needham has no evidence to provide, we should hear from the Metiks. They may clarify this situation. Who will speak on their behalf?"

"That's your cue," Teej whispered to Anna.

They all turned to look at her: Gahan, Gendo, Andre, Marion, Ossian, Eleanor, her friends, even the Black Knight.

Reluctantly, Anna got to her feet. It was time.

"I..." she had so much to say, but the words died in her throat. Where could she start? Should she talk about Wildey's death? Describe her battles with the Mott and Drowden? Explain what happened to Amara? Demand Alby be returned to his brother? Accuse Rayleigh of orchestrating everything from behind the scenes?

Anna stood open-mouthed. Their eyes bore into her. Rayleigh's gaze was expressionless. The soft snow drifted down, wreathing her in ghostly white.

Teej got to his feet to stand by Anna's side. He squeezed her hand, and she turned to see little snowflakes on his eyelashes.

"I have been with Anna since the beginning. If anyone questions her character, I am here to help her answer."

"Good," wheezed Gendo. "Because she has much to answer for."

He gestured to Marion. "If it is our time to speak?"

"This is where the knife meets the bone," said Marion. "I reckon we have two different stories to hear, and it's up to us to choose which one we believe. Let's settle it in the court of public opinion."

Marion walked a few steps closer to the audience to speak more directly to Anna. "You seem to be lost for words. Perhaps Gendo should go first, dear? I don't know you yet, but I want to be fair. Maybe you should hear his argument before you have a chance to share?"

Anna nodded mutely.

"I have something to add, first," said Pappi.

"Please," said Marion.

"Whatever Anna stands accused of, I stand by her also."

"As do I," said Teej.

Teej nudged Elise.

"What?" She was confused but jumped to her feet. "Do I get a vote? Then I stand by Anna, too."

"Very well," said Gendo. "The Metiks have thrown their lot in with the Undreamer."

He turned to Alby, who remained silent. "Most of them anyway. As such, the accusations I will make are specific to Anna, but if proven guilty, the wait of the responsibility must fall, at least in part, on the shoulders of *all* these Metiks. The whole must bear the burden of the one."

"So it must be," Pappi said under his breath.

"And I am right in saying Rayleigh won't be speaking herself?" asked Marion. "Although these accusations come from her?"

Rayleigh shook her head. "Gendo will speak."

"Alrighty then," said Marion far too breezily. "Let's hear what Anna did wrong. What's your version of events, Gendo?"

Gendo made a sweeping gesture with his arm across the whole auditorium. "The Undreamer's crimes have undermined the goals of this Council and cost innocent Dreamers their lives. She has repeatedly made choices that have allowed the Blood Plague to spread, and she has endangered us all. Furthermore, she murdered our brothers and sisters in cold blood. In short, the Blood Plague is the disease killing us all, but the Undreamer is a symptom of that disease. We must excise her from the community if we are to heal."

As he spoke, Gendo's mouth was wet like he was salivating. His words dripped with spite, but he was convincing, and Anna could see several nods of approval around the auditorium. There were many here who agreed with him already.

"I shall begin," said Gendo with relish, "By telling you all the story of how Anna pursued and murdered the Midnight Man."

thirty-nine

Though she knew she should be listening closely, Anna's eyes wandered off to the cityscape beyond the Amphitheater. The clear skies hadn't lasted long. The heavy gray clouds had returned to smother the streets of Plovdiv with a heavy blanket of snow.

As Gendo continued with his long list of accusations, Anna knew she should be defending herself. Instead, all she could think of was running away. Running down the stairs, through the tunnel, out into the snowy streets, then further, all the way back home. Anywhere but here.

Elise nudged her.

"I'm listening!" said Anna.

"It's not that," whispered Elise. She was pointing at her watch. "Merry Christmas, Anna."

It was five past midnight. Anna grinned. "Merry Christmas, Elise."

Anna turned her focus back to Gendo's lecture. His face was red.

"Furthermore, the Undreamer did not only burn Mott alive without showing any sign of remorse, but she went on to pursue his fellow Dreamers. The Undreamer justified her actions by claiming there was a conspiracy she called *'the Doxa'*. Scant evidence for this conspiracy exists. Indeed, the only ones who seem to have faced this conspiracy are the Undreamer and her mentor Donnel, now going by the name *'Teej',* a Metik who shows obvious signs of mental damage following the Spiral of a Haze. A Haze, I should add, where his actions contributed to the death of his previous partner, Linda, and where he aided and abetted the known dissenter and murderer, Wildey."

"Hey!" shouted Elise. "It's not just Anna and Teej. I've seen the Doxa, too. And so have Pappi and Alby. The Doxa killed Vinicaire. You all know the Doxa were real. Why are you pretending you don't?"

Elise's face was red, but Teej motioned for her to sit.

"I know you are angry," said Marion softly. "But you will get your chance to have your say. I promise."

"Ah, Vinicaire," said Gendo as he skipped forward with a cruel grin, obliquely mocking Elise's mentor. "We will get to his death soon enough, but it will take time to catalogue all of the crimes you and your conspirators committed at Avalon."

"Quiet now," said Teej. Though he put his hand on her arm, Elise pulled away. "Why are we just sitting here and taking this?!" she hissed.

"Listen to me," said Teej under his breath, "Look at Pappi. Look at him! Think of how hard this is for him to endure. And *yet* he endures it. Sit *down*. We will have our chance."

Reluctantly Elise lowered herself onto her seat. Anna felt her friend's frustration, but she wanted to hear what preposterous accusation Gendo would make next.

"Destroying Malamun. Traipsing along the Moonlight Road, damaging it as she went. Attacking Andre DeLorde, luring him into a trap, then kidnapping him. There is no limit to how much destruction the Undreamer has wrought. Barely in control of her Praxis, she is a maelstrom, and we can all see it.

"The Metiks talk about the Will, the Word, the Sight, and the Sword, do they not? This Undreamer's Will is to hunt and kill Aesthetes wherever she finds them. She uses the Word recklessly, subjugating her enemies to her commands. For this Undreamer, the Sight is used to find and stalk her targets, and when she tracks them down, her Sword is one of pure, flaming vengeance. This emotional woman is the most dangerous threat we face—self-righteous and powerful enough to wield her flame, but too weak to control it. Angry and volatile, she brandishes her trauma as an emblem to justify the chaos she spreads. My friends, the Blood Plague is a threat to us all, but this Undreamer may be even worse. The Blood Plague is something we all know to be evil, but this Undreamer believes herself to be a force for good. She is mistaken, as are *we* if we do not stop her, now. Today."

The whites of Gendo's eyes were brighter than the snow. His finger pointed at Anna in accusation. This was a witch hunt, and everyone here had already agreed she was a witch.

"Do we get a chance to defend ourselves now?" asked Teej.

Almost everyone.

Teej stood unbowed. "We have a few things to say about Rayleigh. About her support of the Doxa and the attacks she has committed on me and my friends."

Marion opened her mouth to answer, but Gendo sneered and stepped in front of her.

"This isn't a trial to decide if Rayleigh will be deposed. This is a trial to decide if you will all be executed."

"Gendo!" snapped Marion. "This is not a trial *at all!*" He flinched, and Anna felt the tiniest rumble in the stone under her feet. Marion had almost used the Word, and Gendo knew it. Everyone knew it.

"I will not tolerate this! I was asked to adjudicate, and that's what I'm going to do. God help me boyo, if you push me any further, I won't use my Art to put you straight, I'll do it by putting my toe up your arse!"

Chastened, Gendo slithered away from Marion. As she took a calming breath, Anna heard someone laugh. It might have been Gahan.

"I like her," Anna said to Teej, but he was rapt and didn't hear her.

"You have accusations to make against me too?" asked Teej. "Make them now. Mustaine? The Apoth? Are you going to pin them on me? Let's hear your version, Gendo."

"Yes," said Gendo as he smoothed back his greasy hair with one hand. Though the snow continued to fall, his forehead was dappled with sweat.

"Yes, you are surely to blame for the deaths of both Mustaine and John Murray Speare. You may claim they attacked you first, but neither needed to die. Your response was disproportionate. You were cruel and without mercy. But the worst of your sins can't match the worst of Anna's. She committed the ultimate crime. All other infractions may have some explanation or excuse, but for these most heinous of actions, there can be no absolution. No redemption."

"Well?" prompted Marion. "Get on with it. What did she do?"

Once again Gendo stepped to the front of the arena to make his appeal to the crowd. Anna reminded herself that he was just a puppet. This was all about Rayleigh. No matter how innocent she looked or how quiet she was now, Rayleigh was the real enemy.

"The Sump. We all know the name. The older Dreamers know it as Avicimat. A place worse than death. Anna travelled to that accursed place, seeing it as the ultimate prison for her enemies. With malice, she tricked her opponents and trapped them there. Both Ozman and Drowden wasted away till they were consumed by the Black Water. Who amongst you might she send there next?"

Anna shook her head. "You're wrong."

"Am I though? I see the faintest guilt in your eyes. Perhaps some vestige of conscience might yet remain. You grieve for the ones you left behind. The woman and her girl. They showed you kindness, and you repaid them with callous abandon. Does the girl's body lie at the bottom of the Black Water now? A testament to your cruelty?"

"How do you know about Char and Fee?" asked Anna, barely aware of her own words.

"You see!" shouted Gendo with glee. "She denies nothing. She is guilty."

"I didn't want to leave them behind," said Anna weakly.

"I believe you. I do. I think you are not beyond redemption, but first, you must confront your crimes. You must admit what you are doing. You are destroying yourself."

Gendo took a step back as if he had received an invisible command, then Rayleigh spoke.

"No one alive has burned like you burn, Anna. Those flames will consume us all, whether you want them to or not."

Rayleigh scanned the crowd, casting her gaze from one Dreamer to the next.

"*That* is Anna's deepest secret. She cares nothing for *our* world because *her* world is at an end. Anna wants to die."

Elise and Teej both looked at her with concern. Anna put her head down and collapsed into her seat. She waited for them to say something, anything, but her friends were silent. It was too late. Everyone already believed Rayleigh. All she could do now was hold back her flames and try to keep control.

"No," said Pappi. Anna lifted her head out of her hands to see the tall Mctik looking straight at her. The snow seemed to dance around him as if it didn't want to disturb his serenity. He was the most patient, most tranquil man she had ever met.

"The Anna I know is none of the things you claim. You say she is cruel, but I know her kindness. You say she is merciless, yet I know her as someone who fights only when she must. You say she feels the darkness, so she inflicts it on others, but you are *wrong*. Anna feels the darkness and yet she turns it inwards to protect her friends. She would let that darkness destroy her to save them."

The stillness all around the Amphitheater was suffocating. Nervous glances were exchanged.

"I am not the only one who feels this way," said Pappi, finally. He might have been waiting for someone to back him up, but no one else got to their feet. Pappi stood alone.

Anna's head went down again. Pappi was brave to speak, but his word alone would not be enough. The Dreamers didn't trust the word of Metiks. If Anna had any chance, she needed more Dreamers to come forward. More than just her friends.

"I don't know these people well," said Leanan. She rose, her emerald eyes bright like warning lights. "And I don't stand for *or* against the accused. Maybe Anna has committed these crimes. Maybe not. I don't care much for Pappi's opinion, but I don't care much for *any* man's opinion. Long ago, when I believed such a thing as a *'good man'* was possible, I thought Donnel might be one. Or at least a decent one, if a little weak. Now, I think only his weakness remains."

"Revenge of the jilted," muttered Elise.

"But nothing I've heard here convinces me that any of the rest of you want to make things better either. All I hear are the same old squabbles, the maneuvering, the politics. Half of you look at this existential threat as a chance to better your position. The other half sit and watch with quiet fear. Let me tell you, your teeth-sucking attitude will doom us all. If you say nothing today, if you stand for nothing, you doom us all. I don't know these Metiks well, but I know that accusing the Undreamer is not the answer. If Rayleigh is your solution, I want my problem back."

Leanan didn't sit. She had more to say.

"I won't allow you to turn this debate into a mock trial that diverts us from the real problems. If you ask me to take a side in this enmity between you and her, to choose which is worse, the inept leader or the reckless open flame, I chose the latter. I'm with Anna. You *all* deserve to burn."

Leanan sat again, leaving the auditorium in stunned silence.

"Did that… help us?" whispered Elise. "I have no idea what you ever saw in her, Teej."

"I see it," said Anna.

Elise rolled her eyes. "If you say so."

"Alrighty," said Marion as she rubbed her forehead. "Well, if we've heard from everyone who wants to speak either for or against Anna, maybe it's time we heard her defense."

"Wait!" called out Gahan as he swung his legs over his seat and lazily got to his feet again. "I'd better say something."

"Any idea what's coming next?" Teej asked Anna.

"From Gahan? No."

"I've spent some time with Anna. She was going by the name *'Kas'* at the time, and I pegged her as cute but dangerous. Right enough, I believe *everything* Gendo says about her. If I was siding with someone in this debate, it would be Gendo, no question. I could certainly trust his word over Anna's."

"What a bitch," breathed Elise.

"Did you dump him?" asked Teej. "Or run over his mom? With friends like these…"

"No, you don't get it," said Anna with a chuckle. "No one trusts Gahan. No one believes him, and he knows that. He knows what he's doing. This is the only way he can help us now."

"I get it!" said Elise. "I think…"

"I don't see what that added to proceedings," said Marion with a scowl. "But you had your say, Gahan, so please be seated. I believe it's time we heard from Anna."

Marion gave her a nod of reassurance. "This is your chance to defend yourself. Take your time dear. I'll make sure you're not interrupted."

This was it. Anna's chance to prove them all wrong. To make her case against Rayleigh, to propose a peace treaty, to find an answer to the Blood Plague. Was there a combination of words that could achieve all those goals? And could she do it without losing control again?

Anna looked to Teej, and he gave her a reassuring smile. He would be by her side the whole time.

No.

Anna put her hand on his shoulder and shook her head. He couldn't help her right now. She had to do this alone. She pushed him down into his seat and gave him a look she hoped told him she was ready for this.

She took a breath to steady herself. If Anna was going to convince them all, she'd have to be completely honest, even if that meant revealing parts of herself she'd hidden for a very long time.

"Where to start?" she said, her voice weak in her own throat. She swallowed, took a moment to compose herself and spoke louder. "I guess I must seem like some kind of monster to most of you. I didn't ask to be an Undreamer. Or a Metik. If you want to call me reckless, well, that's fair. Most of the time, I have no idea what I'm doing."

Forcing herself to look at their faces, Anna glanced around the arena and realized how many of them were not looking back. Nervous glances were exchanged between some of the Dreamers, while others couldn't tear their eyes away from the Black Knight. Some looked at Rayleigh, but only for a moment, as if they feared attracting her attention. Most looked at Gendo and Marion. Anna's accuser and the adjudicator. Resolutely, Anna decided she would *make* them all look at her. If they were about to condemn her to death, they'd better look her in the eye first.

"When Teej found me, I was clueless. I was with my friend. We'd both been slipped a date rape drug. Do you all understand what that is? I guess you do. I thought the monsters were all in my head, until they killed my best friend."

Anna let out a sigh. Was this the right story to tell? Yes, it was her story.

"I suppose I could have let the Midnight Man surrender, but I burned him alive. I don't feel bad about that. He killed Sue, for no reason—for sport. And I learned later he'd killed lots of other innocent people, too.

"Teen almost died for me that night. Not for the last time. He might not be the best teacher, and I'm sure as Hell not the best student, but he's never let me down.

"Since I joined you all Behind the Veil, I'd heard about the Doxa from day one. It seems they're the worst kept secret society since the Illuminati. Are they real, too? I forget sometimes. Dragons are real but unicorns aren't? Vampires exist but zombies are made up? I don't know how long it took you all to figure this stuff out, but it seems I'm still getting it all wrong.

"Drowden told me about the Doxa on Malamun just before he ordered one of his hench-robots to cut my best friend's head off her shoulders. So, yes, I wrecked that place too. But I was being chased by a ghost bear… or something. So, I really didn't have time to come up with a better plan.

"When I ended up in the Sump after being sucked through a portal in my parent's summer house, I felt like every dark thought I'd ever had was pulled out my head and molded into a world of pure despair. I sat on the edge of the Black Water, and I wanted to jump in so badly. It's a horrifying place for anyone, but for someone whose husband drowned at midnight after jumping off a bridge… well it's worse. It's so much worse.

"So yeah, I didn't save my husband Sam, and I didn't save Ozman or Char or Fee either. I barely saved myself. I somehow scammed my way out of the Sump, partly because my friends sent help, partly because that big, red-cloaked monster was amused by the idea of letting me go. I think in some way he knew one day I'd go back. And I *did* go back."

Anna swung open her red cloak and held her head high.

"This isn't the first time I've met Rayleigh, either, though she spoke through a surrogate back then, too."

Anna shot a dismissive look at Gendo.

"I thought Rayleigh was a man. I guess you were?" She looked directly at Rayleigh.

"You recreated the church where I married Sam. You poisoned me. You sent the Green Knight to kill my friends, and you goaded me from the shadows."

Rayleigh didn't respond.

"Will you deny all this?" asked Anna, her voice shaking. "Will you tell them it didn't happen?"

"I can talk if you want me to," said Rayleigh. "If I do, everything will come out."

"That's a threat," said Anna. "You think I have too much to hide. I don't care anymore. Go ahead."

Gendo stepped in front of Rayleigh to point a finger at Anna.

"It is true you came to Rayleigh. She believed you might talk of peace, of reconciliation. But everything in that Haze you describe was formed by your own Praxis. Rayleigh did not choose the church to frighten you, your own madness shaped it. Rayleigh did not threaten you, she tried to help you. When she learned of the doomed expedition to Avalon, Rayleigh warned against it and even sent her ally the Green Knight to help make the best of a bad situation. At every stage, Rayleigh has sought to help you come to terms with your madness. This desire for conflict comes only from you."

"You poisoned me."

"Self-defense," whined Gendo.

Anna shook her head. "There are witnesses to most of these events, whether you believe them or not. There would be more if we hadn't fought so hard. We lost Vinicaire and Garret to Rayleigh. I guess we've lost Alby too, though we won't stop fighting to get him back."

Alby was glancing at his feet, but Anna spoke to him.

"Alby, I don't know what happened to you, but you're still my friend. When you tried to kill me, I know it wasn't really you."

"More lies," said Gendo. "Alby did not attack you. You were conspiring with the traitor Wildey. While we sought treatment for the Blood Plague, you planned a bloody revolution."

"A treatment?" snapped Anna. "Who has Rayleigh successfully treated?"

"Andre, of course," said Gendo. "And many more, including the one you abandoned at Albion. Alby."

"No," said Pappi as he came to stand by Anna. "My brother did not take the blood. This is a lie. You compelled him."

"No!" screamed Gendo. "*You* compelled him, Pappi. You used the blood of the Apoth's failed experiment to bring your brother back from the brink of death."

"I… no," said Pappi weakly.

"You know it is true. You found his broken body, and you used the Vig from the carcass of the New Motive Power to save your brother. The blood that ran through that dead God's veins was tainted, and it corrupted Alby. Inflicted him with madness. It is a small mercy that Rayleigh was able to separate the two of you, for away from your corrupting influence, Alby is finally regaining his senses. We managed to wean him off the blood. His mind remains troubled, but his thinking is clearer than it was."

Pappi's hands curled into fists. For a moment, Anna felt the swelling of Vig within his body, but it stalled, and he collapsed into his seat, defeated.

Anna put her hand on his shoulder. He thought they were beaten, but for the first time, Anna saw a weakness. Gendo had made a mistake.

"Wait, what did you say?" said Anna. "You knew about the New Motive Power? So, you must have known about the Doxa too?"

"No, not necessarily," said Gendo. "You see…"

"There's no way to weasel out of this," said Anna firmly. "You knew about the Doxa all along. And you, Rayleigh, did nothing to stop them."

"We sent Raguel to stop them!"

"A bit fucking late! You only sent Raguel when Teej and all my friends were already there. And you knew what you were sending him to do. You knew about the Doxa! You knew about the New Motive Power and their Fluxa Haze. You knew how dangerous they were, but you were too busy pursuing your ancient fight with Wildey to do anything to stop them. You let the Doxa grow and swell in power, all the while allowing the Blood Plague to get worse, purely so that me and my friends would get desperate, go to Wildey for help, and lead you right to him. It's clear for everyone to see now."

"We all see how you twist the truth, Undreamer."

"Quiet!" snapped Marion. "You have had your say. Allow Anna to speak."

"Thank you," breathed Anna. She took a deep breath. This was it. This was how they would win. She had to stay calm now and lay everything out as clearly as she could.

"You see we have witnesses to our version of events. More than you have for yours. I bet even Needham and Andre would contradict the picture of me painted by Gendo."

This was where it could all fall apart. Either of them could object. Anna felt their steely glances directed back at her, but neither had anything to say.

"We now know Gendo is lying about the Doxa. But Rayleigh is powerful, and you all fear her. Rightly so. The question then is, do you fear her enough to swallow all of these lies? Because only one of us can be telling the truth."

Anna took a deep breath, closed her eyes, and allowed herself one second of doubt. Was this next move a good one? Or was this where she fell into Rayleigh's trap? She had to go for it. She had to bet that the trust she had for her friends was stronger than the power of Rayleigh's lies and deceit.

"I can settle this whole argument for you right now!" Anna was shouting now, her anger righteous, fueled by both fear and desperate hope. She felt her fingertips hot with her flame, but she forced the fire down into her belly and swallowed it.

"I ask one more person to speak on our behalf. To validate everything I have said, and to prove once and for all that Rayleigh is the real threat here. Alby. Speak now."

There was a buzz around the arena again. Many of the Dreamers shook their heads. When she looked at her friends, Teej was worried, Elise was confused, and Pappi had his head down in dismay. This was a long shot. Had she just doomed them all?

"Alby," prompted Marion. "Will you speak in support of Anna? Or Rayleigh? Can you tell us your version of events?"

The boy's body seemed to tremble. His lips pursed, and his hands curled into tight fists. Alby looked like a bomb about to go off, but as the seconds ticked by, he didn't respond. Marion gestured to Anna for guidance, but Anna held her hand up for more time. Just a little longer.

"I don't remember what happened at Avalon," said Alby finally. His voice was faint, barely audible over the sound of rustling clothes and wind.

"You see!" shouted Gendo. "The boy is broken. Why do you make him confront his abusers? Rayleigh redeemed him. The stress of talking here will only set him backwards on his journey to recovery."

"Alby," prompted Marion gentled. "Is there anything you can say now? Anything you can contribute to this debate?"

"I don't remember," repeated Alby. "I am sure the blood was used to keep me alive. I wished for death, but it did not come. I remember the gunshot. My chest, mostly gone. The smell of my burnt flesh. Then nothing."

"And then you were saved by Rayleigh," said Gendo. "Redeemed! Allowed to heal."

"I was not…" Alby looked up for the first time. He met his brother's gaze. Frozen in place, he opened his mouth to speak but seemed unable to continue.

"This pains him!" shouted Gendo. "Adjudicator, you cannot let this continue!"

Marion bit her bottom lip. "The lad is struggling. I think we need to stop."

"Enough of this!" cried Gendo. He reached out to Alby to pull him back.

Pappi jumped to his feet suddenly. Anna stepped in front of him, fearful he had lost his temper, but when she looked in his eyes, all she saw was grim resolve. She stepped away.

"Brother, they shout to scare us off," said Pappi.

No response.

Pappi refused to sit down, refused to give up. He waited for his brother's reply.

"Confidence is quiet," said Alby finally. "And refuses to bow to fear."

"What is this?" said Gendo.

"Quiet!" snapped Marion. "Alby?"

"I don't remember it well, but I know that my brother did not let me down! I failed *him*! I succumbed to Rayleigh's manipulation. Through Gendo, I was fed her lies. Perhaps she helped me, but something is wrong with me now. I still don't know what is real and what is not, who manipulates me and who seeks to save me. But I know this: my brother did not betray me. Nor did Anna."

"This changes a lot," said Marion. Flushed, she put her hand to her head and leaned on the nearby column. "But without some memory of the events Anna describes, we still can't say for sure who is lying. Can you recall anything of the Doxa? The Blood Plague? Did Rayleigh imprison you?"

"It did not feel like imprisonment. It still does not. But…"

"Gendo," said Rayleigh darkly. "You should not have pushed the boy like this."

"What?!" cried Gendo. His expression was suddenly desperate. "I… You told me to…"

"Of what I understand," said Alby, "I have heard Anna tell no lies."

The whole arena erupted into a raucous debate. Dreamers were shouting, some raising fists, others shaking their heads. Gendo cowered, suddenly in fear for his safety. Alby's head went down again. He looked exhausted. When Anna turned to Pappi, she saw tears in his eyes. Joy, sorrow, and relief all at once. Teej wore a desperate look of hope. Elise just looked confused.

"Please, can we have some order!" said Marion, but her strained voice was drowned out by the din. As Dreamer confronted Dreamer and debates and arguments erupted across the Amphitheater, Anna realized both Alby and Pappi were silently staring at each other. Finally, Alby started to walk towards them. The huge Black Knight blocked his path, but as Alby walked towards him, he looked to Rayleigh. Perhaps Anna was the only one who saw it, but Rayleigh gave him the tiniest of nods, and the Black Knight stepped aside. Alby began to walk up the stairs towards them.

"That was risky," said Teej.

"I know," said Anna. She was glad they had a moment to talk during the disruption.

"Was this your plan all along?"

"No," said Anna with a laugh. "I'm just making this up as I go along."

She rubbed her chest with the heel of her hand, trying to brush away what felt like the worst heartburn of her life.

"This will all be over soon," said Teej. "We can get you healed up. Get you some new clothes. You know, I forgot to eat dinner."

"What's wrong with my clothes?" asked Anna, pulling aside her red cloak to show fragments of burned fabric. "And dinner!? You're thinking of food *now?"*

Teej rubbed his chin. "I've always dreamed of going to Venice, eating *baccala mantecato* by the canal."

Anna laughed. "That's your dream? That's your priority right now? Pasta?"

"Hey! I'm just trying to lighten the mood. It's mean to laugh at people's dreams. You know who else had a dream everyone laughed at?"

"You."

Teej crossed his arms in mock anger.

"Hey, third wheel here!" said Elise as she elbowed her way between Anna and Teej. "We were *supposed* to go back to Japan, remember."

"Can I join you?" interrupted Alby.

"Of course," said Anna, stepping aside so Alby could squeeze past to join his brother.

"Order!" shouted out Marion. The crowd was beginning to settle down, with most of the Dreamers taking their seats again.

Pappi reached out to hug him, but Alby hesitated.

"It is not so simple as you think," said Alby. "My mind is still conflicted. Rayleigh is neither wrong nor right. But for what it is worth, Anna, I am sorry for attacking you. I was not myself."

"We don't need to talk about it right now," said Anna. "You are back."

"Am I?" said Alby doubtfully. "It will never be the same between us."

Pappi looked down on him with a smile. "That is life, my brother. Relationships change. This is normal. We must work at them to keep them alive. I did not give up on you."

"Nor did I," said Alby.

"I knew where the truth of your heart lay," said Pappi.

"This is cute and all," said Elise. "But shouldn't we be ready for what they accuse us of next? It seems like Rayleigh will have something else planned."

"You are wise to be cautious now, Elise," said Alby. "You must have already realized what Rayleigh fears most of all."

"Wildey," said Anna. "But he's dead."

"Still, this is how she thinks. She fears an attack from the grave. You must use this. Rayleigh *does* want to stop the Blood Plague, but her ancient enmity with Wildey consumes her. You all may doubt me, and I do not blame you, but I am not lying when I say she is not as wicked as she seems."

"We'll see," said Anna reluctantly. "Elise has given me an idea."

"Great!" said Elise. "What idea?"

"Here, take this," said Anna as she shook the cape off her shoulders and gave it to Teej.

"You'll freeze," he replied.

"It's about the optics," said Anna. "And I'm sweating. This pain in my chest is getting worse. I'm burning up. I just have to get through this."

Anna coughed loudly and waited for them to notice her. The din was already dying down, and she hoped the sight of an angry woman standing defiantly, half-naked in scorched rags in the snow might attract their attention. It worked.

"Anna," called out Marion. "You have more to add?"

"I do," said Anna. Gradually the noise abated, and Anna felt the weight of everyone's expectation on her shoulders.

"I want to propose something," she said.

"We will hear it," said Marion, "But first, we need to conclude this dispute. The accusations between you and Rayleigh must be set to rest."

"I have more evidence to bring to bear!" said Gendo desperately. "This is just the beginning of Anna's crimes. There is more, much more. We have not even begun to discuss her desire to die. Anna is trying to destroy herself, and everyone else with her, because she caused the death of—"

"No," interrupted Rayleigh. Her ghost-white face seemed to blend in with the snowy cityscape behind her. She stepped to the front of the stage and turned to face Gendo, who cowered in response.

"I do not support Gendo in these accusations."

The whites of Gendo's eyes were huge. His arms went in front of his face like he was being physically attacked.

"No… Wait! Why is this happening? I did what I was told!"

"What is going on here?" asked Marion. "Let me get this straight: when Gendo made those accusations, you did not support them?"

"Did you hear me say that I did?" replied Rayleigh.

"What is going on?" Anna whispered to Teej.

"She's straight murdering him," said Elise. "Right?"

Teej nodded. "We won. But Rayleigh will sacrifice Gendo to save herself."

"Well, this is confusing," said Marion as she shrugged. "Rayleigh, what *do* you accuse Anna of?"

"Recklessness perhaps," said Rayleigh.

"That's all?" said Marion. "Well then, what do you want to do now?"

"Move on," said Rayleigh.

"Do you propose we just forget this all happened? What about the accusations Anna made about you?"

"Which ones?" said Rayleigh wearily.

"Kidnap. Sending Raguel to kill your enemies. Your attack on Anna in the church. Is Gendo not your acolyte?"

"He was, but now he is more of an equal partner and one who has acted on his own devices," said Rayleigh. "I left him with the responsibility to carry out some instructions, and he went entirely too far."

"You're a monster," muttered Gendo.

"Fortunately for you, I am not," said Rayleigh. "Leave now. You're not part of this Council anymore. If we decide on your fate, we won't struggle to find you."

Gendo looked to Marion in desperation, but she just shrugged.

"Undreamer, this cannot stand!" shouted Gendo. "Say something, now! Tell them I was not behind these attacks. It was all Rayleigh."

"Or," said Rayleigh, "Let Gendo leave, let us drop these petty squabbles, and now that you are reunited with your friend Alby, let us talk freely about how we can stop this Blood Plague."

Teej tugged on Anna's sleeve. "We can't just let her off the hook. She killed Garret."

"And Vinicaire," said Elise. "And she took Alby away from us. Away from his brother."

Anna looked at Pappi, but he was shaking his head. "My brother stands by my side. Do whatever you feel is best."

Taking a moment to think, Anna knew what she must do. Though her friends might not like it, she had to walk away from this fight. Her flames cooled.

"We should move past this," Anna said to Marion. "We need to focus on the Blood Plague, and how we stop it."

Marion looked exhausted. She shook her head in disbelief as she paced the stage. "I cannot get my head around this. You lot are a headache, you really are. Alright! Gendo, I suggest you take your leave."

The Dreamer was already halfway down the stairs at the rear of the Amphitheater. Anna didn't know where they led, but she was sure he would break into a run when he got to the bottom. As the Black Knight backed off and Marion stood aside, Rayleigh stood alone on the stage.

"Another mask falls away," said Pappi.

"I'm going to push for something now," Anna whispered to Teej. "Back me up."

She cleared her throat then waited for them to give her their attention. It didn't take long.

"I want to propose something," said Anna as loudly as she could. "Everyone here wants to stop the Blood Plague. We would not have come otherwise. The only way to fight this plague is by helping those who are already afflicted and standing against those who refuse that help.

"We have to form a pact and promise one another we will not give in to temptation. There is no way for me or anyone else to police those who break the pact, but it can be enforced if *everyone* polices it. You will have to become a proper community. More united. Even as your numbers dwindle, this is a way for you to become stronger. And if the Dreamer sitting to the right or the left of you falls, *everyone* must unite in condemning them, and if necessary, standing against them. Together."

Was this working? Unbelievably, Anna saw some heads nodding in agreement. She had to keep pushing.

"We need to draw up a charter. A promise that we will reject the temptations of the Blood. It will be like a…"

Anna turned to Elise, looking for help.

"A Magna Carta," mouthed Elise.

"Yeah! A modern Magna Carta, signed by everyone here today as a first step to not only fighting this plague but ensuring we never spiral into civil war like this again. Who knows, maybe someday peace will become the default. And if fighting breaks out, well, that will be the exception."

There was a faint murmur of approval throughout the arena, but it was Rayleigh who spoke first, and her words stunned everyone.

"There is precedent. Long ago, there were peace accords. They stood between the Ancestrals and the first Dreamers, but it is not impossible to imagine another such arrangement. There would need to be mechanisms in place to protect this peace."

"Are we agreeing on something?" asked Marion, mouth agape. "Now I've seen it all. As regards precedent, I also have record of a similar peace accord in my historical records. And for what it's worth, I agree with you both. A peace treaty could staunch the bloodshed. Further, I think I know of a way to enforce such a treaty."

"Go on," said Rayleigh, her eyes narrowing.

"Well, it's very much as the young lady suggested," said Marion. "We all *want* this peace. I see it in your eyes when I look around. However, we cement that desire for peace—whether we all sign a fancy parchment in blood or swear a solemn oath—the result is the same. We make a promise. A promise to each other. Hear and now. We promise that if one of us here abuses the power of the blood plague, the rest of us unite against them."

"I can go a step further," said Rayleigh. "I can promise the safety of anyone who abides by the peace treaty."

"How?" asked Anna. "How can you protect anyone?"

"With my resources. With everything at my disposal. Anyone who knows me knows I may have faults, but failing to stand by my word is not one of them. And my word here is thus: if you do not partake of the blood, and you come to me for support or shelter, you will find it. I swear it."

Anna guffawed, but Marion held up her hand.

"Do not mock this promise. I know Rayleigh, faults and all, and I know she speaks truth. When she makes a promise, she keeps it. Furthermore, making a promise here, in this place of power, rich in Vig, in front of these Dreamers–well that promise holds a life of its own. Rayleigh will stand by her word. I believe her."

"And so it is," said Rayleigh. "We will draw up a contract and sign it on paper. The document means little, but the intent will be clear. Sign your name, commit to peace, and let us usher in a new age. All we need do now is—"

Rayleigh's words trailed off. All Anna heard was static. She clutched her chest and fell to one knee. It felt like her heart was on fire.

"Anna, what's wrong?" asked Teej. The pain in her chest was blinding this time. She almost collapsed, but he held her. Anna fixated on her white knuckles as her fingers grasped the seat in front of her. She could barely get a breath. *Not now!*

"I… don't know. It's getting worse."

"Do you trust me?"

It was Pappi. He was standing directly behind her. She couldn't answer, but she nodded her head.

The end of Pappi's cane burst through Anna's chest, just below her left shoulder. She screamed in agony, her vision whiting out. Everyone was shouting. Anna was looking down into a pool of her own blood as it formed around her feet. A coin fell to the ground. Wildey's coin. Before anyone could react, Pappi snatched it up out of the snow.

As Anna collapsed, she watched Pappi run down the stairs of the Amphitheater clutching the coin close to his chest. He dashed across the stage to the back of the arena, and silhouetted against the city skyline, Pappi hugged the coin close to his body, fell to his knees and closed his eyes before it exploded.

The shockwave rolled in towards Anna carrying a cloud of rock and debris. She tried to scream, but instead coughed blood and collapsed. With her face pressed into soft snow, Anna felt the Amphitheater crumble under her body as the runes gave way. A moment later, she was falling.

forty

Never freeze, kid. That was the very first lesson Garret taught Teej. When everything goes wrong, the worst thing you can do is lock up. If you can't fight, run. It doesn't matter if you run *from* danger or run *into* danger, just *run.* Action, any action, is better than freezing.

And so Teej started to run. As the ground crumbled below his feet and rocks rained down on him from above, he ran towards Anna.

The Amphitheater was sinking, and the floor tipped underfoot. Just ahead, Anna's unconscious body slid along the ground towards the edge of the cliff. Behind him, the Dreamers were flooding out of the arena through the rear entrances. Pappi had saved them all. His sacrifice hadn't saved the Amphitheater, but it had taken Wildey's explosive coin far enough away that the explosion didn't completely obliterate the platform. Instead, it was slowly crumbling piece-by-piece, and everyone had enough time to make a hasty escape. Everyone but Anna.

The blast knocked them all off their feet, and by the time Teej opened his eyes and got back up, Anna had already slipped away from him.

As he hurdled over broken rocks, the voices of the Dreamers faded into the distance. Behind him, he heard Elise scream. He glanced back, hoping he would spot a clear escape route. The columns and stairs were already collapsing, rocks as big as cars crashing down and filling the air with dust and debris.

"We must go!" shouted Alby to Elise.

The boy had Elise by the arm and was trying to pull her back to safety, but she was resisting, tears in her eyes as she reached for her friends.

"We can't leave her!" screamed Elise.

"Go back!" shouted Teej. "Get her out of here, Alby!"

"You must come too!" shouted the boy. "You will be crushed. Anna would not want this."

Teej closed his eyes, gritted his teeth, and ignored Alby's words. He was right, but Teej couldn't live with himself if he lost her. Wildey had once more targeted someone he cared about, this time from the grave. Teej had to go after her, even if it was too late.

As he ran, memories of Linda's final moments returned. This is exactly how he lost her: a bomb smuggled into the Doxa's Haze, triggered at the worst possible time. How could he have forgotten? This was Wildey's plan all along, and only Pappi's quick reactions had given Anna any chance of survival. It was a chance that was fading fast as her unconscious body slid towards the precipice.

Clenching his fists, Teej jumped over shards of broken rock, dodged between falling boulders and slid over snow and rubble. His tired legs ached, but he didn't let up for a second.

Keep. Running.

Dust and dirt showered his back as a pillar smashed down inches behind him. A chunk of rock exploded outwards and battered the back of his calf, but he stumbled for only a second before pushing on. Anna was almost within reach, her body splayed at the very edge of the stage, poised to fall at any moment.

Even if Teej got to her in time, there was no way back. He had no idea what to do next.

This is it. I either save her, or we both die here.

There was no going back now. As Teej grasped hold of Anna, he tried to feel her pulse. It was there, faint but steady. Pushing a tiny amount of Vig out through his fingertips, he brushed her tattered clothes aside and placed his hand on her chest, then set to work closing the wound and steadying her heartbeat. It didn't take much to stabilize her. He used his Praxis without fear or desperation, expressing his love for her with slow, steady waves of Vig that breathed life back into her body.

"Anna," he said as he stroked her face. She didn't respond. "You have to wake up. You have to wake up so we can get out of here. You did it. You survived Wildey's final trap, and you saved Alby. You even turned the Dreamers! We can still make it out of here. You just have to wake up."

Teej grabbed her with both hands, shook her, but there was no response. He couldn't get through to her. Behind him, another boulder collapsed showering them both in shards of stone and debris. The ground lurched underfoot, and he felt sure they would fall any moment.

Teej grabbed her again and shook her harder. "You have to wake up!"

Still nothing.

Dammit!

He wanted to keep shouting, but his anger stalled, he dropped his head down onto her chest and held it there as tears streamed down his cheeks.

It was no use.

"I'm sorry. I'll stay with you. You won't be alone. Anna… I love you."

forty-one

A heat was spreading across Anna's chest like warm bath water poured over her bare skin. She worried she might be bleeding again, but there was no pain. Her lungs burned, but with each breath, the heat receded. Someone's hand rested over her wound. Anna felt Teej's pain and fear. She wanted to tell him it was going to be okay. That they would be together. That it would be easier if he just let go, and together they could drift away, all the anxiety and fear melting like snow in the sun.

No, it's time to wake up.

Anna cracked open her eyes. She could see the blurry outline of Teej as he crouched over her. All around them, the Amphitheater was collapsing, the solid stone pillars blowing away like sand in the wind. There was a chill in the air as all the Vig flooded out of the arena. The mystical power that held up the ruins was bleeding away, and soon this place would be gone forever, just another ruin littering the Realm, a faint echo of past majesty.

Anna tried to speak, but when the words came out, they sounded strange, like she was underwater. The explosion must have damaged her ears.

"Sometimes you're not like him at all, but other times you're so much like him it hurts."

"Anna!" said Teej in desperation. "What are you talking about? We need to move."

"I can't," replied Anna honestly. "I'm done. *We're* done."

"Not yet!" said Teej. His green eyes shone in the moonlight. Though he was battered and bruised, dirty and tired, Anna decided he had never looked better. His eyes were so kind. Anna almost chuckled to herself. His messy hair was adorable. As she looked deep into his eyes, she felt no pain and no fear.

"It's too late. Did you hear what I said? You're so much like Sam. So kind. So patient."

"I heard you. There's no time!"

"What you said Teej… I can't. I can't love anyone."

Did he understand what she was trying to say? Anna's mind was foggy, and she couldn't find the right words.

Teej let out a sigh and grasped her hand tight. "Whatever you need to hear, I'll say it. Whatever you need me to feel, I'll feel. I just need you to stand up. We can talk after we get out of here."

"If we get out of here, I'm gonna sleep for a month," she said with the best smile she could manage. Anna reached her arm around his neck and let him heave her to her feet.

"This feels like the end of the world," said Anna as she glanced at the destruction all around.

"It was the end of someone's," said Teej glumly as he struggled to hold her upright.

Pappi.

"Which way?" she asked as Teej pivoted on the spot looking for an escape route through the dust and fallen rock.

"We'll try to find a path to the mountainside. If we can make it past this rubble, there should be some steady ground on the north face, maybe a plateau. I don't know if we can make it down to the ground, but at least we'll be safe."

"Safe and trapped up a mountain," replied Anna as she rubbed dust out of her eyes. "Can't you fly?"

"No," said Teej. "Never. Not even once. Why would you think that?"

"Something Pappi said. *We might be able to fly, but you can bring down the whole sky.*"

"He said that? Pappi would never sacrifice a poetic turn of phrase for something as trivial as accuracy."

Anna pushed herself away from Teej and leaned her numb body against the broken boulder.

"Well, if you can't fly, you can at least jump high. Why don't you just… you know?" Anna made guns with her fingers and pointed upwards. "*Zoop*!"

"*Zoop*?" he said, confused.

"It's a real word. It means to *jump over the rocks to safety.*"

"I guess I could—"

Before Teej could finish, a deluge of huge boulders as big as houses rolled towards them. They fell to the ground, the rocks fell to the ground over their heads, crunching into pieces. Though she couldn't see for dust, Anna heard the landslide fall on top of them. More and more boulders fell, more debris, more rubble. Anna closed her eyes, and when she opened them again, they were both in darkness. Buried alive.

She felt the oppressive weight of the giant stone boulders above her. Dust went in her eyes and mouth, blinding and choking her. Somehow, they were alive, but each movement, each breath threatened to bring tons of stone down on their heads. A sliver of daylight shone through a crack in the rocks. Anna reached out for Teej and grabbed his arm. He was shaking.

"Are you alright?" whispered Anna.

"Get out," breathed Teej.

"What?"

"The gap. You can make it. Move quickly."

As her eyes adjusted to the gloom, Anna glanced up to see Teej's palms were pressed into the rock overhead. His left leg was crushed under broken, jagged rocks. He was pinned in place.

"Your leg!"

"Now!" snapped Teej as dust rained down on them. A grinding noise overhead signaled a whole mountain of rock was ready to fall on their heads.

Anna scrambled to the gap, then looked back, waiting for him to follow.

"What are you doing!?" she shouted. "Come on."

"What are *you* doing?!" he countered. "I'm trapped, and I'm holding up this rock. Get out of here!"

Both his arms were over his head, his bare hands pressed against a ton of solid rock. Teej's body glowed faintly in the dark, the tiny amount of Vig he had summoned coursing through his veins as he used his Praxis to supplement his failing strength.

"Teej…"

He shook his head sadly, a bead of sweat running down his cheek. "As soon as I move, this whole thing will collapse. I can't walk. Or even crawl. We can't *both* make it. If you don't escape right now, neither of us will."

"I won't go without you!"

"I can't hold this much longer. If you don't go now, we'll both die here."

"Then we'll both die here," said Anna seriously.

She stopped moving.

"No!" screamed Teej. The rock shifted overhead, and they both flinched.

Teej's body shook with the strain. In desperation, Anna shot an arm up to help him. Maybe she could call on her own Praxis. Split the rock. Smash her way to safety. Anna flexed her fingers and pushed her Praxis through her ring, closing her eyes to concentrate, summoning all her will. She let out a scream, then opened her eyes.

Nothing. Not even a spark of her fire remained. Anna collapsed next to him as her body and Will failed her.

"Listen to me," said Teej softly, his voice quivering. "I'm done. I'm tired. My time is over. This is *your* time. You… have to finish this."

“I can’t,” muttered Anna. The snow was melting. The ground under her body was wet, and as her head slumped into it, she felt like the water was coming up to swallow her again.

“You can. You have to see this through.”

Anna shook her head. “This is what happened to Sam.”

“Anna, your husband, Sam, his death wasn’t your fault. You can’t stop someone from killing themselves.”

“You’re a fool,” snapped Anna. The old coldness rose inside her. How could she have been so stupid? All her fears had caught up with her again. Why bother running anymore?

“He didn’t kill himself,” said Anna. “It wasn’t his choice.”

“He wouldn’t want you to die here,” pleaded Teej. “Neither do I.”

Anna looked up to see the tears in Teej’s eyes. Was this the last time she would ever see them?

“I can’t do it Teej. I can’t lose someone else that I…”

“You’re stronger than you think,” said Teej. “And you can.”

He groaned as the weight above bore down on him, and for a moment his shoulders seemed to fail, but he slowly straightened his back and lifted the rock again. His Praxis was almost spent.

“Remember what I said to you when we first met?”

Anna came close to him and touched his face. Closing her eyes, she waited for the roof to collapse and finish them both.

“I said you were ash that had caught a spark. Flame… spluttering back to life.”

“I remember,” said Anna. She put her forehead to his.

“It’s not yet time… for that flame to go out. Not yet. Anna?”

Reluctantly she looked into his eyes.

“Anna, you have to let me go.” Teej’s grimace faded from his face, and all that remained was a look of calm. “Let me go, Anna. Let me go.”

Her mind as numb as her body, Anna turned away from him.

Crawling in the dark through the rubble, Anna squeezed her body through the narrow gap and then felt the rocks collapse behind her. A mighty crash, then she emerged into the cool night air, rolled over, and went still. She was looking straight up at a thousand tiny, blinking stars. As her eyes adjusted, she started to see constellations and nebula daubed all over the vast, black night sky, like little flecks of white paint dotted across infinity.

When she finally turned to look back at the mound of debris and rock, the tiny gap she'd crawled through was gone. Everything was ruined now. She tried to push out her Haze Sense, but it told her what she already knew. Teej was dead.

It had caught up with her. It always did. Anna was alone again.

Desolation.

She lay in utter silence.

"Anna!"

Who was talking? Why was someone calling her name when she was alone now? Anna recognized the voice, but for some reason, she couldn't identify the owner. The numbness had gotten inside her now, just like it always did. The pain was too much. She couldn't take it. If she called out in sorrow, cried, allowed herself to feel it, it would never stop. Instead, Anna pushed it inwards, made her hands into fists and dug them into the pit of her stomach, swallowed back tears and pushed everything she felt deep down inside.

She'd been here before. Lying on the bank of the river, looking up at the stars. No sirens in the distance, no one calling out from the bridge, asking if she needed help. Just the burbling water and the rustling of the trees in the evening breeze. Sam swallowed by the Black Water, his body sinking so deep she felt sure no one would ever find it.

And Anna lying on the bank, too scared to live or die, yet still, breathing. Was she still there? Had she ever left?

"Anna!"

Why wouldn't the voice leave her alone? It was high pitched, insistent, and irritatingly familiar. Who was calling for her? Where was she?

Anna should be soaking right now. As she curled into a ball, she wondered why her clothes were dry and dusty and not wet and cold. She'd just come out of the river. What would she tell Sam's parents? The Black Water had rejected her. It had spat her back out and now she had to face them all. Sam's parents, her own.

Anna's mind reeled as she saw her future (or was it her past?) flash past in front of her bleary eyes. Dropping out of college, going back home to her old bedroom, Mom checking on her every few hours to make sure she hadn't cut her wrists again, Dad looking over the top of his newspaper at the dinner table, brow furrowed but saying nothing.

But it didn't have to be like that. Anna could fight it. Stay in the city, finish college, pretend it was all an accident. Hide the letter.

The letter...

But she'd already burned it. Or had she? She remembered dropping it in the trash, looking into the flames as it burned away.

"Anna, get up!"

Who was that? Anna didn't have any friends in the city. It was just her and Sam, and now he was gone. Who was calling out to her?

This is all wrong.

The air was cold but dry. Though the snow melted in puddles all around her body, snowflakes were still drifting down. It never snowed here in the city.

Anna was so lost to herself, she almost laughed.

I am completely alone.

Was the Desolation itself calling to her? Had the Desolation imagined a whole world for her: friends and adventures and sunshine and snow, love and kindness. Was all of it created just so she would pick herself up and keep fighting? Only then could the Desolation crush her once more. It was a cruel enemy, invincible and omniscient. It existed across time and reality, and it would remake Anna's whole world for just one more chance to destroy her completely.

There was rumbling below her now. The river sounded more like crumbling stone, but that was just a trick of her mind. She was coming back to reality. Anna absentmindedly twirled her ring around her finger, the cold metal sliding easily as if her hands were slimmer. She had to hold it in place now or it would slip off. Was she wasting away here on the riverbank? How long had she lain like this?

"We have to go!" said the voice. "Alby found a path out. We can't reach you up there. You have to jump! You're so close to safety, Anna."

Elise? Why did she know that name?

"The whole thing is about to collapse. Anna… he's gone. He wouldn't want you to die here too."

Elise and Alby were on a narrow platform jutting out of the mountain face. Elise was reaching out as if Anna was in touching distance, but she would never reach them. She could barely stand, her body's strength spent, her will gone. Anna stared off into the distance and waited for them to leave without her.

"Come with me, girl," said Rayleigh.

On the opposite side of the rubble, Rayleigh stepped closer, clearing a path through the rock with an idle flick of the wrist. The Dreamer looked tiny against the ruined backdrop of the Amphitheater, but a vast flickering green aura surrounded her like she carried the aurora borealis on her shoulders. Her lips were curled into a satisfied smile.

"We need to talk properly. It's all over now. You've done very well."

"Where are we going?" asked Anna as she reached out to take Rayleigh's hand.

"Deep into the Realm. To the Silver Shores of Selmetridon. That's where we will settle things between us."

"No!" called out Elise, but her voice was cut off as the last of the Amphitheater finally collapsed to rubble.

forty-two

Anna woke to the sound of lapping waves. Her hand spasmed and she felt wet sand between her fingers. She was lying on a beach.

Saltwater spray found her face. Her body felt heavy and peaceful, and though the breeze was cool on her skin, she enjoyed the sensation. Her clothes were damp but not wet, and overhead a cloudy gray sky felt too close to the ground, like a low ceiling.

This place felt familiar, but she had never been here before. When she was a student, at the end of a hard day she would fill a bath to the brim, the water so hot it steamed up every window in her apartment. When she was done, she would pull the plug and let the water drain till she was sitting in an empty bath, her skin slowly cooling. Something about the warmth in her body evaporating made her feel deeply melancholy. She felt that melancholy now, a blanket of apathy that lay softly on her soul. She'd be content to lie on this beach forever. Lie here till the tide finally rolled in and carried her silently out to sea.

But the tide didn't roll in. Instead, Anna lay for an hour, for two hours, until all the familiar pains of a human body slowly returned. Lying on her chest with one arm pinned beneath, her shoulder cramped. Her parched throat and tongue cried out for water, any water. If the waves lapped close enough, she would have drunk from the sea just to have something wet in her mouth. Her stomach grumbled like a tiny earthquake at the core of her being. Anna's mind flashed with images of glazed donuts, cheesy pizza with little pepperonis curled up into greasy cups, and hot, sweet black coffee.

When her eyes cracked open again, it was dark. The waves sounded closer now, and she was shivering in the cold night air. Nightmares left her disorientated, though they were already blurry and indistinct in her memory. She'd been dreaming she was with all her friends, but they were swapping faces and laughing at her when she got them mixed up. Sam was there, and he kept pointing at her chest and telling her that she was "undone." When she looked down, she had a tuft of fluff coming out of her skin just below her ribs. When she pulled at it, more and more stuffing came out, like she was a doll. Her hand went inside her rib cage, tearing out wads of herself till she was done. At the end, Sam looked at her with a smirk. "You're empty."

Then she woke up.

Anna's mouth was so dry that even breathing burned her throat. Her eyes were crusty, and her head ached. All the familiar pains of reality were back. Reluctantly, she concluded getting up and finding water, shelter, and food was preferable to dying here on the beach.

With a groan, she pushed her arms under her body, heaved herself up and, with a mighty effort, got to her feet. It felt like someone had set off a bomb insider her skull, and she could only endure the pain by clamping a hand tightly around her forehead and breathing slowly.

After a few practice steps, the dull pain subsided enough for Anna to survey her surroundings.

The stars were bright and clear, though she couldn't find the moon anywhere in the sky. A swirling nebula gave off so much purple and green light that it reflected across her arms and hands when she held them up over her head. The waves lapped lazily up the beach, the sea stretching out to infinity. Between her toes, the silvery sand sparkled like diamonds in the starlight. Along the periphery of the beach, a forest of thick dark trees was so densely packed that they constituted a wall. If Anna was going to go anywhere, her journey would have to begin by following the beach.

She walked slowly, glancing back at her footprints. Strange that they started where she woke up. Had she been washed up by the sea? Or fallen from the sky? Anna had no memory of how she got here, but she didn't push herself to remember.

As she skirted the beach, eventually she came across a washed-up old log. Carved into the wood were symbols she couldn't read. She ran her hand over the smooth oak, feeling where the ocean had eroded the bark, leaving a smooth surface. Without trying, Anna's Praxis manifested, and she felt the life and vigor of the old tree pulse under her fingertips like a faint heartbeat. The forest, the sea, and the air encapsulated in this one piece of old wood. *Through the bitter winter, the sun clung to the horizon, but wood holds both the memory of water and the dream of fire. Though the flames burn out, the fire waits. And it watches.*

The sandy portion of the beach slowly gave way to pebbles and rocks. They were hard on her bare feet and Anna picked her way across them slowly, occasionally falling to her hands and knees as the bank steepened. In the dark, it wasn't clear if this was the end of the beach or just a rough patch she would eventually clear, but she pushed on regardless. After what felt like an hour, her feet once again found soft sand and she was relieved to leave the rocks behind.

Though Anna tried to steer her thoughts away from the past, she couldn't shake one memory that resurfaced over and over again. The Moonlight Road. She remembered rushing along the gossamer path through deserts, forests, ancient cities, ruins, wastelands, swamps, towns, and tundra. She had passed cities in the sky, fields of blue snow, and towers of frozen rainbows shimmering under a green sun. Passing between swaying castles built from the stuff of ghosts, she had rushed past it all, desperate to get to someone she could no longer remember,

How much beauty and wonder had she missed, focused on a man who was probably going to leave her anyway? Anna closed her eyes and shook her head in frustration. She had been a fool. The Moonlight Road could have carried her beyond all her cares and worries, beyond this world into oblivion. Anna wished she could be back there now, with every ten steps taking her into a whole new world and farther from the disasters in her wake.

She consoled herself by admitting that wherever she was now, this world was far from all her worries. This wasn't the Moonlight Road, but it certainly wasn't Basine either. Everything had heavy inertia as though she was still dreaming. The air felt thick and comforting, and the sound of the waves was muffled like her ears were stuffed with cotton wool. This place was far enough from her pain that she could keep walking. She could forget.

Up ahead, she saw a green bottle embedded in the sand. Someone had put it in her path for Anna to find. What would it hold? A message?

Anna knelt and examined the bottle closely, but without touching it. Her nose just inches from the lip, she sniffed without expectation or hope.

Clean water?

Casting aside caution, Anna drank the whole bottle.

Letting out a belch, she coughed a little then chuckled in pure relief. Dropping the empty bottle in the sand, her body shuddered, then she felt her shoulders rock up and down as she began to silently sob.

Teej was dead.

What were her last words to him? "*I can't do it, Teej?*" No, she'd said something after that.

"*I remember.*"

Anna held her head in shame. She *had* to remember him. She couldn't let his death be meaningless. She couldn't let herself become numb just like with Sam. Teej had died for *something*. He had died to make the world safer, to bring peace to the Dreamers. Anna had to keep fighting too, even if it cost her everything. She had nothing left to give but her own life, and she'd spend it willingly to fulfil Teej's dream of a better world. A better world for everyone else but himself, she thought bitterly.

Anna glanced down at her ruined clothes and her scarred body and focused on her clenched fist. Nestled between white knuckles, her ring seemed to shine in the night. This was her Periapt, the focus for her power and the key to finding her way back. Back to what remained of her friends and family, and back to finish what she had started at the Amphitheater. She'd use it as a beacon to find her way home. She'd get back to Elise and Pappi, back home to Mom and Dad. Back to finish the fight.

Smoothing her hands over her rags, Anna pushed out her Will and mended her clothes as best she could. Loose jeans, a sweater, some crude sneakers, and she even managed clean socks.

Not bad, now I just need to—

Anna glanced up to see she was not alone. A figure was coming along the beach towards her. Silhouetted against the stars, a small, slim woman walked slowly and calmly. She was still far away, but Anna could see her arms crossed in front of her body, dark hair waving in the wind. The woman wasn't looking at Anna. Instead, her gaze was fixed on the sea and the dark, rolling waves.

Anna let out a long breath and started walking towards her. As they got closer, the cove straightened out till they were walking straight towards each other. The stars were so bright that it didn't take long for Anna to realize who she was facing. Her Haze Sense was dim, but her eyes didn't deceive her.

They stopped about ten steps apart. Anna adjusted her ring and faced Rayleigh, shoulders square, feet planted firmly in the sand. Rayleigh regarded her with a neutral expression. Her dark eyes were intense, and her hair danced around her face in the wind. Though she was shorter and slighter than Anna, there was something about her stillness that was unnerving. She didn't seem to breathe or blink. Her pale lips were pursed like she was about to say something, but the words didn't come. Her plain black top and pants didn't leave much room to hide a weapon, but Anna knew she didn't need one.

"The make-up around your eyes?" said Anna as she squinted at Rayleigh. "Why do you wear it? It looks like a..."

"A crow," said Rayleigh. Her voice was smooth and calm. "When the men see the crow, they shudder and turn away. They don't stare at the crow, they let it get on with its business. But no one forgets the crow is still there."

"You're so full of shit," muttered Anna. "It's all an act. How you look, how you talk. It's all..."

"Manipulation? Of course it is."

A gust of wind blew silver sand between them. Anna turned away, but Rayleigh looked straight ahead, the dust blowing around her. A moment later the wind was gone, replaced once more with an unnatural stillness.

"Did you take the form of a woman because it makes it easier to manipulate me?" asked Anna.

"Sometimes you change so much your old body doesn't fit you anymore."

"No," said Anna shaking her head. "No cute speeches. It's just us now. Don't play games."

"There are *only* games, Anna," said Rayleigh solemnly. "Now it's just us, we can finally play in peace."

"You think I won't fight you as hard if you're a woman? Because I'm used to fighting men? You're wrong. I don't care what you look like."

Rayleigh shrugged. "The amount of attention you've received has made you conceited. How I chose to live and what form I take has little to do with fighting *you.*"

"Then why?"

"Why not? Gender can be a playground or a cage. Even the sleepers in Basine have learned this. Forcing someone to live as something they are not is monstrous. Man or woman, what does that matter to a Dreamer? Again, you show how little you know of our world Anna. You learn fast, but there is still much you don't understand. The most powerful among us change appearance like you change clothes. This is too easy. I can wrongfoot you by changing the color of my sweater."

Anna shuffled awkwardly. Had she misjudged Rayleigh? Underestimated her?

"Why are we here?" asked Anna as she looked around. "And *where* are we?"

"We're deep in the Realm. As deep as anyone has been for a long time. These are the Silver Shores."

"Selmetridon? Close to the Winterheart?"

"Close. There was a time when you could sail from here across the Caledon Sea and reach the ancient city. No longer. It has all been swallowed by the Fade. And the Winterheart is lost."

"The Fade?"

Rayleigh nodded. "You don't know it?"

Anna shook her head. Though Amara had mentioned it, Anna didn't want to reveal her knowledge.

"It is a primordial mist that swallows the Realm piece by piece. In the regions where Basine and the Realm break down, only the Fade remains. Once a place within the Realm falls behind the old fog door, it is closed off to us forever. The routes to Selmetridon are gone. No one can enter."

"No one but you," said Anna.

Rayleigh frowned. "What makes you say that?"

"Raguel. And whoever that big black knight was. They came from the Realm, right? They were Ancestrals, recruited from Gwinn's court to protect you and terrorize everyone else."

"You are right about the Green Knight, but the other was just a shadow. A shade."

Anna scowled. "Another lie."

Rayleigh smirked. "If you like."

"You have no bodyguards left to bully us?"

Rayleigh sniffed. "I have no interest in bullying anyone."

"You're going to stop terrorizing the Dreamers?"

"I only had one warrior left, and you destroyed him. And then Gendo betrayed me."

Anna shook her head. "Gendo was doing exactly what you wanted him to. You turned on him when you knew everyone else was turning on *you*."

Rayleigh chuckled. "I suppose that's true."

"So why are we here?"

Rayleigh looked up at the stars and sighed. "All I really ever wanted was to talk with you like this, Anna. Alone, without interruption."

"Yeah? For a long time, it seemed more like you wanted me dead."

"Never. I admire you. Look at yourself. You've endured yet another loss, and you're already back on your feet. I can tell how acutely the death of Teej wounds you. No one alive has burned like you burn Anna. And yet it does not consume you. You're facing me now, still ready to fight for something. You have taken circumstance and made it into purpose. Yes, I admire you very much."

Anna scowled. "You think you know what I'm fighting for?"

"Peace. The same thing I fight for, though the path to achieve it looks different for each of us."

Anna pointed an angry finger. "You're telling me you want peace? Are you going to back off and let the Dreamers make their own choices? Are you going to bring the people you killed back from the dead?"

"I'm going to give you a chance to get everything you've ever wanted, including peace."

"I've had enough of this!" roared Anna. She had lost everything, and Rayleigh was playing more games. "I won't let you get away with what you've done."

"Careful," said Rayleigh her voice rising very slightly. "You are a threat to me here, and I will not tolerate threats."

"Just get to the point," spat Anna.

"Wildey's final scheme failed, and with his death, I am no longer glancing over my shoulder. Certainly, I still have enemies, but none like Wildey remain. When that bomb failed, I knew it was over. There was only one loose thread left, and it was time for a reckoning. The only pieces left on the board that count are you and me. Anna and Rayleigh. I knew I must bring you here to the Silver Shores to settle this thing between us."

"So, let's settle it," said Anna as her hand curled around her ring.

Rayleigh took a half step back. "To the girl who controls fire, all problems look flammable."

"Just this one."

"Tell me honestly, Anna, is that really how you want to end our story? One more fight? More blood?"

Anna frowned, put her hands back down at her sides. "No."

Rayleigh turned to look out at the sea and gestured to the rolling waves. "I like it here. Do you?"

"If it's a choice between fighting and talking about the pretty waves or how nice the stars look or how soft the sand feels, I think I'd rather fight. You're wasting my time while the Dreamers tear each other apart. Do you care about peace at all?"

"Lasting peace amongst the Dreamers? You don't know how much I want it. Anna, I've failed more times than you've tried."

Anna sneered. "Well, then you're really bad at it. You should let someone else try."

"Someone like you?"

Anna nodded. "The charter. The Magna-Carta… thing. We should try. There's no other solution."

Rayleigh's brow was furrowed. She didn't seem to like Anna's suggestion.

"What if there was another way?" said Rayleigh. "What if there was a way to stop the spread of the Blood Plague?"

Anna opened her mouth to answer, then checked herself. Where was Rayleigh going with this?

"You have an idea. I sense it."

"So do you," replied Anna. "Or you wouldn't have mentioned it."

"I think we can work something out, Anna. I think we can fix this thing between us."

"I doubt it."

With a sweep of her arm, Rayleigh's Mimesis sparked to life. Anna took a step back and raised her guard, but there was no immediate threat. With a gust of swirling wind and a little dust storm, Rayleigh conjured a table out of thin air. The wood looked solid and old, while the surface was covered in smooth green felt, like in a casino. With a second swoosh of wind and a wave of her arm, Rayleigh conjured two solid oak chairs on opposite ends of the table. She gestured for Anna to take a seat, then without waiting, she sat down and placed her palms on the surface.

"I have you at a disadvantage Anna. I tell you this so you know where we stand. I have watched you for a long time. I have a burning curiosity about one event I watched but did not understand. Would you answer my question?"

"Depends on what it is," said Anna cautiously as she walked to the table. As she pulled up a chair, she allowed her Haze Sense to probe for danger, but felt no obvious threats. Anna twitched as she sat down, her body instinctively responding to some invisible attack that never materialized.

"No need to be nervous. I will not force you into anything. Nor will I try to trick you. You're too clever for my tricks after all, isn't that right?"

"I guess."

Anna didn't know when they had appeared, but between them sat four small shot glasses, each filled to the brim with clear liquid, and an unlit candle with a blackened, smoldering wick. Anna eyed the Dreamer suspiciously and tried to ignore what sat between them on the table.

"What's your question?" said Anna.

"You didn't play Dean's game. How did you know it was fixed?"

Anna was about to pretend she didn't understand, but there was no point. She knew exactly what Rayleigh was asking. The Dreamer wanted to show her how much she knew about Anna's life. She had been watching Anna from the very start. Anna had to play along.

"I just knew."

Rayleigh scoffed. "That's not a good answer. Perhaps you were not certain, but something made you suspicious. Something about Dean's manner. You read him, and you knew that both you and your friend had already been poisoned. This question is a trifling thing to you, but it would mean a lot to me if you were to answer. I will ask it again. How did you *know,* Anna?"

Anna licked her lips nervously. She searched her mind for the most honest answer she could find. She might as well tell the truth.

"I knew Dean had spiked our drinks already because that's what I would have done. If I was him, I would have made sure I didn't lose."

Rayleigh sat completely still. Anna shuddered.

"*If I was him.* Of course. That is how you prevail. You think like your enemies. It is not hard for you to think the worst of others. You think it of yourself."

"Alright, Freud," said Anna with scorn. "Spare me the free therapy. Why are we starring at four shot glasses and a burnt-out candle?"

Rayleigh spread her hands across the table. "Our final game together will be a numbers problem. Or rather, a question of odds. In these glasses we have—"

"No thanks," interrupted Anna. "I'm not here for this. No games, no riddles, and *definitely* no puzzles."

A flicker of impatience appeared on Rayleigh's face, but her voice remained calm. "If you want something from me, you have to listen to me."

"I don't want anything from you," said Anna with a shake of her head.

"I told you before, I can give you everything you want."

"Like what?!" said Anna incredulously.

"Light the candle and I will tell you."

Anna shook her head in annoyance but acquiesced. She grabbed hold of the candle, pinched the wick between her fingers, then snapped her fingers and the flame spluttered to life. Setting it down on the table, she folded her arms across her chest and waited for Rayleigh to continue.

"There are three things you think you want. I can give you all three."

Anna wasn't interested. "I don't believe you."

"There are also four glasses on the table. Three contain water. One contains Eitr."

Anna threw her hands in the air. "Poison? That's your solution. You *already* poisoned me. It didn't work."

"This is the purest form of that poison."

Anna eyed the four glasses with suspicion. "I can't believe I'm back here."

"You have been to the Silver Shores before?" asked Rayleigh, confused.

"No back *here*!" said Anna in irritation as she pointed at the glasses. "Playing stupid games."

"Shall I explain the rules?" Rayleigh licked her lips.

"Get on with it."

"I will not compel you to take part. Instead, I will offer you the three things you desire most in the world."

"Lovely. When do you poison me?"

"I don't," said Rayleigh with a half-smile. "If you want what I offer, you will poison yourself. Or not, if you are lucky or wise."

"I assure you I will *not* poison myself."

"One glass contains Eitr," Rayleigh went on as if she had not heard Anna. "The other three, water. Neither your eyes, nor your tongue, nor your Haze Sense can detect the poison. It is invisible, odorless, tasteless. Eitr is the poison that all other poisons flow from. The source and the end of life. If you drink it in a pure form, there is no cure, no way to undo the damage it will wreak on your body. No Praxis or Mimesis can save you."

"I get the point. Why would I take the risk?"

"Because of what I offer."

"You can't offer me anything that would make me do that."

Rayleigh shrugged. "Maybe you are right. It is time to test your resolve." She leaned forward and pushed one of the glasses towards Anna.

"My first offer is this: if you chose one of these glasses and drink, I will guarantee the safety of your family and friends as long as I live."

Too good to be true.

Anna scoffed. "Bullshit. There's no way I'd believe you."

"Consider for a moment, if I could make that promise and you truly believed me, would you take me up on that offer? A one in four chance of death to protect everyone you love for as long as I live. Surely that is worth the risk? They would be safe from me and safe from any Dreamer that might hurt them. I would protect their lives. A solemn vow I would never break."

Anna furrowed her brow. Under the table, her toes dug into the sand, and she leaned forward to examine each glass. They were identical, clear, and spotless.

Mom. Dad. Elise and Alby. All safe from Rayleigh and anyone else who might threaten them. If the offer had been real, it would be tempting.

"If I believed you, I might."

Rayleigh laid her hands flat on the table. "What if I gave you power over me? Would that convince you?"

"How exactly would you do that?"

"Here, we are evenly matched. Were we to fight each other…"

Anna narrowed her eyes and put a clenched fist on the tabletop.

"Yes," said Rayleigh carefully. "I think you would beat me. You are desperate and angry. I would try to deflect your fire. Conjure monsters and demons from your memories using all the knowledge I have gathered of your past. But I predict it would not be enough. You would prevail. So already, any harm that befalls you here must be your own choice."

"But you don't want to fight?"

"Neither of us want that. We want peace. But you do not trust me."

Anna shook her head.

"And you are right to mistrust me," said Rayleigh earnestly. "I am a manipulator. They call me Old Gray Face. Do you know why?"

"Because your face is old and gray?"

Petty, but satisfying.

A twitch of anger, then a smile. "No. It's from a poem. Sometimes a stanza has a disproportionate effect on our thoughts and our lives. Do you agree?"

"If you say so."

"They wrote a poem about me. They said no one could read my expressions. *Eyes dark as black coals in space, what thoughts smolder behind that old gray face?*

"Manipulation is my Art, but I have to surpass my Art if I am to bring about peace. That is the price I must pay. To do that, I will be honest with you. I will reveal my weakness."

What would Teej say if he were here? Make a joke? Walk away? Anna felt his absence acutely. She didn't have his wit or guile to help her face Rayleigh. All she had was anger and sarcasm.

"Don't let me stop you," said Anna coldly.

"I have a daughter."

Anna reeled. *A daughter?*

"*You're* a mom?!"

Rayleigh nodded slowly. "I… am not accustomed to opening myself up this way. It goes against all my instincts. But yes, I have a daughter. Petra. No one else in the whole world knows, but you."

"A daughter?" repeated Anna. "Ho-lee shit. Why?"

"Why does anyone?" asked Rayleigh acerbically.

"What? No, I just—"

Rayleigh rubbed her brow. "I did not plan for it. But now that she is in the world, and now that Wildey is not, I can envision some future for her. For both of us, together. I don't think I need to explain to you that this information can destroy me. If a single Dreamer learned that I have a daughter, there is no limit to what they could compel me to do by threatening her life."

Anna was confused. "So that's how I make you keep your promise?"

"Correct. You hold my secret."

"But I don't need to reveal that secret to hurt you. *I* could just use it against you."

"Of course, *you* could Anna," said Rayleigh, her eyes intense. "*You* could threaten the safety of my daughter. If you were to threaten to burn Petra alive, I would do whatever you asked of me."

"I wouldn't—"

"Why not? Why would you not burn her alive?" Rayleigh was pressing her, her eyes serious.

Anna opened her mouth to speak but didn't know what to say.

"I have always operated under the assumption that you are not a monster," said Rayleigh. "Nor would you masquerade as one."

"You could be lying about everything. The daughter. The poison. All of it."

Rayleigh reached below the table. Anna tensed up, but when Rayleigh's hand came back all she held was a photo. A photo of a little girl.

"Petra?"

Rayleigh nodded.

"Shit, she does look like you. She has your eyes–you know, minus the..." Anna gestured broadly at Rayleigh's face.

"I know."

Anna leaned back in her seat. "So now you've shared your secret, you think I'll trust you?"

"Enough to believe that I really will live up to my promises, lest you ruin me."

Anna eyed the four glasses in front of her and licked her lips nervously.

Shit, am I really going to do this?

"You said there were three things you can offer me. What are the other two?"

"I'll tell you after you make your choice. Take your chance and take up my promise of safety for your loved ones. Or let this chance slip by and see what I offer next."

"It's not a choice. If I don't take up your offer, you'll kill them."

Rayleigh shook her head. "I did not say that. I wish them no *particular* ill will. I just won't guarantee their protection."

Anna looked out to the waves. The sun was set to rise, the barest hint of dawn peeking out over the horizon as a thin sliver of yellow on the blue sea.

"And if I drink your poison, you'll have no reason to live up to your promise."

"That is true," said Rayleigh. "But I promise I will keep them safe regardless. You'll have to take me at my word."

Anna let out a derisive chuckle. She pointed at the nearest glass. "You know which one has the poison?"

"I did," said Rayleigh evasively. "Maybe I forgot."

"You pushed this one towards me." Anna picked up the nearest glass and sniffed it. "If this one is the Eitr…"

"It would not take long for you to realize. First, your throat would constrict. Your vision would yellow. You would taste bitter berries, and your heart would beat so hard in your chest it would feel fit to burst. Finally, your legs would fail and you would fall, paralyzed. The pain would be unlike anything you've experienced, but it wouldn't last long."

Anna wrinkled her nose in distaste. "What is wrong with you? I mean really, what is your problem? Why would you want to poison me like that? Or anyone?"

"If you'd walked every step I'd taken to get where I am now, you'd make all the same choices."

Anna shook her head. "No. You're just a sadist."

"You speak as if *your* actions can be explained. As if they cause no pain to others."

"I do the best I can," said Anna with a shake of her head. "I don't *try* to hurt anyone."

"Did you do the best you could for Sam?"

Anna slammed her fist down on the table, splashing the liquid. She would not let Rayleigh say his name. Her ring sparked to life.

"Have I reached the bottom of you already?" scolded Rayleigh. "You barely hold the flames in check. Is that all it takes to undo you? Saying his name?"

"Yes," said Anna through gritted teeth. "Or at least it used to be."

To hell with her.

Anna grabbed the nearest glass and drank it in one gulp. It tasted like nothing. Like water. She got to her feet and threw the glass as far as she could. It disappeared into the waves.

Rayleigh clasped her hands together. Her eyes sparkled. "Well done."

Anna wiped her mouth with the back of her hand. No tightness in her throat. No yellow vision. Nothing.

"Sit," said Rayleigh with obvious glee. "You must be curious about what I offer you next."

"You promised," snapped Anna.

"I did, and I will live up to that promise. Your family, your friends, all safe, at least from me and the Dreamers."

Anna put her head down. "That's all I want from you. You can't offer me anything more."

"Take a moment," said Rayleigh calmly. "Settle yourself. We need not rush."

"You're happy?" asked Anna. "If I drank the poison first, the game would be over. You wanted this to keep going."

"Certainly," said Rayleigh. "There is nowhere else I would rather be."

"What if some maniac was making Petra play this game? What if they threatened to poison your daughter?"

Rayleigh's dark eyes sparkled as she spoke. It was as if every moment before now she had been profoundly bored, and now for the first time, Anna was capturing her attention.

"It would not happen. She has done nothing that would deserve such punishment."

"And I have?!" shouted Anna.

"Of course. And you admit it, to yourself if not to others. Why else do you punish yourself? It's because you think you deserve that punishment. Believe it or not, this is helping you more than me."

"You think I blame myself for failing to save Sam? Or Teej?"

"No, Anna," said Rayleigh. "I think you blame yourself because Sam's death is your fault. You blame yourself because you *should*."

Anna was about to smash her hand on the table again, but she restrained herself. Closing her eyes, she focused on her words.

"You're right," breathed Anna. She should be angry, but she wasn't. Anna had always wanted someone to say it. It was true.

Sam's death was my fault.

“What’s the second thing you offer?” asked Anna. She fixed Rayleigh with an unwavering gaze.

“I can offer you what you asked for at the Amphitheater. Your idea is flawed. I do not believe it will work, but I am willing to try. If you drink once more.”

Anna put her hand over her mouth and groaned.

“The Magna Carta? The peace charter? Why wouldn’t it work? You already promised to do it!”

“The Dreamers know the nature of temptation. You can resist any compulsion if there is some indication that it will eventually end. You must remember Anna; the Dreamers’ lives are long. They see all manner of promises broken, eroded by time. The Dreamer who swears off alcohol can never truly forget the taste of a Châteauneuf-du-Pape forever. The Dreamer who loves the company of handsome young men might avoid them for a few centuries, but time and chance will mean eventually they come across a jawline so perfect their heart will melt. If they know that *eventually* their resolve will break, they are likely to decide sooner is just as good as later.”

Anna remembered what Amara had told her at the Blackened Bridge, then again in the snowy blizzard. She had to give the Dreamers hope that the Blood Plague would end, even if that hope was a lie. The cure? The Winterheart. Should she bring it up now? Maybe not.

“You are deep in thought,” said Rayleigh. “You disagree?”

“I disagree,” said Anna. “The Dreamers are not monsters. No one wants their Art to cause this much suffering.”

Anna glanced down at the three glasses lined up in front of her. “Or not all Dreamers, at least. If we can give them a chance to police each other, to come together and try to overcome their urges, then I think we have to try. And besides, you already guaranteed them you would enforce it. You already agreed to the peace treaty.”

“Indeed, I did,” said Rayleigh with a shrug. “And I will hold to my promise. But what I did *not* commit to is another Council meeting. I did not agree to make the Dreamers face each other again and to witness them sign the treaty. I agreed to support the treaty, not to endorse it or do the work to make the Dreamers sign it."

"But it will work!" exclaimed Anna. "You can *make* it work. And it's in your best interests."

"Then drink," said Rayleigh. "Look at the glasses before you. The odds you will get what you want are even."

"How is that? asked Anna.

"Two drinks from four. An even chance."

Anna shook her head and chuckled to herself.

"Is something funny?" asked Rayleigh.

"No, it's nothing. It's just, well, Teej would have laughed. I never thought my undergrad statistics class would help me defeat an ancient witch in a poison-drinking game in a mystical land on a silver beach."

"Witch?" grumbled Rayleigh.

"Well, *whatever* you are," Anna leaned forward. "Look, it's a two in three chance." Anna shifted two glasses to the left and one to the right. "One poison, two safe glasses. After the first guess, the game changes. The problem space has been reset."

"Yes," said Rayleigh reluctantly. Anna wanted to laugh but held back. Rayleigh didn't understand. It didn't matter.

"Fuck it," said Anna as she grabbed a glass and lifted it to her lips.

"Wait!" called out Rayleigh.

"Why?"

"You should consider if you have made the right choice. Take some time to choose."

Anna stared into Rayleigh's eyes. This was it. This was Anna's final move. No delaying, no more tricks. One way or another, their fight was over.

Never play their game… but if you have to play, play to win.

"You lose, Rayleigh."

Anna drank the water in one gulp. They gaped at each other in silence.

"You are an infuriating woman, Anna."

Wiping her mouth, Anna slammed the glass down on the table. "Yeah? Put that on my fucking tombstone."

She got to her feet. "We're done here."

"The game is not complete," complained Rayleigh. "I have one more thing to offer."

"We're done," repeated Anna. "I expect you to live up to your word. Go back and call another Council. When the Dreamers come, tell them this was all your idea. Tell them everyone must sign up for the peace charter. A promise to never partake of the blood. *Make* them obey. I know you can make it work. I'll even help you."

"How?" asked Rayleigh. Anna felt the balance shift. The Dreamer got to her feet. Suddenly Anna was the one with answers.

"You talked about a cure. The Winterheart. I can get it."

"What madness is this? It is lost."

"I can find it. I'll go to Selmetridon."

"Have you lost your mind?" Rayleigh's eyes were wide. Anna enjoyed the change in the Dreamer's demeanor.

"No. You mentioned a way to stop the spread of the Blood Plague. A cure. Amara must have told you. She told me, too."

"She did," said Rayleigh reluctantly. "Amara claimed the Winterheart was a cure. She did not tell me where it was though. But…"

"But what?"

Rayleigh scowled. "But she told me *you* knew where it was. I did not believe her."

"You should have."

"What does it matter? No one can get to Selmedtridon. The Winterheart is unreachable."

"Just leave that part to me," said Anna resolutely. "That's *my* problem. You just have to play your part. Tell the Dreamers they must not succumb to the Blood Plague until I find a cure."

"You are throwing your life away. There is no way to reach the ancient city. The curtain has dropped. The Winterheart lies beyond the Fade."

"As I said, that's not your concern."

Rayleigh shook her head. "I do not understand you, Anna."

Anna shrugged. "Same. I hated the Dreamer that killed Garret and trapped me in a murder church. I hated the Dreamer that poisoned me. Now in that Dreamer's place, I see a woman with a daughter trying her best to intimidate me. Playing her old games, but I don't think her heart is in it anymore. I see a woman looking for a way to escape the role she cast for herself. You changed, Rayleigh, but not in the way you think."

Rayleigh blinked, shook her head. "Do I still frighten you?"

Anna turned away from her and looked out at the ocean. "We frighten each other."

Rayleigh stepped away from the table and came to stand by Anna's side.

"Be honest with me. How will you make this journey?"

Anna reached into her pocket and pulled out a scrap of red cloth. "All I have to do is dip this in any body of water. Charron will come. As long as I hold the cloak, he will sail me to wherever I want to go."

"Even he can't take you through the Fade."

Anna ignored her skepticism. "What is it like?"

Rayleigh took a deep breath. "The Fade? I ventured into it only once. When you get deep enough, it feels like your mind is spinning away from your body. The fog swallows your physical form, and your mind spirals away like water down a drain."

"It almost took you?"

"It was close. I escaped with Raguel and swore I would never go back."

Anna walked across the wet silver sand and crouched down, the crystal-clear water splashing over her new sneakers. She dipped the red fabric in the sea and felt the Vig pulse outwards into the ocean. It was calling for its master.

"Remarkable," breathed Rayleigh.

"You should leave," said Anna. "You have a lot of work to do."

"Anna, there is no treasure at the end of this quest. No magical item that fixes things. No magician is pulling the strings behind the curtain. Your story is not that kind of story."

"We'll see."

Anna stepped deeper into the water, the waves coming up to her knees.

Rayleigh called after her. "You truly do not want to know the third I would have offered you?"

Anna pulled the scrap of Charron's cloak out of the water and wrung it out before stuffing it back in her pocket. Against the horizon, she could already see his boat, a speck silhouetted against the rising sun.

"I was going to help you overcome the darkness inside you," shouted Rayleigh. "That word that haunts you."

Anna didn't even look at the Dreamer.

"I know the word. I don't need your help. I'll do it myself."

forty-three

Charron had done a good job repairing his boat. The first time they fought, Anna had punched a hole in the deck. The second time, she had shattered it completely.

The Ancestral didn't look at her as she waded through the sea towards him. Climbing aboard as it rocked gently on the waves was difficult. The rough stone hull felt immensely solid as her hands clung to the deck. When she finally heaved herself inside, Anna wondered how she had ever managed to damage such a seemingly invincible vessel. Glancing up at Charron, she also wondered how she had ever defeated such a fearsome foe.

His red cape fluttered in the wind, minus a small torn patch in the bottom corner. His skull visage remained implacable, but he gestured with one huge, skinless arm for Anna to take her position at the prow of the boat. She wasted no time, sitting down on a small slab of stone that seemed like it was designed just for her.

Charron pushed off, his huge polearm cast deep into the water. As the silver shore faded into the distance behind them,

Anna stared at the spot on the beach where Rayleigh's little table sat. Two full glasses remained there, untouched.

Rayleigh was gone, swallowed by a portal that took her back to Basine. She promised she would complete the peace treaty process they had both agreed, and Anna believed her. The aftermath would leave Anna with nowhere safe to run to, but it didn't matter. She had no one to run *to* anyway. Her gambit had guaranteed her friends' safety, and her family's, too, as long as she never returned to see them. All she had to do was sail away to her death. As long as Anna was gone, and the Dreamers thought she was on a quest for a cure, her friends were safe.

Anna was at peace.

Leaning back, she stretched her legs and let out a long sigh. Her hand under her chin, she glanced out at the rolling waves with detached fascination. Charron's skull-face slowly turned to look down on her as he sailed them towards the mists. He stared for a long time before he said anything.

"You are different."

His voice rumbled lower and louder than the waves.

"If you say so," said Anna. She wasn't in the mood for talking, and every time he opened his mouth, the air filled with the scent of brimstone. His breath was terrible, but it wasn't his fault.

Charron grumbled till Anna couldn't take it anymore.

"What's wrong with your face, Charron?"

"My face? I do not have one."

"I mean what's bothering you?"

Charron gestured at the mists ahead. "I sense a change in you. We are sailing into oblivion. When you defeated me, I had never before faced someone so defiant of death."

"You worried about me?" teased Anna.

"I am concerned that someone I respect has fallen to despair."

Anna shook her head. "That's not what's happening."

"Then why?"

Anna rubbed her forehead. It was a good question with a complicated answer. "Because everyone I care about will be better off when I'm gone."

Charron seemed unconvinced. "I have a great deal of experience with those who seek to escape life. I often hear people talk like this when they want to die."

"In this one rare case," said Anna with candor, "It really is true."

"Very well," said Charron reluctantly.

"You'll miss me?" asked Anna, expecting no answer.

"It will bring me no happiness to see you die needlessly."

"You're sweet. You need a girlfriend or…?"

"Strange to jest at a time like this," said Charron.

"What else can I do?" Anna smiled to herself. Teej would have laughed.

"After you enter the Fade, as long as you do not go too deep, there is still a chance to escape. Should you change your mind, follow your own footsteps to find your way out. There is no Winterheart. If you see the spires of Selmetridon, you have gone too far. There will no longer be a way to mark your progress. When your footsteps disappear, you won't find a route out. There will be no way back to Basine. The Fade will take you."

Anna frowned. Maybe she shouldn't tease the big monster. His concern seemed touchingly genuine.

"I'm sorry."

"For what?" he asked. "You were a worthy opponent. And when you defeated me, you spared me."

"I've done terrible things."

The bones of Charron's shoulders clacked as he made a gesture that was something like a shrug.

"Not to me."

"I killed one of your kind. Raguel."

Charron huffed. "The fewer of us, the better."

"He's not the only one who died because of me."

"Did you kill them all in combat? Dying in combat is an honor, especially to an Ancestral."

Anna didn't want to think about fighting or combat anymore. "Is that all an Undreamer is, though? A fighter? If that's it, well, I don't think I want to be one anymore."

"An Undreamer has many roles."

"And I don't understand any of them! I don't know how I became an Undreamer. I don't know if there are any others. I don't know what I can do with my powers, or what I *should* do with my powers. I'm clueless."

Charron grumbled. "I've known many Undreamers over the years. Some were heroes, some were monsters. Most lay somewhere in the middle. They developed their abilities by practice and patience. But you gained them through some trick of fate. Some coincidence with your blood, or some misfiring Fluxa Haze imbuing you with powers far beyond your ken."

"And what have I done with those powers?" asked Anna acerbically.

"Given the potential for destruction you possess, I am honored to have been bested by you. I am surprised you have not defeated more enemies. I know destruction is not in your nature, even though an Underreamer's abilities lend themselves to it."

"Am I doing it all wrong? Should I be more like those other Undreamers?"

Charron made a tutting noise. "In my eyes, it is up to you, as the last Undreamer, to decide what your role should be. Who else can carry that responsibility? It can only fall to you."

Anna moved to the side of the boat and looked out at the waves.

"The last Undreamer?" asked Anna.

"As far as I am aware," said Charron.

"Thank you, Charron. I won't burden you much longer. The sooner you get me to the shores of Selmetridon, the sooner I can disappear into the mist, and you can get out of here."

Charron nodded slowly.

"If you change your mind; if you come back from the Fade to the shore, I will take you *anywhere* you want to go."

Anna frowned. "Thanks for the offer, but I'm not coming back."

The mist was so thick that Anna didn't realize they had reached the shore until the boat jerked upwards. She lost her footing, almost tripping on Charron's cloak.

Wordlessly, she climbed over the hull and splashed down into the water. The gray, opaque sea reached her knees.

"We did not come across the Blue Men of Minch. We were lucky."

Anna cocked her head sideways. "Who are the Blue Men of Minch? They must be pretty terrible if the mighty Charron fears them."

Charron leaned on his long polearm with both bony hands. "They take sailors who travel this sea unbidden. The only way to defeat them is to match their rhymes with your own. If your poems do not impress them, they take you down to the depths."

"Like a poetry rap battle?" said Anna. "Just as well we missed them. My poetry is terrible."

"As is mine," said Charron. "Farewell, Anna."

Was that a chuckle? Anna regarded the giant skeleton with fondness as his boat disappeared into the mists.

Turning from the gray sea, Anna waded through murky water till she reached the shore. This one was not silver. Gray sand underfoot, gray clouds above a gray ocean, all wreathed in gray mist. The air was cool and damp.

Where now? With her arms hugging her body, Anna surveyed the horizon, but with no obvious marker to direct her, she had no choice but to pick a direction and walk in it.

Whistling tunelessly to herself, Anna disappeared into the swirls of fog. And ghosts.

forty-four

So, this was the Fade. It didn't seem so terrible. Anna didn't feel fear. She didn't feel anything.

At first, the ghosts seemed like they were from her imagination. The swirling fog obscured the faceless figures just ahead, but as she got closer to them, they danced away. She knew the mind could conjure familiar images when confronted with random shapes and patterns, but this was different. These figures were more defined, more solid. And they were watching her.

Remembering Charron's words, Anna looked down at her feet. She could still see her footprints in the soft gray sand, but they were getting fainter. It wasn't the thickening mist that obscured her passing. Rather, she felt the air itself was getting too thick to see through, to walk through, to breathe. The heavy vapor seeped through her clothes until it seemed she might never be dry again. She felt like she was already deep under water, the surface far above.

"Annie?"

Anna looked up to see the shape of a slender girl wearing a beret over loose braids. Her face was featureless, her whole body made of shimmering fog, but her voice was unmistakable.

"Elise?"

"Come on Annie. Just a bit farther!"

Anna reached for her friend, her pace quickening. But as their fingertips brushed, the mist disappeared in the breeze and the ghost of Elise was gone. Anna felt a pang of loss but pushed on through the fog.

"We didn't touch your room." It was Mom. Her back was to Anna, and she stood at the counter in the kitchen.

"Bring your friend, too. Just a little farther, Anna. Bring him, too. Bring Teej."

Anna reached out for Mom, but something stopped her.

"You mean Paul?"

"Who?" asked Mom.

"Paul. We told you his name was Paul."

"Yes. Yes, of course. Paul."

Mom was a gossamer cloud on the wind. Anna ran to her, but she was already gone, her voice echoing into the Fade.

"That was *not* Mom. She didn't say anything about my messy hair."

Anna's legs were getting heavy, her breathing labored. She wished these phantoms would stop haunting her. Who next? Dad? Teej? Anna couldn't take it. She had run to the margins of existence to escape them all, and still they clung to her. She could escape the people, but not the memories.

"Hi, Anna. It's me."

The voice cut through her, and Anna turned away before she saw the ghost of Sam. Collapsing into a crouch, she shut her eyes tightly and waited for him to blow away.

"It's me. It's really me. I know you don't believe it. But I've been waiting for you."

The voice was Sam's, but the words were all wrong.

"Anna, come on. I know it's hard to believe, but we're *all* waiting. The water tried to take you away from me, but I never gave up on you."

Anna swallowed, then opened her eyes. She knew what she had to say to him, but she needed a moment longer to steady herself. She kept her gaze down. She didn't want to see his face.

"Anna, come on. Keep going. You can do it."

"No," sniffed Anna. "Not unless you tell me what you wrote in that letter. What did it say?"

"It doesn't matter what I wrote," said Sam. "What matters is that I'm here now."

Lies.

Anna wiped away tears with the heels of her hands, stood up and turned to face the ghost. She was ready to shout at him, but dismissed by her incredulous anger, he disappeared on the breeze before she had a chance. A ghost from her past, she would never get to apologize to the real Sam. All she could do was rage at this cheap facsimile of the man she loved.

"When will I stop feeling like this?" She looked down at her footprints. Almost gone. They were fading. A few steps more and there would be no way back.

She kept walking.

Anna stared at the towers that emerged from the mist for a long time before she realized what they were. At first, they looked like a column of fog, but as she got closer, she began to pick out details. Even this far away, she could tell the city was huge. And she'd seen it before. When she'd walked along the Moonlight Road, she'd seen spires of bone-white stone, interlinked with bridges and spires that stretched out to infinity. She saw those same spires now, or the tallest of them at least.

It had to be Gwinn's tower dominating the ancient city of Selmetridon. That's where the Winterheart would be. It was a shame she would never touch it. The Fade was thickening by the second, and her chest heaved with each breath. The sand beneath her feet retained the barest trace of her passing. Maybe even now she could turn back if she wanted to. She could retrace her steps, head back to the shore, and call on Charron. She could return to her life in Basine. A life without Sam. Without Teej.

Anna was about to take another step when she hesitated. Why was her Haze Sense tingling?

Was someone calling out from the mists? She heard a distant echo, but there was something strange about it. The voice was broken, imperfect. The Fade made all the other voices preternaturally clear, as though it wanted the ghosts within to be found, but this one was muffled and indistinct, attenuated by the fog. This was a voice the Fade did not want Anna to hear.

Her footprints were gone now. Anna knelt, picked up a handful of wet sand and rubbed the grains between her fingertips. She tried to push out her Haze Sense, but there was no Vig here. This land was dead. With no Vig, there was no way to emanate any form of Praxis. She was powerless. No longer an Undreamer, she was just Anna from this moment on.

She glanced backwards, squinted, and after a moment of relaxing and focusing her eyes, she saw that the faintest sign of her track was still visible. If she stopped here then maybe, just maybe, she could still find her way back.

"Anna!" The voice sounded like Teej.

"Teej?"

Was it really him? It couldn't be him; he was dead. It didn't really sound like him, anyway; the voice was broken and weak. Hopeless.

Anna hesitated for just a second before calling back louder.

"Teej?!"

"Anna! I… took too long."

He sounded breathless. Anna recognized the wheezing. She felt that same heaviness in her lungs. The Fade was soaking into her, and whatever it was doing to her body now, it had already done worse to Teej.

But Teej was dead. This couldn't be him.

"You didn't make it out!" she called into the mist. "You couldn't have. I saw the rocks collapse on you."

"I made it out," he said with a groan.

"You should be dead."

"I'm not. Yet. Just very soggy."

It *was* Teej!

Anna let out a roar of raw emotion. How could this be? She'd finally been ready to leave everything and everyone behind, and instead, against all logic, he had clung to her.

"*How?*"

He coughed. It sounded bad. His breathing was so ragged she could hear it, even though his words were far away. She dared not take another step towards him.

"After you disappeared, Rayleigh helped me out of the rubble. I was a mess, but there was enough Vig to… to heal me. She told me you had gone to Selmetridon to find the Winterheart. I didn't know what else to do."

"You used the mirror blade," said Anna with dread.

"I used the mirror blade. It was the only way to get here, but when I came out of the ocean at the shore, there was no sign of you. I had to wander into the Fade, and eventually I collapsed."

"Dammit!"

Despite all Anna's schemes, despite all her sacrifices, Rayleigh had sent her here to die, and she'd sent Teej here to die with her too. *No loose ends.* And worst of all, she'd made Anna feel like this was all her own choice.

"Just go back!" said Teej. "If you come any farther, you'll be lost like me."

Anna raged. "Oh, come on! This is some Greek tragedy bullshit, and it is *not* happening. Not like this!"

Teej let out a sigh. "I tried, Anna. I tried to stand. My legs are numb. I can't use my Praxis. I can barely breathe. It's too late."

"I can still see my footprints," said Anna. "Just."

"Then go back!" said Teej pleadingly. "I can see the Spires. I'm too far gone."

"Maybe I can leave a track," said Anna. "You can't be that far."

"No! snapped Teej before another fit of coughing overtook him.

"I'm coming for you. Fuck it."

"Listen to me!" he shouted. "It might seem like I'm close, but when you've lost your footsteps, you've lost them forever. The tracks are more than a guide out. They're a lifeline, and when that line is severed, there's no way to pull yourself back out. I'm too far away. There's just… there's just no way."

"Stop quitting!" shouted Anna. "Don't you get it? I am never leaving anyone to die because of me again. I'll tear off fabric from my clothes to leave a path. I'll dig my heels into the sand. Something!"

"That won't work," said Teej wearily. "Rayleigh thought of everything. She knew I would go too far. Don't you get it? She knew I would kill myself trying to save you, then she knew you would hurl yourself after me. Prove her wrong. Let me go."

"Wait! I know how to leave a path."

Teej was silent.

"You have to trust me," said Anna, her voice trembling.

He coughed again.

"Teej, are you still there?"

His words were faint. "I trust you."

That was all she needed to hear.

Anna's Haze Sense was still there with just barely enough Vig to fuel it. She could feel Teej's presence. Finding him would be easy, but the problem was there was no Vig to find her way back. No Vig except what she carried with her.

Anna ripped a scrap of Charron's cloak. It was a powerful Relic and it glowed here in Selmetridon. It could serve as a beacon.

Taking a deep breath, Anna stepped forward into the mists dropping bits of fabric as she went.

She moved slowly at first, but feeling Teej's presence fade, she quickened her pace. The only sound was her footsteps on the damp sand.

"Teej? Stay awake. I'm coming for you."

She heard a faint groan, then silence. Aware that she was losing sight of both Teej and her beacons, she looked back over her shoulder. She was almost out of range of the last scrap of Charron's cloak, and there was still no sign of Teej.

Wrestling her ring off her finger, Anna dropped it into the soft sand. Another beacon to guide her back, if she needed it. "I'm sorry, Sam."

She set off as fast as she could, her heavy legs struggling to carry her forward. A horrible, wracking sound followed her every step, pushing her to run faster till she realized it was her own breathing.

"Teej! I can't keep the trail going. I've run out of things to leave behind."

There was no answer this time, but though her Haze Sense was fading fast, Anna felt he was close. *Just a little further*!

Anna looked down at the little scar on her left wrist. She'd spent the last four years of her life trying to make sure she never looked at it. Never thought about it. Now, she needed it to save Teej.

Can I do this?

Grasping her forearm so tight the skin of her hand turned white, Anna pushed her thumbnail into the jagged, mountain range scar across her wrist. Shaking with the strain, she scrapped and dug her nail as hard as she could till finally the skin split. Wincing in pain, Anna managed to cut herself, but only a few red drops ran down the outside of her hand. Not enough.

"Fuck it."

Anna lifted her arm to her mouth, locked her teeth around her wrist, closed her eyes and bit down as hard as she could.

"God damn it!"

Big red splotches of blood ran down her hand and dripped off the end of her fingertips. Maybe she had cut herself too deeply. Maybe she had hit an artery. It didn't matter.

Anna ran as fast as her legs could carry her, driven forward by desperation and hope. Her mind went back to Sam. She remembered hearing his body hit the water, swimming to him, reaching for him, trying to grasp his hand as the tide carried him away. She had let hope slip away that night. She grasped onto that hope now. Hope that she could reach Teej before he was gone. Hope that she could use her own blood to find a way back. Hope that she might survive all of this and explain everything to Teej. She wanted to tell him how much she loved him.

forty-five

Wheezing, pale, bleeding, and barely able to stand, Anna appeared from the mist looking like a weary ghost. Teej had never seen a better sight in his whole life.

"You look terrible," he blurted.

He knew he should say something better. He should tell her that she was amazing and that he loved her, but he didn't have the energy.

"Yeah? Should I just leave you here till someone more attractive comes to save you?"

"Not possible," he said with a groan and reached out to her. Collapsing to her knees, she pulled him into a tight embrace.

"Is this enough?" he muttered into her ear. Her hair tickled his nose. She smelled sweaty and dirty and *alive*.

"A hug?"

"No," he said between wheezes. "Making it this far. Being together. Just… resting? Did we achieve something? Did we do *enough*?"

Anna's head went down. He couldn't tell what she was thinking.

"I can't go on," said Teej. "I'm done. I can't even crawl. All I'm saying is, if you can't do any more, it's enough. You did enough for me."

Anna leaned into him again and pushed her damp face into his chest. He put an arm around her.

"We'll just drift off together. We won't be in pain. Other Metiks die. Maybe these two just fade?"

He felt her pull away from him. Even here, even in this damp nowhere, he saw the spark of defiance in her eyes.

"Most flames burn out," said Anna.

Teej smiled, reached out a hand and stroked her cheek. She leaned in and kissed him. Her lips were soft; her mouth tasted like saltwater.

"But sometimes the ash catches a spark" Teej replied.

With a groan, Anna stood, reached out her good arm, grasped his hand and pulled him up.

"My blood can lead us home," said Anna as she pulled him to his feet. "The Vig in my veins can help us escape. I'll carry you to the shore, but then you carry us the rest of the way home. Deal?"

"Sure," slurred Teej, his eyes closed. "No problem."

Pale, exhausted and barely able to breathe, Anna followed a trail of her own blood, and carried them both out of the Fade.

forty-six

Anna woke up first, but when she rolled over and saw Teej sleeping next to her, she wriggled closer to him, closed her eyes, and fell asleep again. She awoke to find herself in his arms as he hugged her tightly. Gently pushing him away, she rubbed the sand out of her eyes and held a hand up to shade herself from the bright sun.

Sitting up with a start, Anna felt a sudden panic. Were they dead? Were they lost? Where was her ring? She shook Teej to wake him, and when his eyes opened, he was already smiling.

"Are we dead?"

He shook his head, then put his hand to his brow in pain. "If we were dead, I don't think my head would hurt so badly."

"Then, where are we?" asked Anna. She glanced around in confusion. They were on a sandy shore, but overhead the sky was clear blue, and the sun shone brightly. The breeze brought the scent of a clean ocean, and seagulls dotted the sky, squawking as they flew past in formation.

"A beach."

Anna slapped Teej's arm. "I know we're on a beach! But this isn't the Silver Shores, and it sure isn't Selmetridon, either."

"It is," said Teej as he squeezed a handful of yellow sand between his fingertips. "This is the beach we were on before, but we're not in the Realm anymore. We're back in Basine. The real world."

"How?"

Teej shrugged. "You were conscious for more of the journey than me. You found your way back through the Fade. You were bleeding. You cut your wrist?"

"Not for the first time," said Anna. She meant it as a joke but realized it was a mistake when she saw the concern in Teej's eyes.

"There was no other way to get out of the Fade. I knew I could use the Vig in my own blood to leave a path I could follow back."

Teej still looked worried. Anna took his hand.

"Don't worry, I don't want that anymore. I don't want to die."

"You don't always act like it," said Teej with a frown.

"It's true. But I have good friends who haven't given up on me yet."

She squeezed his hand.

"Like the big guy with the boat? He waited for us at the shore. Sailed us back to Basine. He didn't say much, but I think he likes you."

"Charron?"

"Yeah, the big skeleton guy with the hook."

"Oh yeah," said Anna with a grin. "I think we might go steady."

"Your kids would be adorable," said Teej.

"He's just my type, you know?"

"Tall, dark and skinless?"

They laughed.

"He took us all the way back to Basine?" asked Anna.

"He did," said Teej. "And I healed your wounds as best I could with my Praxis, but then I passed out."

"And we ended up on a beach!" said Anna with a chuckle. "I think it was *always* going to end on a beach."

"End?" said Teej.

"I need to say goodbye to Sam and I think I know how to do that now. It will help me to talk about it and there's so much I need to say.. Can I say it to you?"

Teej nodded. "Yes. Of course."

Anna opened her mouth to speak, but Teej stopped her.

"Will it be a *long* story? Because I have one too. And some questions."

"You've *always* got long stories," complained Anna.

"We're on a beach, it's sunny, the waves are lapping at our feet, the birds are singing, everyone thinks we're dead. What better time is there to sit and tell stories? What else do we need?"

"Well, we could have cocktails… and a really big pizza."

Teej rolled his eyes.

"You're not hungry?" asked Anna.

"Starving, but I have to ask you something first."

"Shoot," said Anna.

"Did you see the tower? At the top was a pale blue stone that I think was the Winterheart."

Anna shook her head. "I don't think so, Teej. There is no cure. There is no Winterheart. There's only me."

"Maybe you're the Winterheart?"

"It fits," said Anna. She looked at Teej with concern. "But I don't care about any of that. I just wanted to get you back here."

Teej nodded and looked off to the waves. He seemed distracted.

"I'm just glad we found a way to stop the Dreamers from killing each other," said Anna. "I'm not sure it will last, though."

"I think we did what we could," said Teej hopefully. "If Rayleigh said she'll try for peace, she will. It's messy, but I think things are better now. And our friends are safe."

"But according to Rayleigh's plan, we should be dead."

"Then we're dead!" said Teej with a giggle. "And dead people can do whatever they want. So, from one corpse to another, how about we go on a holiday?"

"I think we've earned it," conceded Anna.

"Sounds like a plan. But first, you wanted to tell me about him? About Sam?"

Anna turned away from Teej and looked out at the sea. She didn't know where to start, so she just said the first thing that came into her mind.

"He was kind. That was the main thing about Sam. I could tell you what he looked like or his job or how we met, but none of that is who Sam really was. Sam was kind.

"This might seem dumb, but we used to eat waffles all the time. He wasn't much of a cook, but I was worse. Any time it got bad, or I got really low, out came the waffles. It became our joke. I'd get sad; he'd make more waffles. At first, it worked every time and meant a lot to me. The fact that he saw how low I could get, and he was trying his best to pull me out of it. Even after I got mad one time and threw the plate at the wall, he didn't stop making me waffles. He used to make jokes. He'd tease me about the ghost waffle that lived behind the sofa. We never found it.

Anna shuddered.

"But then waffles didn't make me feel better, and neither did Sam. Everything he did made me feel worse. It was like the harder he tried to save me, the more guilty I'd feel that it wasn't working. I'd pretend to feel better because seeing him struggle with my pain just made the pain worse. There were so many things we couldn't talk about anymore because talking just made me angrier and more distant."

Anna rubbed sand between her fingertips.

"He'd try other things to help. I noticed them. He'd call my mom and they'd talk about how they could look out for me. I'd hear them from the other room. He was always too loud. He was terrible at keeping secrets."

Anna took a deep breath. She had to keep going. It was time to tell him everything.

"The first time I tried to kill myself, it was with a rusty pallet knife. Sam was out with friends for the night. I knew if I killed myself that night then he would feel guilty for leaving me alone.

I knew that would hurt him the most, and even though I didn't *ever* want to hurt Sam, I could never *stop* hurting him. It was like I wanted to hurt my body to show everyone how the pain inside me was real."

Anna wanted to look at Teej to see his expression, but she kept her head down. Still, she felt the warmth of his presence. She felt his love for her like it was a blanket over her soul.

"In the end, he talked with the doctors more than he talked with me. I guess every time he tried talking with me, I snapped or began crying. I pushed him away every chance I could."

Anna stopped and waited for Teej to say something, but he didn't. In the space that he gave her, she let out a long sigh and looked up. Fluffy clouds drifted over the sun for a second, but they were thin and wispy, and the sunshine still felt warm on her face.

"It's like your whole world is under a rain cloud, and everything is muted and dull, and you do anything—hurt yourself, hurt the ones you love—to feel things again. Then one day you wake up and the blanket is gone, and you don't just feel the pain you caused, you have *become* the pain. Instead of feeling nothing, you feel everything at once, and it rips your insides apart like tissue paper."

Teej reached out to her now. He didn't touch her; he just put his hand near hers.

"People like to say that adversity makes you stronger. Sorrow and loss make you tough. Not me. All that pain sticks to me, but it's just *damage.* Sometimes I feel like I'm walking scar tissue."

Anna put her head in her hands and closed her eyes.

"I didn't know," said Teej simply. "I thought losing Sam made you feel this way. I didn't know... you've felt this way a long time. Right?"

"Yes. He was the best man I ever knew, and he couldn't make a dent in my misery. In the end, he just got caught up in it. He would have been better off if he never met me. And even now, telling this story, I'm feeling sorry for myself when all I should feel is guilt."

"And the letter?" asked Teej.

Anna heard it in his voice. He understood what it meant to her.

"In the charity shop, I didn't need to read it because I already knew what it said. When the ghost in the Fade pretended to be Sam, I knew it wasn't him when he talked about the letter. The letter had nothing to do with Sam. *I* wrote the letter. It was *my* suicide letter."

"I knew it already," said Teej. "Somehow, I think I always knew. What did it say?"

"Just one word. The last line of a poem I wrote when I was a little girl. It's the first memory I have of the depression getting really bad. I always felt like that one word soaked up all the horror I could feel, and it chased me wherever I went."

"One word? What was it?"

"It doesn't matter," sniffed Anna. "It doesn't apply to me anymore."

"If it holds no more power over you, why not say it."

Anna shrugged. "Desolation."

Teej nodded. "Sam dove into the water to save you?"

"Yes. And since he died, I haven't shed a single tear for him. I just buried it. Buried him. And when I cried, I cried for me."

"You weren't ready," said Teej softly.

Anna sniffed. "It's like our lives were a tapestry and he was stitched into everything good. When he was ripped out of my life, everything was torn and tattered till there was barely anything left that wasn't ruined."

"You didn't intend for him to die," said Teej as he moved closer.

"I didn't intend it, but it *was* my fault. And because I was too scared to live, I dragged someone else down with me. And I risked doing that again to someone I cared about. Someone like you."

Teej put his hand on hers. Anna turned and looked into his green eyes as they shone in the sun.

"But you didn't drag me down," he said softly. "You dragged me out. You saved me, over and over again. Anna, I—"

She pulled away from him. "I know how you feel. You have to understand, it's too soon. I don't need that from you right now. I need something more important than a partner. I need a friend."

Teej nodded. His smile was sad, but not defeated. "I understand. And we are friends. Forever."

"Forever?" she said biting her lip. "I'm not ready for words that big. Right now, some things are easier done than said."

She threw her arms around him and hugged him tightly. "Thank you, Teej. For saving me."

"Nonsense!" he said with a chuckle. "You saved yourself, and you saved everyone else while you were at it. Thank you for being Anna."

Anna leaned back, put her hands behind her head and looked up at the sky with a shaky sigh.

"I can't believe I told you all that. I can't believe it's all out there in the open now."

"Me neither. Do you feel better?"

"Definitely not," said Anna with a shake of her head. "But I will be eventually."

She looked at his face as he gazed up at the clouds. The little wrinkles and smile-lines around his eyes made him look tired and charming.

"Where shall we go now?" asked Teej.

"I guess we go into hiding? I'll miss Elise. We were going to take her to Japan."

"I have absolutely no doubt she will find us one way or another. And if she doesn't, we'll pick her up on the way. Hell, maybe we can change our identities and we can *all* run away."

"Oh, we should pick new names!" said Anna excitedly. "Our old names don't fit us anymore, right?"

"Right," said Teej with a chuckle.

"So, you wanted to tell me something too, right? Some big rambling tale about a zombie in an airport, or a dragon in a cinema or something."

"It was a shopping mall," corrected Teej. "And I was going to tell you about something different. The Sunrise Train. You've heard of Helios, right?"

"The chariot pulling the sun?"

"Exactly!" said Teej as he leapt to his feet. The years peeled away from him, and he jumped around like an excited schoolboy. "The Sunrise Train is a Staid Haze, like the Moonlight Road or the Malamun, but it *moves!* It's this luxurious 1920's locomotive. It has a dining cart, separate rooms, sleeping quarters. It's the Orient Express but made of brass and luxurious leather, and it skates across the ocean."

"Dining cart?" said Anna. "I'm listening."

"Remember our first proper Haze together? The train at Cannfranc? I think we deserve another shot at something like that."

"I dunno, Teej," said Anna skeptically. "I'm not sure if you're teasing me again. Is this another one of your stories?"

He offered his hand with a broad smile.

"Don't you want to find out?"

Anna hesitated. "Promise me fewer people will try to kill us this time?"

Teej shook his head. "Nope. I can promise you only one thing..."

"What's that?" She looked down to see she was already holding his hand.

Teej pulled Anna to her feet. "Magic!"

The End

Glossary

Aesthete (Dreamer): An artist so pre-eminent in their field that their Art can change the laws of reality and create a possibility space known as a "Haze."

Amara: A Dreamer who wears masks. Though she is old and powerful, her mind is clouded.

Ancestrals: Precursors of the Aesthetes, these ancient and powerful beings have mostly disappeared or fallen dormant. Their nature and origin are contentious theological and philosophical debating points amongst Metiks and Dreamers.

Apoth, The (John Murray Speare): A member of the Doxa and a powerful Aesthete that creates monstrosities known as Pilgrims through unnecessary surgery. Brother to Mr. Ozman.

Art, the (Mimesis): The ability held by Aesthetes to create Hazes.

August Club: A secret nightclub/brothel where every fantasy can be experienced. It is a Staid Haze that is almost impossible to find.

Banille: The pressure that Basine exerts on a Haze. Banille will cause any Haze to eventually collapse.

Basine: The "real" world. Everything outside The Realm that is not inside a Haze.

Behind the Veil: A term used to describe awareness of more than just the Basine aspect of reality. When a person is Behind the Veil, they are able to perceive Hazes and are conscious of their experiences within them.

Black Water: An expanse of malignant, hungering water located at the base of The Realm, spreading from the depths of the Sump to the silver shores of Selmetridon. The Black Water swallows "all lost things that will never be found."

Blood Plague: The ability for Dreamers to take the Vig from Dreamers by consuming their blood. They can also take blood from Metiks or Muses, but this leads to illness.

Charron (the Boatman): An Ancestral that seeks out the lost and hopeless. He never provides aid but will offer an end to suffering to the last person alive in the Sump.

Choir: A collection of Muses that produce more Vig as a group.

Corpa Haze: A Haze that is sustained by the energy of an Aesthete. A Corpa Haze is temporary, but it will influence Basine when it resolves.

Crags: Razor-beaked creatures that exist in The Realm, especially high in the caves of the Sump.

Crit Command (the Word): A verbal command issued by a Metik that compels anything within a Haze to obey. One of the four powers of the Metik (the Will, the Word, the Sight and the Sword).

Decadan: Archaic term for a Haze.

Doxa: A loose collation of Aesthetes united in their desire to bring about a theological change to Basine by creating a new deity.

Dreamer: Colloquial term for an Aesthete.

Dredges: Lost souls trapped in the Sump, these creatures are emaciated and have lost their humanity to the Black Water.

Drowden (the Occultist): A powerful, precocious Aesthete and the de facto leader of the Doxa. His Art flows from arcane symbols and occultism.

Endless Gray Sea: The sea that exists around everything in the Firmament. The end of every journey.

Etune: A living being created within a Haze. An Etune can be a person or animal, but when a Haze ends, they disappear from Basine.

Fetish: A physical object imbued with Vig, exhibiting residual behaviors from the Haze where it originated. A Fetish can seem supernatural to people in Basine.

Firmament: A term used by Aesthetes and Metik to describe "everything," including Basine, The Realm, all of the Staid Hazes, The Moonlight Road, the Endless Gray Sea and anywhere else that may exist.

Fluxa Haze: A form of Haze which is self-sustaining, pulling Vig from those who experience it and growing exponentially. Fluxa

Hazes can change the nature of Basine, but they often Spiral and are always disruptive and harmful to reality. Fluxa Hazes are very rare, the most recent occurring hundreds of years ago.

Gahan: A handsome photographer Aesthete.

Gwinn (King Gwinn, the Monarch): An Ancestral, and the unofficial ruler of the Firmament. By far the most powerful being active in The Realm, he has lapsed into apathy and torpor. His absence from Basine has loosened his influence on the world, and some now doubt whether he still resides in the holy city of Selmetridon. His nature, origins and intentions were once hotly debated amongst Aesthetes and Dreamers, but he is now rarely discussed or mentioned.

Haze: A possibility space created by an Aesthete where they use Art to change the rules of reality. Their power within the Haze is determined by their natural abilities and the amount of Vig they can retain and channel.

Idyll: A place where Vig is present in large amounts. An Idyll is often a place where people will feel inspired. Idylls are essential resources for Aesthetes and are often contested or fought over.

Kanna Island (Avalon): An ancient Staid Haze. Its origins are a mystery, and no one knows who created it. In the Firmament, it is close to—but not part of—The Realm.

Kunlun Mountain: A huge peak within the Realm from which you can see Selmetridon.

Malamun: A Staid Haze that appears to be located on the moon. An ancient and potent source of Vig, Malamun is currently a run-down bar and nightclub, but it has existed in different forms for as long as any Aesthetes can remember.

Metik: An individual with the ability to change the Hazes created by Dreamers. They cannot create within a Haze, but they can change whatever they encounter. Their abilities are sometimes broken down as "The Will, the Word, the Sight and the Sword."

Mott (the Midnight Man): An Aesthete and a founding member of the Doxa. His Art is based on writing, in particular macabre poetry about murdering young women.

Muse: An individual whose presence generates more Vig than normal. Muses are typically very inspiring people.

Night Collectors: Etunes created by the Midnight Man. They are large monsters that capture and suffocate their victims in constricting bags.

Noop: A derogatory term for a person who is neither a Muse nor an Aesthete, but who is nonetheless Behind the Veil and spends their time in the company of Aesthetes. A kind of groupie.

Ozman, Mr. (the Scientist): An Aesthete, formerly the proprietor of the bar on Malamun. His brother is The Apoth.

Periapt (the Sword): The weapon and tool used by a Metik within a Haze. The term "the Sword" is symbolic, and the Periapt can be any item. Often a Metik learns to produce their Periapt within a Haze, while other Metiks will retain a physical Periapt imbued with some Vig and associated with an emotional memory from their past.

Pilgrim: An Etune that has continued to exist after the resolution of its Haze. Pilgrims are anomalies and typically don't exist long as it requires large amounts of Vig to sustain them.

Pinapune: An Aesthete and old friend of Teej.

Praxis: The process by which the Art (Mimesis) is modified and co-opted by a Metik.

Provident, The: A possible precursor race to the Ancestrals, they have long since abandoned the Firmament. The one exception is Gwinn, who may be the last of their race.

Rayleigh (Old Grayface): A powerful and old Aesthete, and the acting leader of the community. Although Dreamers as a whole are too anarchic and disparate to universally recognize his authority, they all respect his judgements and few would contradict him.

Realm, The: The generic term given to a large, mostly empty world ruled over by King Gwinn from his throne in the Holy City of Selmetridon. Whether it is a Staid Haze, a shadow of Basine or a different reality entirely was formerly a contentious issue amongst Aesthetes and Metiks, but it is now seldom visited or discussed. No one knows exactly how big The Realm is, but it encompasses many distinct regions including the Sump, the Silver Shores, Selmetridon and many regions beyond. There are few remaining open gateways into The Realm from Basine.

Raguel (The Green Knight): A powerful Ancestral able to travel through mirrors to hunt his enemies.

Rolo: A Dreamer whose Art is based on games and secrets.

Selmetridon: A sprawling, seemingly uninhabited Holy City in The Realm. Home to King Gwinn, it is now difficult to reach Selmetridon from Basine.

Spiraling: A term for when a Haze collapses, causing harm to people and damage to Basine. Fluxa Hazes are the most likely to

Spiral. Many Metiks interpret their duty to be the prevention of Spiraling Hazes.

Sump, the (Avicimat): A huge cavern and network of underground tunnels and chambers at the lowest level of The Realm. The Sump is where all lost things go that will never be found. It represents both a prison for enemies and a place of exile.

Staid Haze: A Haze that is no longer affiliated with a particular Aesthete, and that endures far longer than a Corpa Haze.

Straight Way, The: A path through the Realm that takes the traveler through every location. It is now blocked and partially ruined.

The Will, the Word, the Sight and the Sword: The four primary abilities of Metiks. They in turn represent the willpower to change a Haze, the ability to command Etunes within a Haze, sensitivity to the flow of Vig, and the Metiks Periapt (weapon).

Torpor: A form of apathetic madness that affects the minds of very old Aesthetes and Metiks. It is characterized with a disinterest and desire to disengage from Basine, and muddled, incomplete and incorrect memory formation.

Undreamer: A rare and powerful form of Metik that has limited ability to change Hazes, but great potential to destroy them.

Vig: The fuel Aesthetes use to create their Hazes. It can only be detected by those who are already Behind the Veil, where a unique sense allows them to experience it as a kind of air current or invisible light.

Vinicaire (The Travelling Troubadour/Thespian): An Aesthete whose Art flows from acting and performance. He holds a deep love for abandoned places and hidden stages.

Winterheart, the – The mythical blue stone at the heart of Selmetridon, imbued with great power.

acknowledgments

For Eva. I hope you never get tired of daddy's stories. For Nana. I hope you never get tired of my nonsense, because I will never be tired of yours.

For my Mum and Dad. I hope you how much I love you both. For Claire, David, Millie and Evelyn. We're a wee family, but we look after each other!

For the old friends. Gary, Lina, Hollie and James, Silviya, Nikola, Robin and MK and more. And for the new(er) friends. Louise, Debbie, Mel, Danny, Catriona, Emma.

And finally, thank you to Emma, Hannah and the Owl Hollow Flock. See you in the next trilogy!

Thomas Welsh is the winner of the Elbow Room fiction prize and has been published in *404 Ink* and *Leicester Writes*. He received an honorable mention in *Glimmer Train's* Very Short Fiction award, and his story "Suicide Vending Machine" is featured on the *Pseudopod Podcast*.

His work has qualified him for induction into the Fellowship of BAFTA, and he has been published on major sites like *Kotaku, Unwinnable Magazine and GlitchFreeGaming*. He loves Neil Gaiman, Ursula K. Le Guin, Roger Zelazny and dark fantasy stories where women save themselves! He lives in Scotland with his wife Nana.

Follow Thomas at

calmdowntom.com

#AnnaUndreaming
#AnnaandtheMoonlightRoad

Printed in Great Britain
by Amazon